I0646777

THE MOOGEM TREE
A Sol-Larrian Adventure

Written and illustrated by

Robert C. Kew

Grosvenor House
Publishing Limited

This book is published by
Grosvenor House Publishing Ltd
Link House
140 The Broadway, Tolworth, Surrey, KT6 7HT.
www.grosvenorhousepublishing.co.uk

A CIP record for this book
is available from the British Library

ISBN 978-1-80381-147-5

Foreword

This book came to me in a culmination of vivid dreams that have been part of my life since my early childhood. The dreams typically unfold like a film running in my mind's eye: all the peoples, lands, names and places you read here all came from these dreams. Sometimes I was just a viewer watching the events come to pass, and at other times I was actually taking part in the adventure. My Guide was Mr Lucian Snuzz, and he first appeared to me at the age of seven years old. He took me to the fantastic land of Sol-Larris, and introduced to me all the characters that are in this book. Sol-Larris also influenced my sculpting and I had two successful exhibitions of my work in 2006. So come on this Sol-Larrian adventure, meet Mr Lucian Snuzz and his friends and accompany them on their quest through the wondrous worlds of Sol-Larris and Empraktos-Larris.

I would like to dedicate this book to Mum and Dad,
and my good friend Geoffrey Bayldon

The Moogem Tree:
A Sol-Larrian Adventure.

Mr Lucian Snuzz in the Pogglin records office.

Sol-Larris Map.

Prologue

Long, long ago, before the age of the dinosaurs when the Earth was still young, there was the ancient land of **Sol-Larris**. This was the continent that covered the whole of the planet's northern hemisphere and was home to many strange races, creatures and animals. To the west lies the land of Quistorrisia. The homeland of the Quistorrisians, an ancient race and gatherers of knowledge. Quistorrisia is one of the most inaccessible of places to reach, being cut off from the rest of the land by the great mountain range known as '*Quistorrisia's Spine*'. To this day, the only way in is via the '*Zelgemar Pass*'.

At the heart of the city of Zarveltem is a high, dome-capped tower; this is the home of the great "*Hall of Knowledge*". Here are deposited all the histories of Sol-Larris, spanning eons of time and assembled in a fantastic library of ancient tomes. The guardians of this priceless library are the six Councillors of Knowledge. Prometheus Zeus, elected ruler of Quistorrisia, heads the council. He is almost as old as the Earth itself, and has seen many races come and go throughout the span of time. The Quistorrisians have foreseen that a great disaster will befall the Earth. The land of Sol-Larris will be destroyed forever, leaving behind an Earth that will be dominated by great saurian creatures; but the Quistorrisians themselves are powerless to stop it! Hope lies in an arcane prophecy of eldritch lore:

Small and stout in copper hollow,
Cave dwellers now,
A child for the morrow.
This is the one destiny will follow,
Not a cave dweller now,
But one to save the land from sorrow.
Time he will narrow and bend,
His time is now,
Saving Sol-Larris from disastrous end.

So it was to this end that their gaze fell more intensely upon the then cave-dwelling Poggs (later known as Pogglins) of Copper Mountain. Of all the races of Sol-Larris, these little folk bore the seed of hope.

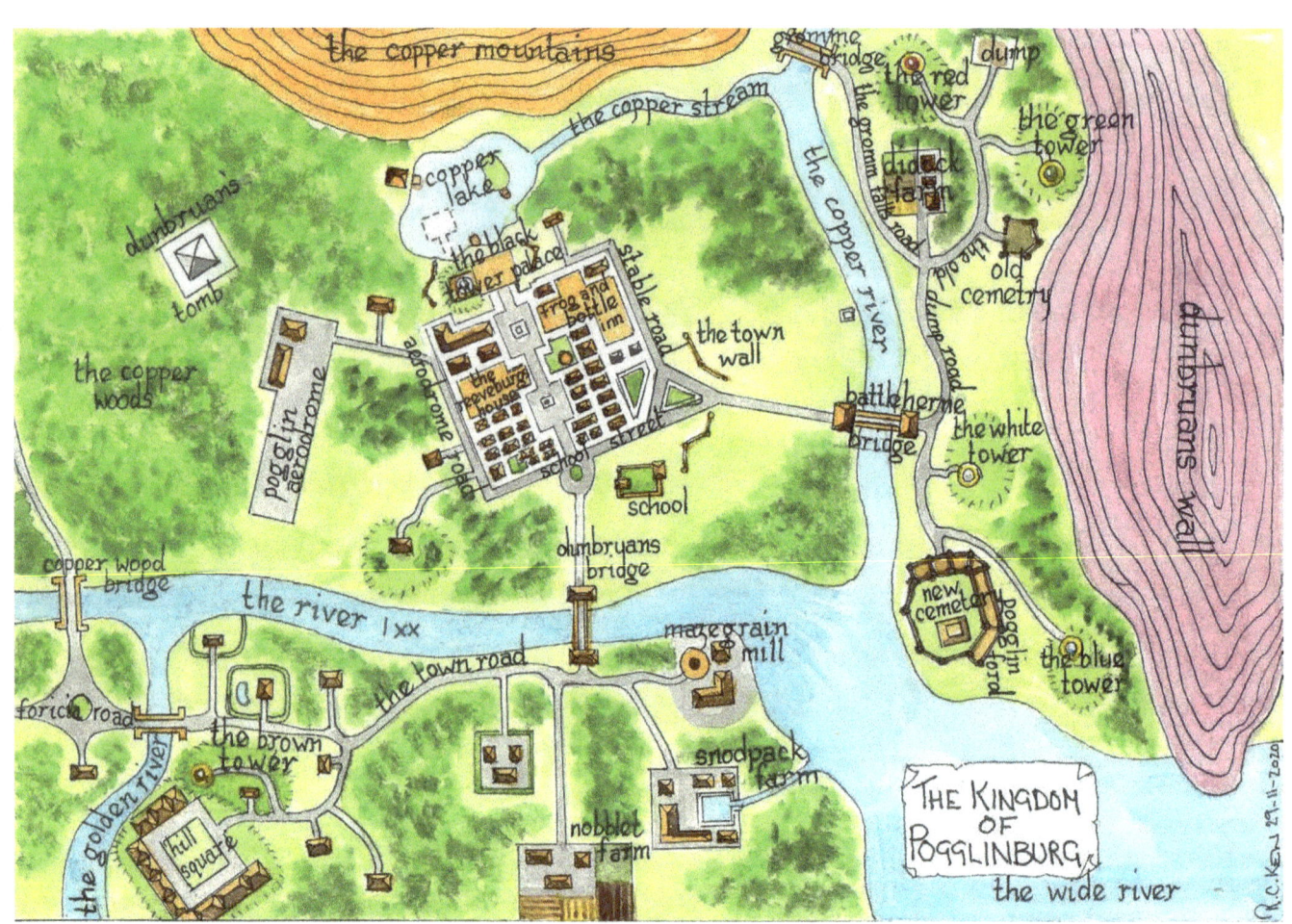

Pogglinburg Map.

Chapter One

Today was a special day in Pogglinburg; it was the morning of the Feast of the Day of New Hope, which celebrates the defeat of the Dondymarian menace back in 3227 BD.

A bright sun shone through the window onto a sleeping figure in a neat little bed. It was a small but comfortable furnished room, with a bedside cabinet and brass bedstead. On the end of the bed were some neatly-folded clothes and hanging on one side of the bedpost was a large, brown 'Mushroom' hat.

Mr Lucian Marius Snuzz woke with a start and looked at his turnip of a watch hanging on the bedstead. "Good Grief, I am late!"

The time was ten past eleven of the clock, and he shot out of bed and over to the bathroom to get washed. He poured some water into the washbasin and looked at himself in the mirror: although he'd had a late night before, he still looked fresh and bright. His large, dark blue eyes inspected his lemon-shaped head: no signs of fatigue through lack of sleep, he thought, and no need to shave either! Lucian was quickly washed and dressed. He ran downstairs, putting on his great brown mushroom hat as he went, grabbed his staff and was out of his front door and away into town.

Lucian rushed to the Gronk stop at the bottom of Hill Square, and was just in time to catch the eleven thirty into Pogglin Town. The coach pulled away as Lucian took his seat at the back, and the coach rattled its familiar way into Town. The coach was pulled by two miserable looking Gronks; they were the beasts of burden that had been used in Pogglinburg for as long as Pogglins could remember. The Gronks were hairy creatures resembling large cows. One had a thick, lush coat of brown hair, while the other was black. Both had a thick fringe of hair that covered their eyes and had very wet pink noses. But the Gronks cheered up as the coach driver began to sing to them as they journeyed into town. Soon the Gronks were at a trot while they sang, and harmonising on the chorus.

A carrion crow once sat on a tree
Singing 'Hey derry, hey derry down dee!'
He cocked his head and winked at me,
Singing 'Hey derry, derry down dee!
Hey derry, derry down dee!'
That old crow that sat in the tree,
Singing 'Hey derry, derry dee!'

The road ran alongside the river Ixx. Great swathes of bulrushes grew along its banks on either side of the river. The sun glinted and sparkled on its waters as giant dragonflies of beautiful iridescent turquoise and green skimmed and darted across the surface in a joyful dance. Some ducks swam in and out of the large reed beds looking for their breakfasts, and a pair of swans with their cygnets glided majestically past.

By now, several Pogglets had boarded the coach, and taken a seat in front of Mr Snuzz. They were delighted and enthralled when he started to point out and name the many varieties of birds and insects that could be seen flying about over the river. He instilled in them his interest and delight of wildlife. He kept them captivated with his enthusiasm and interesting facts about the creatures' lives, and trials of survival in the surrounding countryside. Meanwhile, the other adult passengers, at the front of the carriage were oblivious to this tutorial in progress and continued to sing along with the coach driver and the Gronks. Very soon they were at a canter as the countryside rolled by; the sun peeked out above the lush green treetops, causing finger-like shadows to fall across the fields.

The coach was soon crossing the river Ixx, via the old, turreted, and covered Dunbruan Bridge towards Pogglinburg. Lucian smiled to himself as he realised that he would make it to the public records office before it closed at 12 o'clock, with plenty of time to spare.

The coach pulled to a stop in Dunbruan Square, and Lucian hopped off and waved goodbye to the Pogglets and thanked the driver. Holding onto his large, Mushroom-shaped hat, Lucian rushed towards the Reeveburg's house, home to the public records office. On the way, he noticed that Artimus Whistlecraft's shop was closed. Artimus was a dear and trusted friend of Lucian's and he pondered on the matter: it was a mystery, as Artimus should have been there at this time of day. He had said nothing the night before about closing the shop today?

At last, Lucian came to the Reeveburg's House. Now the Reeveburg's House was the oldest house still standing in Pogglin Town and even predates the royal palace. It was of brick and wood construction, which was brightly painted in green, yellow, blue and orange. The roof, portico, tower and turret were tiled with glorious bottle-green ceramic tiles and had strange twisted chimneys upon the roof. The Reeveburg, who lived here, was originally the elected leader of the Pogglins before the Age of Kings: now he is what could be termed as the equivalent to a Town Mayor. The house was important for another reason, for it also held the Pogglin Records Library.

Lucian walked up the four stone steps that led to the double entrance and passed under the impressive portico. After signing the visiting persons' book in the hall, Lucian made his way down the ancient and immaculate wood-panelled corridor that leads to the Records Office. Knocking on the door, Lucian entered the old library.

"Good morning, Mr Monkclencher," he said, passing by the old librarian, as he made his way to a large reading desk. On the desk were piles of many old files, books and manuscripts. The library was a large imposing room with many bookshelves filled with more books, manuscripts and ancient scrolls. The air smelt of old paper, a smell that even old Monkclencher had absorbed on his person, as he rustled about the place with his long musty overcloak swishing against the floor.

"Good morning, Mr Lucian," replied the librarian in a quivery voice that sounded as old as the room's contents. He followed Lucian over to the bench. "Working late again last night?"

"Too late!" replied Lucian. "But my endeavours were worth it, as I found something of importance."

"Oh, have you really?" asked Mr Monkclencher excitedly.

"Indeed, I have. I found some old papers belonging to the Great Dunbruan, one of which showed an ancient spell for an Earth elemental magic user such as me. I've never seen the like before."

"Goodness me!" exclaimed the librarian, removing his spectacles and fervently polishing them with anticipation. He had the hunched shoulders of a scholar and his high shirt collar came up to his ears. It gave a strong impression that the old Pogglin had no neck. "In all my years as librarian of this depository I have never found any reference to these papers you have found in any of the record indexes. Where on earth did you find them?"

The Reeveburg's House: Home of the records office.

"They were tucked away in the back of this file, and would have been easily missed by even an expert indexer!" replied Lucian to his friend. "I was practising the spell late into the night. It was tricky, but I think I have mastered it now. Would you like to see a small demonstration, Mr Monkclencher?"

"I would indeed, as I find this sort of thing most interesting," replied the old Librarian and eagerly he replaced his by now sparkling spectacles back on his nose.

Lucian took hold of his staff.

"I have always wondered about your staff, Mr Lucian. So beautifully wrought in silver and ebony, and with such craftsmanship! I hope you don't mind me asking, but how did you come by it?"

Lucian smiled. "Three guesses!"

Mr. Monkclencher scratched his bald head while he thought of an answer. "Sir Septimus Pulpit?"

"No, try again, Smiled Lucian.

"Ah, I have it, Mr. Artimus Whistlecraft!" Replied the old Librarian.

"No, one last chance."

Monkclencher rubbed his chin, deep in thought and then said, "Doctor Snuzz! Yes, you're Uncle Doctor Snuzz." Lucian shook his head.

"My mentor! Balferzaar the Black! This staff was a gift from Balferzaar; he gave it to me for my tenth birthday. In fact, Balferzaar made the staff especially for me."

The old librarian nodded his head and continued, "And do you know anything about the beautiful blue gemstone that caps the top of the staff?"

"Indeed, I do, Mr Monkclencher. It comes from the caves of the Copper Mountain and was found by Dunbruan the Great himself."

"Goodness me! You must cherish the staff greatly, Mr Lucian."

"Oh, I do," Lucian said. "It has become an extension of my very being and holds more power than I can possibly tell you." As Lucian purposely but gently tapped his staff on the tiled floor the beautiful gemstone on its top began to glow with a pale blue light. The young Pogglin then sat down at the desk, his eyes closed and his lips moved in silent incantation as he drew the shape of a circle with his index finger on the wooden surface. He then tapped the desktop twice and immediately the wood took on a liquid form within the invisible circle that he had drawn out.

"Crispo!" He said gently, almost as a whisper, and then drew a line out from the circle. The wood suddenly rippled and arched into a crescent, like a wave in water, as it washed across the surface of the tabletop.

"Very impressive indeed, Mr Lucian," the Librarian enthused. "Your skill as a magic smith is coming along tremendously. Balferzaar the Black must be very pleased with your progress."

"Thank you, Mr Monkclencher. For a moment, I didn't think it was going to work as well as it did."

"Umm," said the librarian. "What could you use it for?"

Lucian smiled and said, "Well, with spells the importance can never be underestimated. Even though in truth I do not know the answer to that question as yet, if it is written then it has a purpose."

At that moment there came a knock at the door and an imposing figure entered. It was Sir Gilliethrum Anvilhammer, the Dwarvish Ambassador.

"Why Lucian, my dear fellow!" boomed the Dwarf in his deep baritone voice. "Just the chap I meant to talk to!" he said, crossing over to the bench and shaking the Pogglin's hand.

"Always at your service, Sir Gilliethrum," said Lucian heartily, while standing up to shake the Dwarf's hand. Now, as you probably know, Dwarves are not a tall race, but they still stand taller than Pogglins, even when Pogglins are wearing their hats.

Sir Gilliethrum was a very striking sight, very broad across the shoulders (even for a Dwarf) and stout. He had a great mane of thick brown hair flecked with white and a massive beard that was turning grey. He was dressed in a tunic and robes of pale-blue and sky-blue trimmed with white fur. He had a broad forehead and a bulbous nose, and his kindly deep-set eyes glinted like sapphires beneath bushy eyebrows.

"Of course, you know Mr Monkclencher?" said Lucian, turning to the Librarian.

"I do indeed," said Sir Gilliethrum, shaking Mr Monkclencher warmly by the hand.

"Are you busy at the moment?" asked the Dwarf.

"Just some paperwork and notes to finish, but nothing pressing," replied Lucian.

"Hmm, well, if it's not pressing then maybe you can spare some time to come with me to the Frog and Bottle Inn… Where we can talk!" added the Dwarf, putting his arm companionably around the Pogglin and leading him towards the exit. They departed, leaving Mr. Monkclencher reading the newly-discovered papers belonging to Cosmo Snuzz.

Crossing Pooley 1st Square, Sir Gilliethrum and Lucian talked about his research into the Pogglin archives. Passing 'Bandstand Green' on their right, the two friends came to the entrance of the Frog and Bottle Inn. The Inn was Pogglinburg's second-largest building after the royal palace. They could hear the sound of music and much jollity coming from the inside.

"It sounds as though the celebrations have started early!" laughed Lucian to the Dwarvish Ambassador, as they climbed the steps leading to the door of the Inn. Passing through a small, beamed hallway, and a set of glazed, panelled doors, the two companions entered the great bar-room. The air was filled with the hubbub of talking, laughing, music and the welcoming smell of homely cooking. Down the far end of the bar-room in the left-hand side corner stood a small stage on which a six-piece Pogglin band were playing, a sign proclaiming them as "Fred Ponk and his Frog and Bottle Skifflers". Running down the centre of the room was the covered bar counter, to each side of which there were many tables and chairs: Pogglins, Dwarves, Foricians and Mee-Goggs occupied virtually all of them.

The right half of the room was more densely packed, it being away from the band and hence easier to hold a conversation. At the centre of this portion of the bar was a great wooden staircase, beautifully carved with Pogglin figures, Wallie birds and strange animals, all chiselled in intricate detail. At the top of this staircase (which led to the guest rooms on the upper levels) was carved a depiction of Dunbruan's stand against the Dondymarians in bas-relief: it was Pogglin craftsmanship at its finest.

"You see if you can find a table, Lucian, and I'll see to the refreshments!" said Sir Gilliethrum and moved off through the forest of tables to reach the crowded bar. Mr Snuzz managed to find an empty table by the glazed doors, placed his hat on the table and rested his staff across the chairs. Lucian had recognised a group of Dwarves when he entered the bar: now he crossed over to them to say hello. Lucian motioned to the Dwarves facing him, by placing a finger to his lips, for them not to say anything.

He tapped the Dwarf on the shoulder who had his back towards him.

"I hope you are not drinking too much, Mr Kloons!" he said into the Dwarf's ear and the Dwarf whipped around in surprise. The joy of recognition spread across his features, and his companions laughed heartily at his surprise.

"Lucian Snuzz, thou old blighter!" laughed the Dwarf and jumped to his feet at lightning speed to shake hands and hug with his old friend and travelling companion.

"Hello Elgyn! How are you?" enquired Lucian.

"Why, I be fine, but am feeling the better for seeing thee, my friend!" The Dwarf replied warmly, in the broad accent of the Brown Mountain. Elgyn Kloons was a Dwarf of some renown, and famous throughout the land for his ability to run as fast as the wind itself. He had an immense black beard that was so black that it shimmered to a dark blue in the light. Beneath his black, bushy eyebrows shone humorous eyes of blue-green and he had a red, beaky nose. On his head, he wore a huge fur hat and he wore a tunic of purple trimmed with brown fur. About his waist hung the traditional Dwarvish pouch, embroidered with brightly-coloured silk thread.

Sir Gilliethrum came by with a tankard of brown ale and a glass of Nut Squash for Lucian. "Hello Lads, having a good time? I am sorry to break up the party, but I need to speak with our Mr Snuzz." Winking, he added, "And I will join you, lads, for a jar later at the celebrations!"

Lucian joined Sir Gilliethrum at the table he had reserved. Putting the hat back on his head, and taking his staff from the chairs, he placed it beside him.

"Very kind of you to join me for this chat, Lucian," said Sir Gilliethrum, sitting down and placing a glass in front of Lucian. He then tapped his tankard twice on the tabletop, as is the Pogglin tradition, and raised it to his lips; "Cheers!"

"Down the hatch!" replied Lucian, tapping his glass of Nut Squash, and they both swigged at their drinks.

"Now," continued the Dwarf, "we have the King and Queen arriving from Dwarveshire within the next hour or so. They will be accompanied by the Crown Prince, and Borryn Cobalt the Champion of the Mountain, and also...."

"The Chancellor, Lord Torryn Silverore!" cut in Lucian excitedly. "I am so very pleased that he is well enough to make the journey. I went to see him when he fell ill, and it's been too long since Pogglinburg has had the pleasure of his company. Thank Thremgould that he has made a full recovery!"

"Aye to that!" replied Sir Gilliethrum, nodding in agreement. "It was a trying time for all; King Vardiemar was most concerned and had the very best in Dwarveshire to treat Lord Torryn. By the grace of Thremgould, he has made a full recovery. He was most touched that you made the journey to see him, Lucian. And that is why I wanted this talk, as Lord Torryn wants very much to see you and hopes that you would take some refreshment with him at the celebrations?"

"Why, I would be most honoured and would not reject an invitation from a valued friend. Please tell Chancellor Silverore that I will partake in a drink to his health tonight!"

The two friends clinked glass and tankard together and sealed the appointment. At that moment Grand King Pooley IV, Queen Grizzelda, Arch Duke Lexius Morton-Chump and Sir Hector Rumsbiggot walked into the Bar. Everyone stopped talking, drinking and eating, and stood up with a loud rumble of chairs and benches. Fred Ponk and the Skifflers started up the Pogglin anthem.

"Please," said King Pooley, waving his hands, "No need for formalities! The wife and I have just popped in to unwind with some friends before tonight's festivities. Please continue in your merrymaking."

Everyone returned to their seats, and the hubbub of voices and music returned as the royal party moved up to the Bar. Mr Tiberius Frogbukett gave up his stool to Queen Grizzelda for her to sit down, and the royal group chatted merrily with the throng around the bar. Mr Snuzz and Sir Gilliethrum continued their conversation. The exploits of Chancellor Silverore as a young Dwarf were recounted and the finalisations of arrangements for the evening's festivities were made. It was at this point that their conversation was abruptly interrupted.

"Snuzz! I thought I would find you here!" said the voice, continuing with, "Good afternoon, Sir Gilliethrum."

Before the group stood a stout, smartly dressed, ruddy-faced Pogglin wearing a monocle and a beaming smile. "I have also brought you some much-needed refreshment," he added, and placed three tankards of Brown Ale and Nut Squash on the table. "I hope you don't mind me butting in like this?"

"Not at all, Sir Septimus," replied the other two in unison as their newest arrival sat down.

"I was around the other side of the Bar; I saw you come in and thought I would leave you two to chat awhile, before coming around."

Sir Septimus was the last of a line to one of the oldest families to exist in Pogglinburg. A devout bachelor, he lived alone up at Pulpit Manor on the hill with his two servants, the dutiful Mr and Mrs Bunch. He was of middle age and was, as I said, a well-groomed Pogglin with a liking for checked patterned suits. He had a small tuft of hair, parted in the centre, an enormous moustache and a small pointed beard. He was rather considered by all to be eccentric. Picking up his tankard of Ale and tapping it twice on the table, he chanted, "Chin, Chin, Snuzz and may your beard never grow thin, Sir Gilliethrum!" before drinking deeply from the tankard.

So, the conversation between the three friends was inevitably about the topic of the day, the 'Feast of the Day of New Hope'. During the lull, Lucian noted the strange character wearing a large, wide-brimmed hat standing up at the bar next to the Queen. He was an odd fellow, taller than anyone else at the Bar and dressed from head to foot in black with a very large black cloak about his hunched shoulders. The strangest thing about him was that he wore a black cloth mask. Only his eyes and mouth could be seen through holes cut out in the cloth, and he drank his Ale through a straw.

"I see THE SHADOW is in!" commented Lucian. Sir Gilliethrum followed his gaze and Sir Septimus turned around, having had his back to the Bar.

"Humph! When isn't he!" remarked Sir Septimus and turned back around to face his friends? "No matter what time of day you come into the Frog, you'll find our resident Dondymarian Spy propping up the bar! Still, rather have him in here where we can keep an eye on the rascal than have him snooping around out of sight!"

"It still amazes me that you tolerate him about the place," said the Dwarf, taking a swig from his Ale.

"Ah, there is a method to our toleration, Sir Gilliethrum. The Shadow gets so 'pie-eyed' on Antwhistle's Ale, that he tells us more of the Dondymarians' secrets than he ever gets to report back of ours," chuckled Lucian, "And all that he does report back to his master is the total nonsense made up for his ears alone; I'm surprised that he is still in a job!"

They all laughed and once he had recovered himself, Sir Septimus leaned forward. "I've heard it said that he is so useless that the Dondymarians just send him here to keep him out of their wigs!" Shushing his laughter, he added more seriously, "Mind you, the strange thing is I couldn't get a word out of him this morning!"

"Now that is odd," agreed Lucian.

"Dashed odd!" concluded Sir Septimus. "The blighter is usually so chatty!" His monocle popped out of his socket and plopped into his ale, fishing it out of the tankard; he sucked it before polishing it with his handkerchief.

Lucian grinned at Sir Gilliethrum, "The Shadow is not the only one getting 'pie-eyed' on Antwhistle's Ale!" he twinkled, and they both started to laugh as Sir Septimus looked up, placing the monocle back in his eye-socket, and wondering what joke he had missed.

Then Lucian remembered Artimus Whistlecraft's absence from the shop. "Have you seen Artimus today, Sir Septimus? I noticed the shop was closed."

"No, I haven't seen him since last night", replied Pulpit.

"I saw him this morning in his cart, it looked as though he was making for the Dwarveshire road," interjected Sir Gilliethrum.

"Well, if he was going to Dwarveshire this morning, he said nothing of it last night," Sir Septimus said, finishing his ale.

"I wonder what business Artimus has in Dwarveshire?" pondered Lucian, and then he got up to go to the bar for more refreshment.

Time passed more quickly than usual in such a jovial atmosphere, and Lucian spent more time in the Frog and Bottle than he expected. Lucian hurried over to call for his aunt and uncle. They were waiting on the step for him. "That was excellent timing!" said his uncle, and the three of them quickly made their way towards the green. All of Pogglinburg had turned out for the festivities, along with many Dwarves, Forician and Mee-Gogg guests, and the overflow spilled off 'Bandstand Green' and onto Pooley 1st Square.

Before the bandstand a podium had been erected, on which sat the kings and Queens of Pogglinburg, Dwarveshire, Mee-Gogg, and King Fronos III of Foricia, along with their ambassadors. Lucian could just about see his old friend, Chancellor Silverore, sat next to Sir Gilliethrum. On the Bandstand was Fred Ponk with the Skifflers dressed in sky-blue and green waist jackets. In front of the bandstand stood two lines of six boys and six girls. They wore sky blue and green clothes with red ribbons and large, tall, dark blue hats with orange bands and bells attached. At the head of the two lines stood Pogglinburg's Chancellor, Sir Amias Dore. Resplendent in his best court attire of blue and black, he held his staff of office proudly in one hand, his watch in the other, and his large white moustache seemed to twitch in time with the second-hand of his watch. The whole crowd hushed in anticipation as he started to speak.

"Your Highnesses, Lords, Sirs, Ladies and Gentlepoggs. It is six o'clock!" He thundered in a booming voice and thumped down his staff on the ground, at which the musicians instantly began to play a merry, rhythmic jig. The Pogglin children began to dance: they weaved in and out of each other, the bells jingling on their hats, and the crowd started to clap in time with the music. After some excellent choreography, the dance came to an end with a crescendo, the children bowed to each other and then to the royal party on the podium, the bells jingling like laughter as they did so.

Everybody applauded: Grand King Pooley VI stood up, applauding enthusiastically, and turned to address the crowd. "Your Highnesses and fellow Pogglins, friends; today is the fifth of July and we remember the signing of the treaty of 3227BD; the Day of New Hope – LET THE FESTIVITIES BEGIN!"

A great cheer went up from the crowd and the band struck up with another lively tune. Suddenly from the skies above came a cry of "YOHAY! YOHAY!"

The crowd looked skyward as the Royal Pogglin Flying Corps flew over in formation, much to the crowds' cheers of delight. At the head of the triangular formation flew Wing Commander "Ginger" Wingnut on his Hobbdrak mount, Red. Hobbdraks look a little bit like Dragons, but are much friendlier. They like to talk, and they love to drink mugs of tea! Red had beautiful, deep metallic upper scales of crimson, which sparkled in the evening sunbeams: his orange underbelly glowed like a summer's sunset. Coming up behind was Flying Cadet Ignatius Ffaph on Greenie the Hobbdrak, and Flying Cadet Thaddeus Morton-Chump on Bluey the Hobbdrak. You could say that the Flying Corps were not exactly adventurous in their selection of names for their mounts!

Long streamers of blue, green, red and orange had been tied to the Hobbdraks' tails and flowed out behind in rippling lines. The Wing Commander and the Cadets waved to the crowds below, whilst the crowds cheered and applauded in appreciation of the spectacle. With another cry of "YOHAY! YOHAY!" the Hobbdraks flew off over the royal palace. Once they were out of sight, the Royal party moved off towards the Palace.

"That was a really nice touch with the streamers on the Hobbdraks' tails!" said King Vardiemar, slapping Grand King Pooley across the back.

"Yes indeed - one of my dear Grizzelda's finishing touches!" replied King Pooley.

As they followed the royal party, Chancellor Silverore and Sir Gilliethrum caught sight of Lucian in the crowd and made their way over to him.

"Lucian, my dear Pogglin! By Thremgould it's good to see thee!" said the Chancellor, shaking Lucian warmly by the hand.

"It's a pleasure seeing you looking so fit and well, my lord," said Lucian.

"I'm a tough old bird, Lucian, and I mean to be about for a long time yet. It will take more than a chill on the lungs to carry me off!" said the old Dwarf in good humour.

"Aye to that!" replied Lucian, and patted his arm warmly.

"Of course, you know my aunt and uncle?" said Lucian, introducing his relatives to the Chancellor.

"I certainly do," he said warmly and shook Dr Snuzz's hand. "Nice to see you again", he murmured, kissing Aunt Samantha on each cheek. As they stood talking, Sir Septimus Pulpit and Mr Artimus Whistlecraft joined the group.

"Look who I have found!" said Sir Septimus, indicating Mr Whistlecraft with his thumb, and then shook Chancellor Silverore's hand. "Wonderful to see you again, Lord Torryn."

"And you, Sir Septimus." replied the Chancellor as Artimus greeted the others.

"So, what business took you to Dwarveshire this morning?" inquired Sir Gilliethrum as he shook Artimus' hand.

"Oh, nothing of any importance, Sir Gilliethrum," replied Artimus as he shook the Chancellor's hand.

"We meet again, Mr Whistlecraft," the Chancellor smiled and shook his hand in return.

"Come, let us make our way to the Hall of Celebration," continued the old Chancellor and he motioned them all to move along to the palace. Lucian caught a 'twinkle' in Chancellor Silverore's eye. "He knows something of Artimus' business to Dwarveshire," he thought to himself.

Outside the palace, the Pogglin Army stood in full dress uniform, all five of them! Captain Rumsbiggot stood with his sword at the salute as the royal party moved towards them the Sergeant Major Trump saluted stamped his foot and turned to the three soldiers.

"PRESENT ARMS!" he bellowed, and the soldiers moved in unison and presented arms as they stamped their feet to attention. Turning around smartly on his heel, the Sergeant Major saluted the royal procession. King Pooley saluted them as he passed and the royal party entered the palace.

"Nicely done, boys!" said the Sergeant Major out the corner of his mouth after the royal party had gone. Then the Pogglins, Dwarves, Mee-Gogg and Forician crowds began to file past into the palace and made their way up to the grand banqueting hall; 'The Hall of Celebration'. After all had entered the palace, Captain Rumsbiggot gave orders for the soldiers to stand down, and left to join the feast.

"Well done, boys," said the Sergeant Major. "Now, let's go and get some well-earned nosh!"

The Hall of Celebration was a huge room that could seat a thousand people: its walls were decorated with mirrors and beautiful mosaics of varying shades of amber. At one end of the Great Hall was the high table where sat the Kings and Queens, Royal families and guests. The rest of the hall was laid out with long, polished wooden tables that sat twelve to a table. The only exception was one table, situated in front of the High Table, which was laid out for six places. The royal party was already seated when the first of the throng began to arrive. After many minutes all were seated, and Chancellor Dore thumped his staff on the floor for silence.

"Your Royal Highnesses, Lords, Sirs, Ladies and Gentlepoggs! Pray be upstanding for the order of the Six, their Eminences the Grand Wizards of Pogglinburg," he said in a booming voice that echoed around the Great Hall. A grand and lengthy fanfare started up from the minstrel's gallery above the main entrance, as an ornately gilded door opened at the side of the hall and the precession of the six Grand Wizards entered. At the lead was Balferzaar the Black, the head of the order, followed by Westerin the White, Glondin the Green, Roondar the Red, Baaras the Brown and Bableglum the Blue. All held their staffs of office and capped with a Gemstone for their namesake.

The order of the Six Grand Wizards was set up by the Great Dunbruan himself. He had selected the six best magic smiths of Pogglinburg and took them to Quistorrisia, where he had trained them in the arts of magic. On their return from Quistorrisia, Dunbruan the Great laboured on the six staffs for the Wizards. Wrought in Silver and ebony, he capped the top of each staff with a coloured gemstone mined from the Copper Mountain. Great towers were erected capped with a great gemstone, mined by the Dwarves of the Brown Mountain, and the Six Grand Wizards installed in the tower of their colour.

They lined up before the High Table and bowed; the Royal party bowed back and then sat down, followed by everybody else in the hall. Balferzaar the Black remained standing while the other Wizards took their places.

Balferzaar could be a stern-looking Pogglin at times, but his eyes always twinkled with kindness and warmth. He was dressed in his black and silver robes of office, a brimless hat that came to a point and ended with a silver tassel. Around his waist, he wore a sash of silver and sky blue, which was tied into an ornate bow at the side.

"You're Royal Highnesses, Lords, Sirs, Ladies, and my dear fellow Pogglins, Dwarves, Foricians, and Mee-Goggs," he said in a warm, mellow voice. "We welcome once again our friends from Dwarveshire, Foricia, and Mee-Gogg. Their Royal Highnesses King Vardiemar III, Queen Ellgah and Crown Prince Vardiemar. King Fronos III, King Mimboo XII and Queen Teebon to this happy feast".

There were cheers and applause from the crowd, and King Fronos III acknowledged them by raising his goblet in salutation. Balferzaar the Black continued after the cheering and applause died down.

"On this day 1592 years ago a treaty was signed by the then Reeveburg, Silvarnus Jupp, and Mumbeldok 1st of Dondymaria. The ancestors of our Dwarvish, Forician and Mee-Gogg Royal guests were also present. It was a 'Day of New Hope': the Dondymarian-Pogglin wars were at last over, and a great feast of celebration was held. A celebration that has come down to us through time, and a tradition as cherished as the Six o'clock skiffle," and raising a goblet in toast, "My friends, I give you the Feast of the Day of New Hope!"

A cheer went up from the crowd and the doors at the far end of the hall opened. Out came countless waiters holding silver trays and terrines containing Great Spotted Puddock, poached Fudock, stewed Fiddok and Carpet Fish. They were led by the Royal Butler, Mr Archibald Duckposture. While the feast was being served, music played and Yorik the Jester performed balancing acts and yoyo tricks for the enjoyment of the High Table. Pogglin and Dwarvish waiters were serving the Royal party. A Dwarvish waiter with an extremely thick, black beard and wide-set eyes was serving Queen Grizzelda with some poached Fudock.

"May I suggest to Your Majesty the Chef's speciality, Sortie Pencil Wrasse?" he said and flipped a long, thin, weedy fish onto her plate. She thanked him, tasted a small piece and smiled.

"My compliments to the Chef," she said, "This is very good indeed!"

The waiter nodded, "He will appreciate that, it's been prepared specially," and then he passed along the table offering the poached Fudock, leaving the Queen to enjoy her meal.

"Just a moment!" said Chancellor Silverore, as the waiter was about to leave. "You're new to the service, aren't you?" he enquired of the Dwarf.

"Yes, your Chancellorship," replied the Dwarf, "I only came into His Majesty King Vardiemar's service last week," he said and left for the kitchens to replenish his tray.

"What's wrong?" asked Sir Gilliethrum.

"Oh, nothing really. It was just that waiter looked familiar, something about the eyes?" replied the Chancellor as he tucked into the poached Fudock.

A merry hubbub of talking and laughter filled the Great Hall as the feast continued. Lucian was sat at the end of a table that ran parallel with Grand Wizards table. He was in the company of his aunt and uncle, Sir Septimus and Mr and Mrs Bunch. Also, at the table were Artimus Whistlecraft and his son Marius; Orlando Whistlecraft (Artimus' brother) and his wife, Sophie and children, Augustus, Emma, and Orlando Jr.

It was the first opportunity that Lucian had to ask Artimus about his trip to Dwarveshire, but Artimus proved as tight-shut and stubborn as an oyster on the subject. "Yes", he said calmly. "I did go to Dwarveshire this morning, but will say no more of my business there."

"And Chancellor Silverore knows of it?" said Lucian.

"That he does," said Artimus with a smile, "But again, that can also wait until later!"

"You are being over mysterious tonight!" laughed Lucian.

"So, he is too!" cut in Sir Septimus who had been listening.

On the table opposite were those who advised Grand King Pooley: Chancellor Dore, Field Marshal Sir Gilley Mandergast, Admiral Sir Horatio Loomboggle, Secretary Sir Cecil Grunther-Pulpit and all their families. And there at the end of the table, next to her father, sat Miss Sara Dore. She was in a dress of scarlet and blue, which contrasted beautifully with her raven black hair and sapphire-blue eyes. Around her neck, she wore a pearl and emerald necklace, which was a gift from Lucian; he had had it specially made for her. Sara caught the attention of Lucian and she smiled: he smiled back, raising his glass to her, his eyes twinkling with delight.

Chancellor Dore looked at Lucian and frowned in disapproval; Lucian quickly put down his glass! The feast continued and after the first course, another five courses followed, and the feast ended with Mrs Duckposture's famous 'Strawbeat Trifle'. After the waiters had cleared the plates away, Grand King Pooley VI stood to thank the Royal Staff and in particular Mrs Duckposture for cooking such a fine meal. There then followed speeches from the various Kings, with King Fronos III causing much amusement by stating that although Foricia grew the best Strawbeats, Pogglins make the best trifles from them! Grand King Pooley then asked everybody to move into the ballroom where there would be entertainment and music, which was met by more cheers and applause.

Minutes later everyone was gathered in the palace ballroom and the musicians struck up. Some danced, some stayed in little groups, and others chatted to the seated guests around the perimeter of the ballroom. Lucian was in a group consisting of Dr Snuzz, Sir Septimus, Artimus and little Marius, but he wasn't really listening: he was too busy looking to see if he could glimpse Sara Dore among the seated groups. There was Sir Amias Dore, talking to King Fronos III, but no Sara. Then Sir Septimus pulled him back into the conversation.

"Pardon?" said Lucian.

"By Dunbruan, Snuzz! Haven't you been listening to a word we've been saying?" replied Sir Septimus.

Dr Snuzz looked over his spectacles at his nephew.

"I suppose you have been too preoccupied looking for young Sara Dore? I saw you both mooning at each other across the hall of celebration during the entire feast!" his uncle smiled.

"I thought we were being discreet!" Lucian blushed.

"You were being about as obvious as the beard on Obadiah Thrasskin's chin!" said Sir Septimus, and they all laughed. Obadiah Thrasskin, by the way, was a famous character in Dwarvish legend, and renowned for his immensely long and thick growth of beard.

At that moment Chancellor Silverore approached. "Ready for that drink, Lucian?" he said and took Lucian to the refreshments table, around which stood many Dwarves, including Sir Gilliethrum and Elgyn Kloons.

"To your good health and everlasting friendship, Lord Torryn," said Lucian, raising a glass of Nut Squash to the Chancellor, who nodded his thanks and they both drank. A few moments later Lucian felt a tap on the shoulder: he turned, and it was Sara Dore.

"I thought we were to have the first dance, Lucian?" she said, smiling.

"Please excuse me Lord Torryn, Sir Gilliethrum, Elgyn. My attention is needed elsewhere!" Lucian took Sara's arm and led her to the centre of the floor. Taking off his hat in an arching swoop, he bowed low.

"May I have the honour of this dance?" he asked.

"You may indeed!" she laughed in reply and curtsied. They linked hands and joined the rest of the dancing couples. The Dwarves watched on as the couple danced around the floor, smiling deeply into each other eyes.

"I don't think it will be too long before those two are spliced!" said Sir Gilliethrum.

"Not if Chancellor Dore has his way," said Chancellor Silverore.

"Thou thinkest Chancellor Dore will give leave for Lucian to marry Sara?"

"I think so Sir Gilliethrum. Chancellor Dore is a shrewd Pogglin and recognises greatness in one. Yes, I should think Lucian will get his bride!" replied the old Dwarf, smiling.

Further down the ballroom, Sir Septimus and Artimus (holding young Marius in his arms) were virtually having the same conversation.

"So, what are your odds-on old Sir Amias Dore giving the happy couple leave to marry?" asked Sir Septimus of his friend.

"Come, Sir Septimus, there is no doubt there," replied Whistlecraft. "You are forgetting that Lucian has a powerful ally in Balferzaar the Black. And a friend of Balferzaar is a passport to Sir Amias Dore's patronage!"

The monocle popped out of Sir Septimus' eye. "Why Artimus Whistlecraft, you old cynic!"

"Maybe, but they are happy and that's all that matters," he replied and under his breath, "As I was once," he murmured, looking at his son who was sleeping in his arms.

Replacing his errant monocle, Sir Septimus said, almost as an uninterested aside, "So just what were you up to in Dwarveshire today?"

No reply.

"You are being most mysterious about it; you are up to something, my lad!" Then he added, "Just what have you been spending my money on? I hope it's better than your Der-Werga-Werga machine!"

"Let me just say, Sir Septimus, that it is something that would be frowned upon by the Grand Wizards, Balferzaar in particular," Artimus replied.

Then Sir Septimus looked at his friend with excitement and rubbed his hands together. "Ah-ha! Yes, I think I have an inkling of what it could be. Is it what was spoken of about eighteen months back? Eh what, what?"

Artimus just smiled in reply.

The music stopped and there was applause from the crowed the dancers left the floor. Yorik the Jester took to the floor.

"I say, I say, I say. Why did the Manu cross the road?" he jovially asked the crowd as he flapped around the ballroom floor.

"Why did the Manu cross the Road?" asked the crowd in reply.

"Because he had lost the way!" laughed Yorik as he stepped forward, his hand out, waiting for applause, but applause came there none!

"Not a fellow of infinite jest, is he!" whispered Chancellor Silverore to Sir Gilliethrum.

Yorik quickly produced his yoyo and started to perform tricks that were much more to the appreciation of the onlookers than his appalling jokes! After finishing their dance, Lucian and Sara returned to the company of the Dwarves, where the conversation once again returned to the subjected of the feast and past adventures of Elgyn Kloons and Lucian.

Yorik finished his act to little applause.

"It's amazing what he can do with that Yoyo!" said Grand King Pooley excitedly to a rather bored Queen Ellgah, who was yawning discreetly behind her hand. The band struck up again and the ballroom floor was again awash with dancers, among them were Sara and Lucian. After the dance finished the couple returned to the company of Sir Septimus and Artimus.

Sara stroked Marius' hair who was asleep in his father's arms. "Oh bless, the little Pogglet, he has fallen asleep!" And Sara offered to take Marius to give Artimus a rest. "The evening has been too much for him," said Lucian, looking at his nephew with pleasure.

Sir Septimus gleefully said; "I believe I have guessed what Artimus' latest invention could be!" And he whispered the answer into Lucian's ear.

Suddenly a wretched and blood-curdling scream echoed around the ballroom, followed by mutterings of disbelief and finally culminating into a full-blown panic! The noise startled Marius from his sleep, and he clutched Sara to him in fright.

The Pogglins rushed over to where the crowd had gathered around the centre.

"What has happened?" asked Lucian as they pushed through.

"Tis the Queen!" was the reply and then a terrible sight met their eyes.

In the centre of the crowd lay Queen Grizzelda like a fallen lily, deathly white and gasping for air. Her face gleamed with perspiration, and her lips had turned a deep blue. By her side was a very grave and distraught-looking King Pooley. He patted her hand: "Grizzelda my dear, speak to me!" he said, in the forlorn hope of a response.

Dr Snuzz was also by her side and was examining the stricken Queen. He leant forward and smelt her breath, shaking his head as he tutted to himself, and then he wiped her face and smelt the sweat on his fingers. Again, he shook his head, "My word, it's not possible!"

King Pooley looked at the Doctor's shocked expression. "What is it, Doctor Snuzz? What has happened to Grizzelda?"

Dr Snuzz looked sadly at the King. "Your Highness, the Queen has been poisoned!"

Gasps of disbelief and horror came from the crowd, at the dreadful statement. With great sadness and resignation, the Doctor added, "And I deeply regret, Sire, that she is beyond my help."

The assembled crowd began to mutter again in disbelief and some of the ladies began to cry.

"SILENCE!" boomed Balferzaar the Black stepping forward. "This outpouring will not help her Majesty." He bent down to the Queen's side, placing his hand above her head while murmuring words of incantation. A violet light glowed from his hand as he scanned it along the Queen's still body from her head to her feet and back again.

The King looked anxiously at the old Wizard, "Can you cure her, Balferzaar?"

The old Wizard shook his head sadly. "It is beyond my magic to save her life, my liege. It is a very potent poison that has been administered, but I will be able to temporarily postpone her death!"

At this, the old Wizard raised his staff and began muttering words of magic. Suddenly a blazing green light encapsulated the Queen's body and she began to breathe easier as calmness spread over her face until her breathing was almost a whisper.

"There, it is done," said Balferzaar. The King had the Queen taken to her bedchamber with Dr Snuzz in attendance, and then he called an end to the festivities. As the crowd began to file silently out of the ballroom, Balferzaar called for a council meeting in the Black Tower, with Lucian, Sir Septimus Pulpit and Artimus Whistlecraft to be in attendance.

Artimus sought out his brother and asked if he could please take care of Marius. Orlando took Marias from Artimus, and he kissed and waved goodbye to his son as Orlando and his family left the Ballroom.

Outside the Palace, it was now dark and the moon was high in the night sky.

On the uppermost turret of the palace sat a large, scrawny specimen of a bird. It watched in interest with beady little eyes as the guests left the building far below. From on high it heard phrases and exclamations of poison and murder. The bird chuckled to itself, and then took off eastward on long wings and headed for Dunbruan's Wall.

★ ★ ★ ★ ★

To the east, over Dunbruan's Wall and into the land of Dondymaria, and further southeast, lay the island fortress of Dondymar City; the capital of the war-like race. Dondymarians were not a very pleasant looking race. They were naturally bald, round-shouldered, pot-bellied, and bow-legged individuals. Surprisingly, for creatures of such singular ugliness, they were very vain indeed, choosing to wear flamboyant clothes and outrageous wigs – in fact, the more outrageous the wig, the better. The Dondymarians were also very argumentative, conceited, and selfish. They had sworn oaths that they would not rest until Pogglinburg had been erased from the Sol-Larrian map and swallowed up by the Kingdom of Dondymaria.

Dondymar City was not constructed for beauty, but for the tactics of war, being built on a huge island in the middle of "The Great Wide River". The island could only be reached via four, massive, iron drawbridges that could be raised in times of siege, making the city impervious to attack. The Dondymarians were the most technologically advanced race in Sol-Larris with the power of steam and gunpowder at their command, which had spawned diabolical weapons of war and destruction. Most of the city was one vast industrial estate, which worked day and night in the perpetual task of turning out weapons of mass destruction. The furnaces were stoked to capacity and the great chimneys belched forth a sulphurous smoke and smog into the air that created a cloud of pollution about the island. The dense cloud reflected back a sickly yellow light. Factories about the city shores also spewed chemical pollution into the waters of the fast-moving Great Wide River.

Perched on a great outcrop of rock, above the smog, stood the fortified Royal Palace - a sturdy edifice built to with stand any attack, and fortified with a spread of cannons. A broad, dome-capped tower stood majestically at the centre of the palace, at the top of which was housed the throne room. The throne room commanded spectacular views of the surrounding countryside and mountains. Dondymarians weren't impressed by such sights. To them, it was just a strategic vantage point to see enemy armies moving against the city; in fact, King Mumbeldok II found the views rather dull!

It was to this Royal edifice that the strange, scrawny bird flew and landed on the windowsill of one of the large turrets. There was a tapping sound at the window. Lord Fangdom Creep smiled to himself and put down his quill, went to the window and opened it. And in flew the large, strange-looking bird. It flapped over to the desk and landed on the lamp, its ungainly wings blowing some papers onto the floor. Lord Creep closed the window. Walking back over to the desk, he sat down, looking at the bird. The bird ruffled its feathers and started to preen with its long beak under its wing.

"You can do that later, Shrigg!" said Lord Creep. "Now give me your report."

The bird squawked, and then looked around the room with mischievous little eyes. "Are we alone?" it said, and Lord Creep nodded in answer.

"Password," said the Gweeley bird.

"There is no time for that! Just get on with your report, Shrigg," Lord Creep snapped, leaning forward menacingly.

Shrigg turned his head and looked at Lord Creep with a beady eye. "Look! You wanted all this cloak and dagger nonsense, so give me the password!" And Shrigg squawked again in annoyance.

"Oh, very well. 'Ghost Fish'. Now Shrigg, let's have the report!"

The Gweeley bird leaned forward and spoke almost in a whisper. "All has gone to plan my Lord, with complete success! The festivities have come to an abrupt end, the Queen has fallen and all have left the palace in a right tizzy!"

Lord Creep gleefully rubbed his hands together. "Excellent!" he said and grinned with evil satisfaction. "The Queen will be dead by the early morning! The Pogglins will hold the traditional two weeks of mourning, their morale will be low and that is when we will attack, my dear Shrigg!"

The bird began to cackle, but stopped, as Lord Creep fed him a piece of raw meat on a fork.

Lord Creep feeds Shrigg a piece of raw meat on a fork.

★ ★ ★ ★ ★

In the council chamber of the Black Tower, five of the six wizards were ploughing through the many books on the bookcases. At the head of the great table sat Balferzaar the Black with King Pooley VI; around the rest of the table sat King Vardiemar, Chancellor Dore, Field Marshal Mandergast, Admiral Loomboggle, Sir Cecil Grunther-Pulpit, Sir Septimus, Artimus and Lucian.

"Your Highnesses, Sirs, Gentlepoggs, this is indeed a very grave matter," said Balferzaar the Black. "The Queen will be dead within a fortnight if we cannot find a cure; she will be totally beyond our help in twelve days."

Everyone around the table looked glumly at each other. King Vardiemar said to King Pooley, "You have the full backing of Dwarveshire, Pooley, if there is anything we can do. It is there for the asking."

King Pooley nodded his thanks; he was to overcome with worry to speak.

"Who could have done such a dreadful deed?" asked Chancellor Dore, looking around him.

"Dondymarians!" said Field Marshal Mandergast, without hesitation. "They have been spoiling for another war with us for the past forty years," he explained, twirling his white moustache.

"That's impossible," said the royal secretary, Sir Cecil Grunther-Pulpit. "There was no way the Dondymarians could have administered the poison."

Field Marshal Mandergast looked at Sir Cecil, "Not at the feast I grant you, but…"

He was interrupted by Sir Septimus, "But at the Frog and Bottle Inn!" His monocle was practically popping out of his socket.

Chancellor Dore swivelled his head around at Sir Septimus and thumped his fist down on the table. "THE SHADOW!" he exclaimed.

This started everybody talking over each other, but the hubbub came to an abrupt stop when Dr Snuzz entered the chamber and sat down. "I have carried out a blood test on the Queen and there is no doubt about it, she has been poisoned; *poisoned twice*!"

This caused an outburst of exclamation, and the Doctor waited until it had calmed down before he continued. "Two poisons are reacting with each other. Together, they have almost totally broken down her immune system. If Balferzaar had not put a blocking spell on this process, the Queen would most certainly not have made it through to the morning," he said gravely.

The King began to weep while King Vardiemar tried to console him.

The other five Wizards returned to the table looking very dejected. They could find nothing in the spell books or books of medicine that would reverse the Queen's ailment.

Balferzaar rubbed his chin. "Then my friends, we have only one chance." He turned to Lucian. "Lucian, I think it's time you consulted the secret book!"

Lucian nodded and stood up. Tapping his staff three times on the stone floor of the chamber, he pronounced the words; "SHAR CHALBERASH!" There was a flash of blue light and a battered book, about the size of a quarto, appeared on the table before the young Pogglin.

Lucian sat down and went through the pages, his lips moving as he read the different headings to himself. The others waited for what seemed like an eternity for Lucian to speak. Finally, he closed the book and looked gravely at the group around him.

"There is nothing specific that will cure the Queen, no spell or antidote to the known world. There is only a vague reference; a legend of an antidote. There is a mythological tree called the Moogem, the fruit of which cures many ailments of the body including poisons." He continued, parting his hands as if to picture a map before him. "The only clue the books gives to the whereabouts of the tree is to look in the *Undiscovered Lands*."

More mutterings of "just a myth" and "impossible" came from around the table.

"It is a very slim chance that Lucian has put before us," said Balferzaar the Black as he pondered the matter. "But it is the one, and sadly *only*, hope we appear to have for her Majesty. Therefore, it is a quest we must undertake and hope that the legend is true!"

Balferzaar stood up and moved next to King Pooley VI who had by this time managed to bring his grief under control.

"My Liege," said Balferzaar. "May I have your permission to arrange matters for this quest?" The king nodded, and Balferzaar continued. "Then may I suggest that Your Majesty retires to his chamber for some rest? Doctor Snuzz will accompany you."

King Pooley VI left the chamber in the company of Dr Snuzz and King Vardiemar, who hoped they might be able to distract King Pooley from his present state.

After they had left, Balferzaar sat back down at the table. "What do you propose?" asked Chancellor Dore.

"I think our next step is to send Lucian, Sir Septimus and Artimus here on a long journey. It falls to them to attempt the honour of finding the Moogem Tree!"

"Why them?" asked Admiral Loomboggle, with a glint in his voice that might have been jealousy.

"Because, Sir Horatio, these three Pogglins have travelled about Sol-Larris more than any other Pogglin. If the Moogem Tree exists, then these three will find it," replied Balferzaar.

Sir Septimus, Artimus and Lucian looked at each other and smiled, honoured that Balferzaar had so much faith in their abilities.

"So, what is your plan of action?" asked Chancellor Dore.

Balferzaar stood up, rubbing his chin, and paced around the council chamber. "We are on a race against time, gentlemen. We have a maximum of twelve days to administer the antidote before it is too late to save the Queen. I suggest that our first move will be to get our three young Pogglins off to Quistorrisia. The High Council of Knowledge will most likely to be the ones who will be able to know the truth of the legend, and therefore help locate the Moogem Tree."

"Quistorrisia is eight days' journey from Pogglinburg. They will never make the deadline in time!" protested Chancellor Dore.

"Then they shall be flown there by Wing Commander Wingnut and the Royal Flying Corp!" retorted Field Marshal Mandergast.

During this conversation, Sir Septimus leaned over to Artimus and whispered out the corner of his mouth.

"What about your machine? Could that get us there quickly?"

Artimus' eyes twinkled and nodded his reply.

Lucian caught what the two were saying.

"That's a splendid idea!" he said, just as Chancellor Dore was saying, "But even flying by Hobbdraks, the journey to Quistorrisia will still take three days!"

Artimus Whistlecraft stood up, hands on his lapels, and spoke. "Gentlemen, I think I can solve this problem by reducing our travelling time to Quistorrisia to *one* day!"

The group looked at him in stunned amazement.

"He's insane!" muttered Admiral Loomboggle.

"Preposterous piffle!" exclaimed the Field Marshal.

"Totally impossible!" said Chancellor Dore.

Balferzaar the Black smiled, and said, "I do believe Mr Whistlecraft is going to be unveiling another of his inventions for us. Pray tell, Artimus!"

★ ★ ★ ★ ★

Minutes later the council had assembled in Whistlecraft's large workshop at the back of his shop. Artimus lit some candles. In the corner of the room was a tall, bulky object covered by a large sheet of tarpaulin. The Pogglins walked over to it and Artimus reached out a hand for the tarpaulin. Artimus pulled off the tarpaulin with a flourish, revealing a machine to the onlookers.

"Behold, my friends! Seventeen months of work and it is complete, my flying machine! It only needs the rotor blades to be attached. Then Lucian, Sir Septimus and I can go on the journey."

"Behold, my friends! Seventeen months of work and it is complete, my flying machine!" Said Artimus.

Balferzaar the Black patted Artimus' shoulder and laughed. "You have come very close to breaking Dunbruan's teachings, young Artimus –its border-line! But I am very pleased that you have made this fine contraption!"

The Flying Machine was crafted from brass, oak and mahogany. It stood on five brass legs that ended in flat circular pads. Mounted on these legs were two discs of oak sandwiched between four discs of brass: a row of lights went around each of the oak discs. On the top disc sat an octagonal body made of mahogany with brass inlay and above which sat an octagonal window frame, fluted out at the top. On top of the windows were another two oak and brass discs, larger than two below and also had a row of lights around each disc. It was capped off with a low dome made of polished mahogany and into which were cut deep grooves. These would eventually house the rotary fins of the machine.

Artimus climbed up the three brass steps to the cockpit and unlocked the door so that his friends might inspect the interior. After opening the door, he came back down and let his friends go up. Sir Septimus and Lucian excitedly rushed up the steps. They were like children given a new toy, as they entered the cockpit.

"It's going to be a tight squeeze with three of us in here, Artimus!" said Lucian calling back to his friend. Before the two Pogglins was a control panel of mahogany with inlaid brass and covered with many dials and lights. There were two control levers that Sir Septimus took to be the flight controls. Atop the control panel were three glass bells that protected an intricate mechanism of coloured glass and metal, and the two Pogglins were at a loss as to what they could be. To the right of the control panel was a large lever with a carved handle of ivory. A large thick spindle ran from floor to ceiling. Around the wall of the cockpit were brass grabbing-rails, and the panels of the wall were upholstered in lush, vibrant red velvet.

They came back down and patted Artimus across the back and congratulated him.

So, it was agreed by the council, the three adventurers would leave for Quistorrisia first thing on the morrow in Whistlecraft's Flying Machine.

Lucian and Sir Septimus helped Artimus fit the rotary blades to the dome of the Flying Machine, and they did this in double-quick time! Then they went home to snatch what equipment and what little sleep they could before tomorrow's journey.

The following morning of the 6th July, the Flying Machine was pulled out of the workshop and up onto Bandstand Green by the town guard. A great crowd had once again assembled like the night before; although the mood was sombre, there was much chatting caused by this new contraption. King Pooley VI made a speech and gave his thanks to the three Pogglins for their bravery and courage in undertaking what could be a very dangerous quest.

The six Grand Wizards each sent praise to the three Pogglins. Balferzaar the Black told Lucian that he had sent a Wallic bird on ahead to tell the Quistorrisians to expect the Pogglins. Like the Gweeley birds, the Wallie birds were the means of communication between Pogglinburg and her allies.

While Lucian and Sir Septimus wound up the Flying Machine with the large brass key, Artimus had climbed the stairs and was standing in the cockpit making final checks. After winding the mechanism, the two Pogglins stowed away the key under the machine and climbed the stairs and closed the door behind them. The crowd and the gathered dignitaries moved back as the rotor blades of the machine slowly began to turn and gradually picked up speed. Faster the rotor blades went, until they became a blur. The three glass bells on the control panel pumped up and down furiously. As the centre glass bell dropped into the control panel, so the two on either side rose up.

From the window, the three Pogglins waved a final farewell as the flying machine lifted off.

The flying machine shot straight up into the air and then hovered; a steering set of rotor blades sprang out the back of the machine and it zoomed off into the west. The crowd cheered and waved, shouting their good wishes and a successful journey.

While Artimus stood at the controls, Sir Septimus and Lucian looked excitedly out of the windows.

"So, this is how Pogglinburg looks from the air! I can see why Pogglins want to join the Royal Flying Corps," said Lucian.

Sir Septimus pointed excitedly. "Look Snuzz! There's my house, Pulpit Manor!" he laughed.

Soon the Flying Machine was zooming over the Brown Tower and Hill Square, and then out over the border into Foricia. Suddenly the machine was hit by turbulence and jostled its occupants, wiping the smiles off their faces as the machine began to plummet towards the ground. Artimus pulled back on the control sticks; the gears of the machine squealed as the driveshaft to the rotor blades span faster. The drop began to slow as Artimus got the machine back under control, and it began once again to gain in height.

"By Obadiah Thrasskin's beard, that was a narrow squeak Artimus, my lad!" said Sir Septimus, mopping his brow with a handkerchief. Lucian patted Artimus on the back.

"Well done, I thought we were finished back there!" he said. Artimus just nodded: he had thought they were finished too!

Hours later, the Pogglins were still flying over the green waste of Foricia. Artimus checked the controls. "We are going to have to make a landing shortly. The mechanism needs to be wound again."

Lucian and Sir Septimus looked out of the windows for a place to land. Artimus had been following the Green Woods, keeping it on the right and the Green Waste to the left; this way he could be sure that they were going west and on course for Quistorrisia.

"Look!" said Lucian, "There is a clearing in the woods down there, just beyond that hill with the old watchtower on it."

"I see it," said Artimus, and brought the Flying Machine around and started the descent.

Shortly the flying machine descended to land by some rocks in a clearing. Sir Septimus opened the door and walked down the steps on to the grass. He stretched and yawned, his monocle predictably popping out of his socket. Soon Lucian and Sir Septimus pulled out the brass key and started to wind up the machine.

They hurriedly stowed the key away once the machine was fully wound and ran up the stairs. Once the door was closed, Artimus took off. The flying machine sped through the night towards Quistorrisia, only stopping briefly to wind up the mechanism when needed. By the early hours of the 7th July the Pogglins had flown over "Quistorrisia's Spine", the mighty, snow-capped mountain range that separates Quistorrisia from Sol-Larris.

They were now in Quistorrisia, which was many thousands of feet above sea level, and by dawn, they were flying over the great Silver Lake. Before them in the distance was the great city of Zarveltem, the capital of the Quistorrisians, the 'Tower of Knowledge' dominating the city skyline. The flying machine flew in over the city and came to land in the great square in front of the tower.

As the Pogglins disembarked, the head of the Council of Knowledge came down the stairs to greet his guests.

"Good morning my friends," said Prometheus Zeus, "and welcome again to our city of Zarveltem." Prometheus Zeus was a striking figure. He was very tall and slender (like all the Quistorrisians), with white skin and very large blue eyes. His face was very narrow with high cheekbones and a long, chiselled nose. His baldhead caught the pale moonlight as he bent down to shake each Pogglin gently by the hand.

"Come!" he said turning and walking up the stairs to the tower's imposing entrance. "You are expected, and we have prepared the information that you seek."

The Pogglins followed the tall figure up the stairs, his flowing robes billowing in the early morning breeze. They entered the tower and walked up several more flights of stairs until they came into 'The Great Hall of Knowledge'. It was a room of massive proportions that even managed to dwarf the eight-and-a-half-feet tall Quistorrisians. In the centre was a strange podium, on which "floated" a globe of the Earth: around this podium was situated many desk-like tables with ornate brass lamps above them. Behind the podium, a staircase led up and on to a landing. The landing housed many bookcases of huge proportions. Although the Pogglins had been in the hall many times before, they were still moved by the sheer scale of the place and magnificence of it, and looked around in awe. 'The Great Hall of Knowledge' contained almost the entire history of Sol-Larris as the Quistorrisians were the great gatherers of knowledge, and these histories were contained within the many volumes of books that lined the many huge bookcases at the back of the hall.

The Quistorrisians welcome the Pogglins into 'The Great Hall of Knowledge'.

The rest of the Council came down the stairs and greeted the Pogglins. "Welcome, my friends," said Pandora Nyx, bowing to the Pogglins and kissing them on each cheek, her silver hair flashed in the now rising sun streaming through the skylight above. She stood next to Prometheus Zeus and smiled. No sign of age showed upon her white skin, but she was as old as the stars themselves.

"My sister and brothers have prepared the information that you require. So do not worry and let me put your minds at rest, for your quest is not in vain. But before you look may I suggest that you retire, followed by some refreshment. You will work better after some rest." The Pogglins nodded in agreement, thanked their host for their hospitality and followed Pandora out of the Hall.

Minutes later they were shown to their separate bed chambers. Each of the Pogglins went straight to bed after their exhausting journey and fell into a deep restful sleep. Just before dusk, Pandora woke the Pogglins and she took them to a dining hall where the Pogglins ate a substantial meal. After which they were again ushered into

'The Grand Hall of Knowledge'. Some desks had been prepared for them, the seats being raised so that they could reach the tabletop; Pandora lifted up each of the Pogglins and sat them down.

On the table were many maps, old volumes of books (most of which were written in Quistorrisian) and a map. Sir Septimus and Artimus couldn't read these, but Lucian understood a little and managed to read 'Empraktos-Larris' on the spine of one of the smaller tomes. Luckily, he didn't have to rely on his translating the books as Prometheus Zeus and Pandora stayed with the Pogglins, while the rest of the Council returned to their researches among the great bookcases.

"The Wallie bird sent by Balferzaar told us what has befallen your Queen," said Prometheus Zeus in a gentle voice. "He told us that you had consulted the 'Secret Book', and that referred you to the legend of the Moogem Tree. You will be encouraged to hear that The Moogem tree is not a myth, my friends! The Moogem Tree really does exist and grows still, though very few know of this fact. It is secret and sacred and it must be protected. You, my dear friends, are the exception and we will help you in your quest."

Sir Septimus asked if the Quistorrisians knew who had poisoned the Queen.

"The Queen was poisoned twice, yes?"

The Pogglins nodded in response.

"Your Queen was poisoned, as you correctly guessed, by the Dondymarians. Our intuition tells us that the Dondymarians have shown their hand in the matter, along with the help of the Grodium Dwarves," continued Prometheus Zeus.

"At the moment," said Pandora, "how the deed was done is of no importance, as you will find answers to these questions later. While you were resting, we had news from a Wallie Bird sent to us by Balferzaar the Black. The news is the Grodium Dwarf that poisoned the Queen has escaped from Pogglinburg, but has been captured and now lies in a cell deep within the Brown Mountain."

"Why would the Grodium Dwarves want to poison our Queen? We have never been bothered by the Grodium Dwarves before," Lucian asked.

"What is more important now is the quest for the Moogem Tree," she replied. Lucian looked deeply into her kind blue eyes; the depths of untold centuries of wisdom reflected back.

"The Secret Book told us to look in the Undiscovered Lands," he said, and pointed to the small book on the table, the old tome whose title he had managed to translate. "Is this land of 'Empraktos-Larris' the one we seek?"

Pandora looked at Lucian and smiled, "You are correct in your assumption. Empraktos-Larris is the land that you seek. Empraktos is an ancient word and means *beneath*."

Empraktos-Larris Map

Sir Septimus slapped Lucian across the back. "Good old Snuzz, we can never go wrong while he's with us!"

Artimus, in the meantime, was studying the large map and it was in a language he understood. It showed Quistorrisia's Spine and the land just east of the mountain range, but it also showed most of the lands to the north. Artimus concluded that this must be where the lands of Empraktos-Larris must lie. He looked up from the map as he heard Prometheus Zeus say that the Pogglins must take the Zelgemar Pass in the mountains to the north.

Artimus pointed to the map. "So, this must be the land of Empraktos-Larris."

Prometheus Zeus shook his head. Explaining as he went, he traced his long, slender finger across the map. Through the Zelgemar Pass, around the Mouth of Zelmekh (a massive lake of molten lava), past the Dead Lake and he stopped at the foot of Mount Zelmekh. "My friends, the entrance to Empraktos-Larris: The Zelgemar Gate!"

The Pogglins looked blankly at him, not understanding his meaning.

"So Empraktos-Larris is inside the mountain?" asked Sir Septimus.

"Not inside the mountain, Sir Septimus, but there we will find the entrance to Empraktos-Larris!" Lucian cried. "Empraktos-Larris is underground, remember? Empraktos means *beneath*!"

Prometheus Zeus made a gesture of his hand towards the many old volumes of books laid on the table. "These books, my friends, are histories of Sol-Larrian races that refer to Empraktos-Larris and the Moogem Tree in their

25

histories." Picking up the small book, he opened it. "In this book are the accounts of races that have come up from Empraktos-Larris to visit Sol-Larris!"

The Pogglins looked surprised. "There are people down there?" they asked.

Prometheus Zeus nodded as he turned the pages of the small book, looking for the map, while Pandora spoke.

"We Quistorrisians have never ventured to Empraktos-Larris ourselves, but we have managed to talk with visitors from that land and this small book contains some of their accounts." Finally, Prometheus Zeus came to the page he was looking for and laid the book before the three Pogglins. It was a map, although it was a very crudely-drawn map, with many blank spaces.

"This map was drawn by one of the subterranean peoples that inhabit the land. As you can see, there is nothing east of the 'Valley of Zaark'. We believe that the Moogem Tree lies beyond - further to the east, by the 'Lake of Wonders'." He returned his finger to a crudely-drawn staircase in the far west of the map.

"These are the Zelgemar Stairs: these lead down from the Zelgemar Gate. You will then have to make your way through the Fungoid Forest and then to the Valley of Zaark. It is then down to your own counsel and initiative as to how you reach the Lake of Wonders."

Pandora picked up another of the books and read to the Pogglins a passage about the magical qualities that the waters of this lake held. Putting the book down she said, "It would be wise that you also bring back some of the waters from the Lake, as I have a feeling that they will also aid you in your quest to save Queen Grizzelda."

Both the Quistorrisians stood up from the table.

"We will leave you now to study this map and make your plans. We cannot say that your journey will be easy, for many dangers will you face in Empraktos-Larris. But I believe you will find also allies as well as enemies," Prometheus Zeus said.

"We will return in an hour and then it will be time for you to leave and begin your quest," said Pandora. The Pogglins thanked her and she gave them a warm smile. They both withdrew and walked away up the stairs toward the bookcases at the far end of the hall.

Sir Septimus polished his monocle as the Pogglins gathered around the map to study it more closely. While they talked, Artimus copied the map onto a sheet of paper and placed it in his overcloak pocket.

On the map, they had two paths which to follow: northwest through the Fungoid Forest, or southwest across open country past the volcano that was 'Mount Uoplaax'.

"I don't like the sound of going through this Valley of Zaark," said Sir Septimus. "Too much open country for my liking, and we don't know what blighters live there!"

Artimus agreed and pointed to the map.

"I think we should go through the Fungoid Forest and head towards the Vunolf Peaks. The forest will give us cover and there may be a way around, avoiding the vale."

"Sounds good to me," nodded Lucian in agreement.

The three Pogglins were now in agreement and time was of the essence. Taking one of the large Quistorrisian pencils, Artimus cut nine notches with his quill knife into the pencil, which he placed in his waist-jacket pocket.

"Each day we are in Empraktos-Larris, I will cut off a section of pencil and we can keep track of the days," he explained to the other two.

"A good idea," said Lucian, and patted his friend on the shoulder.

The hour was soon up and the whole of the Quistorrisian Council of Knowledge came to them. "It is time," said Prometheus Zeus, and he gestured to three of the Council, "My brothers have prepared these for you to take on your journey."

They stepped forward and gave the three Pogglins each a large pouch with a shoulder strap. "This food and water should last you on your journey until you return to us." The Pogglins thanked them for their kind help and hospitality and then stepped back into line.

Pandora then stepped forward and gave Lucian and Sir Septimus each an ornate glass bottle and a jar. "These I have prepared for you. The fruit of the Moogem perishes quickly; it will keep the fruit of the tree fresh and the waters of the lake pure."

The Pogglins thanked her and placed the bottles and jar into their new pouches.

The Council took the Pogglins to the Flying Machine. By now night had fallen, and the full moon shone brightly in the night sky. Lucian and Sir Septimus wound the mechanism while Artimus checked the machine's instruments. The Quistorrisians' white skin seemed to shimmer in the moonlight as they lined up to say farewell to their guests.

Pandora stepped forward. "Fare thee well, my little ones," she said, kissing them on each cheek. "Beware the 'Tower of Eybraas', and come back to us safe."

Finally, Prometheus stepped forward. "I shall send a Wallie Bird to Balferzaar and give him news that you have started out on the historic quest. Take care on your journey to Mount Zelmekh, as there are many spies in the pay of the Dondymarians. Come back safely to us, my friends."

The Pogglins bade farewell to their hosts and climbed aboard the Flying Machine, waving as they went. Artimus started up the machine and took off the brake. The machine lifted into the air, with the Quistorrisians waving a final farewell from below.

"You did not tell them that they will not be the first of their race to visit Empraktos-Larris?" enquired Prometheus Zeus of his sister.

"No," Pandora replied, "I thought it better that Lucian should discover this for himself."

"A wise move, Pandora. The prophecy, it begins!"

The machine was soon rushing northward, over the great lake towards the 'Quistorrisia's Spine' mountain range. Flying over the Zelgemar Pass, the Pogglins were now into the land known as the 'Grey Waste': a vast and soulless desert of grey sand, broken only by the occasional mountain peak. An hour later they saw a deep red glow lighting up the night sky on the horizon; it was the Mouth of Zelmekh.

"Fly to the west, Artimus – I don't like the idea of flying over a lake of molten lava!" said Lucian.

The flying machine veered to the left of the great lake of lava, whilst the Pogglins looked on in awe.

"I wouldn't fancy the idea of making a crash landing into that little lot, what, what?" said Sir Septimus, shuddering at the thought of it.

The flying machine rushed on into the night and was soon passing The Dead Lake, which was a huge mass of water in the middle of the desert. The water's surface reflected a vile sickly green colour in the moonlight. Beyond the lake, the Pogglins could make out the black peak of Mount Zelmekh.

Lucian pointed to an outcrop of rocks just on the shore of the lake, and Artimus brought the Flying Machine down to land under cover of the rocks.

The Pogglins disembarked and stretched themselves, as it was rather cramped in the cockpit with nowhere to sit. Sir Septimus walked over to the lake and bent down; the smell was enough as the water was putrid! He got up quickly. "No good for drinking then!"

"Right!" said Lucian, picking up his staff and putting on his mushroom hat. "I think we should make a start for the Zelgemar Gate; we have about half a mile to go." Sir Septimus and Artimus nodded in agreement. Artimus then went up to the flying machine cockpit and unscrewed the two levers that controlled its flight and put them in his pouch, and then he locked the door behind him.

"Will it be safe to leave the machine here?" asked Sir Septimus.

Artimus nodded, "Yes, I have removed the control leavers and the machine is immobilised without them. Apart from some gang of rascals dragging the craft away, it should still be here when we get back."

Artimus checked the time by his watch: 6.05 a.m. The three Pogglins moved off towards Mount Zelmekh, with their pouches at their side and Lucian holding his staff. Their feet sank into the soft, grey sand as they walked; it was hard going and tiring for their little legs, but the Pogglins none the less discussed the plan of action that they had laid down the night before. They still agreed that the best route to take if they were to succeed would be via the Vunolf Peaks.

The mountain drew ever nearer and grew in size, as they trudged wearily toward it. Then, they saw it: there, at the foot of the mountain, they could just make out a dark shadow —the Zelgemar Gate. Finally seeing this come into view gave them all renewed vigour and they strode purposefully toward it.

As they approached the Zelgemar Gate, they realised it was not at all what the Pogglins had been expecting from their glimpse of it the night before. They imagined the gate to be a wrought-iron affair, but it was just an opening that had been roughly carved out of the mountainside. Strange beast-like creatures were carved at either side of the entrance; above the opening were stones that looked as though they were carved to represent teeth.

Soon the Pogglins finally stood before the entrance of the Zelgemar Gate. The rocks above the entrance were indeed the representation of teeth: the entrance gave the impression of a yawning mouth with the two stone guardians either side of it and above these, etched in the stone was hieroglyphs that the Pogglins could not read. Sir Septimus eyed the stone guardians suspiciously and became a little ill at ease.

"Any guesses as to which civilisation wrote that, Lucian?" asked Artimus pointing up.

Lucian shook his head, "I've never seen the like of it, Artimus." His eyes were sparkling with wonder at this marvellous sight, as it had awakened the archaeologist in him.

"You are not going to read that mumbo-jumbo aloud, are you Snuzz?"

"No. Why do you ask, Sir Septimus?"

Still eyeing the statues with unease, he replied, "Because I can remember the last time, we were in a situation like this with statues and strange hieroglyphs. You read the words out and the blooming statues came to life and chased us!"

Lucian chuckled, "Fear not, Sir Septimus, I won't be doing anything like that again. To be sure I wouldn't even know how to pronounce these hieroglyphs, let alone read them!" And then he took out a notebook and pencil from his waist-jacket and copied down the hieroglyphs, muttering to himself as he worked: "This really is most interesting!"

Moments later he was putting away his notebook and pencil while saying, "Maybe a member of the Council of Knowledge will understand this writing and tell us its meaning."

Artimus consulted his watch. "We have made good time, my friends." The smile dropped from his face as the realisation that they now had to pass through the entrance into unknown territory dawned coldly upon him.

The Pogglins looked into the gloom and beyond into inky blackness of the entrance. Occasionally they could hear the roar of the wind as it whistled down the tunnel towards them.

"There must be another opening at the other end to cause this draft of wind," said Sir Septimus. For a moment they all hesitated.

"Shall we?" said Lucian, leading the way.

The Pogglins entered and were swallowed up by the blackness; it would be a long time before they were to see sunlight again.

Chapter TWO

In the Dondymarian capital, Dondymar City, a door opened to the main laboratory of the *Research Unit for Advanced Technology and Science* (R.U.F.A.T.A.S. for short). Professor Inglenook Frumpton-Stone walked into the laboratory. He was as ugly, rounded-shouldered and bow-legged as any other Dondymarian. But unlike other Dondymarians, he wore no wig. A gold monocle was fixed in his right eye. He wore a long, white laboratory coat stained with grease and oil. A black bowtie hung at his neck like a vampire bat. He had a mustard-yellow waistcoat, heavily stained down the front with half of his lunch. Black breeches and grey stockings completed his shabby and grubby attire.

Professor Frumpton-Stone was the head scientist at the *Research Unit of Advanced Science and Technology* or R.U.F.A.S.A.T. for short. Doctor Munggo Meltabossokk, the head scientist of R.U.F.A.T.A.S. had called for him to attend. They were arch-rivals, but both had grudgingly agreed to work together on the top-secret project.

Operation Steam-Powered Mass Destruction. The development of the new secret-weapon; the Steam-Powered War Robot. Both were the scientific geniuses of their age, and both were barking mad! Frumpton-Stone eyed his rival from the doorway, "What did the old fphool want now?" he lisped to himself, closing the door behind him. "It had better a good reasphon thisph time, having crosspshed half the cphity to get here!" He shouted in his lisping voice. But reply there came none from the little Doctor. "Well, what do you want?" he inquired of Meltabossokk.

Meltabossokk didn't hear; he was too busy working on an intricate, steam-powered device on his bench. His rubber-gloved hands were working feverishly with an infinitely small spanner, with which he connected a wire to the device.

Frumpton-Stone tapped him on the shoulder. "What do you want?"

Meltabossokk looked up from his work with a manic smile. "Ah-ha! Frumpton-Stone, just the fellow! Here - hold this!" He said in a low, creepy voice, and he gave Frampton-Stone the other end of the wire to hold.

"If you insphispht!" said Frumpton-Stone and took hold of the wire. Instantly he was thrown across the laboratory with the jolt he received from the electricity, hit the wall; and slid down into a heap on the floor.

"Thank you," said Meltabossokk, looking over at the tangled heap on the floor.
He grinned maliciously to himself. "I thought that was the live wire: so kind of you to confirm it for me!" He bolted the wire onto the apparatus, laughing maniacally as he worked.

Eventually, Frumpton-Stone came to in a daze. He saw Meltabossokk standing by his bench, grinning down at him with that idiotic lopsided grin. Doctor Meltabossokk was almost of Dwarfish proportions, and even more round-shoulder than was usual for a Dondymarian. His head was large, with a long top lip and low-set ears. He too wore no wig. To other Dondymarians, this was a sure sign of his madness! In his left eye was a monocle framed with blackened pig-iron. He too wore the obligatory white coat (the badge of all mad scientists!) and a red waistcoat. A frill of black cloth was about his throat. His wide-set bowlegs were clothed in dark blue breeches and white stockings. And of course, those black rubber gloves; Frumpton-Stone was certain that he slept in them!

"I'm glad to see you are with us again, Professor," he said, and moved to one side of the bench. "Look! The adjustments to the steam-powered positronic brain are complete!" He maniacally rubbed his rubber-gloved hands together as Frumpton-Stone marched over to the bench and glared at Meltabossokk ominously. He jammed his monocle back into his eye, before turning round to examine the little positronic brain on the bench.

Frumpton-Stone sniffed grudgingly as he examined Meltabossokk's work, which had been expertly carried out. The little Doctor stood beside Frumpton-Stone with an evil grin fixed on his face. "Yesph," lisped Frumpton-Stone, nodding his head. "Excellent work – and you are sphure the adjusphtmentsph will work?"

"Oh yes, Professor, it will work!" he replied, frantically nodding his head and chuckled in a weird, crooning manner. Doctor Meltabossokk called for his assistant. Philbinn Dropjaw hurried into the Laboratory; he was thin-faced and fat-bodied, and very eager for promotion. "At your service, Doctor," he fawned.

"Take the positronic brain to the activation room, Dropjaw."

"Yes, certainly Doctor Meltabossokk." Dropjaw picked up the little positronic brain with reverence and hurried out of the laboratory. The two followed him. Presently they came to the activation room, wherein the centre of the room stood a large, bulky object covered with a sheet. The little Doctor walked over to the object and pulled off the sheet revealing their new secret weapon; the War Robot!

★ ★ ★ ★ ★

The three Pogglins walked slowly as they passed through the entrance to the Zelgemar Gate and into the gloom. A warm breeze arose hitting them in the face and causing the brim of Lucian's hat to flap. He pulled it down tighter on his head; he did not want to lose it in the dark and dismal gloom of the tunnel. As they moved further down the tunnel and away from the entrance, their sight was consumed by impenetrable blackness. The sounds of their tentative footsteps were amplified by the acoustics of the tunnel and echoed around them like the tapping of dwarven hammers. Lucian tapped his staff lightly in front of him, finding the way, the metallic sound echoing around the walls.

"I say Snuzz old thing, could you throw some light on the matter?" asked Sir Septimus. "I've a feeling we're going to run into something nasty, and I would rather see it first!"

"Ever the optimist, Sir Septimus! Better I conserve my magical powers for an emergency, rather than wasting it on a light," replied Lucian, his own thoughts now turned to what could be watching them in the darkness.

As they moved along, the Pogglins felt their shoes scuffling along the rock floor. "The tunnel must have been cut through the solid rock of the mountain." said Artimus. The daylight, although dwindling fast, still penetrated a little from the entrance along and into the darkness of the tunnel, causing strange shadowy images and shapes to dance over the walls. As their eyes slowly became accustomed to the dark, the Pogglins realised that the strange shapes were in fact carvings cut into the wall, but without more light, they could not make out what they depicted.

"By Dunbruan, look at those carvings!" The other two looked, craning their neck and squinting into the gloom. "They seem to run along the entire length of the tunnel," said Lucian excitedly.

Artimus could hear something below the sound of the rushing wind. "What's that noise?"

"What's what?" replied Sir Septimus.

"Sshhhh!" hissed Artimus. "That! You hear it?"

The three Pogglins listened intently. "Blowed if I can hear anything other than the wind!" said Sir Septimus, and then he stopped. Now that he thought about it, he *could* hear something, something bubbling and something that almost sounded like the sea. Then Lucian caught the sound of it.

"What an interesting noise! Sounds like a boiling sea," he exclaimed. "I wonder what it could be?"

Artimus too was fixed by the strange noise. "Whatever it is, my friends, it's coming from the other end of the tunnel and seems to be quite close!"

"I don't remember seeing any sea marked on the map that the Quistorrisians showed us?"

"There wasn't," replied Lucian in answer to Sir Septimus' question.

The Pogglins' eyes were becoming accustomed to the gloom and began to move off again down the tunnel towards the strange noise.

"Look! There seem to be red light somewhere near the end of the tunnel," said Lucian with a whisper.

The tunnel walls eventually began to veer off to the right, and it was then that Lucian noticed more carvings on the walls as the tunnel started to widen again, much to their great relief.

"What a pity we have to move on! I would have very much liked to have recorded these carvings," said Lucian in disappointment, "but we simply haven't the time, we must keep going."

The wind was rushing past them and seemed to be louder now than it had been earlier. The noise became more perceptible above the wind, the bubbling noise being the louder of the two noises that they had heard earlier.

"We must almost be at the centre of the mountain!" said Artimus.

Sir Septimus nodded his head, "I agree."

"It's getting warmer too" added Lucian, as he continued to make out what he could as the carvings passed him by.

"Goodness me, it's getting hot!" said Artimus and he loosened his bowtie.

"Stifling!" agreed Sir Septimus, mopping his brow and then taking a water bottle from his pouch and taking a sip.

"Be careful how much you drink, Sir Septimus. We may have to ration ourselves in case we cannot find any drinkable water in Empraktos-Larris," Lucian advised.

They moved closer to the end of the glowing tunnel: fear had oddly been replaced now by curiosity as to what was emitting the glow and the unusual noise. After several more minutes, the Pogglins reached the tunnel's end where they encountered a very similar carved gateway, which replicated the one at the entrance.

Walking through, they came to a narrow bridge across a chasm, which had a sheer drop on either side down into the red-tinged blackness below. Turning around to his friends, Lucian warned them of the drop. Moving over the bridge, the three Pogglins now had to tread extremely carefully as lumps of rock fell into the seemingly bottomless abyss at their side as they planted their feet tentatively on the path. Sir Septimus fixed his gaze ahead of him; he hated heights and *particularly* heights where you couldn't see the bottom!

The bridge led the Pogglins to a pathway around the rock-face to the left. They kept close to the rock, as there was another sheer drop to the right of their path. The rock was warm and the air around them was roasting hot: not even the breeze had a cooling effect, and they soon began to sweat profusely. Around the Pogglins went, the path still veering to the left and the sheer drop all too present the right.

Artimus, who was at the back of the group, happened to look up and noticed the narrow rock bridge above them. "We are descending around in a circle; this path is taking us downward!" he exclaimed to the others.

Suddenly the path narrowed into roughly hewn steps in the rock, whilst the rock face started to grow thin and stretch until it resembled an elongated column. The Pogglins realised that they were now traversing a very roughly cut spiral stairwell, like a corkscrew, which seemed to be suspended in mid-air with nothing but the void around them.

"These must be The Zelgemar Stairs, my friends!" shouted Sir Septimus, above the bubbling noise still rising from below. Downward the Pogglins went, downward for what seemed like an eternity, and at their every step a danger; the same danger that with one false move would send them plunging to their deaths far below.

They kept in tight to the column of rock, the bubbling noise throbbing in their ears and the sweat streaming down their backs. Their eyes were accustomed to the light by now, which was of a deep red colour, and with the aid of that glow they could now see what was making the bubbling noise. Below them was a massive sea of heaving lava, red as molten rubies, that seemed to stretch off into infinity in all directions—and worryingly, the Pogglins seemed to be descending right into the middle of it!

Artimus was edging down the stairs as quickly as he dared; the lava seas below seemed to invite him to plummet to a ghastly death. As he made his way around the column, his overcloak snagged on the rock surface, causing him to stumble and he only just managed to keep his balance. His overcloak was becoming a danger to his safety! He kept his back to the wall of the column of stairs, and all the while the bubbling lava below captivated his gaze. Slowly he shrugged off his pouch over his head and then removed the overcloak. He replaced his pouch over his head and placed the map in his waist-jacket pocket and, stepping up his pace to catch up with the others, he gingerly hugged the rock-face as he descended towards the sea of lava.

Lucian was weary with the exertion of leading the descent. The red glow from the lava below them was making his eyes sting. He had to keep blinking to try to not only alleviate the stinging, but to clear his vision. Amidst the sulphurous vapour and smoke rising up from the lava he thought that he could make out another light to the east, but he couldn't be sure. He began to feel dizzy with fatigue: each step was painful to him, and with all his heart he wanted to sit down and rest. Knowing his companions were in the same state made him push on, in the hope that they would soon reach the end of the stairway.

Suddenly Sir Septimus shook Lucian out of his melancholy. "WOULD YOU JUST LOOK AT THAT?" He shouted, the monocle flying from his socket, as he pointed excitedly and lost his balance. Within the space of a heartbeat, he had stumbled and plummeted over the edge with a cry.

Artimus rushed forward and caught the sleeve of his friend's waist-jacket just in time to save him from a boiling death below. "I'VE GOT YOU!" Artimus yelled. "NOW TRY TO SWING UP ONTO THE STEPS IF YOU CAN!"

Sir Septimus started to swing his body towards the steps, while Lucian hurried back up the steps to help Artimus.

"My grip is slipping! LUCIAN, HELP ME!"

Lucian rushed forwards and grabbed hold of Sir Septimus' hand, while the latter desperately tried to swing his legs up over the edge and back onto the steps. Suddenly there was a sickening noise of ripping cloth as the stitching on the sleeve began to tear along the shoulder seam.

"Try and swing your leg up!" cried Lucian, as he pulled with all his might. His strength draining fast, he felt a wave of panic rush over him. Fearing he was about to lose his dearest friend; he gave one final heave at the same time as Sir Septimus swung his leg for the umpteenth time onto the ledge above him.

At last, after what seemed like a hopeless venture, Sir Septimus finally managed to swing his boot up and onto the ledge of the steps as the other two Pogglins caught his weight and heaved up their friend to relative safety. Suddenly the map fluttered from Artimus' waist-jacket pocket and made its slow, mocking descent into the Lava waiting below.

"The Map!" cried Artimus, and the three of them stood there frozen by shock. They couldn't believe their bad luck, as they were lost even before they started on their journey into Empraktos–Larris.

Lucian patted his friend on the back in reassurance. "We'll find our way, Artimus," he said reassuringly.

While Sir Septimus recovered, Lucian and Artimus saw below what Sir Septimus had been pointing at so excitedly before his near-fatal fall. To the east of them lay a great and vast forest of giant mushrooms that stretched off into the horizon. The mushrooms were of subtle pastel shades and they seemed luminous. for they lit all around them with a greenish-blue glow. The Fungoid Forest: it was an eerie a sight as it was a beautiful one.

The successful rescue, short rest and promise of beauty that awaited them, encouraged the Pogglins onward and they moved with infinite caution down the Zelgemar Stairs. It soon became obvious to them as they descended the stairs that the great sea of lava actually laid to the north-west.

It took another hot and tiring hour of effort before the Pogglins finally made it to the bottom of the stairs. The stairs terminated in an outcrop of rocks, and the Pogglins looked about them. They were on the hot and rocky shore of the lava sea that covered the whole of the west and north-western horizon. Although there was no daylight in the sky itself, the Pogglins could see by the red glow generated by the lava sea.

Miles above them the Pogglins could make out a vast, rocky roof, and they realised that they were standing in a cavern of tremendous size, deep within the bowels of the Earth. The bubbling from the Lava Sea and strange noises from the forest filled their ears as they took in the panorama about them. Artimus checked his watch: 4.30 p.m.

The Pogglins then turned east and headed towards the luminous Fungoid Forest, ever mindful of what could be living here and whether it was friendly or not. This encouraged the trio to move as quickly as possible, and shortly they were on the outskirts of the great forest. Exhausted, the Pogglins made their way to cover under the first of the smaller mushrooms and lay down on the soft, peat-like soil. Breathing rapidly, they slowly regained their composure and fell easily into a much-needed deep and refreshing sleep.

★ ★ ★ ★ ★

An early evening sun was shining bright in Pogglinburg, and Balferzaar the Black was sitting by the open window in his study within the Black Tower. He was writing at the desk, but his attention and thoughts were in the west when a bird landing on the windowsill distracted him.

Balferzaar smiled and gestured to the bird. "Come in, my friend," he said to Sedgwick.

The bird nodded its thanks and hopped in on to the old wizard's desk. Sedgwick was of medium size for a bird, and quite plump. The Wallie bird's eyes were bright, with a touch of mischievous humour about them. He had beautiful powder-blue feathers that shaded into green towards its clawed feet. His bill was large, somewhat like a dodo's and was of a bright burnt-orange colour.

"Greetings and salutations, O Balferzaar the Black," said Sedgwick, and he bowed in reverence. The old wizard poured a little wine into a silver bowl and placed it before the Wallie bird. "You must be parched Sedgwick, after your journey from Quistorrisia!"

The bird began to drink, sipping at the wine and then throwing its head back to swallow. "Thank you. Most refreshing and my favourite vintage!" said Sedgwick, and continued, "I bring you good news, O Balferzaar, from Prometheus Zeus. Lucian and his party have arrived safely in Quistorrisia."

"That is excellent! Well done, young Artimus!" interjected the wizard.

"The Quistorrisians gave the information that you requested to Lucian and his party. They set off late in the evening for Mount Zelmekh. If all has gone to plan, they should be on the Zelgemar Staircase."

The old wizard gently stroked the top of the bird's head.

"Thank you, my friend; your news has been of enormous help. Should you and your friends hear any more of this matter or any other Dondymarian affairs; I would like you to bring me news of it here?"

Sedgwick nodded. "This we shall do, O Balferzaar."

★ ★ ★ ★ ★

The War Robot was a strange-looking contraption, and built like a tank. Its body was cylindrical in shape with tank-like caterpillar tracks. These were driven by a large piston on either side of the body. At shoulder height jutted two propeller-like props where one would expect to find arms. The prop had three steel blades attached to it; the blades had been keenly sharpened and were razor sharp!

Professor Frumpton-Stone and Doctor Munggo Meltabossokk with the war robot.

In between the rotary blades, on the Robot's chest was emblazoned the Dondymarian coat of Arms, which was the Royal Crown. Beneath that, at about the height of a Pogglin belly were situated two screw-like spikes. The Robot's head was hexagonal in shape with two circular eyes; these stuck out a little from the head, and were covered with red glass lenses. The jaw, which resembled a Knight's helmet's visor, had been bolted at either side of the head. It had antenna-like objects in the place where the ears would be on the head. On top of the head was a red, glass-domed light.

While Doctor Meltabossokk fetched the positronic brain, Dropjaw laid out a set of metal steps by the side of the Robot. The Doctor then ran up the steps, flipped open the top of the War Robot's head and placed the little steam engine of a positronic brain inside. Dropjaw was already standing by with a set of operating tools.

"The spanner if you please, Dropjaw!"

The Doctor was handed the tool and he bolted it into place. He then stoked the engine and lit the boiler; slowly, the little pistons began to rotate. He smiled to himself, wringing his hands as he watched the flywheel pick up speed. Satisfied with his work, he closed down the top of the head and locked it into place. The red glass lenses of the War Robot's eyes began to glow with life. He ran quickly down the steps and over to Frumpton-Stone.

"It is done, Professor. You may now start him up when you are ready," he giggled with mad glee.

"Then I sphall proceed immediately!" He proclaimed, throwing his arm into the air and waggled his finger, in an over-theatrical gesture. Clapping his hands together, he rushed over to the War Robot. At the back were situated six exhaust pipes, three down either side of the back. They stuck out horizontally at 90-degree angles and then curved at 40-degree angles up into the air.

At the top, in the centre of the back, there protruded a cylindrical vent with a lid. Frumpton-Stone flipped open the lid, and he was given a large canister full of water by Dropjaw. The Professor filled the War Robot's boiler with water and snapped the lid shut when it was at full capacity. Towards the bottom of the War Robot was the furnace door, which was unlatched by the Professor. He opened the door and stokes the furnace with coal.

It was at this point that Lord Fangdom Creep entered the Activation Room with the Royal Secretary, Sir Kyaphaas Gittoid.

The Professor lit the furnace and used bellows to help it burn more quickly and the coals were glowing into activity. Frumpton-Stone closed the door and dropped down the latch. He then closely observed the pressure gauges mounted into the engine pipes set between the six exhaust pipes and then turned the pressure valve to increase the output pressure.

"We are all mospht at full pressure and we will shortly be coming up to activation point," Frumpton-Stone informed them as he stepped back away from the War Robot.

Lord Creep looked nervously at the crimson-painted steam-powered monster.

"You are totally sure that this machine is now safe?" enquired the Lord Creep in his thin, reedy voice.

"Oh yes, my Lord, quite sure!" nodded Meltabossokk, wringing his hands

"Then you had better start the demonstration!" Lord Creep wheezed.

Professor Frumpton-Stone activated the War Robot by pressing in a button and turning a small pressure valve. The domed light on top of the War Robot's head illuminated and the eyes glowed intensely.

"I-AM-READY-TO-RECEIVE-ORDERS," said the War Robot in a harsh, grating voice. Frumpton-Stone moved quickly away, eyeing the screw-like spikes nervously. He handed over the proceedings to Doctor Meltabossokk, who went and stood next to the War Robot.

"I am pleased to report the modification to the steam-powered positronic brain has now been completed," he announced and patted the chest of the War Robot.

"Robot: move forward!"

The pistons on either side of the War Robot slowly began to move, and the six exhaust pipes began to belch smoke. With a sound of hissing steam, the War Robot rolled forward on its tank-like tracks. It headed straight towards Lord Creep and Sir Kyaphaas Gittoid; the anxiety started to show on their faces as the War Robot drew near.

"Halt!" shouted Meltabossokk, and the War Robot instantly stopped.

"Reverse." ordered the doctor, and the War Robot reversed back to its starting point.

A smile began to curl on the lips of Lord Creep. "The old fool has perfected voice control!" he thought to himself.

"Turn left." The War Robot did as commanded. "Move forward and come about," cackled Meltabossokk with glee as the War Robot perfectly followed his directions.

"Halt." The Robot stopped, the steam hissing quietly from the pistons as they idled in readiness.

"Remarkable, Doctor Meltabossokk! You have done an excellent job!" chuckled Lord Creep with glee. "Now can we see a demonstration of the War Robots weapons, Doctor Meltabossokk?"

"Certainly, Lord Creep," and he turned to the War Robot. "Activate primary weapons system!"

The War Robot's eyes blinked; "I-OBEY." The rotary blades on the props began to turn, gaining speed until they were a blur and made the air hum as they whirled around.

"Attack system!" commanded the cackling, Doctor. Instantly the rotary blades shot out on pistons four feet in length, making a buzzing noise as they moved.

"Activate secondary weapons system!" The two screw-like spikes on the War Robot began to turn until they were whirling around like drills.

"Deactivate weapon systems and power down!" he said, wringing his hands with obvious pride while he watched the War Robot retract the rotary blades and the spikes slowed down and came to a halt.

"Excellent!" called Creep and Gittoid, applauding loudly.

"This is a machine to conquer the whole of Sol-Larris!" rasped Lord Creep.

Gittoid whispered in Creep's ear, Creep nodded in agreement. He turned to the Professor and the Doctor.

"Sir Gittoid and I are extremely impressed with the weaponry, but feel we would like to see a full demonstration of it in action."

Frumpton-Stone eyed Meltabossokk, "Thisph might be my opportunity in ridding mysphelf of thisphfphool," he thought to himself. In fact, Meltabossokk was having precisely the same thoughts for Frumpton-Stone! Then they both began to smile evilly at each other and nodded in total agreement.

"Dropjaw, would you mind coming in for a moment!" bellowed Meltabossokk.

Dropjaw came rushing into the room. "Yes Doctor, could I be of service?"

"Yes," said the Doctor, and told him to stand on the spot marked X by the table. Dropjaw eagerly hurried to the spot and stood there with a stupid smile on his ridiculous face. He watched the two guest observers and the Professor and the Doctor, as he eagerly awaited further instruction.

"ANNIHILATE!" screeched Meltabossokk. The War Robot's eyes began to blink on and off, the rotary blades whizzed into action, as did the screw-like spikes. The War Robot trundled forward, belching smoke from the exhausts. It moved towards Dropjaw, who still wore the stupid uncomprehending smile on his face.

The War Robot bore down on him, the blades a whirring blur.

"YOU-WILL-BE-ANNIHILATED!" grated the War Robot as the rotary blade pistons came shooting out towards him.

Dropjaw's smile fell from his face as the realisation of what was about to happen hit him, a split-second before the blades did!

Doctor Meltabossokk wiped his face with his coat sleeve. He shook his head. "Dear old Dropjaw; he was so eager to contribute to the project, and now he has finally had his wish granted."

"Excellent!" grinned Lord Creep evilly. "When will the army be ready to attack Pogglinburg?"

"The factories are at full capacity, my Lord, and will be at full muster when you require them!" replied Doctor Meltabossokk.

"That is music to our ears, Doctor!" said Lord Creep, with Sir Kyaphaas Gittoid nodding in agreement.

★ ★ ★ ★ ★

Artimus was awoken by something tickling his face; there was a dark green muzzle sniffing at him as he opened his eyes with a start. His startled movement frightened the creature, and it darted back into the Fungoid Forest just as Sir Septimus and Lucian sat up.

"What was that?"

"I don't know. Whatever it was, it was quite large and green!" He quickly consulted his watch, at 7.15 pm. But his glance was so quick that he did not notice that it had stopped.

The glow from the luminous mushrooms lit all around the surrounding area and gave the impression of a blue and misty twilight. The Pogglins stayed where they were, and peered into the depths of the Fungoid Forest.

"It didn't mean us any harm, or we wouldn't be sitting here," said Sir Septimus, and then stopped; there were several pairs of glowing golden eyes staring at him from the darkness of the forest undergrowth. "You see them?" he said quietly out the corner of his mouth.

"Yes!" came the reply from his friends.

"Nobody moves!" said Artimus.

Suddenly the air was filled with a dreadful wailing sound, and all three clapped their hands over their ears. The noise ended as suddenly as it started. They sat stock still in dread for what seemed like hours, until one of the creatures began to venture forwards. It emerged from the shadows, and the Pogglins saw that it was a large green cat!

The cat sniffed the air; it's extremely large ears pricked up high on its small head, and it took a slow step forward. Presently it was joined by four more of its kind. They really were quite the strangest-looking cats. They were long in the body, long in the leg and very sleek. The tail was as long as the body and the head seemed disproportionably small. They had very large orange-coloured eyes. In the luminous glow from the mushrooms, the cats looked to be lime green with darker green patches over their bodies, which were totally hairless.

The leading cat came a little closer to the Pogglins and then sat down, its head cocked to one side as it studied them. The Pogglins in return sat quietly and waited to see what would happen next. The main cat made a mewing sound and the other cats sat down a little way behind. After a long pause, the lead cat broke the silence.

"Not very talkative, are they?" it retorted in a throaty voice to its companions and they nodded their heads in agreement.

The sight of a talking cat did not particularly surprise the Pogglins; for almost all creatures of the Sol-Larrian Earth could talk.

"You are not Fungiglook," continued the cat. "Nor are you Subterranians. Are you Baalzionians, then?"

"Neither," replied Lucian. "We are Pogglins from Pogglinburg, and who may you and your companions be?"

"Never heard of Pogglins before." said a cat sat just behind the leader.

"No, I have never heard of the Pogglins of Pogglinburg either." The lead cat agreed. He raised his paw, a claw sprang out and the Pogglins flinched, wondering if he was about to attack them, but the cat merely scratched his nose and retracted it again.

"As to us, we are the cats of Empraktos-Larris. I am Fontahl, leader of this scouting party." The Pogglins introduced themselves, as the cat nodded in acknowledgement.

"You are obviously strangers to this land," said Fontahl. "But where do you come from?"

"We come from above," said Lucian, pointing to the Zelgemar Stairs. "From the land of Sol-Larris. My friends and I seek the Lake of Wonders and the Moogem Tree. Do you know of it?"

Fontahl narrowed his eyes. "From above, you say? I have heard tales of a land at the end of the Zelgemar Stairs, but I have yet to meet anyone from there." He pondered the matter, examining his ivory claws for some moments. "Very well, I shall take you at your word," he said. "The lake that you seek is to the east beyond the *Valley of Zaark*..."

His ears picked up a sound in the forest; he meowed, and all the cats vanished into the Fungoid Forest in a twinkling of an eye!

"By Obadiah Thrasskin's beard! What a rotten time for those cats to dash off like that. Just as they were giving us directions!" said Sir Septimus, thrusting his hands into his breeches' pockets in annoyance.

"Those cats heard a noise, and it must have meant danger for them to run off like that? This means we had better make ourselves scarce as well!" Artimus replied in agitation. Before they could move, they heard a noise of something flying through the air.

Acting instinctively, Sir Septimus hurled himself at his companions, bowling them over into the undergrowth of the Fungoid Forest. A great mass of liquid struck the spot where they had been standing. It dissolved the soil and the part of the mushroom's stem, causing the mushroom to come crashing down. The liquid appeared to be a quick-acting acid!

Lucian and Artimus recovered from their shock and thanked Sir Septimus for his diligence.

"That was acid, but where by Dunbruan did it come from" whispered Lucian.

Suddenly the Pogglins squatted down as the answer to their conundrum came slithering into view. The newcomer was a giant slug. The Pogglins quivered with revulsion at the sight of the great glistening and pulsating beast. The slug was of tremendous size, being over sixty feet in length, it was a sickly yellow colour, and pale blue veins crisscrossed its vile body. Small eyes stuck out on stalks from its head. Above its head was a mass of puckered blisters and growths that were crowned by a protuberance which was nozzle-like; this was the creature's acid gun. A thick, beaded skirt ran around the base of its body, which rippled as the creature heaved its massive bulk along on a bed of slime.

The Pogglins' stomachs heaved at the sight of the vile creature until they could take no more; they turned and rushed in panic further into the Fungoid Forest.

★ ★ ★ ★ ★

Minutes later they came to a halt, panting for breath, and totally lost. The Pogglins were now very deep into the Fungoid Forest, and in their haste to escape the slug they had lost all sense of direction. The undergrowth was made up of dead pieces of mushroom that had turned to mulch. Out of this clearly fertile soil grew long, thin blade-like grasses and small mushrooms of differing shapes, sizes and colours. Sprouting everywhere about them were the larger mushrooms, ranging between anything from one-and-a-half feet up to six feet tall. Then there were the giant mushrooms. These impressive specimens reached up to a height of one hundred feet. They were all of delicate pastel colours of pinks, reds, purples and blues. Some were spotted, some were not, but all gave off the same greenish-blue glow. The eerie silence was interrupted now and then by a shriek or a call of some kind. The constant rustling in the undergrowth depicted unknown animals or insects present. Whether friendly or otherwise, the trio were yet to find out!

"I'm getting too old for all this running about!" exclaimed Artimus, collapsing to the ground with exhaustion. The Pogglins' arrival on the ground disturbed a creature that was feeding, and out of the undergrowth marched a small, three-legged thing with large eyes and a quiff of green tendrils on its head.

"*Quibervezy!*" it angrily mumbled at Artimus and stomped off back into the forest.

The three Pogglins looked at each other, somewhat fazed by the thing's abrupt arrival and departure, and Lucian shrugged his shoulders. "Must be having a bad day!" he said, leaning on his staff and trying to catch his breath.

"I know how it feels!" replied Sir Septimus.

"Of all the adventures we have been on, this is the first time I have forgotten to pack a compass —and now I have lost the Map!" bemoaned Artimus.

"Well, we did have to leave Pogglinburg in a hurry, Artimus, and there is nothing we can do about it now. Don't be so hard on yourself, and I know you are missing Marius already because you are getting grumpy."

Artimus gave Lucian a look.

"We'll rest here for five minutes and then see if we can find our bearings," said Lucian calmly.

"I wish I had a sack of salt! I would have shown that slug a thing or two!" said Sir Septimus, and they all began to laugh.

They stopped abruptly, above the whoops and squawks of the Fungoid Forest they heard a slithering noise heading toward them.

"The Acid Slug!" cried Artimus and the Pogglins leapt to their feet and dashed through the forest as fast as their little legs would carry them, the grass blades whipping at them as they rushed by. Suddenly they skidded on a slime track and went hurtling headlong into the side of another of the forest's giant slugs. The Pogglins closed their eyes and braced themselves for instant death.

"That was a rather rude and blunt introduction I must say!" said a low gurgling voice. "Not a good way to start a friendship at all!"

The Pogglins opened one eye and then the other. Staring down at them were two very large eyes on the end of very long stalks! Realising that this was no acid slug, the Pogglins started laughing with relief, for it was a giant snail and a friendly one too!

"Well now, you come hurtling through the forest at breakneck speed, not having the courtesy to look where you are going, you go crashing into me and then start laughing at me –and all without a proper introduction! "Dear me, what strange little fellows you are," the snail continued, grazing on one of the giant mushrooms without another word.

"We are very sorry." the Pogglins apologised. "We thought you were a slug."

The snail whipped his head around. "Do I look like a giant slug?" He said indignantly. "What do you think that is on my back, a hump?" Pieces of mushroom sprayed all over them as he spoke.

The Pogglins wiped themselves down as much as they could and then introduced themselves to the snail. The snail nodded approvingly as the Pogglins went through the formalities of introduction.

"Very pleased to meet you, I am sure. Now if you had done that in the first place, we would have gotten off to a much better start," said the snail, taking another bite of the mushroom and munching on it slowly, "Now what can I do for you?"

The Pogglins told the snail of their quest for the Moogem Tree, and while he listened to them the snail continued to eat. "The Moogem Tree? Now let me see," and he munched on some more of the mushroom. "That can be found to the east –beyond the Valley of Zaark I believe – and southeast from the outcrop of Uutroc." he said, turning his head and pointing with one of his eyestalks behind him, "which is over in that direction."

The giant snail was getting fed up with the mushroom and he began to move off for grazing pastures new.

"Be careful of the slugs, my friends! Once they get a scent of you, they will follow you to the ends of the earth." Then, seemingly as an afterthought, he added, "Better roll in my slime, as it will help you avoid the slugs!"

The Pogglins watched the snail move slowly off deeper into the forest, whistling to himself.

The three Pogglins looked down at the slime and grimaced. Pogglins are very smart and tidy people by nature, and take a great deal of care over their appearance.

"I don't like the sound of rolling in that slime for the sake of it!" Sir Septimus said with disgust. "You two can roll in it if you wish, but I am messy enough as I am, thanks very much," he said, polishing his monocle and then patting down his hair and twirling up his moustaches.

Artimus looked at his clothes and sighed, "I hate to get any dirtier, but it if it keeps those vile slugs away then needs must!" and he quickly dived into the slime, followed by Lucian. The slime was of a sticky, stringy texture and stuck to the Pogglins' clothes in patches. Sir Septimus quivered at the sight of seeing his friends rolling in the slime.

"This is a mighty strange place indeed!" announced a sticky and uncomfortable Lucian as they moved off in the opposite direction.

The Pogglins moved along at a reasonable pace, only pausing to pull off dead blades of grass and tiny mushrooms that had stuck to their clothes due to the slime. But all the while they constantly listened out for the giant acid slugs and any other creatures that they might come across. The air smelt damp and the heat of the Fungoid Forest was like that of a cool summer's day, nowhere near the stifling heat of the Zelgemar Stairs.

Strange noises rang out now and then; weird mutterings of howls and shrieks filtered through the forest gloom. They were nothing like anything the Pogglins had heard before - any known bird certainly didn't make them, or animal. Every so often they would see the familiar outline of dragonflies flying silently overhead above the mushroom tops. Familiar they may have been, but their size was way beyond anything they had seen before.

As the Pogglins moved along they became conscious of being watched. They heard rustlings among the grasses that were definitely not insects, and sometimes they would see dark shapes moving swiftly through the gloom to either side of them. Occasionally, they glimpsed luminous eyes watching them from the depths of the undergrowth then disappear in a flash.

Every time the Pogglins looked in this or that direction, they saw nothing to confirm who or what was behind these eyes, but the continuous rustling noises from the undergrowth told them they were still around.

"We're being stalked!" said Artimus anxiously.

"Probably those cats?" said Sir Septimus.

"I don't think so? The eyes are too big!" replied Lucian worriedly.

"They're also the wrong colour and size too! Whatever they are, they have been following us since we left the snail," said Artimus with growing fear, his eyes looking from side to side as he walked. He readied himself for the ambush that he thought was bound to come at any moment. He also wondered why they had not considered bringing any weapons into unknown territory!

"Come out and show yourselves, whatever you are!" he shouted.

The Pogglins came to a halt and listened: there was no sound, no movement.

Then suddenly they saw a thin, nimble creature bounce up and onto the high mushroom top, leap-frog over another, and then somersaulting back on to the ground with a soft *thump* in front of the surprised Pogglins. Pausing only to look at them, the creature darted back into the depths of the forest. But in that few seconds, the Pogglins made out that the creature's skin was of a pale mushroom colour and it had large, emerald-green eyes.

The monocle popped out of Sir Septimus' socket with surprise. "By the beard on Obadiah Thrasskin's chin! There are more life forms in this forest than you can shake a stick at! What on Sol-Larris was that?" He said in dismay, just as another of the creatures somersaulted to the ground before them and darted back into the forest at lightning speed.

"Whatever they are, Sir Septimus, they find us a curiosity, but I think they mean us no harm," said Lucian. The Pogglins decided to stop and rest where they were in the hope of making contact with the timid creatures. They sat down in a semi-circle of mushrooms that stood about three feet tall. The caps above the stalks gave them cover from any passing acid slugs. They pulled from their pouches something to eat and drink, while they discussed the best way of finding their way east.

"If I had some iron and a magnet, I could make a compass," bemoaned Artimus once again and felt through his pockets again. "Yes, I know I am getting grumpy again!"

Lucian smiled, then he saw the creature; the thin-bodied thing was peering at the group from behind the stem of one of the smaller mushrooms. It hid when it saw the Pogglin had spotted it. Quietly Lucian told the others to keep their voices down, the creatures were near and that he did not want to frighten them off. The Pogglins talked quietly among themselves and before very long a creature appeared again, peering from behind the mushroom. It was listening intently to what the Pogglins were saying, its big eyes luminous in the shadows.

To the Pogglins' amazement, the creature began to climb up on top of the mushroom and sit down. Another of the creatures appeared from behind the mushroom, and soon another. Now that the creature was in the light, the Pogglins had the opportunity of seeing it in detail, as it sat there listening to them. The Pogglins continued their conversation, not wanting to frighten the creature away, but all the while they kept their eyes on it.

The creature was very small; Lucian guessed that they were sixteen to eighteen inches tall when standing and its eyes shone like emeralds lit from within. The pale mushroom-coloured skin was perfect camouflage for life in this forest. It was thin and wiry, with large hands and long fingers. Their feet were large and flat. It had an oval face, there was no nose but it had a wide and pleasant mouth like a frog. The ears were big and pointed. The head was bald and elongated at the back and it sat atop a long thin neck. The creature was totally nude but for a loincloth of grass that was about the waist. Another of the creatures slowly climbed up the mushroom to join the other. The first broke off a piece of the mushroom, broke it in two and passed a piece to its companion; they then casually started munching on it as they listened to the Pogglins.

"So, they eat the mushrooms; I wonder if they are edible to us? It would be useful if our food runs short," mused Artimus.

Very slowly, Lucian began to stand and move cautiously toward the creatures. The ones beneath the mushroom darted back for cover in the forest. One of the creatures on top of the mushroom began to climb slowly down and peeped over the top of it at the approaching Pogglin. He stopped just short of the mushroom that the creature was sitting on.

"Hello," he said, "I am Lucian Snuzz, and these are my friends, Artimus Whistlecraft and Sir Septimus Pulpit." Lucian held out his hand, making the creature shy away. Then the creature cautiously moved nearer to Lucian and then in a rapid movement placed the piece of mushroom it was eating into his hand.

"You're not getting through to him Snuzz; he thinks you want the mushroom," said Sir Septimus cautiously.

"We are your friends," said Lucian and then tried a piece of the mushroom; the creature had given him, and as he did so a beaming smile spread across the creature's pale little face and he nodded his approval.

"What does it taste like, is it edible?" asked Artimus.

"It tastes surprisingly good!" replied Lucian.

The other two Pogglins went over to join him and greeted the creature. Very cautiously the creature broke off two pieces of the mushroom and passed a piece each to Artimus and Sir Septimus. They both tried the mushroom,

"It's very good!" said Artimus turning to Lucian.

"It's a pity we can't take some of these mushrooms back with us; the others back home would love it!"

Sir Septimus in the meantime had broken off another piece of the mushroom and the creature was nodding and smiling happily at him.

"This is excellent," he said enthusiastically. "I think I'll be eating this for the rest of our visit!"

The other creature climbed back on top of the mushroom to re-join his companion, intently watching the Pogglins. The other leaned over to whisper in his ear, and he began to look less worried. The Pogglins were trying to decide how they could make the creature understand when the situation was taken out of their hands.

"You are now my mushroom brothers," smiled the creature, with nothing but friendliness in his emerald-coloured eyes, "and I welcome you to the great Fungoid Forest."

The creature spoke in a singsong fashion and the voice was soft and full of warmth.

"We are honoured by your kind gesture and welcome," said Lucian holding out his hand again to the creature, which looked at him puzzled.

"Please? You want more mushroom?"

"No thank you. You don't understand my meaning; the shaking of hands is a gesture of welcome and friendship," explained Lucian. The creature, though puzzled, graciously took Lucian's hand and shook it obligingly.

"Then it is a custom I willingly accept!" smiled the creature.

A shrill, chattering noise like that of a monkey came from nearby and all the creatures darted off for the cover of the forest. "We must go!" gabbled the Pogglins' new friend and grabbed Lucian by the hand, trying to drag him away.

"Acid slugs are coming!" Picking up their pouches, the Pogglins hurriedly followed the creatures deep into the forest.

The Pogglins had a hard job trying to keep up with their new little friend and his companions. The other creatures, jumped, leap-frogged and somersaulted from mushroom to mushroom at a rapid pace; only the Pogglins' new friend stayed with them on the ground. One of the creatures stopped atop of one the bigger mushrooms and called down, "Acid slug coming in from the north!" He then cupped his hands and cried, "Bar-yorooo! Bar-yoroo! Bar-yoroo!" A little way off to the east there came a low reply "Bar-yoroo! Roo! Roo!"

The creature smiled and called down, "Follow me! Quickly!"

They hurriedly followed him, becoming aware of the slithering noise of a slug behind them. After about five minutes they came into a clearing where a giant snail was grazing on mushrooms. The creature called to it; "Roo! Roo!"

The little creatures leapt up on to the snail's tail and ran along its back to the shell and crawled under it. The Pogglins friend told them to get under the shell as quickly as possible. The creatures helped the Pogglins up, and they crawled under the shell followed by the others. They made it under the shell's protection just in time as the acid slug slithered into the clearing and then suddenly recoiled with revulsion at the sight of the snail. Turning about, it went back into the forest.

Inside the shell, the Pogglins found the light was quite dim but bright enough to see, as it was being reflected around the shell by the mother-of-pearl that lined the interior. They were in the lower chamber of the shell and the noises from outside echoed about the chambers above, and they could see the snail's body snaking upwards. Smooth ridges of mother-of-pearl had formed into little ledge shapes poking out of the shell's wall, making very comfortable seats for the passengers to sit. The Pogglins new friend gestured for them to sit down.

"The nasty has gone!" they heard the snail say from outside.

"Which way are you headed?" called the little creature.

Suddenly there was a gurgling sound, like water going down a plughole, as the snail retracted its body back into the shell; the head and eyestalks entered the small chamber where the passengers were sitting.

"North." replied the Snail.

"How far will you take us north?" asked the little mushroom eater.

"Until I get bored with going north!" answered the snail, looking at the Pogglin's shoes. "I thought we had strangers aboard – those things on your feet were tickling my back!" He looked more closely at the Pogglins. "Why are you covered in slime?" He asked quizzically.

Lucian looked at Artimus and then down at his own clothes before answering,

"We ran into another of your folk, and he told us to roll in the slime to protect ourselves from the acid slugs."

The mushroom folk began to giggle among themselves as the snail sniffed Lucian and he too began to chuckle.

"That was Sidney; I'd know his smell anywhere! You ran into him, you say?" and the Pogglins nodded in reply and explained that they did literally "run" into him.

"You've been properly had! Slime wouldn't put the slugs off your scent. That's Sidney's sense of humour all right; he had you roll in the slime by way of a joke!" The snail turned an eyestalk towards the mushroom folk, while keeping the other on the Pogglins. "Give 'em a rub down of my milk, why don't you. We can't have 'em blundering about the forest into slugs now, can we!"

Still chuckling, the snail withdrew from the shell and they felt it begin to move off.

Sir Septimus looked at his companions' shocked expressions and burst out laughing; his laugh was so infectious that all the party were soon in fits of laughter. After they had recovered themselves, the Pogglins thanked the creatures for getting them to safety. "Many thanks indeed for getting us out of there," said Lucian, "Where are you taking us?"

The creature looked at him and then smiled. "Why, we are taking you to the safety of our Village of Mushentar. Our people would like to meet you; it is not every day that strangers visit Empraktos-Larris from Sol-Larris."

The Pogglins looked at the creature in amazement!

"By Dunbruan the Great, how do you know that?" exclaimed Lucian.

"There is no mystery, my mushroom brother! The cats told us where you are from and we came to help you. As for me and my companions, we are Fungiglooks."

The other Fungiglooks nodded their heads and smiled.

"You have no personal name other than Fungiglook?" enquired Lucian.

"Yes, you may call me Fengook!" He shook the Pogglins' hands once again, as though they had just been introduced for the very first time. Fengook then pointed to his companions, "This is Ongook, Dargook, Songook and Reclook." The four little Fungiglooks waved at the Pogglins in greeting as each name was called out by Fengook.

The passengers fell quiet for a moment as the snail's body rippled slowly beneath their feet, the silence suddenly broken by strange calls and shrieks from outside that echoed around the shell. After this had died down, they could hear the snail quietly humming to himself as it moved along through the mushroom forest.

The Pogglins asked Fengook to tell them more about the forest. Fengook told them that the Fungoid Forest covered many hectares of land. To the far north of the forest was Mount Vunolf; it was below the mountain that his village of Mushentar lay.

"Many creatures inhabited the forest, and the only real predators were the giant slugs. They would eat anything that they could catch, so one had to be cautious when venturing out of the village and had to find the help of a giant snail as soon as possible. The snails excreted milk that was foul-smelling to the acid slugs, for only they can smell it and makes them stay away! The cats could be a problem sometimes, but only when they had a hard time finding food do they become a nuisance to the Fungiglooks. They are on good terms otherwise.

"The Mijapillars keep very much to themselves and keep to their part of the Fungoid Forest to the southeast. The Mijapillars are insectoids and look like a cross between Mosquito and a Grasshopper. You have to be careful that they do not sting you; otherwise you would get the sleeping sickness. They have been known to fly over Mushentar, but only very rarely."

"Mount Vunolf? Is that near to the Vunolf Peaks?" asked Sir Septimus.

"They are to the northeast," replied Reclook.

"So how far away are the peaks from your village?" asked Lucian.

Fengook considered and replied, "They are about half a day's walk from the edge of the forest. That is as far as I have ever ventured. But I have gone beyond the forest threshold to the south, to Mount Uoplaax."

Sir Septimus was flicking his moustache in thought and then said: "Right then! If it's only half a day's walk to the Vunolf Peaks, we will stick to the original plan and go that way."

Fengook's eyes widened and the other Fungiglooks shook their heads, their large ears slightly flapping.

"No, you cannot go that way, for there lies great danger for those who venture to the Vunolf Peaks!"

"What is there? What is the danger, Fengook?"

The other Fungiglooks started to whisper to themselves, as Fengook replied. "There are caves in the Vunolf Peaks where dwell the Night Husks! They are the unseeing, the unhearing servants of the Subterranians. Please listen to me and do not take that path."

"Yes, you must not go that way!" implored Songook.

"Fontahl mentioned the Subterranians when he met us. Who are the Subterranians, Fengook?" asked Lucian gently.

"They are the 'white faces' that live in a great city of Naarunkesh, which is beyond in the Valley of Zaark," Ongook replied. "Our folktales tell of a place of dread!"

The Pogglins looked at each other with fear in their eyes.

"Fontahl of the cats said that you are all on a quest?" Fengook asked the Pogglins.

"That's right. We are looking for the Moogem Tree. All we know is that it lies east beyond the Valley of Zaark." said Lucian.

"Why do you seek the Tree?" he smiled, his pale eyes blinking in the dimness.

"Because those blighters the Dondymarians have poisoned our Queen, and the legends say that the Tree's fruit cures all known ills," replied Sir Septimus.

"We have less than seven days to get the Moogem fruit and back to Sol-Larris. We then have a day and a half to get back to Pogglinburg by 16th July," said Artimus.

The Fungiglooks started to shake their heads.

"You have less time than that, my mushroom brother. You and your friends slept for a day before you awoke," said Ongook.

The Pogglins looked at each other in shock. Artimus pulled out his watch, still 7.15 pm; "It's stopped!" he exclaimed and took out a key from his pocket and began to wind it furiously. He then estimated the time and adjusted his watch accordingly.

"The cats thought you were dead because you had not moved from their last patrol the day before," continued Ongook. "When they went back to you the second time, they planned to drag you away. You gave them a shock when you sat up!" The other Fungiglooks began to chuckle at the fright that the cats had received.

The Pogglins smiled, but this latest news had put them in a real predicament. Artimus took off his pince-nez and polished them in his handkerchief.

"That gives us just five days to get to the tree and back up to the surface!" He clasped the pince-nez back onto the end of his nose and then took the Quistorrisian pencil he had cut the notches into out of his pocket and snapped off two pieces. "That just gives us five days! It's going to be very tight indeed for making it back for the 16th, my friends" said Artimus, gloomily.

"Fengook, thank you for your kind hospitality, but we will not be able to stay in your village. As you have heard, our time is short and we must set out for the Moogem Tree as soon as possible," said Lucian apologetically.

"We, I and my scouts will come and help you find the Tree," replied Fengook.

"But why are you willing to help us? You are volunteering to go on a dangerous journey and there is a great danger for us all!" said the Pogglin.

"You are kind and your heart is pure; you are a good person Lucian Snuzz, and we want to help you in your quest", replied Fengook, and his companions all nodded in agreement.

"We appreciate what you have already done for us." said Lucian. "And we are very grateful for your help in our quest for the Moogem Tree!"

The snail interrupted the conversation. "Off you get, my friends! I'm bored going in this direction now, and I want to go left!"

"How far left?" called Fengook.

"Why, as far as the forest's end at the Valley of Zaark." replied the snail.

"Then we will be staying on, if you don't mind: there has been a change of plan!" said the Fungiglook.

"Very well," called back the snail and the occupants of this shell felt the change of direction as the snail moved off to the east.

Fengook touched a finger to his lip. "Of course, you are not the first of your race to visit the great Fungoid Forest." He looked deeply into the eyes of the Pogglins. The Pogglins were dumbstruck with the implications of what it could mean; finally, Sir Septimus broke their silence

"By Obadiah Thrasskin's beard! We are not the first Pogglins to come here?!?" The monocle dropped from his eye socket in disbelief.

"No, you are not!" replied Ongook, with some surprise.

"It is true," replied Fengook. "I remember our great wise one telling us the story when I was but yet a young Glook."

Lucian was pulling at his moustache, deep in thought of the news, "Who on Sol-Larris could have been a visitor from Pogglinburg?"

★ ★ ★ ★ ★

King Pooley sat by his Queen's bed. His expression was one of love and concern for his wife, and he held on to her hand in the hope that she would not slip away from him. He was not alone as the six Grand Wizards and Chancellor Dore also stood in attendance. Grizzelda looked as white as a marble statue: all colour had drained from her face, and yet there was an aura of peacefulness in her expression. Well-plumped pillows supported her head, over which flowed her flaxen ringlets. The king looked up from his wife as the door opened and Dr Snuzz entered the chamber.

The old Pogglin bowed and walked over to the bed; putting his bag on the bedside cabinet, he began to fumble inside. While the doctor plugged his stethoscope into his ears, Balferzaar the Black was conversing with his fellow wizards. He stopped and turned around to face the doctor who was listening to his patient's heart.

"How is she, Doctor?" asked the King.

"No change, You're Majesty, but she is stable thanks to Balferzaar's magic," Dr Snuzz replied as he mopped the Queen's brow with a damp cloth. He then dropped the cloth into a bowl of water and wrung it out as he continued.

"I can do very little, Your Majesty, apart from checking to see that she is stable."

"I have done all that can be done", replied Balferzaar, "The Queen's life is out of all our hands, and it lies in the balance. All our hopes lie in the return of Lucian with the fruit of the Moogem Tree."

"Is there any news of my nephew's progress?" inquired the Doctor.

Balferzaar nodded. "Yes, I have received word that Lucian and his companions have left Quistorrisia on the evening of the 7th and they should now be deep within the land of Empraktos-Larris."

★ ★ ★ ★ ★

"Now that we are not going by way of the Vunolf Peaks, which way do you and your scouts suggest that we go?" enquired Artimus.

"I would go south, keeping to the western edge of the forest and make my way down to the Emprak Mountains. This way we will avoid the Night Husks and most of the 'whiteface' scouts from the city. Our only major obstacle will be in skirting Lake Naar and the petrified jungle. Not only will we have the beds of quicksand to contend with, but also the Naara frogs. These creatures may look clumsy and docile, but they are deadly!" Fengook warned.

"Excuse me, but just who are the whitefaces?" asked Sir Septimus.

"Subterranians," answered Lucian.

"Indeed," replied Reclook.

"They are the inhabitants of the City of Naarunkesh," said Fengook. "He is their leader and master of the Night Husks. We must avoid the city and its inhabitants at all costs, otherwise, we will be doomed forevermore!"

Sir Septimus' moustache twitched a little on hearing the reply.

"Who on Sol-Larris is 'He?" asked Artimus, a little confused.

"He is the Necromancer!" said Fengook, in a hushed voice. "We do not talk of him."

"Can you tell us anything more about the Night Husks, then?" enquired Lucian.

Fengook held him in his gaze for a few moments before answering. "The Night Husks are an abomination to behold!" came his tremulous reply. "One look upon their hideous faces can turn your blood to ice. They scream and bellow in mindless misery, soulless creatures doomed to endless toiling at the bidding of their master within the city of Naarunkesh. They come in many forms and sizes and, should you have the misfortune to come into contact with a Night Husk, you are instantly stupefied and dragged off to the city."

The little Fungiglook shook a little as the horror came into their eyes.

"This is far as I go", called the snail. The Fungiglooks and the Pogglins crawled out from under the snail's shell and jumped to the ground below. The little group thanked the snail for its help, while it was busy munching on a nearby mushroom.

"Not at all", replied the snail. "Always pleased to help. If ever I or my sister-brothers are going your way, you only have to call." As the snail moved off the Pogglins followed their new friends into the depths of the Fungoid Forest.

They moved as quickly as possible through the forest, stepping over small mushrooms, between mushrooms or around mushrooms, according to the size. Fengook stayed on the ground with the three Pogglins, while Ongook, Songook, Reclook and Dargook went on as scouts. The three Pogglins hurried after Fengook, he was setting quite a pace for them; Sir Septimus was finding it hard trying to keep up with the little fellow.

Above them came series of hoots and whistles and Fengook suddenly halted and held up his hand for the Pogglins to stop. Sir Septimus tried to catch his breath while listening for other movements in the surrounding forest. But all he could hear was his own heart pounding in his ears. Suddenly there was a whooping noise and Fengook motioned the three Pogglins to move on.

"Not far now my mushroom brothers, but it is not safe to linger in this part of the forest!"

"Best foot forward, my friends," said Lucian.

Ongook and Dargook moved off quickly ahead, while Songook and Reclook stayed close by Fengook and the Pogglins.

"We have a long road ahead of us, and time is short." Lucian's two friends nodded in agreement.

"How long before we come to the edge of the forest, Fengook?" asked Artimus.

"It will take a few minutes to reach the western edge of the forest, then we turn south and it will take a half-and-one day to reach the southern edge of the forest."

"That's going to be cutting it too fine!" interjected Sir Septimus, his monocle popping out in surprise.

"Agreed!" replied Artimus gravely.

"Then we shall have to make sure that our march is quicker," said Lucian.

"We have to get to the southern edge of the forest today, if possible!" He then asked Fengook if it were possible to do this.

"Only with great haste," replied the Fungiglook, and he called in a chirping whistle to his fellow scouts ahead of him. The reply followed and Songook and Reclook fanned out into the forest, and Fengook was off at a trot.

"Hold onto your hat, Lucian, we're off!" called Artimus as he dashed off after Fengook. Lucian chuckled and trotted off after his friend holding his hat. "Come on, Sir Septimus!" he called, trotting quickly around a clump of waist-high mushrooms and out of sight.

Rather surprised by his sudden desertion, Sir Septimus looked back into the depths of the Fungoid Forest. Suddenly the thought of an acid slug came into his mind, and he raced off after his friends with a cry of "Wait for me!"

The party decided to move on to the safe spot that Fengook knew, and fifteen minutes later the Pogglins were brought to an extraordinary part of the forest.

The giant mushrooms were tightly packed close together, making a roof-like canopy in a large area. The stems were the thickest the Pogglins had yet seen, and all about were white semi-opaque spheres stuck to the floor.

"We will be safe here, my mushroom brothers."

"What a strange place!" marvelled Artimus and as he touched one of the spheres and the surface gave a little to his touch.

"What are these strange spheres?" asked Lucian. The spheres came up to just above his waist in height and it vibrated as he touched it. Lucian pulled his hand back sharply. He peered into the sphere and could just about see something moving inside.

"They are eggs, my mushroom brother. This is the nursery of the snails; no acid slug would dare to venture here!" Lucian smiled at the Fungiglook's cleverness. "Right then, I think we can spare ten minutes before the next march."

Suddenly a great booming alarm rang out, followed by a wailing noise like that of a banshee's scream. It froze the Pogglins with fear.

"Great Dunbruan, what is that awful noise?" said Lucian as fear gripped him.

"It is the Night Husks. It is the changeover of shifts down the mines," replied Ongook. "It is a noise one must get used to hearing while you are in Empraktos-Larris." The mournful wail slowly ground down to a halt and the Forest returned to normal.

"I hope never to hear that noise again!" moaned Sir Septimus

"You will get used to it," replied Reclook.

The little group found themselves a comfortable place and then sat down for some well-earned rest - albeit a short one. Lucian was just settling down when he heard a funny noise, like someone munching on an apple. He took off his hat only to find that something had taken two bites from out of the brim. And there was the little creature, still clamped onto the brim by its teeth.

Lucian managed to pull the three-legged creature off his hat and placed it on the floor. It ran off, with the green tendrils on its head flapping about, and darted back into the undergrowth of the forest floor. Lucian frowned and examined his hat, and then he noticed that Fengook was sitting up, watching him.

"What was that little creature?" he whispered to Ongook.

"A Mushi-Muncher. He must have mistaken your hat for a mushroom!" He whispered back with a broad smile. Lucian shook his head in amazement and settled down for a quick nap.

Artimus could feel himself drifting off into sleep when his eyes popped open and his nerves were all of a jingle.

"What was that noise?" he whispered to himself as he sat up abruptly, it wasn't the Night Husks' siren. His ears strained to catch the sound again on the breeze that rustled the tongue-like blades of the long grass. He didn't have long to wait. Above the sound of the breeze was a distinct, wailing sound, almost like someone chanting; it chilled Artimus to the bone! The wailing sound rose in pitch and then fell to a guttural moan. Artimus could take no more and shook Lucian from his sleep.

"Lucian!" he said urgently.

"What is it, Artimus? What is wrong?"

Before Artimus could answer his friend, Lucian heard the sound for himself as the chanting noise rose higher on the breeze again. It was a horrible sound, and it instantly struck the Pogglin with fear.

"By Great Dunbruan, what is that?" he exclaimed.

"I don't know", replied Artimus, "it started a few moments before I woke you."

Suddenly the two Pogglins saw the change in the light about them; a pale, sickly yellow light began to permeate the forest. The light was coming from the east, from the Valley of Zaark, and from which a great roar of guttural chanting screamed through the forest. The sound startled the Fungiglooks and Sir Septimus awake, and all turned quite white with fear. The chanting now progressed to a rhythmic gurgle as Lucian moved off cautiously towards the edge of the forest. Fengook and the Fungiglooks moved to stop him.

"You must not go!" implored Fengook to the Pogglin. "It is the Necromancer and the white faces. They are calling the Night Husks!"

"I must see what is going on, Fengook. My fear has become a curiosity. I will be careful, my friend," as he picked up his staff and turned towards the edge of the forest and thrust his hat onto his head.

The Fungiglook guides muttered to themselves, shaking their heads, while Artimus and Sir Septimus looked at each other.

"Well, I for one am not going to let Snuzz face this alone!" said Sir Septimus, trying to smile, but he was white to the lips with fear.

Artimus nodded fearfully and the two Pogglins moved off after their friend.

Lucian crouched down low as he got nearer to the clearing at the forest's edge. The chanting filled his ears as he spotted a large boulder to his right and made his way towards it. Gathering his wits, he fearfully peeped over the top of the rock and his eyes widened in the horror at what met his gaze.

Before his eyes lay the Valley of Zaark; far off in the distance was a Great Lake before which stood a dark and twisted altar. Either side of the altar stood a pair of foreboding obelisks: the light from the lake danced over their surface, and Lucian could just make out that they were carved with some sort of hieroglyphs. He pulled out his miniature spyglass from his pocket for a better look.

On pulling it open, and looking through it, he saw an extremely tall and thin personage standing at the altar, clad in a flowing robe. Lucian couldn't make out what type of being the creature was, but it stood with its arms outstretched and the head was thrown back. The Pogglin caught a glimpse of flesh, as white as marble, and what he thought he saw a glint of red eyes. Two other figures stood back from the altar at either end. One was tall and muffled to the neck and lower face. Thick lenses covered his eyes, and his head was crowned by a shock of bright, flaming red hair. The other figure was shorter and wore thick lens spectacles that stuck out beyond the bridge of his nose. He was also muffled to the neck and lower face, and his head was topped by a shock of grey-white hair. Of what Lucian could see of their faces, they too were deathly white and looked to have been carved from the coldest marble. They both stood with their arms crossed against their chests, and the shorter of the two seemed to have a staff or rod clasped in his hands.

A great plume of yellow vapour arose up out from the lake in a high column and crept slowly across the rock ceiling far, far above. In the distance, in silhouette, appeared a multitude of figures behind the plume of vapour. From their shaded faces beamed eyes of glowing orange. They walked with a listlessness that made Lucian shiver with revulsion as they staggered towards the altar at the other side of the lake.

Breathing heavily, Lucian sank behind the rock when he saw his two friends crawling towards him. As the new arrivals reached the rock the chanting ceased; the silence was so profound that the group held their breath in fear of being heard. The silence was then suddenly broken by a great screech that echoed around the valley. The sound rang in the little trio's ears; it was a horrible sound of unimaginable pain and torment, a sound as though a soul had been twisted out of its very being. The Pogglins looked at each other in dread.

As the wailing screech came to its crescendo the chanting then struck up again. Lucian looked into his friends' eyes and saw their fear, and he hoped that his own fear was not so easily read.

"So... so what do... think that was Lucian?" stuttered Artimus.

"I don't know Artimus, but it sounded like an incantation - and a very powerful one at that!"

Artimus pondered on this, trying to ignore the chanting, but he could feel it penetrating to the heart of his being.

"You must ignore it, Artimus!" replied his friend, as if he could read Artimus' mind. "You must both ignore it and try to think of happy memories past; we must not succumb to this enchantment!

With that, he popped his head up over the rock to see if he could see more of what was going on in the vale below with his spyglass. Seconds later he was joined by his two friends. The three Pogglins looked down onto the same scene that Lucian saw minutes earlier, except the group at the altar had been joined by three more figures. One was immensely tall and wore a cocked hat that had seen better days. The second was stout and a lot shorter than his companion, and the third was even shorter than the second.

"So those mountains over there must be the Vunolf Peaks?"

"That's correct, Sir Septimus, and those creatures must be the Night Husks!" said Artimus in horror.

The three Pogglins watched from their vantage point as the shambling figures shuffled towards the altar in the valley below. They walked four abreast, and there must have been hundreds of them trailing back in a straggling column towards the Vunolf Peaks.

The Pogglins look on in shock and fear.

Lucian passed the spyglass over to Artimus for him to have a look. The Night Husks gathered around the lake while the vapour pulsed different shades of yellow and green, each sicklier than the last. At the altar, the thin creature gesticulated and fiddled with an item.

"It looks like a puppet," said Artimus, handing the spyglass back to Lucian.

"So, it is!" whispered Lucian in surprise.

As he leaned over, Artimus suddenly jumped as Fengook placed a hand on his shoulder.

"I wish you wouldn't do that Fengook!"

"I am sorry my mushroom brother, but we must go now. The 'white faces' have called down the Night Husks from the Vunolf Peaks. If they sense we are here, we will be doomed to their fate forevermore."

"What do you mean, old chap?" asked Sir Septimus.

"The Necromancer will sense that we are here and send the Night Husks after us, my mushroom brother."

The figure at the altar then passed the puppet to the stout figure, which had a wooden box on his back. He bowed his head in reverence as he took the puppet. He then flipped the thing into the box on his back. The stout creature turned and waved to two of the group to follow. A little figure, with another box-like object on his back, and the tall thin creature with the cocked hat left the group to follow their companion back towards the city along the candlelit trail.

The three Pogglins and the Fungiglook bobbed back down behind the rock.

"What do you think that was all about?" mused Sir Septimus in a fearful whispered aside.

"No idea! This is more your field, Lucian?" replied Artimus.

"Well, I can tell you that it is a ritual of some sort," answered Lucian. "That yellow vapour, I am sure, contains the souls of the Night Husks. That's how the Subterranians hold power over the Night Husks. And, I think we shouldn't get entangled with those fellows!"

"Who is the tall fellow at the altar?" enquired Sir Septimus of his friend.

"That is the Necromancer, Sir Septimus. Someone I have read of in many magical books!"

The three Pogglins and the Fungiglook got up and had another look.

At that moment the chanting rose again in pitch and the Necromancer at the altar picked up a large, ornate staff and raised it above his head and made again that horrible screech that Lucian would never forget for the rest of his days. As the screech died down, the column of vapour began to spiral down into the lake and its waters seemed to boil and bubble. The Necromancer gestured for the Night Husks to come forward and for the first time, the Pogglins got to see them in the dying, sickly light from the lake.

They were hideous to behold. Their skin was rough and wrinkled, and they were deathly pale. They were terribly thin, as though all the goodness had been sucked out of them. They wore tattered rags; some only clad in loincloths. Some had shoes; some had rags tied around their feet, but most were barefooted. Their heads hung on their chests and lolled from side to side as they shuffled towards their master. But most terrible of all was their faces: their skin was like parchment, and they were eyeless! Once where there were eyes were now glowing sockets of orange, the eyelids having been stitched open with fluorescent lime green thread. A twisted "smile" had also been stitched mockingly onto their faces in the same thread to finish off the ghastly apparition.

"We must go!" said Fengook as he darted back towards the forest; Artimus closely followed him; he had seen enough.

"Come on, Snuzz. I think we had better take the little fellow's advice," Sir Septimus said, patting Lucian on the back. "And don't forget, we are short of time."

As Sir Septimus turned to head off to the forest, Lucian pulled him back with an urgent whisper for him to come back. Sir Septimus returned to the rock and Lucian gave him the spyglass. He peered through it to see what had upset his friend. There around the side of the lake, near the altar now stood about fifty extremely short Night Husks – empty shells that had once been Pogglins!

Sir Septimus' mouth dropped open with shock. He turned to Lucian. "Pogglins, Snuzz, they must be..."

"Yes, Sir Septimus, they must be the remains of the lost colony; and we must save them!"

"But you can't, Snuzz. Remember why we are here. We have the mission for our Queen to fulfil," he said, handing back the spyglass to Lucian.

At that moment a low muttering mumble came up from the Valley below, it was the harsh tongue of the Subterranians. The two Pogglins looked down, and saw the Necromancer at the Alter give a small object to one of the Night Husks. He then turned to one of the Pogglin Husks, and his language changed to a lighter sounding tongue.

"Great Dunbruan! That's old Pogglish he is talking," exclaimed Lucian in shock.

"Are you sure, Snuzz? No Pogglin has spoken Pogglish since Dunbruan's day. Only the six Grand Wizards now know the dialect."

"And me, Sir Septimus, I too also read and speak our ancient tongue."

"Yes, well you would do, wouldn't you?"

Below them in the valley, a Pogglin Husk shuffled forward to their master and received orders and returned to the group of Pogglin Husks. They too had the same horrific mutilations as the larger Husks, with stitched open eyes and the mouths stitched shut. Then they departed, heading back towards the Vunolf Peaks.

The Subterranian tongue was then heard again, and Lucian peered through the spyglass as a group of Night Husks peeled off from the group and headed southwest towards the Fungoid Forest. The others returned to their toil within the mines of the Vunolf Peaks.

"That could mean trouble!" whispered Lucian.

"What could?" asked Sir Septimus.

"A group of thirty or so Night Husks have split off from the main group and are heading towards the Fungoid Forest!"

"Oh, Corks!" exclaimed Sir Septimus.

Suddenly the short figure with the shock of grey-white hair, turned his head in the direction of the forest, and Lucian dropped down behind the rock with fright. He had a strange feeling, sharp as a razor's edge, that he had been "seen". He trembled violently with fear as he put away his spyglass.

Sir Septimus popped down to his friend with a look of concern, "What is wrong, Snuzz?"

"That Subterranian, the short one, I think he is a "Seeker". He is a danger to me, Sir Septimus; we must be very careful as I believe he has "seen" me."

"A Seeker? What is a Seeker when he's at home?" frowned Sir Septimus.

"A Seeker is a powerful magic user who can seek out fellow magic smiths and destroy them! We must get away from here, as we are now in deep danger!"

With that Lucian got up and moved back towards the forest, closely followed by Sir Septimus, his mind full of questions. Soon the two Pogglins were back at the little clearing where the agitated Fungiglook guide s were sitting, while Fengook and Artimus came up to meet them.

"Where did you get to, Lucian? I thought you were following behind."

"Sorry Artimus, we would have been, but we lingered a little too long and now we are in mortal danger."

"Quite so, he's right!" interjected Sir Septimus, wiping his monocle.

"What more did you see, Lucian?"

"Something horrible Artimus! Something I wished that I hadn't witnessed; that our poor kinfolk should live a *living death* like that," he said and wiped his face with his handkerchief. For the first time, he was tormented by doubt as to whether he was up to the task given to them by Balferzaar the Black.

It was Artimus that brought him back from his thoughts. "Kinsfolk? You are not making sense, Lucian. What kinfolk?"

"What Snuzz and I saw, Artimus were Pogglins! Some of those poor devils were Pogglins!"

Artimus gasped in shock and sat down. "Pogglins as Night Husks, how could that be?"

"They must be the remnants of the lost colony, Artimus, the families that left Pogglinshire back in 4495 BD after the last great swarm of the Grommians and the Karaarsin. The last contact from them was in 3297BD and they have not been heard of until now!"Lucian looked sadly into Artimus' eyes.

"No, Lucian, you can't. I know that look, but you cannot do anything for them, and we have to stick to our quest."

Lucian nodded, "Yes, I know Artimus, but I must try and save those poor souls. Some of them are our relatives."

"No! Lucian, you can't. We were sent here to carry out a task by Balferzaar and at the King's command. We cannot save the Queen *and* the Pogglin Night Husks!"

"Artimus is right, Snuzz. The Queen first, and if we get through all this, we can come back and release our kinsfolk."

Lucian was quiet for a moment, and then looked forlorn again as he thought of the Pogglin Night Husks.

"Then once we have fulfilled our oaths, I vow that I shall return and save the lost colony. Remember they were once all just like ourselves, they have not always been the creatures that we saw in the Valley. Now, my friends, we must MOVE, and quickly!

"So, who was the Subterranian that stood at the altar?" asked Sir Septimus as they ran and followed their Fungiglook companions.

"The shorter figure, I am sure, is a "Seeker". As for the other, I don't know."

When he caught up to Fengook, he asked: "Do you know who they were, my friend?"

Fengook nodded his head. "They are the white-faces, led by the Necromancer. The tall one, with eyes but no eyes, is the maker of Night Husks," he replied.

"As I guessed, the Necromancer! The other is the Needleman, maker of the Night Husks," said Lucian. Then he frowned. The thought of a Seeker worried him greatly, as it meant the mission was now made even more perilous than it already was. He was suddenly aware of his silence and that Sir Septimus was looking at him intently as he ran along by his side.

"So, Snuzz, are you going to tell them what this *Seeker* is, and what it means to us?"

"I can't run and talk easily at the same time when we are safely able to pause for a short rest; I will tell what I know."

★ ★ ★ ★ ★

After running as fast and as far as their little bodies could take them before collapsing, they hid as well as they could amongst the grass and mushroom stalks. They needed a breather, some food and water. As they recovered and refreshed themselves, Lucian explained the position to the others.

"A *Seeker* has two very powerful talents at their disposal. One, they can sniff out a Magic smith. And two, they have the power that covers all four elements of magic, which means they can easily destroy a fellow Magic smith like me."

"So that's what you meant when you said you had been *seen*!"

"Indeed, Sir Septimus. Regrettably, my presence has put the quest into great danger. Now we do not only have time against us but a powerful enemy. Tell me, what of the other three that returned to the city - who were they?" asked Lucian of Fengook.

"The first to leave was the soul-stealer, the master of puppets; he was followed by his kin, the enchanted music player. The third was the collector, he that has a face but no face! They are very dangerous as they walk abroad in the land, whereas the other three always remain within sight of the city."

"I'm not sure I understand all this or what's going on," said Artimus. "All I do know Lucian is that you have put us in even more danger, added to which we have the extra burden now of trying to make up all the time lost back at the Valley if we are to stand any chance at all of saving our Queen!" The tone of his voice was harsh, but Lucian knew it was down to tension and fear rather than bitterness.

A great cry came up from the Valley and silenced the little group. After a short pause, they gathered themselves together and hurriedly moved off again southwards.

Chapter Three

Two hours later, the little group of Pogglins and Fungiglooks had put a good distance between them and the small clearing near the Valley. The forest had changed in atmosphere since the cry from the Valley: it seemed to have lost its tranquillity, and now it seemed as if a creeping menace could strike at any time.

Suddenly Lucian stopped and clapped his hands over his ears; the dreadful noise of the Night Husk siren rang out through the forest, and instantly reminded them of their poor wretched country folk's torment. It was a memory which now haunted Lucian's conscience. He felt like he had deserted them; he had seen them in such a state of horror, but had left them to it and run away. He was even more determined to do the right thing and release them from their misery as soon as was possible.

The four Fungiglooks had paired off and were scouting out the land ahead; Fengook stayed closed to the Pogglins. For a change, Sir Septimus was not lagging behind the others now. The image of the Night Husks was still fixed in his mind; he had no wish to join them! A hoot came from ahead of the party, and Fengook held up his hand for the Pogglins to stop.

"What is it, Fengook?"

"It is a warning that an acid slug is to the south-east of us. We must be ready, should it come this way."

"What do we do if it comes near?" asked Artimus.

"We have no snail to hide inside now!"

"Do not fear, for we will guide you away from that particular danger." Another yelp came from the scout ahead; they listened for a few seconds and moved on in haste.

"So how far to the southern end of the forest, Fengook?" puffed Lucian.

"We should be there in six or so hours if we keep to this pace."

Three more hoots and whoop rang out, a signal to say that the acid slug was moving off to the east, which was followed by a whistle and a hoot. It was something that the Pogglins had not heard before from the Fungiglook scouts. They looked at Fengook for an answer.

"There is a scouting party of cats ahead; they wish to speak to you, as they have news which concerns us," he replied.

The group came to a clearing that was encircled by the smaller of the Mushrooms; the heat had cooled just a little here, which they were grateful for. Movement and rustling made them jumpy, and their heart rate soared every time a bush or mushroom came alive. Any sudden movement seemed more threatening to them now, even though it was always just a forest animal or insect going about its business.

Within the mushroom circle were the Fungiglook scouts and five green cats. They stopped talking as Fengook and the Pogglins approached. The largest of the cats padded towards them, then settled himself down. He narrowed his orange eyes and waited.

"You should nod to him," Fengook whispered to Lucian. "Oh, right, of course," Lucian acknowledged. He took off his hat and bowed, and the cat nodded back.

"You are Lucian Snuzz from the land above?" enquired the cat in a purring voice.

"I am," he replied.

"Then you should know that a group of Night Husks have entered the forest north of here," said the orange-eyed cat. The three Pogglins groaned in the realisation that this threat was not going away!

"Then that must be the group of Night Husks that I saw peel off from the main party," replied Lucian.

"The Night Husks normally do not bother to enter the forest; their concern is usually within the mines that lie deep within the Vunolf Peaks," continued the cat. "You must be a great treasure to the Subterranians, for them to send the Night Husks here."

"How far off are they?" interjected Artimus.

The cat sneered at him for his rudeness, but answered his question. "They will be here within the hour. They are lumbering oafs, but can move quite quickly when urgency is required." He continued, "It seems that urgency is required now, judging by their actions!"

The Pogglins pondered this news. Fengook had already told them that once a Night Husk got onto your trail, they would not cease until they caught or killed you!

"What's to do, Lucian?" Artimus said at last. "We stand a chance if they come at us within the forest, but I don't fancy our chances in open country between the forest and the Emprak Mountains."

"Actually, my friend, we will have the advantage, believe me, if we head for the open plain," replied Lucian.

"I agree with Snuzz," Sir Septimus cut in. "The blighters would have more of a chance of ambush in the forest. If we make it to the plain, they can only attack from one way and we'll be ready for them!"

"But should there be too many of them, we would at least have a chance of cover in the forest!" Artimus retorted.

"Yes, if you are a Fungiglook and can leap up mushrooms," said Sir Septimus, patting Fengook on the back. "No offence, old chap, but we haven't the nimbleness for scaling Fungoids, now do we Artimus!"

Lucian sighed. "Look we do not have time for the usual Pogglin debate. We must make a decision and make it now. We head for the open plain. Yes?"

"Yes," Sir Septimus said and Artimus agreed: he knew that Lucian was usually right.

Sir Septimus turned to the orange-eyed cat, who seemed amused by the Pogglins. "Now my dear sir, could your scouts keep us informed of the Night Husks' progress and when they are near?"

The cat looked at Sir Septimus, but said nothing. Lucian elbowed his friend gently in the ribs. "What's the matter, Snuzz?"Sir Septimus said in annoyance. Lucian looked at him and did a quick nod of his head. "What are you...Oh yes, I see what you are getting at!" he said in belated recognition. Hastily, he walked forward a little towards the haughty-looking cat, and then took the deepest, most respectful bow that his little pot-belly would allow.

The cat nodded back and said, "Oh, you will not need us to tell you when they are near; you will know, alright! But I am here to offer you help from my scouting party."

In the great Fungoid Forest.

The Pogglins looked at the cat in surprise.

"Fontahl told me of you at our last quorum, and I am curious to know more about your kind." The cat's orange eyes flashed at the Pogglins as he smiled.

"That is indeed most kind, but I am afraid we have no way to repay you for your kindness," replied Lucian.

"My payment will be that you take me back with you to the land above, that I may see for myself."

"It will be a pleasure to take you to Sol-Larris," smiled Lucian.

"*If* we survive!" added the cat, which made Lucian's smile falter for a moment.

"Err, yes quite!" he replied.

"Then it is a bargain," said the cat, holding out his paw. "I am Zontahl of the Cats of Empraktos-Larris."

"And I am Lucian Snuzz of Pogglinburg, Sol-Larris", he replied, shaking the cat gently by the paw.

"Well, I hope he doesn't expect me to put him up at Pulpit Manor," Sir Septimus whispered into Artimus' ear. "Mrs Bunch would never allow him in the house!"

For all his whispering, Zontahl heard Sir Septimus. He smiled wryly to himself, ignoring the Pogglin's cutting remark.

One of the other cats came over to the group and whispered into Zontahl's large ear. Zontahl nodded and then turned his attention back to the Pogglins.

"This is Parrdoo; she is one of my best scouts. She suggests that we get moving as soon as possible."

Parrdoo nodded her greeting to the Pogglins who nodded back in return.

"My other scouts," continued Zontahl, "are Amukah , Rumshesh and Sarlizahl."

Zontahl then meowed orders to his companions, and they shot off quickly in a northerly direction.

"I have sent my scouts north; they will watch our backs from attack." He nodded to Fengook. "Your scouts can cover our front." Fengook nodded, smiled in agreement, and called to his scouts to pair out ahead before following them.

Lucian hesitated, deep in thought, his hand gently rubbing the stubble on his chin. "Stand behind me everyone; I am going to try something that I have never tried before. I am going to try and put the Night Husks off our track."

Allowing time for his party to move away, Lucian struck the ground with his staff and the gemstone which crowned its top sprang into life. Lucian closed his eyes in concentration and, as the blue gem throbbed and darkened in colour, he spoke the words: "*MUTATIO VENTUS.*"

A light breeze stirred the forest. "It is done; I hope it works!" said Lucian.

"What have you done?" asked Zontahl.

"I have cast a spell which should put the Night Husks off our scent and send them off in the opposite direction." With that, he held his hand out for Zontahl to lead the way.

"After you, Lucian," said Zontahl and trotted alongside the Pogglin as they briskly moved out of the clearing at a trot.

The four Fungiglook scouts fanned out among the mushrooms and moved quickly ahead, running along the ground, leapfrogging over mushrooms and leaping up onto the taller ones. Their agility was quite astounding: not once did they falter, fall or misjudge the distance. All the while they whooped and hooted, signalling back to Fengook on the path below. Fengook himself remained on the ground with the Pogglins and translated what his scouts were saying. Zontahl remained close to Lucian, with Artimus following behind.

The forest was growing a little darker with every step, now that they were nearing its edge. The mushrooms were not so large and tall, like the ones at its centre, and most were bell-shaped. They seemed a little grizzled, and did not emit so much of the beautiful blue-green glow as the rest of the forest mushrooms.

As they moved along, the Pogglins became aware of the growing silence. The only calls they heard were from the Fungiglook scouts. "Why is it so quiet, Zontahl? Does nothing live in this part of the forest?"

"Only the Mijapillars and the Acid Slugs, Lucian," replied the cat in a matter-of-fact fashion and then continued to explain. "Neither species are vocal; therefore, the unwary do not know they are there until they are upon them, at which time it is too late. But we have nothing to fear from the Mijapillars, as they are in hibernation during this season. It is only the Acid Slugs that we have to be aware of," he explained with a fanged smile.

As the endless forest rolled by, the party ran at full pace. Soon it started to thin out as at last they saw that they would soon be at the forest's outer edge. After the six-hour march, the party came to rest among a few small mushrooms and grasses. Before them lay a great expanse of a desolate-looking landscape, known as the Plain of

Uoplaax. It was entirely open country and was only broken by a large mass of stone in the centre. On the far distant horizon was an uninviting mountain range, the Emprak Mountains. To the right, a volcano glowed lividly in the dusk-like light. It was then Artimus noticed that at the far end of the forest he could just make out the foot of the Zelgemar Stairs.

They had come around in a circle! This trip through the Forest could have been avoided and precious time saved, if we had only known it. He sank onto the floor in exhaustion and misery. "Why did the Quistorrisians tell us to go this way?" he thought.

Sir Septimus just fell on his back; puffs of sand flew out around him on impact. He had never done so much exercise in his life. "Why do adventures always have to be so exhausting?" he thought to himself. He lay there for a few moments, panting for breath, and it was a while before he could speak.

Lucian was not much better; he sat on a small mushroom and leaned on his staff. He was tired and parched, but this was soon forgotten when he saw how miserable Artimus was.

"Artimus, what is wrong?" he puffed. "We have been in tighter spots than this, and we have the support of our friends here."

Artimus looked around at his friend and attempted a smile. "Oh, I am so tired, and just finding out that we were almost at our starting point upset me a little, Lucian. But as you say, we have our friends to help us." Then it dawned on him! "*You will find allies,*" the Quistorrisians said. "Of course! THAT'S WHY they sent us this way. The forest was the only place to find help!" This time, a smile lit up his face: he was his old self again.

"That's it Artimus, there's always hope!" beamed Lucian, forgetting his own fears for the moment. He knew that all three must be alert, optimistic and willing, to give them any chance of survival.

The Fungiglooks gathered up some mushrooms to eat and then fanned out along the forest edge, up into a convenient mushroom, and kept a lookout for the slugs. The Pogglins, however, were in discussion with Fengook and Zontahl about their next march across the desert. Lucian was drawing a map into the dirt with his staff. He was following instructions from Artimus, who had memorised the map as best he could before he lost it on the Zelgemar Stairs. About him sat his companions, and one would point now and then if Lucian had left anything out of the map and he would make the correction.

"Now", he said, "this is everything on the map, and as you can see it shows nothing east of the Valley of Zaark. I think we should head for this outcrop of rock here."

"Uoplaax's Fang," Zontahl cut in.

"Oh right, Thank you, Zontahl. So Uoplaax's Fang would be a place to camp before the final push for the Moogem Tree. All agree?" he said, pointing at the map with his staff. They nodded in agreement.

"Right then, from Uoplaax's Fang we head south for the mountains, and keep close to the foot of them. I don't want to risk going east over open ground. Pandora Nyx warned me of the *Tower of Eybraas*; if we go that way we'll be in full view."

"I think it would be even riskier if you think you have now been sussed by this *Seeker* fellow," said Sir Septimus.

Suddenly a mew rang out from the depths of the forest; Zontahl sprang to his feet, his large ears pricked in alertness. "It is my scouts. The Night Husks are approaching from the north-east!"

"That puts them right behind us!" exclaimed Artimus.

"Blast! That means my spell has failed. Sorry, my friends. Then we must make for Uoplaax's Fang!" cried Lucian, and quickly rubbed out the map with his foot. While Artimus and Sir Septimus gathered their few possessions, Fengook called in whistling tones to the Ongook, Dargook, Songook and Reclook. Three of the scouts came running to Fengook's call. "Where's Reclook?" asked Fengook.

"Reclook is returning to Mushentar to tell the Wise One where we are going." Ongook replied. Fengook bowed his head in sorrow.

"Not to worry, old boy – somebody has to report back!" soothed Sir Septimus.

Soon the little party were racing out into and across the open desert; the breeze blowing their clothes so strongly, that Lucian had to hold on to his hat with one hand. The force of it also dried their sweat-soaked clothes, and gave a little relief to their discomfort. All had their sights set on Uoplaax's Fang that lay before them in the distance. Each had their own thoughts of uncertainty. Would they survive and make it to the safety of the rock? Except, that is, Lucian; he was too worried about how to deal with the Night Husks.

Looking behind, Sir Septimus saw the four cat scouts come racing out of the forest. They meowed to Zontahl who translated that the Night Husks were about five minutes behind, and that there were thirty of them!

"What do we do? And how did they get to us so fast? We have been running like mad for hours and they can only shuffle along –it doesn't make sense that they could be so close!"

"We keep running, Artimus, and worry about the how and whys of that later! The more distance we can put between them and us, the better. Out here on open land, we can see if they are getting closer or not!"

Very soon the four cats had caught up with the rest of the party when suddenly the Pogglins heard an awful roar that chilled their bones. Sir Septimus forced himself to look around and saw the thirty Night Husks charging out of the Forest. Upright, focused, ruthless: they didn't look like the slovenly, listless things he had seen earlier in the Valley of Zaark.

"There's your answer, Artimus!" Sir Septimus groaned.

Most of these Husks were once Manu (as the Pogglins called the race of Man), but there were a few Dondymarians and Grodium dwarves amongst the ghastly horde. The Night Husks looked even more hideous as they roared and bellowed while running towards the fleeing party. The fluorescent lime-green stitching around their mouths ripped open in their fury and left deep gashes in their cheeks. The eye-sockets burned bright orange from deep within the mask-like faces. Lucian looked behind; the Night Husks were gaining on them far quicker than he anticipated. Then he saw it.

One of the Night Husks was waving something limp above its head; the limp thing was a Fungiglook corpse! Lucian's heart sank. So little Reclook never did make it back home.

Suddenly Lucian stopped in his tracks. "This is the place to make our stand. All of you, behind me now!" yelled Lucian.

"What? Against thirty of them?" Artimus cried.

Lucian stood defiantly in front of his companions and struck his staff on the ground. Once again, the gemstone on top of the silver mount sparkled into life. It grew brighter as Lucian muttered incantations in a low voice and as his voice rose in pitch, so the gemstone began to burn brightly, turning from sapphire-blue to white. The Night Husks were almost upon Lucian and his party.

Fengook looked in open-mouthed horror as he saw the Night Husk thrashing the corpse of his friend about his head, and it was all Sir Septimus could do to hold him back.

Finishing the spell, Lucian parted his hands and then threw out his arms and held his staff aloft.

"*CRISPO!*" he shouted, and then thrust down his staff hard on to the ground.

A tremor went through the sand, causing a rippling effect to fan out from the bottom of the staff. The sand took on a liquid form. The ripple turned into a high wave of sand and earth that went rushing headlong into the advancing Night Husks.

The great wave of sand smashed into the oncoming creatures like a tidal wave. Some of the Night Husks were instantly buried by the force of the wave; others screamed in horror as they were thrown into the air and were silenced as they fell to the ground with sickening thuds as bone ripped through flesh on impact. Some lay on the ground all pell-mell, while others were half-buried.

Lucian dropped to his knees, holding on to his staff, his resources spent. He knew it would be a long time before he could use his magic again, but he was also thankful that he had learnt that recent spell. Suddenly groans filled the air, and they realized that not all the Night Husks were dead.

"Thank you, Lucian, for your timely intervention. We owe you, our lives. I think me and my scouts can take over now!"

With that, Zontahl and his scouts bounded over to the scattered bodies and tore at the throats of the Night Husk survivors. This horror was too much for Lucian and he turned his back on the grisly scene; he could only hope the Pogglin Husks were not among the carnage. The cats' teeth ripped into the dry skin with ease, and soon the task was done.

(Meanwhile, back at the Lake Naargrah, the scene of the Necromancers blasphemous incantations, thirty gossamer-like shapes rose upward out of the lake and shot skywards. If Lucian had been there to witness it, he would have known them for what they were. For they were the departing souls of the Night Husks imprisoned in the lake, and upon their faces was a look of peace.)

Fengook soon found Reclook; a bony Night Husk's hand sticking incongruously out of the sand had the lifeless little body dangling from it. Fengook dropped to his knees and wept. It was the first time his young eyes had witnessed death. Sir Septimus was with him and he comforted the little creature, as he too tried hard not to weep himself. They had all become very fond of these kind and brave little creatures.

While the cats dug a hole in the sand, the Pogglins, Fengook and the Fungiglooks removed the body from the grasp of the Night Husk. They then laid the body to rest, and the cats filled in the grave. They patted down the sand, and then the Fungiglooks each laid a mushroom on the grave (as was the Fungiglooks' tradition). In respect, the Pogglins and the cats each did the same. They pondered a moment over the grave; maybe each wondered if that was what their own future held. They then said a final farewell and moved off towards Uoplaax's Fang.

★ ★ ★ ★ ★

A tall figure with a shock of flaming red hair was bent over a table, deep in his work. He judged the still face before him for a moment, then looped the thread through the eyelid and started to stitch the lower eyelid firmly onto the upper cheek.

The Needleman was skeletally thin and tall. About his neck and chin was a high shirt collar that was muffled with black cloth and gave the impression that he was chinless. His high forehead sloped down into a long, beak-like nose, and dark, thick green lenses in place of his eyes. His swept-back red hair, which elongated his head still further, gave the impression that he was permanently caught in a high wind. His hands were thin with long, dexterous fingers and were the tools of his trade. They could expertly thread a needle in a twinkling of an eye.

Suddenly he was disturbed as the doors at the far end of the chamber flew open and a stout figure came marching in.

"I knew I sensed something at Lake Naargrah; there *IS* a magic-user in our territory!" the newcomer bellowed in a high-pitched, throaty voice.

The Needleman turned and peered at the disturber of his work. The newcomer was not unlike the Needleman himself; he was shorter and stout. His shirt collar was set higher around his face and the cloth muffled his chin and mouth to his nose, His jacket collar was also set high up his neck so that it gave the impression that his head was disappearing into his shoulders, which made him look even stouter than he truly was. His forehead sloped back even further than the Needleman's and was crowned by a spiky shock of grey-white hair. His nose was even longer and more aquiline than the Needleman's, and even more beak-like if that was possible.

The Seeker and the Needleman.

But the most striking thing about his face was his spectacles, for the lenses were so thick that they almost looked like binoculars.

"And what of The Master?" enquired the Needleman in a high-pitched, emotionless voice, pushing the Seeker away from his worktable.

"He will know about it!" The Seeker replied.

"Then shouldn't you be telling him instead of me?" he replied flatly.

"I meant that he would have felt the presence for himself. The Master does not need me to tell him!" he replied, somewhat petulantly.

"Then that makes your position of *Seeker* rather obsolete, does it not?"

The Seeker started tapping his staff on the chamber floor with annoyance.

"Stop that, it annoys me!" retorted the Needleman in his flat tones, as he dropped a stitch. "Why do you bother me with this news, Seeker? Can you not see I am *very* busy?"

"It concerns you, my dear Needleman, because this user of magic has destroyed thirty pieces of your handiwork!"

The Needleman looked at the Seeker unmoved.

"We have plenty more at our disposal and, thanks to Memleket, I have more work." He pointed at the corpse laying on his worktable.

For a moment nothing was said; the Needleman continued to work at his table, while the Seeker moved over to the window and looked out over the Valley of Zaark and the land beyond. "They were destroyed by *him* just there on the Plain of Uoplaax."

No reply. The Seeker looked over his shoulder at the Needleman who was still stooped over his worktable; he smiled to himself. "Yes," he continued, "It was on the Plain of Uoplaax that three of the largest from the tribe of Menton were destroyed!" The Seeker watched as he saw the Needleman stiffen slightly at this news: he smiled to himself again. "Three examples of your best work taken out with a meagre and yet clever trick."

"What?" he asked flatly, while continuing his work at the table.

"A simple earth-shifting spell; he is an Earth elemental-based user!"

The Needleman spun around on his heels. "Interesting."

"Yes, I thought that would interest you."

The Needleman stuck the needle into the table, covered his work with a grubby sheet and joined the Seeker at the window. "Tell me more!"

"The magic-user is weak, but his power is growing, although he is unsure of his capabilities. If these capabilities are realised then our world, as we know it, would change forever."

"And the Astral-Ley Plain, has he appeared on it?" he enquired, putting his long hands behind his back and leaning forward to observe the Seeker more closely.

"Indeed, he did, and he performed his incantations where two of the Ley lines crossed!"

The Needleman drew himself upright (the nearest he ever came to being shocked) at this news and was silent for a few moments, deep in thought.

"For a creature so unsure of his power and capabilities he has chosen his place well," he murmured, and moved away from the window. Caught by a realization, he suddenly spun around and pointed a long, white and bony finger at the Seeker. "I can now see why you came to me with this news: you have felt him on the Astral-Ley Plain, but cannot see his physical form!"

"True." The Seeker simply replied in his shrill voice.

The Needleman beckoned the Seeker to follow him with a waggle of a long finger. The Seeker followed the Needleman into the centre of the octagonal-shaped chamber. Hanging about the walls were hundreds of puppets, a dangling crop of glove puppets and marionettes. They were crudely made; some were made of cloth, others from wood or both. Some of the puppets looked new, while others looked many hundreds of years old. If the heads were not of carved wood, then they were made up from quarters of brightly-coloured cloth and stitched into a ball. A twisted smile was crudely stitched on to the faces, but most horrific of all was that instead of buttons for eyes, real humanoid eyes were stitched into place!

"Three were from the tribe of Menton, you say?"

"Correct." replied the Seeker.

"Now where did I put them?" The Needleman said as he looked about the walls, he clasped his hands together and touched his forefinger together, and placed them just under his beaklike nose. He spun slowly around on his heels as he looked.

"Ah-Ha! There they are!" he said, moving his forefingers from under his nose and pointing with both at three blackened puppets hanging on the second wall by the door, the third row down from the top. He walked over to them, though his motion was to glide along the floor, rather than walk: to any observer it gave the impression that his legs were on wheels instead of feet. He went up to the three puppets and took them off the wall. They were no longer brightly coloured: they looked charred, as though they had been burnt in a fire. Apart from the eyes, which glistened brightly as they did in... life!

"Such a pity, Memleket makes such wonderful puppets. He will be most upset when I tell him." said the Needleman flatly, and he pulled at the eyeballs, which made a squishing sound as he plucked them off the three puppet heads.

"I want to see too!" cried the Seeker, who instantly grabbed them from the Needleman and held one eyeball up at a time to his binocular-like spectacles. He closely examined the retina of each eyeball. "It's not that one," he said, and discarded the eyeball by throwing it over his shoulder. "Nor that one!" The eyeball followed its companion over his shoulder.

"You have mixed them up!" he shrilled in agitation, as he discarded another eyeball, then he fell silent as he examined the next.

"So that's what you look like, you little magic user you!" he loudly exclaimed. "Success!" he crowed, as he found the crucial image burnt into the retina.

"Let me see!" demanded the Needleman.

"Very well," replied the Seeker and cast the other two eyeballs onto the floor like unwanted trash.

The Seeker then started to mutter some eldritch, cabalistic words of magic, and then crushed the eyeball in the palm of his hand with a loud squelch! A red vapour began to rise from the jelly-like gore that squeezed out between his fingers. It rose into the air and started to form into an image. As the image formed, it changed colour, until the final image was that of the Night Husk's last vision before its destruction. There, floating in the chamber between them was a three-dimensional coloured image of Lucian Snuzz. He stood frozen in time, with his arms outstretched and staff in hand.

The Seeker and the Needleman walked around the image as they studied it closely.

"Not very impressive, is he? And yet you say this midget will one day wield more power than the world has ever seen; interesting!" said the Needleman emotionlessly.

"What is he? Do you know?" asked the Seeker.

"A Pogglin," replied the Needleman. "We still have a few of them left working the mines. If you want the eyes, you'll find their puppets over there," and he nodded towards a group of puppets on the wall to their left.

"I'm not interested in Pogglin Night Husks. I am only interested in this one!" the Seeker replied sharply.

The image of Lucian Snuzz faded and disappeared. The Needleman looked at the Seeker blankly.

"I was expecting more information than that," he said bluntly.

"If you didn't stitch up the ears, then maybe we might be able to have sound as well!" The Seeker retorted sarcastically.

The Needleman could never fathom sarcasm, so ignored it. "Yes Seeker, maybe you are right about the ears."

"I've heard of getting blood out of a stone, Needleman, but only you would expect to get sound out of an eyeball!"

With that he flounced out of the chamber, slamming the door behind him, leaving the Needleman to glide about the chamber, picking up the discarded eyeballs. He placed them in a jar and sealed the lid.

"You never know when one will need a spare eyeball," he said to himself and then returned to his worktable, flipped back the sheet and started to stitch, the Pogglin's image deep in his thoughts.

The Pogglin's image was also on the mind of the Seeker of Naarunkesh as he left the Needleman's chamber, and he huffed up the next flight of spiral stairs in the Tower of Eybraas to the chamber above. He rapped on the iron chamber door with his staff, the clanging echoing down the spiral staircase of the tower. From within the chamber, the Seeker heard the sounds of an organ playing. Presently the door opened, creaking on its hinges.

In the doorway stood a short Humpty-backed figure, a malign grin fixed upon his face and with skin was as white as marble. Dull grey strands of lank hair hang heavily about his head. His grin split his face even more as he surveyed the Seeker with pale pink, watery eyes. The light from the stairwell caught the yellowing stumps of his rotting teeth.

"I wish an audience with the Master, Memleket."

He stepped aside to let the Seeker pass and then closed the door, which clanged shut and echoed around the tower.

After closing the door, Memleket followed the Seeker into the main chamber. The chamber was immense and at the far end, there was a throne on a dais with six steps. On the wall behind the throne was drawn a large pentagram which was just about visible in the dim light. On the third step of the dais sat an ugly dwarf that maniacally played an air organ - the pipe box being strapped to his back. He was the Organist of Naarunkesh. In a way, Gemek's face resembled his brother, Memleket, The Master of Puppets, except that Gemek's nose was more beaklike, and unlike Memleket, Gemek was totally bald and had a long straggly, goat-like beard on the end of his chin. His face was fixed into a permanent frown but with a mad grin about his lips. He nodded to the Seeker in salutation as he entered, while his hand moved across the keyboard and his other hand frantically pumped the organ bellows.

The throne was carved with a screaming torso on the left side, which looked like it was trying to tear itself free of the wood. A look of agonised terror was depicted on the face: the hollow sockets of the eyes showed despair as well as horror. Draped over the right side of the throne was a deep crimson cloth. The rest of the throne was carved to depict a mass of screaming souls, contorted and intertwined in excruciating agonies. In the throne itself sat an extremely thin figure.

It sat askew in the throne, with a thin leg thrown over the left arm of it, and the leg dangled languidly over the side. In the right hand, it held a staff of twisted souls, wrought in iron and blued steel. In its lap was an ancient tome of eldritch spells; it traced a long, pale finger across the page as it read. The figure suddenly looked up from the skin-bound book, the face in deep shadow due to the great cowl of cloth that shrouded the head. But from the shadow burned eyes of the deepest red.

The Necromancer sat askew in the throne.

Memleket sat back down on his chair and continued work on his puppets; he looked up from his work now and again to look at his Master and the Seeker. He sat by the chamber door, in the right-hand corner of the chamber, and had a very good view of the proceedings. The Seeker stood in the middle of the chamber facing the throne (his back to Memleket) while the figure sat silently on the throne, holding the Seeker in his gaze. Only the insane notes of Gemek's music filled the chamber.

The enthroned figure suddenly snapped the tome shut and Gemek stopped playing. Finally, after many minutes, the Necromancer of Naarunkesh spoke.

"I created the position of *Seeker* to free my vigilance on this land and allow me time on other pursuits. Yet two hours have passed since I felt the disturbances on the astral-lye plain, and you have only now condescended to report to me."

He spoke quietly in rich and mellow tones, with perfect diction; every vowel and syllable were pronounced perfectly and dripping with menace. The Seeker went to reply, but the Necromancer stopped him with a raised finger.

"Did you ever meet your predecessor?" asked the Necromancer, in a menacing whisper, narrowing his eyes.

"No, my Lord," the Seeker replied hesitantly.

"Memleket!"

Memleket rose quickly from his stool and raced over to the corner opposite his own. He sorted through a few puppets and found what he was looking for. He pulled it out by the neck and trotted up to the dais, still holding the thing by the neck. He smiled evilly at the Seeker and held aloft a large doll about two feet in length. The head of the doll lolled to one side over Memleket's fist. A twisted smile was crudely stitched into the sack-like cloth and the eyes were large buttons. The body stretched down from the neck due to the stuffing and it bulged grotesquely about the belly. The cloth was heavily stained around the doll's belly and little legs that dangled below. The Seeker looked at the grubby doll with some disdain; it was not one of Memleket's best pieces of work.

The head of the doll lolled to one side over Memleket's fist.

"Meet your predecessor, my Seeker!"

"*What?*" he asked with some confusion.

"The doll, my dear Seeker, *IS* your predecessor, or should I say part of him." whispered the Necromancer with malign delight. "He *SO* disappointed me one day that I had to dispose of him. But I wanted a memento of him, a little keep-sake, so I had Memleket stuff that doll with his entrails!"

Memleket smiled (thrusting the sagging doll nearer the Seeker's face) and winked.

"Take the thing away, Memleket," ordered the Necromancer.

"Yes, my Master" intoned Memleket, and still holding the doll out in front of him, he trotted back down the chamber, threw the doll into the corner and sat down on his stool to continue working on his puppets.

The Necromancer leaned forward. "You're not going to disappoint me, are you now?"

"No, no, my Lord!" came the nervous reply.

"Good!" said the Necromancer, leaning back into his throne; he remained silent as he gazed at the Seeker, his deep red eyes blazing from the shadows of the cowl. "So, the Pogglin has shown his hand?"

"Yes, my Lord, on the Plain of Uoplaax. He conjured an earth shift, destroying thirty Night Husks," he replied, recovering slightly from his earlier discomfort. "And losing me thirty souls from my power base!" he added coldly. "But we have other Night Husks to replace those destroyed, my Lord."

"Idiot!" whispered the Necromancer icily, "The Night Husks are only a secondary by-product in the care of the Needleman. Souls are my *first* and most *needed* priority."

The Necromancer simmered in silence, and the Seeker's discomfort rekindled; his Master could be very unpredictable in these silent moods, so he tried to continue with his report.

"The Pogglin magic-user conjured the earth shift at the conjuncture of two ley lines. He is unsure of himself, but his power for magic is grow…"

"I know all this!" cut in the Necromancer with menace. "Tell me something that I don't know!"

The Seeker paused; this was going to be a tricky question to answer, as there wasn't much his master didn't know. "But there must be something?" He thought, but nothing sprang to mind for the moment.

"Have you considered why the Pogglin was on the Plain of Uoplaax?"

"Because of the conjuncture of the Ley lines, which…"

"No!" The Necromancer's eyes narrowed with contempt for his underling,

"That is only a part of it – think!"

The Seeker was flustered and thought furiously for an answer. Never before had his master treated him so.

"Then I shall tell you! The Pogglin was too far east of the Zelgemar Stairs to have just arrived on the Plain of Uoplaax. Therefore, he is making for somewhere; yes?"

The Seeker nodded.

"I say he is making for the Lake of Wonders!" He banged down his right fist on the arm of the throne.

The Seeker regained some of his swagger. "Then my Lord, we have him! The Pogglin will be weak from his expenditure of magic, and I can send out the Night Husks to fetch him back here."

"No!" came the cold reply.

The Seeker was shocked by the reply. "But my lord, in his weakened state I have the opportunity to crush him!" he protested.

"Being in a weakened state has nothing to do with it; you could swat him like a fly at any time. You know only too well that he has not the power to withstand you! But he *does* have the power to destroy my Night Husks, and *you* will not squander them by sending them in pursuit for the moment."

"What then am I to do, my Lord?"

"What you were trained for, you fool! Observe, calculate and then *seek*!" replied the Necromancer in a harsh, cold whisper. "I want to know what the Pogglin wants at the Lake of Wonders; once I know, you can have him and do with him as you please."

The Necromancer paused and then leaned forward. "But we don't want to make his road too easy to the Lake of Wonders," he said maliciously, the warmth returning to his rich voice. "Meet me in the Needleman's chamber."

At this point he disappeared, leaving the ancient book to hover in mid-air above the seat of the throne. The Seeker turned and headed for the chamber door as Gemek struck up again on his organ. Memleket got up from his stool and opened the door of the anti-chamber to the stairwell.

"I bet you wish you were a prestidigitator yourself?" He smirked at the Seeker as he passed. "Better hurry, the Master will be waiting for you downstairs!"

The Seeker looked at him coldly as he passed.

"And I don't like you either!" laughed Memleket, reading the Seeker's mind, and closed the door with a clang which echoed in the Seeker's ears as he hurried down the stairs to the Needleman's chamber.

The Seeker opened the Needleman's door and found the Necromancer and the Needleman waiting for him in silence; he closed the door behind him. The Necromancer stood in the centre of the chamber, towering a good foot and a half above the Needleman.

"You must learn dematerialisation, Seeker; there are a lot of stairs in this tower!" remarked the Necromancer coldly to his minion.

"I can my Lord, but I find it more exhausting than climbing the stairs," he replied.

The Necromancer's eyes narrowed, "I sometimes wonder about you!"

For a moment there was a chilling silence, which was broken by the Necromancer. "The magic-using Pogglin has destroyed thirty Night Husks, thus taking thirty souls away from me. This – will – *stop*!" His eyes turned to the puppets hanging about the chamber walls. The Necromancer thumped his staff on the floor while holding out his right hand, and a purple ball of light formed in his palm.

"*Fleghmarh Dakkhtum-Oum*!" he said, blowing on the ball of light.

It rose into the air above their heads: many hundreds of deep purple spines of light shot out of it, piercing the chest of every puppet hanging on the walls. For a moment the puppets glowed with a bright green light and in a blink of an eye, the eerie glow faded away.

"It is done!" The Necromancer proclaimed with a laugh in his voice. "The next time our little magic-user tries to disperse the Night Husks he will find his magic confounded!"

"What have you done, my Lord?" enquired the Seeker.

"What I should have done years ago Seeker. Until now no one has dared to confront the Night Husks. Their appearance alone conquered all who tried to withstand them and they never suffered defeat, but this little trickster has proved only too well how easily the Night Husks can be destroyed. But not anymore!"

The Needleman and the Seeker looked at their Master in eager anticipation.

"The Night Husks are now under your care Needleman, for they can never be destroyed until these puppets are *first* destroyed," he said gesturing to the puppets hanging around the walls. "Keep them safe, for they are your charge and responsibility."

The Needleman bowed his head in reverence to his Master.

The Necromancer turned his finger to the Seeker. "You have my permission to harry the little trickster on his way to the Lake of Wonders, but be warned!" he leaned menacingly over the Seeker. "Do not over-do it; I want to know why he is going to the Lake of Wonders. This charge I give to you; it is your responsibility, Seeker, and remember the fate of your predecessor. Do not *fail* me!"

With this menacing warning, the Necromancer vanished from the chamber, but his burning red eyes remained, suspended in the empty air, to gaze intently at the Seeker - before they too vanished.

★ ★ ★ ★ ★

The Pogglins and their party had made camp on a ledge about twelve feet up the side of Uoplaax's Fang. There was a hollow in the rock at the back of the ledge that gave some protection from the wind that blew across the Plain. They had just finished eating a mushroom supper, along with some of the food that was given to the Pogglins by the Quistorrisians, and started settling down for some well-earned rest.

"My scouts will take the first watch," Zontahl informed the party, "followed by myself, Lucian, Sir Septimus and Artimus. Fengook and his scouts will take the third." He gave several orders to his cats and they bounded off down the side of the rock and fanned out at the base of the outcrop. There they sat, keeping their bright eyes fixed on the horizon. In their posture, there was an alertness common with all feline species.

Fengook and his scouts bade everyone a good rest and then snuggled down to sleep. The Pogglins were restless for all their tiredness; too many questions filled their heads. Even Sir Septimus could not sleep and he could normally sleep anywhere, under any conditions.

"I want to thank you, Lucian, for what you did. You got us out of a nasty situation back there," and he patted Lucian awkwardly across the back. Lucian smiled, as Sir Septimus never used his first name unless in times of affection, thankfulness, or sternness. Artimus just held up his thumb in thanks to Lucian and smiled. Lucian smiled and nodded back.

Zontahl observed the scene unfold and clearly found it touching. "I see you hold each other in great regard, and I can see that you three are old campaigners of many adventures. I like that, for we Cats of Empraktos-Larris also hold dear those same qualities of camaraderie."

"You agreed to join us, Zontahl, and yet we know nothing about you. Why did you want to come along with us?" asked Artimus.

"When Fontahl told me about you – he is my brother, by the way – and that you were from the land above, I was intrigued. I was curious to know more about you and my scouts had reported to me that you were still in the forest. So, I decided to seek you out, and then I received news that the Night Husks had entered the forest. I realised that you must be their quarry and it was now imperative that I found you before they did."

"Does your chief not mind you accompanying us on our journey to the Moogem Tree?" asked Lucian.

"No, he doesn't mind," replied the cat with a smile.

"Nor accompanying us to Sol-Larris after we are done here in Empraktos-Larris?"

"No," came the reply.

"Your chief must be a most understanding fellow," said Sir Septimus.

"Oh, he is," replied Zontahl with satisfaction. "I *am* the chief of the cats!"

The Pogglins looked at each other, then jumped up and bowed to Zontahl in reverence.

"Oh, there is no need for all that nonsense now we have formally met!" Casually, the orange-eyed cat waved to them to be seated. "I would only expect that from my fellow cats," he said with a broad smile.

"I am very pleased that you did agree to join us, Zontahl," Lucian said.

Zontahl nodded his thanks and spoke. "Lucian, you must be very special to the Necromancer of Naarunkesh for him to send Night Husks into the Fungoid Forest. Never before have these creatures bothered us in the forest."

"But just what are the Night Husks?" Artimus enquired

"They are servants of the Necromancer. They do his bidding and toil in the mines of the Vunolf Peaks. They are relentless in their pursuit if they catch a scent of you. If a Night Husk should touch you, then you will receive a visit from the Needleman!" Zontahl answered, in a tone so matter-of-fact he might have been discussing porridge or last year's rainfall.

"Yes, I knew most of that," continued Artimus, "but just what is the control the Necromancer has over them? How does he manipulate them into doing his bidding?"

"That I do not know," replied Zontahl.

There was silence for a few moments while they considered the question. Finally, it was Lucian who came forward with the answer.

"I believe I know the answer, dreadful as it may be." He had everyone's attention as he spoke. "What we saw at Lake Naargrah – that ceremony –was the Necromancer manipulating his power over the Night Husks. That yellowish, smoke-like substance was not smoke that I and Sir Septimus saw…"

"What was it, Snuzz? It looked like smoke to me."

Lucian turned to face his friend. "They were the souls of the people who are now the beings we know as the Night Husks, Sir Septimus."

His moustache twitched and a look of appalled horror flickered across Sir Septimus' face. Artimus gasped in shock. Upon hearing this news, Zontahl's eyes narrowed.

"Yes, my friends," continued Lucian, "The Necromancer has the souls entombed in the lake. He keeps them there in torment, and that is his power over the Night Husks."

"That is the most dreadful thing I have ever heard!" exclaimed Sir Septimus, his monocle popping out from his socket in dismay.

"It's horrible!" nodded Artimus in agreement.

"Indeed, it is, my friends," said Lucian quietly, and fell silent, deep in thought.

"But the Night Husks are dead," said Zontahl. "They are corpses. How can you kill a thing that is already dead? Why were they so *easy* to kill?"

"Zontahl has a point there, Lucian," said Artimus.

"They are not truly dead, my friends; just soulless creatures. I would say they still feel pain as much as the next Manu. But maybe there is a flaw in the power the Necromancer holds over their bodies? I don't know. But I do know the key to the Necromancer's power over them is Lake Naargrah."

"Also known as the *Lake of Lost Souls*!" chipped in Zontahl.

Lucian didn't look surprised by this news. "An interesting piece of information, Zontahl, which just goes to help substantiate my hypothesis."

"So, Snuzz, what happened to the souls of the Night Husks when they were destroyed?"

Lucian thought on this for a moment. "I can only assume, Sir Septimus, that the soul is released from its torment when the body of the Night Husk is destroyed."

"A happy release then? They are now at peace and beyond the Necromancer's torment," said Artimus.

"That is very comforting," said Sir Septimus, "but there is no hope, then, of ever saving our Pogglin folk from this Night Husk damnation without sending them off to join Dunbruan in the here-after."

"Maybe that is the only release we *can* give them. Far better than the torment they are suffering now," Artimus stated plainly.

"I will discover a way when the time comes. That I have vowed myself to do!" said Lucian with conviction,

"But what about their eyes, Snuzz? They will have no eyes!"

"That will be remedied, Sir Septimus. You can be sure of that," replied Lucian in firm tones.

"So, your plan is still to head for the Emprak Mountains on the next march?" enquired Zontahl.

"Yes," replied Lucian.

"Then I suggest," said Zontahl, "That we shall skirt the foot of the mountains, keeping clear of Lake Naar as much as possible. Then, keeping the Petrified Jungle to our right flank, we should come to the Outcrop of Uutroc, at the foot of which lies the Lake of Wonders and the Moogem Tree."

"You do realise that you will still be visible to the Tower of Eybraas?"

"That I understand, Artimus, but at least we will have some cover – something we wouldn't have if we went via the open route past the city. And if there is a seeker in the city of Naarunkesh, I would already have alerted him to my presence by the use of my magic back there on the plain."

"Then we shall have to be doubly vigilant!" said Zontahl.

Artimus and Sir Septimus nodded in agreement.

"Well, I only hope we meet nothing on the way to the Lake of Wonders as we will be without the protection of magic until then," said Lucian.

Zontahl looked at him in surprise, "No magic? Why?"

"Because my magic level is depleted, Zontahl. Conjuring and casting spells does take it out of you as much as running or weight-lifting; one needs time to recover. Magic-users draw their power from one of the four elements, air, water, fire and earth. Powerful magic-users, like the Necromancer, will have the cleverness to draw on all four elements for their power. I only have the power to draw from the earth elements, and even then, I am only a level three magic-user. So, I need time to recover my strength."

"I see," said Zontahl "Then we must rely on your cleverness and my cunning!"

"We had better get some rest," said Artimus, looking at his pocket-watch. "We have a long march ahead of us, and it will soon be our turn for the watch."

★ ★ ★ ★ ★

Fengook lightly shook Lucian. "It is time for the next march, my mushroom brother," he said gently in his singsong tones. Lucian sat up to find the rest of the party awake and finishing off some more mushrooms.

"You shouldn't have left me so long," he protested as Artimus gave him some mushrooms and water.

"You took quite a draining of your magical abilities on the plain, Lucian, and you need to build them up again, so you needed the extra rest. Anyhow, we don't know what the Necromancer's next move will be."

Sir Septimus was standing by the edge of the ledge, looking out eastwards where the foot of the Emprak Mountains met the Petrified Jungle. It looks a good day's march, if not more. He turned around to face the rest of the group. "Artimus, I fear to ask, but what state are we at, with the time we have left to complete our quest and get back?"

Artimus looked at his timepiece and frowned. "It's taken us longer to get here than we anticipated and I make it the twelfth of July," he said, cutting off a day on the Quistorrisian pencil, "Leaving us four days to get back home by the sixteenth of July. I would say we have another day and a half to get to the Moogem Tree."

The plan relied on many factors – staying alive being the most important!

Sir Septimus drew back from the edge. "I would say the blighter will attack again either at the Petrified Jungle, or he is more likely to attack us on the return journey. That would make sense, as we will be very fatigued."

"We must be ready and alert at all times, Sir Septimus," replied Zontahl. "We must not lull ourselves into a false sense of security, as that will be our downfall."

"My brothers and I do not know this land about," remarked Fengook, "and this is the furthest I have been from the Fungoid Forest. But we feel that we wish to put our scouting skills at your disposal."

Dargook, Ongook and Songook nodded in agreement.

"My scouts have been as far as the Mouth of Zoulgaar," Zontahl explained, "and that is the other side of the Lake of Wonders. So, I suggest that Parrdoo and Sarlizahl go on ahead, followed by three of the Fungiglook scouts. Fengook can be fall-back with Lucian, Sir Septimus and Artimus. I will then follow from the rear with Rumshesh and Amukah to watch our backs."

Everyone agreed that it was a good plan, and once Lucian had eaten, they gathered their things and started to climb down Uoplaax's Fang. They then headed south until they came to the foot of Mount Uoplaax itself. Its top glowed eerily, lighting the cavern roof with a deep red radiance. The little group then swung southeast and around the foot of Mount Aplaax. It was here that the ground dropped into a steep crevasse and started to descend into the Valley of Zaark. A putrid smell of sulphur and stagnant water filled their nostrils. Traversing the climb down into the Valley of Zaark was far trickier than they had anticipated. But after a lot of sweat and toil, they made it safely into the Valley.

A wailing sound of the Night Husk siren was faintly heard far off in the distance. Artimus consulted his pocket-watch once again; 4.09 am. He was surprised because they had made good time, but there was still a long march ahead of them. He replaced the watch in his pocket. From their viewpoint, they could see a glowing dark-green mass way off in the distance.

"That is Lake Naar," Zontahl informed them.

"Is that where the stench is coming from?" asked Lucian. Zontahl nodded.

"It is a lake of stagnant water. The only things that live there are the Naara Frogs and the bloated mosquitoes that infest the waters."

"It sounds very picturesque," mused Sir Septimus "I must remember never to take a holiday there!"

Everyone laughed; it was a good morale booster that came at the right moment.

Far off to the left of Lake Naar was the great walled city of Naarunkesh, home of the Necromancer and the Subterranians. At the southern end of the city was a pinnacle of black rock, and perched on top was the mighty Tower of Eybraas. The Pogglins looked at it in awe.

"A place to be avoided," said Lucian quietly.

★ ★ ★ ★ ★

On the Eastern side of the city, along the outer city wall, and well out of the view of Lucian and his party, a group of Night Husks waited in readiness for their ambush.

★ ★ ★ ★ ★

"I want to make it to the Lake of Wonders before our next stop," Lucian informed his colleagues. The party moved off as before. They followed the foot of the Emprak Mountains, keeping close to the rock face. The smell from the stagnant Lake Naar, even though it was still a long way off, grew stronger as they drew closer to it.

It was darker in the Valley and everything was tinged with the red glow that emitted from the volcanic tops of Mounts Uoplaax, Aplaax and Zarplaax. Sir Septimus looked back up and along the cliff face that ran the entire length of the Valley of Zaark; at the far end, he could see the welcoming green-blue radiance of the Fungoid Forest.

The cat scouts bounded out around the rock face ahead of the party, while the Fungiglook scout followed behind, their large green eyes glowing in the dim light. Dargook and Songook were very nervous: they didn't like remaining on the ground, and it was the first time they had left the confines of the Fungoid Forest. Songook was beginning to think he should never have come this far, and then he remembered his friend Reclook who had decided to return home. He never made it back to Mushentar and he was still within the forest when he died at the hands of the Night Husks. This thought resolved his decision to continue and he hurried along with more confidence.

Fengook was also feeling a little anxious: the furthest he had ever been was to Uoplaax's Fang, but none the less he felt safe in the company of Lucian. If there was any danger to be faced, he felt sure that his new mushroom brother could deal with it. He smiled up at Lucian; he smiled back at the little Fungiglook. Yes, he felt safe in the company of our Mr Lucian Snuzz.

"What more can you tell me of the Subterranians, Fengook?" asked Lucian, as they hurried along, puffing a little as he spoke.

"Not a lot, my mushroom brother," he replied. "According to our legends, the white-faces once lived in peace and harmony with all in the land of Empraktos-Larris. Then centuries ago, the *Necromancer* came! He purged the City of Naarunkesh of goodness and the great Tower of Eybraas was thrown up. Then Memleket, the stealer of souls, Gemek and The Collector began to stalk the land and the Needleman walked abroad. It is said that the Necromancer found him in the dark city of Kesh."

"The city of Kesh? Where in Empraktos-Larris can this city be found, Fengook?"

"I do not know for sure, my mushroom brother —only that it is far, far away to the east, beyond the city of Naarunkesh."

"At about the same time as the appearance of the Needleman," he continued, "the Night Husks slowly began to appear in the land of Empraktos-Larris and it was plunged into misery and darkness."

"That is indeed a very interesting story," puffed Lucian as he trotted along.

"I wonder where the Necromancer came from?" he thought to himself.

Artimus, Sir Septimus and Zontahl had also been listening to Fengook's story as they moved rapidly along. Listening to Fengook had taken Sir Septimus' mind off the trek. "I wonder who this Needleman chap is?" he puffed heavily with the exertion of the rapid march.

"He is an ancient Demon of eldritch lore," answered Lucian, "And an acquaintance you should not wish to make!"

"Oh, righto Snuzz, righto," he said, rather surprised by how quickly he got his answer. "But what does he do?"

"He is the maker of Night Husks, Sir Septimus. He operates on the victims by removing their eyes after stitching their eyelids open and then stitching their mouths closed," replied Lucian flatly.

"That's horrible!" interjected Artimus.

"*They can see all, but will never speak of it,*" quoted Lucian. "The Needleman was originally a demon of revenge and malice. If you want to get your own back or silence somebody, you would get the Needleman to pay him or her a visit!"

"How do you know all this Snuzz?"

"I read a lot, Sir Septimus!" he replied. "However, it looks as though the Necromancer has taken it a step further by having the Needleman create the Night Husks."

★ ★ ★ ★ ★

Captain Chalaaze "Flash" Gunkfopp joined the table, back from his secret mission to Pogglinburg. He resembled a younger version of his father, General Gunkfopp, except that he had excellent hearing and sight in both eyes. Unlike his father, Captain Chalaaze had not an ounce of honour and had not seen any action in the field. The captain was perfect to be a minion and fellow conspirator to Lord Creep.

"*Operation Steam-Powered Mass Destruction* is a total success!" wheezed Lord Creep to his fellow conspirators sat around the table of the conspirator's chamber.

"WHAT?" roared the old Field Marshal, moving his ear trumpet nearer Fangdom Creep.

"Could you do the honours, General Sidok?"

"What?" bellowed the Field-Marshal again.

A green pill was dropped into a glass of wine.

"Have a drink, Field-Marshal Gunkfopp," said General Sidok, moving the glass over to the Field Marshal. He heard the mention of drink: he drank deeply from the glass and fell instantly to sleep.

Lord Creep nodded his thanks to the General and continued.

"The modifications to the War Robot's positronic brain have been carried out! Sir Gittoid and I attended a secret meeting with Professor Frumpton-Stone of R.U.F.A.S.A.T and Doctor Meltabossokk of R.U.F.A.T.A.S. I am pleased to report that they have put aside their friendly rivalry to work on *Operation Steam-Powered Mass Destruction*. They demonstrated the War Robot's weaponry for us on Dropjaw, who was eager to help. He always wanted to make a useful contribution to our plans, and so he did... *With his life!*"

"Serves him right for wanting to help the cause," Cut in Lord Humbart Krank, the Lord Chief Justice. He grinned widely; it was a repulsive sight to behold.

"How comes you were invited to this secret demonstration and we were not?" enquired Colonel Tantermount. "I suppose you thought your fellow conspirators were old fools who were not important enough to attend? Well, that's all well and good, and you may be right," he said, answering his own question. "But I'll have you know" his voice rising, "That we ARE AS IMPORTANT, AND THAT WE *IS* IMPORTANT ENOUGH TO COME TO SECRET MEETINGS, **AND HOW DARE YOU THINK THAT WE ARE OLD FOOLS! SO THERE, LET THAT BE AN END OF IT!!!**" He roared, raising himself from his chair, turning purple with outrage.

Doctor Jenks drew a pistol and shot the raging Colonel in the head with a sedative Dart. He collapsed unconscious onto the table with a loud crash. Every one applauded Doctor Jenks.

The Doctor smiled at his fellow conspirators. "Merely a Hypodermic Pistol; I use it on all my difficult patients!" he said and replaced the pistol in his pocket.

"If it were me, sir," wheezed the Lord Chief Justice, "I would have used a *real* pistol!"

Lord Creep bowed his head in thanks to Doctor Jenks, his wig slipping forward, and straighten it before continuing.

"As I was saying before the interruption, the War Robot's weapons were a total success and will make triple-minced meat of those who stand in the way of our might!"

The conspirators applauded, and the Lord Chief Justice tapped the floor with his sticks. Creep raised his hands for silence. "Tomorrow, after an audience with the King – hopefully my last! –I leave for the Grodium Mountain for a secret meeting with Yorgrinn the Sly for the final phase of our plans. After tomorrow, gentlemen, we can kick out this feckless king of ours and begin the Sol-Larrian domination by the new Dondymarian Empire," he winced to himself at this slip of the tongue, "Sorry; the New Dondymarian *REPUBLIC* can begin!"

Feeling very smug with himself at his own gift of oratory, he sat down to a round of applause.

★ ★ ★ ★ ★

The elongated expanse of Lake Naar now lay before Lucian and his friends. The water of Lake was darker than pea soup with highlights tinged red, the light being reflected from the cavern ceiling high above. About the shore of the lake were many reeds and bulrushes; the occasional boulder broke the surface of the water. The smell of putrid stagnation filled the air. To the right of the lake was the start of the Petrified Jungle, which hugged the shore. In some places, the white stone trees of the jungle stuck out of the shallows.

Suddenly Parrdoo's paw sank into the sodden Earth; she meowed with shock, and quickly pulled it back with a loud plop."There is quicksand! We will have to try and keep to the rocks. It's going to be hard going; some of the rocks are set far apart in places." she said to Sarlizahl behind her, and he passed it onto the Fungiglooks who relayed the message back to the main party.

Artimus slapped his cheek. "Quicksand, and now pesky mosquitoes!" he fumed.

"You can expect more now we are at the water's edge!" said Zontahl with irritation as he too was bitten despite his thick skin. The mosquitoes were about the size of a ten-pence piece, with large bloated bodies. Their wings buzzed furiously about the heads of the expedition, and they flapped the mosquitoes away with annoyance. The persistent mosquitoes slowed the Cats' progress, although the Fungiglooks seemed not to be bothered by them. It was indeed hard traversing the rocks: as Parrdoo had predicted, the tops were covered with slippery moss. Ongook slipped and let out a little squeal as his foot went into the cold water of the lake. The noise from his squeal made the mosquitoes back off and something stirred in the water.

"Did you see that? The noise the little fellow made annoys the mosquitoes!"shouted Sir Septimus.

"Yes, it did! Fengook, do you think you and your scouts could replicate that squeal?" Artimus asked their little friend.

"I don't think that is such a..." started Lucian, but he was drowned out by the shrill noise.

Instantly the mosquitoes flew away and Artimus patted Fengook on the back,

"Well done indeed!" he said joyfully.

"I don't think that was such a good idea," said Lucian, finishing what he was going to say.

Suddenly a heaving, red bulk surfaced from the waters of the lake, and a deep red tongue lassoed the leg of Ongook! Fengook tried to grab his companion, but it was too late. Ongook was pulled, screaming, into the massive mouth of the Naara Frog; the monster clamped down its mouth with half of the Fungiglook still hanging out. Ongook screamed with terror, his arms thrashing about as he was pulled under the water. The water bubbled with expelled air and then there was complete silence. The others looked on in mortified horror.

The waters erupted again and another deep red tongue whipped through the air and wrapped around Amukah at the rear of the group. He disappeared into the water before anyone could even move!

"We've got to get away from the water's edge!" screeched Rumshesh to Zontahl.

Suddenly another tongue flashed out of the water: it lassoed Fengook around the middle, and he screamed in horror and panic! Zontahl leapt through the air and seized the Naara Frog's tongue in his mouth and bit down hard on it! The Naara Frog surfaced and gargled in pain as Zontahl bit through its tongue, whilst the whiplash sent Fengook flying backwards and somersaulted him into the quicksand. The Naara Frog sank below the water and a small amount of blood bubbled up onto the surface. Zontahl thrashed dreadfully in the water as Sir Septimus and Artimus desperately tried to fish him out.

Lucian instantly turned with his staff as Fengook hit the quicksand. He held out his staff with the silver-mounted gemstone facing Fengook. "Take it, Fengook, and I will pull you out!"

Fengook flailed about trying to reach the end of the staff, causing him to sink rapidly. Very soon he was up to his neck, just his head and arms were free. Lucian was at full stretch when finally, Fengook managed to grasp the end of the staff. "Hold on!" he cried and heaved with all his might; slowly, Fengook moved a little and Lucian heaved again.

Dargook and Songook were now holding onto Lucian around his legs as he grappled with the exhausting battle with the quicksand. He gave a final heave and pulled Fengook free! They then turned and helped to get Zontahl free of the water.

"Stop thrashing about!" shouted Artimus at Zontahl.

From out the corner of his eye, Lucian saw two large yellow eyes appear amongst the reeds. In a flash, he turned and brained the hideous amphibian with the end of his staff.

"We must get out of here fast before we are all eaten alive by these vile frogs!"

At last, Zontahl was free and they quickly made their way over the rocks. They bounded over the rocks, Parrdoo to the front, followed by Lucian and his party and Rumshesh following at the rear. The encounter with the Naara Frogs had improved everyone's balance!

"How far does the quicksand go?"

"I do not know, Lucian," said Zontahl "It is many years since I have been this way."

Just as Lucian jumped to another rock, a Naara Frog's tongue whipped past his head; a few seconds earlier and he would have been the frog's supper.

"The Frogs are everywhere!" cried Sir Septimus, with panic sounding in his voice.

The company dodged, ducked, slipped and ran for all their might and with more luck than judgement they edged further away from the stinking lake and its deadly inhabitants. Just as they started to relax a little, thinking the danger had receded and that they could find respite amongst the petrified trunks, they stopped dead in their tracks and the terror returned.

For there, waiting for them, just ahead was a Night Husk.

"We're trapped!" shouted Artimus as Parrdoo leapt up into the bough of the petrified tree.

"No, we're not!" shouted Lucian as the Night Husk rushed forward. With great dexterity Lucian pole-vaulted over the Night Husk's head with his staff, just as a Naar frog lassoed the Night Husk and pulled the foul creature down into the water.

"Well done, Snuzz, that's taken care of the blighter!" shouted Sir Septimus gleefully. "I didn't realise the water stretched this far – I thought we'd left the damned frogs behind!"

"That's the end of him!" said Artimus as he rushed past the bubbling water.

Suddenly the water erupted and foamed red as the Night Husk surfaced, headfirst and upright. Artimus turned in horror. Behind the creature floated the corpse of the dead Naara Frog.

"It's not DEAD!" squealed the Fungiglooks.

Another Night Husk came rushing at Lucian (who had turned in shock at Artimus' cry, and saw the first Night Husks surfacing from the water). Just in time, he turned back to see the Night Husk rushing towards him. He sprang into the air as his staff began to emit a pale blue light, "***Mortalitas Cos Cotis***!" he cried, as the gemstone turned white. The Night Husk jerked and turned to stone! It rocked back and forth before falling into the water as Lucian landed on his feet.

Artimus had picked up a large rock and hurled it at the first Night Husk as it tried to scramble out of the water. The rock smashed into the side of its head, but still, it continued to try to wade ashore.

"They won't die!" cried Artimus in dread, as he and the Fungiglooks pelted the ghastly monsters with rocks and stones.

"It seems the Necromancer has remedied their weakness!" said Lucian in unfaltering astonishment. Another tongue pulled the Night Husk back under the water as it thrashed wildly in the air with grasping hands.

"Look out!" cried Parrdoo from the bough of the Petrified tree to Lucian as a third Night Husk came at him. Using all his might, he smashed the Night Husk in the side of its body with his staff, sending it into the water. Two Naara Frogs immediately descended upon the Night Husk, dragging it under the water.

"Hurry!" called Lucian to the others. "Hurry, while the way ahead is clear!"

The others rushed past where the last Night Husk had entered the water, and the unquiet surface bubbled and foamed in a frenzy. The land began to open out ahead and Lucian gambled that it was the end of the quicksand and jumped off the rocks onto the ground. To his everlasting relief, it was firm.

"It's safe to get back on the ground. To me, my friends!"

The two Pogglins, Fengook, Dargook, Songook, Zontahl, Parrdoo, Sarlizahl and Rumshesh ran for all they were worth along the final row of rocks and down onto the ground where Lucian waited for them.

A mighty roar went up and much thrashing of water was heard as the Night Husks were once again ashore.

"Quickly, said Lucian, "The Naara Frogs didn't hold them for long and I have not yet fully recovered my powers!"

They rushed quickly east, keeping the Petrified Jungle on their right flank. On the horizon ahead they saw a pinnacle of rock thrusting up from the desert.

"That is the Outcrop of Uutroc, and beyond is the Lake of Wonder and the Moogem Tree," said Zontahl.

"Look!" cried Fengook.

In front of their path were six pairs of glowing orange sockets: more Night Husks!

"The two Night Husks are coming at us from the rear too!" screeched Rumshesh.

"They have our scent," said Zontahl bitterly. "They will pursue until we are dead or captured!"

Suddenly Parrdoo charged at the two Night Husks that were coming from the direction of Lake Naar. She bounded at the Night Husk that had half its head staved in by Artimus and the Fungiglooks, and tore at its throat. Whilst it flailed helplessly under her onslaught, the other Night Husk pulled Parrdoo off by the scruff of her neck, stretched her between its arms and savagely broke her back across its knee. The Night Husk bellowed with anger, and its eye-sockets turned red with rage as it threw Parrdoo's limp body at the little group. The corpse landed at Zontahl's paws in a crumpled heap.

Zontahl roared with rage at the two Night Husks that were closing in fast.

Dargook cried out in terror as he saw the other six Night Husks bearing down on them from the east. Quickly Lucian began to draw a circle around the group in the dirt.

"They will not take me like a rat in a trap; I will not die without a fight!" bellowed Sir Septimus at the Night Husks.

"And I will be by your side!" said Artimus.

The two Pogglins and Zontahl were about to make a charge when Lucian jumped in front of them. "Stop!" he ordered, "There will be no more senseless sacrificing of lives!" And he finished drawing the circle.

"Now everyone, quickly get into the centre of the circle and keep your eyes shut tight until I tell you to open them!" He said with great authority and thumped his staff on the ground and under his breath, "I don't know how long I'll be able to hold out." The gemstone glowed —and not a moment too soon as the first two Night Husks were almost upon them!

"**ORBRIS LUMINATRIUM!**" He called, and snapped his eyes shut.

"ORBRIS LUMINATRIUM!" Lucian called.

Instantly a ring of white light appeared around the party, causing the Night Husks to back off. They staggered and reeled from the light, covering their eye sockets and screaming in pain. The light was intense and, being creatures of the half-light, they greatly feared it!

★ ★ ★ ★ ★

Meanwhile, the Seeker was watching the puppets on the walls in the Needleman's chamber. "Interesting! This one's eyes have just turned to flint!"

"More of the earth elemental trickery," said the Needleman from his workbench, calmly putting the last stitch into the eyelid. "The Husk's body may be lost to us, but the soul is still safe. The Master will be pleased!"

"Yes, but it was a potent spell, not just stone but *flint*. He is becoming more confident with his abilities as a sorcerer!"

Suddenly thin beams of hot white light shot out of the eyes of the other six puppets. The Seeker fell back with a scream of disbelief and pain. His large binocular-like spectacles magnified the beam; it felt as if the retinas of his eyes had been burnt out!

"My eyes!" he bellowed, his voice rising to a scream. "*My Eyes!*"

Chapter Four

The ring of light still burned brightly around Lucian and his party, but he could feel himself beginning to weaken. Though he could not hear the Night Husks anymore, he didn't dare open his eyes because of the light. *A few seconds more*, he thought, straining against the toll it was taking on him, *please, just a few seconds more*. Then he thumped his staff on the ground, and the ring of light disappeared as he slumped to the ground with fatigue. He quickly opened his eyes, and could see no Night Husks in the vicinity.

"You can open your eyes now, it's quite safe; the Night Husks have retreated," he said in short gasps.

The others gradually opened their eyes and scanned the area where the husks had been. All were half-expecting them to still be there despite Lucian's reassurance, but were overjoyed that Lucian had saved them again and they thanked him enthusiastically.

"There is no need," said Lucian with all modesty. "Besides, I do not know how long we have before the Night Husks return to finish their task. I suggest we make for the Lake of Wonders while we have the opportunity."

"My dear chap, you can't go anywhere at the moment! You look, and obviously are, completely exhausted!" said Sir Septimus.

"I confess the spell has taken what I had left out of me, but we must move now! I am not sure how much time we have taken under the protection of the ring of light. So, let's push on," said Lucian with a determination that rallied the others to him.

"I will not leave my best scout here for those Frogs to devour!" said Zontahl.

"We are all desperately upset with the death of brave Parrdoo, but it is not safe to tarry here, Zontahl," pleaded Lucian.

"Then we shall carry Parrdoo until we have the chance to bury her with dignity." Zontahl meowed to Sarlizahl and Rumshesh to help carry the corpse of their comrade. They picked her up gently and padded off towards the Outcrop of Uutroc. Artimus, Septimus and Fengook stayed very close to Lucian, in case he collapsed again with this added effort that his body had to endure.

The Pogglins and the Fungiglooks hurried along, followed by the three Cats, when suddenly they heard a howl echoing through the Petrified Jungle.

"Hurry, my friends," said Lucian, holding his hat as he ran. "We do not want to be outflanked by whatever that is in the jungle!"

★ ★ ★ ★ ★

The Needleman had helped the Seeker into a chair and he was now recovering from the light that had emanated from the puppets' eyes. The Seeker looked at the Needleman looking down at him, but his vision of the Needleman was covered with a cluster of green spots.

"They will go!" The Needleman said in his emotionless tone, as if he knew what the Seeker was seeing.

"Yes, they are going, slowly. I thought the little trickster had blinded me permanently!" he said with some bitterness.

"But you *are* blind! That is what enables you to be a Seeker!" retorted the Needleman.

Ignoring the remark, the Seeker continued, "He cast a Light Ring spell. He is getting clever as well as confident in his conjuring."

"And stronger!" said the Needleman.

"It wasn't that powerful – merely a Light Ring!" he replied indignantly.

"You are missing the point! You yourself predicted that he would become more powerful as he gains in confidence in his sorcery. The Light Ring; is it not a spell for a fire elemental user?"

"I see what you mean, yes... And he is only an earth elemental user!"

"Until now!" replied the Needleman coldly. "But how did he do it?"

They both pondered the question. Suddenly the Seeker jumped to his feet, his senses tingled, a disturbance on the Astral Ley Plain; it was the Pogglin magic user!

"He is nearing the Lake of Wonders!"

"He has indeed done well to get that far on his own. One does wonder how he made it past Lake Naar? The Naara Frogs are hungry at this time of the season, and he also had to contend with the Night Husks."

The Seeker thought on these points until the Needleman interrupted them with another question. "Are you certain there is only one magic-user out there?"

"Only one shows up on the Astral Ley Plain, therefore yes, there is only one!"

"Just checking," said the Needleman, now bored with the conversation and heading back to his workbench, "as you haven't been performing at your best of late, have you?" He paused as he took up his needle and threaded it with a new piece of silk. "Twelve Ley lines converge at The Lake of Wonders; our little magic-user isn't going there for nothing!" he muttered, and stuck the needle into a fleshy cheek and started to stitch.

★ ★ ★ ★ ★

Lucian rounded the foot of the Outcrop of Uutroc and stopped in amazement at the vista that lay before his eyes. He was joined by the others and apart from Zontahl (who had seen it before), the company was struck silent in amazement at the scene in front of them. The most beautiful green meadow of lush grass and flowers stretched out before them. After the relentless desolate, barren, and rocky features they had just trudged through, this sight was as big a surprise as it was welcomed! At the centre of this verdant pasture was a stunning blue lake that shone as bright as any sapphire. The waters were the clearest the Pogglins had seen since leaving Pogglinburg and they all felt a slight pang of homesickness at the thought. The atmosphere and light had also changed. It was lighter and brighter than before.

It was like walking out into the sunshine on a summer's day. You would never imagine that you were underground. About half a mile away, at the side of the lake, there was a beautiful silvery and amber glow, coming from the area.

It was shimmering and glorious. "There it is," whispered Lucian in reverence. "We have found it, my friends, for there is the Moogem Tree!"

Their spirit and resolve rose: for the first time in many hours did they feel hopeful of success.

They could just make out that the trunk and branches were the colour of golden amber and the leaves were glistening with silver. It radiated all the light and goodness that was all around them.

"It is beautiful!" was all Lucian could say.

Behind the tree was a great plateau of rock and many strange spires could be seen rising towards the cavernous roof above.

"What is that place, Zontahl?" asked Lucian of the cat.

"That is the Plateau of Uutroc on which stands the city of Kesh. It is a foreboding place; none of my race has visited the city, as it is regarded as a place of ill omen."

The grass was soft beneath their feet as they continued towards the tree. Just walking beside the lake seemed to rejuvenate the party. Its magnificence only growing, the nearer they got to it.

"I think we will not be bothered by the Night Husks while we remain here, so no need to post a watch. We can all get a decent sleep here," said Lucian to his friends as they arrived at the Moogem Tree.

Walking through the meadow was like walking through a bubble that transported them back to Sol-Larris. The light emitted by the Moogem Tree was bright and warming, and, absurdly and impossibly, the lake appeared to be tidal as they could hear it lapping gently along the banks. All that was missing was the sky, the sun and birdsong. If it were not for the dark stone ceiling above and the dark plateau that dominated the horizon to the west, you would think you were in the fields of Pogglinburg.

"This is quite wonderful. Who would have dreamt that such an oasis would exist in a desert such as this!" marvelled Sir Septimus.

"It looks like a piece of Pogglinburg had descended into the centre of the Earth!" said Artimus, picking a bluebell and remembering a time in his life that was not too distant. He blinked: no, he hadn't imagined it. For a moment she was before his eyes once again.

His breath caught in his throat. Yes, there was Jossie with little Marius, playing under the canopy of trees. They were all back in that warm day in May, the day they had decided to take their son for a picnic in the Copper Woods. "Come and sit down and have a drink, before it gets warm!" he heard himself calling.

"Just coming!" replied Jossie, then she picked up Marius and strode back to where Artimus sat on the wide woollen blanket, he'd spread out over the forest floor. She sat down beside her husband, and took a long swig of the refreshing juice. "It's beautiful here at this time of the year. The bluebells look spectacular. Just look at that carpet of blue!"

"Blue was always your favourite colour," nodded Artimus in agreement, and passed Jossie a sandwich.

"I want to remember this day - just the three of us, with not a care in the world!" Jossie said triumphantly, and took a bite from her sandwich.

"A perfect day indeed, with my dearest surrounded by a shimmering sea of blue – but your beauty outshines even the bluebells!" Artimus said happily, watching for that wonderful smile.

Hard to think that three days later she would be taken from him.

A tear welled up in his eye, and then she was gone and he found himself back in the present, back with the pain.

"It could be the fields at the back of Hill Square," said Lucian and smiled at Fengook. He was looking around the meadow in joy and wonderment, just as he had done when entering the Fungoid Forest for the first time. Songook and Dargook went over to the lake and laughed at their reflections in the water, as they bent down to the water for a drink. The water tasted very good. While Songook was drinking, Dargook pushed him into the water with a splash, and then jumped in himself. Fengook went running over to stop them. He felt they had broken something sacred; there was something mystical about the lake and meadow. The two little Fungiglooks had gone through too much and took no notice of his chastisements – in fact, when he got to them, they pulled him into the water for his trouble!

The Pogglins watched all this with amusement. It was nice to see the joy on the Fungiglooks' faces again, and Fengook now seemed to be enjoying the fun. Then Artimus looked around at the Cats, they had laid Parrdoo's corpse on the grass and started to burrow out a grave for her. The Fungiglooks saw that the cats were digging the grave and they stopped splashing the water and came over to help the cats lay their companion to rest.

Then Lucian noticed Fengook's back. The large livid weal caused by the Naara Frog's tongue had completely healed. Lucian slapped his forehead: what was he forgetting!

"Zontahl! Stop!" he cried before running off to the lake and filling one of the glass bottles that Pandora Nyx had given him back in Quistorrisia.

He came running back. "It's not called the Lake of Wonders for nothing! Pandora said the waters of the Lake have healing properties, and she was right!" He turned the dead cat over so that the head was tilted back, while Zontahl and his scouts looked on in astonishment. Lucian opened Parrdoo's mouth and poured the water down her throat, while he gently massaged her neck.

"By the stars above and the sun internal, let the waters of the Lake release their secrets and grant us our wish that Parrdoo is returned to us," he said quietly to himself. A blue aura appeared around his hand as he continued to massage the lifeless cat's throat.

The blue aura flowed over Parrdoo, but it seemed to the group that this was a step too far and a hope too futile even for the lake's water. Lucian wouldn't give up and worked on the cat's body for some minutes. Suddenly, there was a slight twitch: one of her green paws started to move, then she took a breath, coughed and started to stretch out her legs. The twisted body was now straight. Parrdoo blinked and then opened her eyes and smiled up at Lucian and a shocked-looking Zontahl.

"But she was slain – the Night Husk broke her back!" said Sarlizahl in wonderment.

Parrdoo got to her feet and stretched again.

"How do you feel?" enquired Lucian with a smile.

"Very good," replied the cat. "I heard your call from beyond and it brought me back. I thank you for my second chance of life." She bowed her head in reverence.

"I thank you too, Lucian," Zontahl said. "When I called you a *treasure* on our first meeting, I did not know how true my words would be. You are an exceptional being, Mr Lucian Snuzz!"

Lucian blushed and smiled. He picked up his staff, a little embarrassed. "Err, many thanks, but we should be making a move to retrieve the fruit."

"Snuzz never did know how to handle compliments," Sir Septimus said to Artimus. Artimus nodded with a smile, still holding the bluebell as he watched his friend walking the last few steps towards the beautiful Moogem Tree. They followed him, and were then accompanied by the Fengook and the Fungiglooks. The cats, along with their revived companion, went to the lake for a refreshing drink.

The meadow was so peaceful, and strangely far away from the dangers of Empraktos-Larris, that they had lost all their fears and strolled at a leisurely pace in the golden light. It was a wonderful feeling, but Lucian knew that they should not be complacent and should hurry back to the Zelgemar Stairs as soon as they were rested.

Standing under the Moogem Tree, Lucian basked in its radiance. The Moogem Tree was even more exquisite than he could ever have thought. The trunk and branches seemed closer to crystal than wood. It was a beautiful warm amber, and the light shone through its crystalline trunk and fractured the light in an unworldly way.

He touched the trunk. The tree emitted a wonderful humming type of sound that was very soothing on his ears. It was almost as if the tree was singing its welcome to him. The trunk was as smooth as glass, and from it, Lucian felt a warmness that flowed through him. He looked at the beautiful silver leaves that twinkled in the light radiating from within the tree. Lucian could see that the leaves where shaped like a bay leaf, but were larger in size. Then he spotted them; the fruit of the Moogem Tree! They grew in clusters of three and were dotted about the branches. The fruit resembled a cross between a pear and a mango, and it too was translucent, being a rich amber colour. Inside Lucian could see a large stone.

"It was worth the journey just to see you!" he said to himself.

The tree, in turn, hummed and rustled its leaves in delight at the compliment(or so it seemed to Lucian), and he smiled broadly at the amazing tree.

It then dawned on Lucian that although the Moogem Tree was emitting the light, he was actually standing in the shade under its leaves and branches; he really could be standing in Pogglinburg on a summer's day! Sir Septimus, Artimus and the Fungiglooks joined him. They too were full of appreciation of the Moogem. The Fungiglooks cooed and whooped in their own language, they were in awe of the tree. In fact, it was the first tree they had ever seen.

"Are all trees like this, my Mushroom brother?" asked Fengook.

"No Fengook, this is a unique specimen. All Trees are beautiful things indeed, but nothing like this grows in Sol-Larris," replied Lucian to his friend. Artimus was pointing out the fruit to Sir Septimus when the cats arrived.

"I think we should all eat and rest before we do anything else," suggested Lucian. "I think we can be safe in the knowledge that we are under the protection of the Moogem Tree, and so will have nothing to fear while we sleep. I doubt if any evil thing can venture into the meadow without consequences."

Everyone nodded in agreement. Artimus sat under the Moogem Tree, still holding the Bluebell, and gazed into the waters of the lake while the others prepared to eat. It was then that Lucian saw what Artimus was holding and it caught his breath. He came and sat down next to Artimus.

"Bluebells were Jossie's favourite flowers. You still miss her very much?" he said quietly.

"Every minute of every day, Lucian. It has been three years since the accident took her from me and it still feels as raw as the day it happened! I warned her not to take out the cart and to take the Gronk coach instead, but no, she wouldn't listen."

"On that day I lost my sister too." Lucian said quietly.

"And young Marius lost his mother – and his father, who cannot face the fact that she is gone, and runs away on adventures rather than raising his own son." Artimus bit his lower lip and dropped the Bluebell.

Lucian put his arm around his friend and comforted him as best he could. Sir Septimus looked at his friends with sorrow, but thought it best to leave them alone.

★ ★ ★ ★ ★

The Royal Dondymarian Throne Room was a massive circular chamber with a great domed ceiling. It was situated at the top of the main tower in the Palace. The floor of the Throne Room was patterned with deep blue and white marble tiles and these were highly polished. About the white- and red-striped walls many windows looked out over the city below, the Great Wide River and the land beyond it. The windows were curtained with deep crimson velvets of the finest quality. In between the windows hung portraits of the past Kings to have ruled Dondymaria.

At the top of the Throne Room was a dais which was carpeted in red and upon which stood the Royal Throne. This was a highly decorative gilded affair with purple upholstery. High above the throne was a huge replica of the Dondymarian Crown, from which flowed a canopy of crushed purple velvet. The decoration was quite superlative and far beyond the skills of the Dondymarians. Dwarf artisans from the Grodium Mountain made all the interior decorations. Dondymarian talents were in science, industry and war. They had to import all the finer niceties of life from the workshops of the Grodium Mountain.

One step down and to the left of the King's throne stood the Queen's throne, above which hung a portrait of her father-in-law, old King Frampton IV. Three steps down and to the right of the throne was the Lord High Chamberlain's seat, and above that hung a portrait of King Mumbeldok II himself, painted by the renowned artist, Sir Gander Mull.

Sitting in his splendid Lord High Chamberlain's seat, Lord Creep consulted his watch and huffed with irritation. "The King is late – again! I cannot dally, as I have to be at the Grodium Mountain before noon," he thought to himself. He replaced his watch in his pocket and sat back in his seat, tapping his staff of office on the marbled floor with simmering annoyance. His little eyes surveyed the chamber that was filled with courtiers; all the usual scroungers, crawlers and spongers were present.

"Most of them will *go* when I am ruler!" he chuckled cunningly to himself. He could see most of his fellow conspirators in the chamber.

Then his eyes fell up on that fool of a Court Wizard. Now he would most definitely go if he didn't buck his magic up! Creep's mind recalled Mysterio the Wizard's last fiasco.

"Before performing my next great feat of magic, I shall look up my Necronomicon."

"He could have phrased that better!" thought Lord Creep.

"I am going to crush Dunbruan's Wall by the same magic that put it there!" the sorcerer boasted.

"The statement turned out to be a damp squib! Crush a wall? All he achieved was cracking every piece of crockery in the Palace! I had to dock his pay in lieu of damages. He was nothing but a third-rate conjuring act, and that's being generous!" Creep shook his head at the memory, as if trying to dislodge a wasp from inside his skull. "The people I have to work with!" he sighed.

He became aware that the chamber had become quiet, and looked up to see six trumpeters standing either side of the grand entrance to the chamber. He stood up in readiness to receive the King and Queen.

The King slapped the trumpet out of the player's mouth.

The trumpeters were dressed in the livery of the Dondymarian household. They played the royal fanfare as the King and Queen of Dondymaria entered the Throne Room. While the fanfare played, the Royal couple walked over to the thrones. As they walked past the courtiers, they nodded their heads in acknowledgement of the bows and curtsies. Now and again, Queen Baalshibah had to pull her pet Snoog Lug-Lug's chain to bring him to heel. Lord Fangdom Creep greeted the couple as they climbed the steps of the dais.

"Good morning, Your Majesties, and thank you so ver…"

"Cut the flannel, Creep! Let's just get on with it, shall we!" interrupted the King, marching up to his throne. Lord Creep bowed gracefully and backed away to his seat, but he was flushed with anger by the king's snipe. The instant the Royal couple sat down on their Thrones; the orchestra struck up with the Royal National Anthem. The King (he grumbled with irritation) and Queen got to their feet and everyone in the room started to sing:

Hail to thee Your Highness,
Ruler of the land.
We, your loyal subjects,
Are here for your command.
You, our sovereign leader,
Always know what's right.
The Army stands ready,
Ready for the fight...
Dondymaria! Dondymar.....

The King had had enough. "We have the gist of it, so you can all shut yah cake holes now!" he said ungraciously and, in a manner not at all what you would expect of a royal personage! The King threw himself down on his throne with all the grace of a sulky toddler. From his splendid seat, Lord Creep looked at King Mumbeldok II with cold eyes.

"We will not have to suffer this pig for much longer," he thought to himself.

"Soon they shall be singing to me; Hail to thee our *Emperor*!" A broad smile crept across his ugly face at the thought of it.

The King waved a hand at Lord Creep. "Let's get on with this dreariness!"

Lord Creep bowed low, causing his wig to slide forward over his eyes and he jerked up quickly in fear of losing it altogether.

"Idiot!" sneered the King.

King Mumbeldok II slid down into his throne.

Creep straightened his hairpiece and ignored the insult as he started to address the court. As he did so, King Mumbeldok II slid down into the throne; he cupped his heavily jowl-cheek in his hand and leaned on one padded arm-rest. His crown slipped to a tilt on his head and he tapped the arm of the throne with his fingers. His eyes glazed as his mind wandered; he didn't register a word of Lord Creep's speech.

Queen Baalshibah, on the other hand, took great interest in Lord Creep's speech. She watched him intently; his magnetism for power corrupted her years ago, and ever since then the Queen had been Lord Creep's mistress. She loved Creep. It was his voracious appetite for power that was the thing that captivated her. Queen Baalshibah had lost all her love for her husband, the King, well before she became involved with Creep. Mumbeldok was impotent when it came to wielding power, and yet he was supposed to be the most powerful man in the entire Dondymarian Kingdom. The power he was born with didn't interest him; it just bored him, and it made him behave like a child dodging some detested obligation. He also had no interest in expanding the Kingdom – unlike Lord Fangdom Creep, who had many expansion plans!

She looked at her husband. "Look at him slumped in the throne, not a care in the world. The ungrateful, good-for-nothing slob!" she thought, and shook her head.

When she really thought about it, she didn't really love anything apart from her darling little Lug-Lug. She leant forward and patted him, and he rubbed back against her hand with contentment. Lug-Lug was a Snoog of the lesser variety. He was a strange-looking creature; like a cross between a bulldog and a reptile. His skin was red and scaly. His head was large, and he had big, floppy jowls that hung down the side of his smiling mouth. He was broad of chest and, like his owner, had pronounced bow-legs! About his neck was a black leather collar studded with the finest pearls. Spines ran from his head down to his long tail. Yes, Queen Baalshibah loved her Lug-Lug the Snoog more than her own children, who she loved purely out of being a dutiful mother.

The Queen was dressed in all her refineries of silks and lace, but for all these fine garments she still looked like a sack of potatoes tied in the middle with string! On her head, she wore a white, powdered wig of enormous height. Her face was caked in white makeup and blusher heavily applied to her cheeks. A vibrant and thick red colouring glossed her lips. Heavy black eyeliner was applied to her wide-set eyes, and her eyelids were highlighted with pale green. Great earrings dangled from her ears and pearls were about her neck, from which hung a medallion of gold, pearls and sapphires. From any objective viewpoint the Queen was as ugly as a baboon's backside, and yet she was regarded as the most beautiful female in the Kingdom. This should give you an understanding of what the other females assembled in the room looked like!

Lord Creep finished his speech and returned to his seat, and looked at his watch. Peatrea, the King's Jester, took to the floor and he bowed deeply to the King and Queen and turned to the courtiers.

"I say, I say. Why did the Pogglin...."

"*I say* you should shut up!" interjected King Mumbeldok, now at his wits' end with boredom. "I've just had to sit here and listen to his rubbish –" the King jerked his head towards Lord Creep (who looked coldly back at the King) – "and now you expect me to sit here and listen to your inane jokes; well, I won't! I'm off, mush!" With that, the King walked down the steps of the dais and slouched out of the Throne Room, taking especial care to slap Peatrea around the head as he passed by him. "You've lost it mate!" he said, and headed for the door, mumbling under his breath. The assembled attendees were obliged to follow suit, and paraded out behind him.

Peatrea's eyes flashed with resentment. He had once been the King's favourite, and he had kept him amused; now His Majesty had cast the jester aside, and Peatrea hated him for it.

The King headed for the door and the trumpeters started up the Royal Fanfare once more. "Shut it!" bellowed the King and slapped the trumpet out of the player's mouth. On his way out he was heard to mutter, "I've had enough pageantry to last me a lifetime!"

Lord Creep smiled to himself. "Yes, how fortunate for you that it won't be lasting much longer!" He knew that having Peatrea perform would hasten the King's departure: with him out of the way, he could now leave for the Grodium Mountain and his meeting with Yorgrinn the Sly. Lord Creep stood up as the Queen made her way over to him in her enormous dress.

"I am getting worried about Mumby," she said, using her pet name for the King.

"Yes, so am I," intoned Lord Creep dryly. "His phrases are becoming more *common* by the day!" He smiled the most charming smile his ugly face could muster. "Are we still on for tonight, my dear Baalshibah?"

"Of course, we are, Fangy," smiled the Queen, using her pet name for Lord Creep. In fact, the Queen had pet names for most of the courtiers, some of which are unprintable!

Lord Creep smiled broadly, showing the yellow stumps that were once teeth; he had a liking for eating sugar. He bent down to pat the Snoog. "Pppphrrrrrrrrrrrrrrrrrrrph!" recoiled the Snoog, and Creep withdrew his hand hastily.

"Lug-Lug dear, don't be nasty to Lord Fangy. He's Mummy's special friend." As she chastised the Snoog by pulling on his chain, Creep sneered at the animal.

"That creature will most certainly have to *go* when I am Emperor!" he thought to himself, and then flashed the Queen another of his repulsive smiles.

"Until tonight then my dear!"

"Until tonight!" the Queen repeated coyly. She smiled and left to follow her husband.

★ ★ ★ ★ ★

Lord Fangdom Creep, General Sidok and Captain Gunkfopp were waiting in the ornately decorated antechamber of Yorgrinn the Sly's palace inside the Grodium Mountain. Although they were closely related to the Dwarves of the Brown Mountain, the Dwarves of Grodium Mountain looked quite different. They were very hot-headed and more aggressive. They were shorter than their cousins and very stocky, with large heads, hands and feet. They also had very wide-set legs. Their foreheads were more angular, with deep-set eyes that were set far apart.

Unlike their cousins of the Brown Mountain, the Grodium Dwarves trimmed their beards and hair short. The Grodium Dwarves also had no loyalty; they sold it to the highest payer in gold. In fact, they would sell their grandmothers for it, and there were countless examples throughout history of certain Grodium Dwarves having done just that; yes, they loved gold very much!

Lord Creep looked at the floor of the antechamber. It was an intricate pattern of marble mosaics, and the walls were lined in marble and granite. "I will have something like this put into the palace when I am Emperor," Creep mused to himself.

The doors to the throne room opened with a jerk. A short, broad and burly Dwarf stood in the doorway. He was Gorgrinn the Hot-headed, brother of Yorgrinn the Sly. He was golden-haired; his hair parted in the middle and his beard was trimmed to a point. Gorgrinn wore a tunic of red, trimmed with brown fur about the shoulders and at the cuffs of his sleeves, and adorned with gold brocade down the front. About his neck hung a thick chain of gold, encrusted with emeralds and sapphires.

"My brother will see you now!" he said bluntly with a thick accent, and stepped aside to let them pass.

They entered a low ceiling chamber that was decorated with a predominantly yellow marble floor. There was a pattern in the shape of an X that went from corner to corner, made up of grey squares with a border of green and orange marble. At the centre of the squares was a black diamond pattern with a white centre. A dark green border ran around the perimeter of the floor. The walls were inlaid with pale blue marble with a geometric square pattern of dark blue. The skirting was cobalt sandwiched between gold and it also ran around the doorways in the chamber. Surprisingly, and asymmetrically, Yorgrinn had his throne tucked up into the top right-hand corner of the chamber. This was arranged so that no-one could creep up behind him in an assassination attempt.

The throne room of Yorgrinn the Sly.

Yorgrinn the Sly eyed the Dondymarians suspiciously as they entered the chamber. He sat forward in his high-backed wooden throne, with his left hand resting on the arm of the throne and his right hand laid on his axe-half that was resting across his lap. Yorgrinn the Sly was never without his axe, as he made most decisions with it!

He had a mane of jet-black hair, black bushy eyebrows and a trimmed beard of silver-grey. His face was craggy, with high cheekbones and hollow cheeks. He had wide, deep-set eyes that sparkled with cunning from beneath his eyebrows. Below his wide, broken nose was an immense black moustache; Yorgrinn was very proud of his moustache. He was dressed in a simple tunic of yellow ochre with gold brocade and fur trim on the sleeve cuffs. Above his large brown boots, he wore dark blue leggings.

"Good to see you again, Lord Creep!" he said in his thick accent from behind the great moustache, for there was no outward visible sign of his lips moving.

"And you!" said Lord Creep, bowing slightly.

However, Yorgrinn was not looking at him: his interest lay in the large casket that General Sidok and Captain Gunkfopp carried between them. His eyes sparkled with the thought of its contents and he characteristically started to twiddle his moustache with his left hand. Lord Creep smiled wryly to himself as he noticed Yorgrinn gaze fix on the casket. He stopped smiling when he saw Ikbold the Bitter frowning at him from under his grey, bushy eyebrows.

Ikbold the Bitter could always be found by Yorgrinn's side, unless he was on a mission of great importance. Ikbold was Yorgrinn's first cousin. That is how Yorgrinn had managed to maintain his power all these years over the Grodium Dwarves. He placed relatives in a position of power, and through them he ruled with an iron fist and showed no mercy to his enemies.

Ikbold was the most sour-looking Dwarf you could ever wish to meet, and his tiny, wide, deep-set eyes of jet shone with bitterness and malice. On his head, he wore an immensely tall brown leather hat. He had high cheekbones and a hooked nose and even his white beard could not hide his massive lantern-jawed chin. He was a hunchback, with a massive barrel chest and long thin arms. He wore a tunic of green cloth with gold brocade and fur-trimmed cuffs. About his neck, he had a chain of gold and emeralds. He wore black legging and his bow legs were tucked into large, brown leather boots. Ikbold was also a dwarf of a Dwarf; hence the tall hat to give him height. Yes, Ikbold the Bitter had a lot to be bitter about!

Gorgrinn now joined Yorgrinn's side, and he too looked suspiciously at the Dondymarians. It was a strange alliance brought together with gold, neither side not really liking or trusting the other. Yorgrinn sat silently, twirling his moustache and watching the Dondymarians. Finally, it was Lord Creep who broke the silence, as Yorgrinn had hoped; it was easier to pry gold from the old fool when he was nervous.

"How is the tunnel coming on?" Creep asked.

Yorgrinn smiled, but his features showed it not. "On schedule," he replied coolly.

"Good," said Creep, rather hoping for more information, "and when will the tunnel be finished?"

"On schedule," came the blunt reply.

"And you are mustering your men in readiness for the attack from the Gromm Bridge?"

"On payment of gold," Yorgrinn said coolly.

Lord Creep waved a hand to General Sidok, who gave a key to the captain to open the casket. He unlocked it and lifted the lid. The eyes of all three Dwarves sparkled brightly when they saw the gold contained within the casket. The captain drew out seven ingots of gold and handed them one at a time to Gorgrinn, who placed the ingots by the side of Yorgrinn's throne.

"Then you *will* attack Pogglinburg from the Gromm Bridge on the appointed day!"

"And I will receive the third payment of gold as agreed?" said Yorgrinn, ignoring Creep's statement.

"On my word of honour!" said Creep, making a flourishing gesture with his hand.

Yorgrinn looked at him, unimpressed. "What is honour?" he growled. "Nothing but words! I prefer something more tangible than words... like the gold you have in that casket!"

"I am a gentleman, Sir, and a gentleman never..."

"You are no gentleman, Creep; you plot against the King to whom you have sworn an oath of allegiance. So don't fill my ears with such nonsense!" Yorgrinn fingered his axe-half, meaningfully. "Were I your King, I would have your head for such treachery!"

The colour drained from Lord Creep's face, causing Ikbold the Bitter to smirk with contempt. He quickly whispered in the captain's ear, then he retrieved another four ingots from the casket and handed them one at a time to Gorgrinn.

"I shall make payment of another six ingots after you have fulfilled your obligations in attacking Pogglinburg," said Lord Creep, a little shakily.

Yorgrinn considered this, still twirling his moustache. "It has been good doing business with you, Lord Creep. You will have your tunnel and invasion of Pogglinburg from the Gromm Bridge as agreed."

"Good," said Lord Creep, smiling.

"Now this audience is at an end. You can go!"

The Dondymarians hurriedly left the throne room, and Gorgrinn slammed the doors shut behind them.

"Well," said Lord Creep, adjusting his wig, "I think that went very well!" He marched off, ignoring the peals of deep laughter that were coming from inside Yorgrinn's throne room!

★ ★ ★ ★ ★

Lucian sat on a rock by the side of the Lake, quietly contemplating the future journey they must endure. Suddenly he snapped out of his thoughts as he became aware that the Moogem Tree was humming to him. Turning his head to see why this was, his eyes caught it! A fleeting flash of amber light, coming from within the Lake. The waters of the Lake had fractured the beam of light, so it must have come up from the lake's bed. And then it was gone.

"Why did the Moogem Tree draw my attention to that light? Was I meant to see it for a reason? If so, I wonder why?" He pondered the matter, but nothing would come to him. "Could it have been a sign, a signal? If so, what for, and from what?"Perhaps, at a later date, he might know what it was supposed to mean, but for now, it was a mystery and one that he didn't have the time to figure out.

Artimus sat under the Moogem Tree with Sir Septimus, and looked at his watch; 12.55 pm. He replaced it in his pocket and then retrieved the Quistorrisian pencil; he tugged at his beard while he calculated the days and time. Suddenly he let out a gasp of anguish!

"What's wrong with you, Artimus? Speak up?"

"We only have a day and a half left to get back to Pogglinburg, Sir Septimus. We'll never make it back in time to save Queen Grizzelda's life!"

"What! Are you sure?"

"Of course, I'm sure! I have just been sitting here working it out, Sir Septimus. We left Pogglin town on 6th July and we arrived in Empraktos-Larris on the 8th. We fell asleep after the journey down the Zelgemar Stairs, you remember?"

Sir Septimus nodded.

"Fengook told us we slept for a whole day, so we lost the 9th to sleep! I was calculating to be back up to the surface by the 14th, giving us two and a half days each way on the journey to the Moogem Tree. Half a day I allowed for being in Quistorrisia, and then back in Pogglinburg for the afternoon of the 16th. Today is the afternoon of the 14th July; we are never going to make it back in time to save the Queen! All this fear, the anguish, the exhaustion, the worry and death are all for nothing - we are going to FAIL!"

The monocle popped out of Sir Septimus' eye socket!

When Lucian returned to his friends, he sensed the note of urgency in their conversation.

"What is wrong?" he asked.

"We only have a day and a half to get back to Pogglinburg!" announced Artimus. "We'll never get back in time to save the Queen."

"What should we do?" enquired a worried Sir Septimus.

Lucian pulled at his beard, deep in thought; "According to your calculation it has taken us seven days to travel from the Zelgemar Stairs to here, and we have only a day and a half to get back?" He pondered aloud "We will not have to journey through the Fungoid Forest this time, remember, so we can save time there."

"Still not enough to return on time," Artimus said sadly, "and that's if we don't get held up or attacked!"

Lucian came to a rapid decision. "Then we have only one choice open to us, and that is to cross the Valley of Zaark between Lake Naara and the city of Naarunkesh! It will be hard going and very dangerous, but it could save us a day and half's march!"

"But what about the Subterranians and the Night Husks? And what of Pandora's warning of the Tower of Eybraas?" said Artimus.

"We have no choice, Artimus, but to take the quickest route back. That is by going across open country, across the Valley of Zaark to be precise! Now I suggest we prepare for the journey. While there is time left, there is still hope!" He gave Artimus and Sir Septimus the glass vials and sent them to fill with the water from the lake.

He also sent the cats and Fungiglooks away with Artimus and Sir Septimus, while he retrieved the fruit from the Moogem Tree. Once they were gone, he took two glass jars from his pouch.

"That light you wanted me to see at the bottom of the lake –it's important, isn't it?" he asked the tree with a smile. The Moogem Tree hummed its reply to the Pogglin and slowly rustled its leaves.

Sir Septimus looked over at Lucian from the Lake; to the Pogglin's gaze, his friend was just standing under the tree holding the jars and staring at nothing."What's he doing?" he thought to himself. For no one but Lucian could see the Moogem Tree move!

Lucian smiled with delight at the tree's gentle answer to his question.

"I will understand the significance of it in time?" he asked. Again, the Moogem Tree hummed and rustled its leaves in gentle reply.

"Thank you!" he said warmly. "You have been of great help and comfort to me." He held out the two jars. "May I ask one final request of you? I have journeyed to this land to seek you for the life of our Queen, who will be taken from us if I do not return with the fruit that you bear. May I have your leave to pick two?" he asked. The Moogem Tree rustled its leaves and dropped a branch laden with fruit to enable Lucian to take his pick with ease.

Lucian very gently picked two of the large fruit and dropped them into the jars and sealed the lids.

"My thanks again to you!" he said bowing his thanks to the tree and placed the two jars in his pouch. The branch remained and the Tree rustled its leaves.

"You want me to take another?" he enquired, and the Moogem Tree hummed its reply, but this time Lucian heard the crystalline words of the tree in his ears!

"*Please do, my little one; it will help, should you meet those from the city on your journey home.*"

The voice was sweet and warming, and it filled Lucian with hope and joy. "Thank you again," he said quietly.

"*Use it with wisdom, little one, and we will meet again,*" said the Moogem Tree, and fell silent. Lucian was putting the third fruit in his pouch when the others returned. Sir Septimus looked at his friend quizzically; he knew something was afoot, but didn't have the slightest idea what.

"Are we ready?" said Lucian to his friends.

"We are," said Artimus and they moved off, leaving Lucian alone with the Moogem Tree.

"Good-bye," he said, "and thank you. I will be back to visit you again, that I can promise!"

The Moogem Tree rustled its leaves in farewell.

★ ★ ★ ★ ★

King Vardiemar Ironhammer III sat on his carved throne in the Great Hall of Thremgould within the Brown Mountain. He stroked his beard as he listened to Chancellor Silverore, and the light from the burning brazier twinkled in his eyes.

Borryn Cobalt, King Vardiemar Ironhammer III and Chancellor Silverore.

"So, there is no doubt that the Dwarf who served Queen Grizzelda with the poisoned plate was from the Grodium Mountain!" said the Chancellor.

The King pondered the matter; "And has he said as much?"

"Nay, Majesty," came the old Dwarf's reply. "But a false black beard was found in his back-pouch. Proof enough that he was the doer of the deed, and most likely he was acting on the orders of Yorgrinn the Sly."

"Let me have words with the scoundrel, Highness," cut in Borryn Cobalt. "I'll get a confession from this Grodium whelp!"

The King's eyebrows rocketed at Cobalt's suggestion and he smiled. "Nay, Borryn. We'll have nought to do with such heavy-handedness. I think we should let the prisoner cool his heels in the cells for a few weeks. Sheer boredom and fear will loosen his tongue!"

The Champion of the Mountain folded his arms in frustration.

"Never mind Borryn, the time will come when thou will again do battle with those of the Grodium Mountain," said the old Chancellor wryly. "And it may be sooner than we think!" he added pensively, pulling at his long moustache.

"But the King has judged wisely. We should not deal with our prisoners, as the dwellers of Grodium would do. A time in the cells will break him before long, and there are many questions that I wish to put to him!"

At that moment the braziers suddenly flickered by a rush of wind, and a blurred shape sped into the Great Hall. It came into focus at the foot of the stairs leading up to the King's throne. A figure bowed low at the three Dwarves.

"Yes, Elgyn?" said the King, and his rich voice bounced around the stonewalls of the Great Hall. "It must be of great importance indeed for thy boots of magic to have carried thee thus into our presence?"

"My Lord Silverore bade me report should I have news from the East, your Majesty," replied Mr Elgin Kloons, panting slightly.

Chancellor Silverore looked gravely at the newcomer. "What is it, Elgyn?"

"It is as you had feared, my Lord. The dwellers of Grodium are excavating a tunnel far beyond their territory and deep into the realm of Dondymaria. Yorgrinn the Sly is in allegiance with the Dondymarians!"

The old Chancellor sighed, and King Vardiemar sat forward in his throne. "Thou art sure of this, Elgyn?"

Elgyn Kloons nodded.

"Then war is coming! The Dondymarians are in collusion with the Grodium Mountain, and they mean to attack Pogglinburg!" said the old Chancellor, thumping his staff on the flagstones in anger. The noise echoed around the Great Hall.

The King shook his head impatiently. "Where is the termination of the tunnel, Elgyn?"

"They are excavating under Dunbruan's Wall, your Majesty. It leads back to Grodium City…"

Chancellor Silverore held up a hand for Elgyn to stop. "Wait! There is more to this than meets the eye. We know that they are already off tunnelling in the east and have been for months – why have they spent their energies on all that, if tunnelling the other way to Dunbruan's Wall was their true aim?"

"Thou hast a valid point, Chancellor; why has Yorgrinn the Sly been digging up the Eastern lands of Dondymaria?" said the King, sitting back in his throne and stroking his beard.

The Chancellor's eyes brightened. "I think, Your Majesty, that Yorgrinn the Sly is trying to out-sly the fox! He is using the excavations of the tunnel as cover for seeking Thremgould's Rune stone!"

"Yes, Chancellor, we are inclined to agree with thee!" The King turned to Borryn Cobalt. "I want thee to bring the Queen, the Crown Prince and Marshall-General Cavernhollow here immediately, Borryn!"

Chancellor Silverore walked down the steps to Master Kloons and patted him on the back. "Thou hast served me well again, Elgyn, but now thy boots of magic will have to carry thee with even greater haste to Pogglinburg. Thou must get a message to our Ambassador, Sir Gilliethrum Anvilhammer. Tell him everything thou hast learnt in this matter. I fear by tonight we Dwarves of the Brown Mountain will once again be on a war footing!"

Master Kloons lowered his head, grimly bracing himself for the task ahead.

"Wait for word from Sir Gilliethrum after his audience with Grand King Pooley, and then report back here to me. The poisoning of Queen Grizzelda was just one part of the jigsaw puzzle: the others are only now falling into place, and I have been too slow to see it! Make haste my friend, and return at thy first opportunity."

Master Kloons bade farewell to the Chancellor, and then took off at great speed out of the Great Hall.

The Chancellor's voice echoed around the stone walls. "I only hope we have not uncovered this treachery too late!"

★ ★ ★ ★ ★

Lord Fangdom Creep was at his desk when a knock at the chamber door made him look up from his paperwork. "Let them sweat outside the door: it always pays to make them wait!" he thought to himself, a smile creeping across his ugly face.

"Enter!" he finally said and General Sidok entered the chamber. "What can I do for you, General?" the Chamberlain asked smugly.

"I have come to report that all is ready. The War Robots are still in production, they stand at 500, but the factories will have at least another hundred by the appointed deadline," he said gruffly.

The Lord Chamberlain threw down his quill and sat back in his chair, interlocking his fingers and smiled with delight and satisfaction.

"That is excellent news, General. Time for a little celebration, I think!" He got up and moved across to a small table on which stood a decanter of wine and slender glasses. He poured only himself a glass, and the General looked evilly at him for his lack of hospitality. Lord Creep caught the General's expression.

"Would you like a glass in celebration, General Sidok?"

"I would indeed Lord Creep, thank you!" came the reply.

He poured a second glass and took it over to the General. "To the success of the mission!" The General clinked his glass and they sipped at the wine. The General sat down opposite Creep and he looked into his glass, and said, "What will happen after the operation is fulfilled?"

"As was agreed at the first meeting!" replied Lord Creep with a wave of his hand.

"I mean, what will *really* happen?" smiled the General.

"Oh, I see what you mean! You want the Field-Marshalship for yourself?" replied Lord Creep, putting the glass down on his desk. "Well, it's yours, as you knew already. Once the King is put out of the way and the army is fully over to our side, feel free to do away with the senile old fool!"

The General nodded approvingly. "And what of you, Lord Creep? You will not be interested in Dondymaria remaining a Republic for too long. I think you have set yourself a higher position than that?"

The smile on Creep's face broadened; "My dear General," he began, but his eyes remained cold and he made a note to himself that after the demise of old Field Marshal Gunkfopp, the General would have to quickly follow. He continued, "You have me completely wrong. My interest is only for a stronger Dondymaria, and nothing more!"

General Sidok was still unsure of Creep's intentions, but he was happy to go along with his plans for the moment. "What news do you have from Pogglinburg?"

"The Queen is dying," replied the Chamberlain, "so all is going to plan!"

"Do they suspect our involvement?" asked the General, holding out his glass for more wine.

Lord Creep's smile dropped for a moment, disgruntled by the General's impertinence for demanding more of his vintage wine. The smile clicked back onto his face as he got up to fetch more. He returned to his desk and gave the General the glass. "They may suspect the Shadow of poisoning their Queen, but I doubt it. If they do, however, it will get the idiot off our hands altogether!" he replied before taking a little sip from his glass.

"Yes," replied the General, "Captain Gunkfopp did well in his impersonation of the Shadow. He said none of the Pogglins suspected him of his subterfuge!" He chortled.

"The captain did an excellent job, indeed; if The Shadow dares to show his face again in Pogglinburg, then I am sure the Pogglins will kill him!" Sipping more of his delectable vintage, Creep continued, "But I have tied a far cleverer knot of intrigue than that, my dear General."

"Oh, how is that?" inquired the General. "The Pogglins will think we ordered the poisoning, even if it wasn't the real Shadow who carried it out."

Lord Creep leaned forward, placing his elbows on the desk, and linking his hands together. "Because, my dear General, the Pogglin Queen was *also* poisoned by a Grodium Dwarf! The Pogglins have not discovered that our Captain Gunkfopp, disguised as the Shadow, poisoned the Queen first at The Frog and Bottle Inn. I had Yorgrinn the Sly send one of his men to carry out a secondary poisoning. It was a reactant to Gunkfopp's poison, but the Grodium poison will be the one detected. So, the Pogglins will suspect Yorgrinn the Sly's hand in this plot, not mine!"

He sat back in his chair and beamed at his own cleverness at the General, who looked very impressed by this news. "The Pogglins will expect an attack from the Grodium Dwarves, not from us! Their eyes will be on the Gromm Bridge, and whilst their attention is distracted, we shall attack from the rear, with our War Robots and armies!"

"A very clever knot indeed Lord Chamberlain, and one which they will find hard to untie! And even if the Pogglins do... It will be too late!"

"Precisely!" replied Lord Creep, and they clinked glasses again.

★ ★ ★ ★ ★

Lucian and his party were making good progress. They had cleared the meadow of the Lake of Wonders and the Outcrop of Uutroc. They were once again in the Valley of Zaark, but this time in open country! The terrain was not too dissimilar from the Plain of Uoplaax, just a little darker and with a deeper reddishness in the twilight. The vile stink of the Naara Lake, which was off to their left, started to invade their nostrils once again. On the right, way off in the distance, was the City of Naarunkesh. They could see the pale walls that were stained red in the light from the cavern roof. On the walls they could just make out the strange, cabalistic hieroglyphs, like the ones they saw on the altar and obelisks at Lake Naargrah.

Rising above the city was the finger of rock on which stood the Tower of Eybraas. Lucian looked at it as they hurried along and wondered if they had been seen. Apart from some large boulders heaped about on their left flank, there was no cover from the sight of the tower.

"Night Husks!" squealed one of the Fungiglook scouts. Ten Night Husks appeared from nowhere and came charging at the little group from their right flank.

"Into the rocks!" shouted Lucian. "We will have a better chance of defence amongst the rocks!"

They all hurried into the rocks and boulders, with the Night Husks in pursuit. They paired off and hid among the boulders. Lucian and Sir Septimus crouched down behind a large boulder. Suddenly the 'boulder' heaved around and both found themselves staring into the yellow eyes of a Naara Frog!

★ ★ ★ ★ ★

The Needleman heaved a body effortlessly onto his work-table; he pulled open an eyelid and looked into the glassy, staring eye of the Dondymarian. He was about to dig out the eye when the Seeker burst into his chamber.

"Our little magic-user has left the Lake of Wonders and is now within sight of the city," he said, rubbing his hands together. "The Night Husks have him pinned down amongst the boulders!"

The Needleman ignored the Seeker and continued with his work.

"It is time to confront the little trickster, and make him pay for the loss of the Night Husk souls!"

The Seeker rubbed the top of his staff and disappeared from the room, unseen by the Needleman, who was too engrossed in his work. "Have you reported this to The Master?" he said, as he finished removing one of the eyes. He looked up; the Seeker had gone. He placed the eyes on the table, and started to thread a needle with a skein of florescent lime-green silk.

★ ★ ★ ★ ★

The Naara Frog blinked at the two Pogglins; they had woken it from its slumber. To the Pogglins' horror, there were two more Naara Frogs behind them! In the twilight of the valley, there was no telling them apart from the boulders. The three Naara Frogs looked evilly at the two Pogglins.

The monocle dropped from Sir Septimus' eye socket and his moustache went limp with fear. "It was nice knowing you, Lucian my friend. It looks like this is the end of the road!"

Lucian didn't answer his friend; his mind was on the Naara Frogs, and his eyes on the Night Husks that were only a short distance away!

The Naara Frogs shuffled towards the two Pogglins, but could hardly move. One of the Naara Frogs made a strange noise followed by a great belch, blasting a vile-smelling gas into the Pogglins' faces. "I thought the gas pigs back home smelt bad enough, but these horrible creatures take the prize!!" Sir Septimus cringed, then added in a whisper, "Snuzz, why aren't they finishing us off?"

The realisation dawned on Lucian that the Naara Frogs had eaten their fill of earlier prey and were neither hungry nor mobile enough now to move on them. He pulled Sir Septimus down amongst the Frogs (who were thankfully once again beginning to doze off to sleep) as a massive Manu-type Night Husk came dangerously close. Not far away, Artimus and Fengook were also crouching behind a rock, but they were not so lucky. They looked up in horror as a Dondymarian-type Night Husk stood above them. It reached out to grasp Artimus by the throat, when a voice shouted out for the Night Husk to stop; it instantly froze and looked around, waiting for its next order.

"You will all come to me, now!" said the Seeker. The Night Husks dropped Artimus, and turned to obey the Seeker.

Artimus looked at Fengook with relieved surprise."That was a narrow squeak, but what are we in for now, I wonder?"

Lucian and Sir Septimus were wondering the same thing as they slowly moved away from the sleeping Naara Frogs, crawling on all fours.

"I know you are in there, little Magic-User. You would be wise to come out!"

Zontahl could see the Seeker impatiently tap his foot.

"Then let me put it another way," said the Seeker. "Your friends' lives, for yours."

Lucian went to move out from the cover of the boulders, but was pulled back by Sir Septimus; "Don't be a fool Snuzz, it's a trap!"

"One of you will have to make it back to Pogglinburg. This might make your journey easier," he quietly replied and moved out from the rocks.

The Seeker stood waiting for him. "You are smaller than I thought!"

Lucian ignored the remark and bowed low while placing a hand in his pouch.

"You have caused me and my Master much annoyance."

"And you and your master have caused those poor creatures that stand behind you much torment and pain!" replied Lucian.

The Seeker laughed mockingly; "Big words indeed, from such a little fellow as yourself. But be warned: my temper is swift and I can crush you like an insect!"

The other two Pogglins came out of the cover of the rocks, followed by the cats and the Fungiglooks.

"Two more Pogglins, some Fungiglooks and cats. What a strange band you are!"

"Enough of this mockery and dismiss the Night Husks; keep your word, Seeker, and let my friends go!"

The smile flicked off the Seeker's face. "You dare to command *me*!" he shrieked.

"I dare, sir, because you fear me!" Lucian replied sternly, and then added, "Why is that, I wonder?"

The Seeker was taken aback; he was confused, as he did indeed fear the little Pogglin. He took control of himself. "You came into our land to seek the Lake of Wonders; you will tell me why. You do not ask questions of me!"

Lucian smiled, and drew a line in the earth with his staff and stepped back.

"Well Seeker, if you wish to know, cross this line… If you dare?"

Lucian had a plan and was hoping his bluff would work. He gripped his staff and his hand remained in the pouch, at the ready.

"Do not anger me, trickster, or you will pay with your life!"

"Yes, yes," said Lucian calmly. "I took that as read anyway!"

"What's Lucian up to?" Artimus whispered out the side of his mouth.

"No idea old chap, but I hope he knows what he's doing!" Sir Septimus whispered back to him.

"Have a care; you do not know the power with which you play!" said the Seeker taking a step forward.

"I think you *are* afraid!" Lucian chuckled, while thinking to himself; "And I hope he doesn't realise that I'm absolutely terrified of what *he* could do!"

"Jackanapes!" roared the Seeker. "Prepare to meet your death!"

He lurched forward with his staff when, quick as a flash, Lucian jumped back and pulled out the Moogem fruit. Lucian had counted on the Seeker's poor eyesight, for the Seeker stopped in his tracks when he saw a flash of amber light leap from the Pogglin's hand.

"No! It is not possible. You possess the power of the Amber stone!"

Now this piece of information startled Lucian, and he hoped it didn't show on his face; he tried to keep smiling. His bluff was working, but not for the reason on which he planned. The Seeker's words made the image of the amber light that he saw at the bottom of the Lake of Wonders flash into his mind. The Seeker had given him a vital clue that would help him in solving the mystery of Naarunkesh! Quickly he said, "Now you know the power that I can control!"

A double bluff; but it worked. Lucian and his friends could clearly see that the Seeker was mesmerised with fear by the amber light that shone from the Moogem fruit. Lucian quickly replaced the fruit in his pouch, before the Seeker realised that he had been duped.

The Seeker took a step towards the Pogglin, then a step back, attempting to claw back what remained of his dignity. "You may leave, Pogglin. But mark you well; if you ever return to these lands again, then you will *pay* a high price!"

"Oh, I will come again," replied Lucian with conviction. "There are things that need to be put right!"

"Then I shall be watching for you, Mr Lucian Snuzz!" spat the Seeker and very quickly disappeared.

"By Dunbruan the Great, Lucian! What did you do?" exclaimed Artimus.

"No questions, not now Artimus. First, let us get out of here and back to Sol-Larris."

Zontahl padded forward too and sat before Lucian, blocking his path.

"Firstly Lucian, I must thank you again for saving our lives. You are an excellent fellow, and I will follow you wherever you wish!" and bowed his head low.

Lucian blushed: he was uncomfortable with these types of situations, and never knew quite what to do. He patted the Cat's head. "Thank you, Zontahl," he smiled. "I appreciate what you say, but there really was no need to thank me."

★ ★ ★ ★ ★

"MEMLEKET!" roared the Necromancer as he sat down. Memleket put down his puppet and hurried up to the throne.

"Yes, Master?" he grinned.

"Where is The Collector?" inquired the Necromancer. The Master of Puppets thought for a moment and then replied, "He's looking for some fresh skins!"

"Find him! You and Gemek are to take him on a venture to Larris. I need more souls, fast!"

"Yes Master!" said the puppet master. Trotting off to his corner, he strapped his box of puppets onto his back and placed the Mantra glove puppet on his hand. He smiled at it, flashing his yellow stumps of teeth. The glove puppet waved back at him, and he smiled menacingly.

"We have our work to do, Qoonk; more souls to ensnare for the Master!" he said to the puppet, which nodded its head knowingly.

He opened the door and turned as his master called to him.

"I need those souls if I am to carry out my plans – I need souls to destroy that Pogglin! Do not fail me Memleket; do your job well!"

"You will have your souls, Master! You will fulfil your destiny and rule over a world of darkness!" smiled the Master of Puppets and closed the door behind him, leaving the Necromancer to brood alone on his dark throne of souls.

★ ★ ★ ★ ★

Meanwhile, the Seeker had closeted himself away in his own chamber in the Tower of Eybraas. He feared the wrath of his Master for failing to destroy the magic-using Pogglin. The Seeker sat in his chair and tried to feel the Pogglin's presence on the Astral Ley Plain: *no! Nothing!* He gripped the bridge of his long, beak-like nose and closed his eyes tightly in the hope of tracing some spark of his magic or his spirit, but still nothing. This was impossible; the Pogglin was still within the land of Empraktos-Larris, so, therefore, he must register! Why could he not sense him?

"Unless," thought the Seeker, "Unless the Amber Stone is cloaking his presence. If that is the case, then he would be invisible to me if he ever re-entered this land!"

He sat back in his chair, gripping the arms in fear.

★ ★ ★ ★ ★

Grand King Pooley looked very drawn and weary. He was sick with worry over his wife - worry which only increased as the time ticked by, and now he had heard that his realm was in danger of attack, and his people needed him to be strong. He sat in the council chamber, flanked on either side by his advisors. All of the six Wizards were present, along with Chancellor Dore, the Royal Secretary; Sir Grunter-Pulpit, Field Marshal Mandergast and Admiral Loomboggle. On the other side of the table sat Sir Gilliethrum Anvilhammer and Elgyn Kloons along with the Ambassadors of Foricia and Mee-Gogg. He had listened to the Dwarves story and he pondered on it for some moments.

"And there is no doubt, Sir Gilliethrum, that Yorgrinn the Sly is involved in the plot?"

"No doubt, Your Majesty. Elgyn here himself caught the Grodium culprit."

Elgyn nodded in agreement.

"We are indebted to you," said King Pooley.

Sir Gilliethrum continued, "We have him now in one of the deepest cells. We found the proof of his involvement, but we are waiting for him to confess."

"We thought the Dondymarians would carry out an attack, but we never thought Yorgrinn would go so far as to play along with the murder of my Queen!"

"I see the hand of Lord Creep behind all this," said Balferzaar the Black. "King Mumbeldok's interest would not extend to these plans; he would have grown bored with them long ago, and war has never interested him. No, this is Creep's work, Sire. Yorgrinn the Sly is only after gold, and will probably betray Creep on receipt of the payment!"

"I agree with Balferzaar," said Westerin the White. "Creep hopes we will only be looking towards the Gromm Bridge and not to our backs."

"Gold or not," said the King, "Yorgrinn has still signed his name to the cause by attempting murder."

"That is true, Your Majesty, but Creep is still trying to use him as his cat's paw. Thanks to the watchfulness of our friends here, we know of his treachery. Now what should we do in countering these attacks?" said the old Wizard.

"You are forgetting the Shadow!" piped in Chancellor Dore.

"Yes," agreed Field Marshal Mandergast. "We were agreed when the deed was first perpetrated that it was done by the Shadow's hand!"

Chancellor Dore nodded in agreement.

"We knew the Queen had been poisoned *twice*," replied the old Wizard. "We now have our answer!"

His five counterparts supported him on this. Suddenly the table exploded into a debate, each putting forward their theories on the matter in hand. The King held up his hands wearily. "Gentlemen, please! We know the deed was done and why it was done. How precisely it was done does not come into this council. The matter at hand is how we are to defend the realm!"

"Dunbruan the Great will defend our land, your Majesty!" replied Balferzaar the Black. "The great tower that he installed will be our chief weapon of defence and myself and my five colleagues will control them through the power of Dunbruan."

"Ahem, excuse me, my Lord," said Chancellor Dore. "The defences installed by Dunbruan the Great have never been tested. The Dondymarians have never actually invaded our land since their instalment. How do we know they will repel the invasion forces?"

"The Chancellor does have a point there, my Lord!" cut in the Field Marshal.

"I will ignore your blasphemy, Field Marshal Mandergast. The defences will be tested when the invasion is repelled by the power of Dunbruan's legacy to us!" snapped back the old Wizard.

Sir Grunther-Pulpit, the Royal Secretary, tactfully put his views forward. "My Lord, no-one is questioning the power that the Great Dunbruan has handed down to us. May I suggest that my fellow advisors would feel a little easier if we could have a back-up plan in place?"

The rest of the advisors nodded in agreement with the Royal Secretary's statement. Balferzaar the Black sat back in his chair in exasperation.

Roondar the Red spoke up for the first time. He was a solitary figure, living at the furthest outpost of the Towers. He rarely came into the town, and was more at home with the Pogglin country folk. He pulled at his long, thin ginger beard as he spoke. "Being that the Red Tower is furthest away from the town, it would also be the first line of defence from a Grodium attack. Their only way into Pogglinburg would be by the Gromm Bridge, as we know. Being that I am the master of said tower, I am rather surprised by the doubts raised by the advisors of his Majesty. Dunbruan's legacy will not fail us!"

"Well said!" agreed Glondin the Green, and added, "You forget we are Wizards, installed to our duties by the Great Dunbruan himself!"

"We have not forgotten," replied the King with reverence. "We still hold faith to the law laid down to us by Dunbruan the Great."

"Well, if any of the blighters do get through; I'll give 'em a broadside from my man of war, The Diamond!" said Admiral Loomboggle, in a whisper to the Field Marshal.

The King turned his attention back to Sir Gilliethrum and Elgyn. "We would like to thank you for giving us this vital information and for your vigilance. We also convey our thanks to King Vardiemar, and hope that he will keep us informed on the Grodium prisoner."

"I will indeed convey your thanks to my King, Your Majesty," replied the Dwarvish Ambassador. "And may I thank you for granting us this audience in your hour of sorrow. King Vardiemar has put Dwarveshire on a war footing. He is ready to come to your aid, should you require it."

"Thank you," replied the King. "We will indeed call upon King Vardiemar, should we need his aid in repelling the invasion forces of Dondymaria and the Grodium Mountain."

Chapter Five

After the audience, Sir Gilliethrum walked with Elgyn Kloons to the gate of the Royal Pogglin Palace. "Do ye think the Dunbruan defences will work, Sir Gilliethrum?"

"By Thremgould, I don't know lad!" he replied to Mr Kloons. "But I think it wise to have our army ready; just in case. Now hotfoot it back to Dwarveshire, and report to the King and Chancellor Silverore," he said, clapping the messenger across the back.

"I will, Sir Gilliethrum. By 'Eck! Lucian's going to miss all the fireworks if he doesn't hurry back."

"It will be more than fireworks if he doesn't make it back. Don't dally, lad—off ye get to Dwarveshire, and be quick about it. And by Thremgould have a safe journey, thou dost not know who will be on the road during these troubled times!" With that Elgyn Kloons dashed off, a blur trailing a billow of dust behind him.

★ ★ ★ ★ ★

Zontahl leapt from one rock to another with ease as he climbed up the cliff from the Valley of Zaark. His three scouts followed him, and behind them followed the Fungiglooks and the Pogglins. They had raced along the Valley of Zaark, thankfully unhindered this time. Neither Night Husks nor the Naara Frogs appeared on their horizon.

Lucian smiled to himself in amazement and gratitude. His bluff with the Moogem fruit worked far better than he had ever expected. The radiance from the fruit must also be cloaking his presence from The Seeker. He was now focused on getting back home and saving the Queen from an untimely death.

★ ★ ★ ★ ★

The massive gates to the City of Naarunkesh creaked open on their great hinges of bronze. Three figures moved out through the gates and they slammed shut behind them. Memleket was to the front, slightly hunched over by the weight of the wooden box of puppets on his back. He had an evil grin fixed on his face, whilst his Mantra hand puppet Qoonk looked about them with interest.

"Yes, it's exciting," Memleket said in a whispered aside to his hand puppet. "Yes, wery exciting! We have a lot to do on this trip, Qoonk!"

He laughed with delight to be back on the road again, and it echoed around the rock walls of the crevasse around him. Memleket turned around to his brother, who was walking behind.

"Gemek! Let's have some music while we walk. Play something that will carry us quickly to Larris!"

The organ wheezed into life as Gemek started to pump the bellows with enthusiasm; very quickly there was enough air to play. Suddenly the crevasse in which they walked was filled with the insane tune that Gemek feverishly played upon the keyboard.

Memleket and Gemek was the deathly thin figure of the Collector.

The trio's shadows were horribly distorted on the wall of the crevasse by the candles that lit the path. Loping along behind Memleket and Gemek was the deathly thin figure of the Collector. His iron-clad feet fell lightly upon the path as he followed behind. His legs were extremely long (as were his arms) and were out of proportion with his short torso. In his hand, he clasped a small wooden collection box with a slot in the top, for money. On his head, he wore a dark-blue cocked hat. He was clothed in bright colours of checks and striped cloth. His face was hideous, with a long carrot-like, twisted nose. He had a wide, narrow frog-like mouth that twisted into a malicious grin. The eyes were distorted sockets, but leering deep within were pinpricks of red. These were the Collector's true eyes, for horrible to relate his face was nothing more than a mask made from a mass of stolen human skin, stitched to the remains of the flesh on his head! When this started to decay and rot, he simply went out and by gruesome means replaced it with a fresh supply from the people who gave him money.

Accompanied by the maniacal piping of the Organist of Naarunkesh, the ghastly trio slowly made their way along the path leading up to the Valley of Zaark.

★ ★ ★ ★ ★

Grand King Pooley had returned to the bedside of his sick Queen. He took her hand in his; at first her hand felt deathly cold, but after a few moments he could begin to feel some warmth.

Balferzaar the Black could read his expression. "Queen Grizzelda will grow steadily colder as the poison takes hold, your Majesty," he said gently as he put his hand on the King's shoulder in comfort. "But while there is warmth, there is still hope."

The King nodded. "Has there been any word of Lucian, Balferzaar? Have the Wallie Birds had sight of him?

"Not as yet, Your Majesty, Sedgwick will bring word to me the moment any of his bird friends sight Lucian."

The old Wizard smiled at his King. "Lucian will be here on time. He will not fail in his duty."

★ ★ ★ ★ ★

Colour-Sergeant Frampton Nagg came to attention, stamping his booted foot on the floor and saluted: "SIR!"

"At ease, Colour-Sergeant," replied General Sidok from behind his desk. The General's office was rather spartan in furnishings compared to other Dondymarian chambers in the Royal Palace. The General might be frugal in furnishings, but he was by no means frugal on ambition. The Colour-Sergeant's eyes fleetingly left those of his officer and fell upon the figure who stood by the General's chair. The figure was an extremely short, fat and pompous-looking Dondymarian. He had thick-lensed spectacles that magnified his eyes alarmingly.

"A change of plan today, Colour-Sergeant..."

Nagg's eyes snapped back to his officer.

"The Queen will not be accompanying the King today. Instead, Sir Nausious Nojj here will travel with the King."

The pompous little Dondymarian nodded in acknowledgement to the Colour-Sergeant. The General leaned forward on the desk. "Once you have escorted His Majesty to the coach you and your guard will stand down; you are not to accompany the King further. You understand?"

"OH, I SEE SIR," roared the Colour Sergeant; he always spoke as though he was addressing the parade ground. "I TAKE IT, SIR, THAT FIELD-MARSHAL GUNKFOPP KNOWS HOF THE CHANGE IN PALACE GUARD ROUTINE?"

"The Field Marshal is incommoded by another urgent matter, and he ordered me to convey his orders to you!"

"I SEE, SIR. THANK YA, SIR!"

"Carry on, Colour-Sergeant," and the General waved to the door.

"SIR!" stamped Frampton Nagg. Then he saluted, turned on his heels and left the room.

"Do you think he suspects anything?" enquired Sir Nausious Nojj.

The General shook his head. "No, Nagg is an unthinking dullard! Typical NCO class; crank him up with orders, and he will unquestioningly carry them out to the letter!"

Sir Nausious smiled, reassured by the General's words.

★ ★ ★ ★ ★

Colour-Sergeant Nagg closed the courtyard door. He scratched the back of his baldhead, causing his large, tricorn hat to tip even more alarmingly forward on his head. Nagg really was deep in thought, causing his great lantern jaw to jut out even more. He didn't even seem to notice the soldier walking across the parade ground. "THIS AIN'T RIGHT, SUMMINK'S WRONG 'ERE!" he thought, and the uncomfortable feeling that arose from his pondering was transferred to the unfortunate soldier as he approached.

"OI! WHERE ARE YOU GOIN'?"

The soldier started to protest his innocence.

"DON'T GIVE ME LIP, LADDIE...HAND GET YA 'ANDS OUT HOF YA POCKETS WHEN YA TALKIN' TO MEEE!" He bellowed, as he bore down on the unfortunate soldier and marched him off to the glasshouse.

★ ★ ★ ★ ★

Queen Baalshibah was in her bedchamber sitting at her vanity desk. She powdered her ugly muzzle while looking in the mirror, which not only reflected this vision of beauty (or so she thought!) but also that of Lord Creep, who was standing directly behind her.

"Today is the day we have worked towards, my dear," Creep cooed in Baalshibah's ear. "By tonight you will be rid of your husband, and so too will Dondymaria!" The queen caught a flash of his yellow teeth in the mirror as he smiled.

"Will it be a quick exit for Mumby?" she murmured, putting a final dab of powder.

"He will be too bored to notice it, my dear!" replied Lord Creep with a grin.

"That's good," said the Queen casually, and turned around to the Lord Chamberlain. "And who is to do the deed?"

"The Royal 'REMOVER' himself; Sir Nausious Nojj!"

Queen Baalshibah turned to face Lord Creep and threw her arms around his neck.

"Pppphrrrrrrrrrrrrrrrrrrph!" protested Lug-Lug loudly from the Queen's bed; he hated it when she showed affection towards the Lord Chamberlain. Lord Creep curled his lip and growled back at the disgruntled Snoog.

"Don't be horrible to Lug-Lug, Fangy. And Lug-Lug, don't you be nasty to Fangy!" She kissed the Lord Chamberlain.

"Pppphrrrrrrrrrrrrrrrrrrph!" again protested the Snoog.

Creep eyed the creature with a sneer, which went unnoticed by Queen Baalshibah. She looked up at him and he flicked back to his repulsive smile.

"Let us seal our covenant with marriage, my dearest. After all, you will be free to do so by tonight!" His eyes twinkled with lust for power.

"But you're married, Fangy! Will not Lady Frumptunella have something to say about that?"

"I have already lodged a file for divorce with Lord Justice Krank. It will be a mere formality, my dear!"

"Then of course I will marry you, Fangy!" said the Queen with delight.

"Then let us seal it with a kiss!" beamed Lord Creep. He took the Queen in his arms and dramatically threw her backwards; he leaned forwards over her heaving body and kissed her deeply on the lips. The wrinkles in their skin seemed to entwine, and it gave an eerie impression of their heads growing out of each other.

"Pppphrrrrrrrrrrrrrrrrrrph!" Lug-Lug protested again, killing the moment.

★ ★ ★ ★ ★

At the heart of the Brown Mountain lies the sacred grotto of Thremgould, Father of the Dwarves. It is a massive cavern of iridescent stone that fragments the light into a kaleidoscope of rainbow-coloured rays. To the right of the great natural pool lies a rampart of stone, leading to a balcony carved from Snow Stone. This is the holiest place in the grotto, for here stands the great anvil and hammer of Thremgould, and it is before these sacred artefacts that all the ceremonies and rituals of the Dwarves take place. The most important ceremony is "The Coming of Age", when a Dwarf in his forty-fifth year (a young age by Dwarvish standards) comes of age and is initiated into the clan.

No Dwarf who is not of age is allowed to enter the grotto. Not even Lucian knew of the existence of this sacred place. Here dwells the Dwarves' biggest secret: Murren, the Mage of the Brown Mountain!

Chancellor Silverore waited by the pool for Murren to arrive. The atmosphere was buzzing with ethereal warmth, so that one instantly felt at peace on entering the holy grotto. Occasionally drips of moisture fell into the pool from the stalactites hanging from the cavernous roof above. As the drops hit the water, it sounded like ringing crystal and caused great circles to ripple the water's surface.

The ripples distorted the Chancellor's reflection in the pool. He felt at one with the earth in the grotto, and it gave him so much peace and solace in the cathedral-like cavern. Chancellor Silverore smiled as another reflection appeared in the pool next to him. Murren was dressed solely in white silk, and it shimmered in the rays of light that emitted from the rocks around. The neck, shoulders and sleeve cuffs were trimmed with sky blue fur. Around the hem of the garment was gold and sky-blue brocade. About his waist was a leather belt from which hung the traditional Dwarvish pouch. Hanging down, on the left and right of his breast, were the holy bands of Thremgould. On his head, he wore a long, pointed hat made of pale blue fur and in his right hand, he held his staff of office. It was made from the purest silver and ebony, and the top of the staff was fashioned into an anvil.

"Thou art deep in thought, Torryn, my son," said the old Mage. His voice was deep and warm, and it echoed around the great cavern of Thremgould.

"Aye, that I am, my Lord," replied the Chancellor, going down on one knee and bowing his head in salutation to the aged Mage.

"Come Torryn, there is no need for such formalities," smiled the old Mage as he helped the Chancellor to his feet. Murren's large kind eyes twinkled in the light as he smiled at the old Chancellor. Murren's beard and hair were as white as snow itself, and a thick curl peeked out from under his hat at his forehead.

Silverore looked at Murren's round face, the white, bushy eyebrows and round nose. Nothing had changed, he thought; Murren had still looked that way back when he was forty-five years old.

"I wonder how old you really are?" thought Silverore, as he looked at the aged Mage. "You must have been born at the dawn of Thremgould – as old as the mountains!"

"I am as young as I wish _to be_, Torryn," smiled the old Mage.

"I forgot you can read my thoughts," the Chancellor laughed, and they linked arms as they walked to a seat carved out of the rock and sat down.

"What troubles thee?" asked the old Mage.

"I am worried about the Pogglins. Elgyn has returned from an audience with Grand King Pooley. They are putting all their faith into the defences laid down by Dunbruan the Great." Murren nodded his head and put a crooked finger to his lip as he listened to the Chancellor.

"Dunbruan was a very powerful Wizard, a little arrogant and headstrong, but powerful none the less."

"You met him?"

"Nay, I never met him, Torryn, but my eyes can see far beyond the confines of this mountain."

"So, you _do_ believe that Balferzaar counselled Grand King Pooley correctly in relying on Dunbruan's Towers?"

Murren tapped his finger to his lip before replying. "Balferzaar and his Wizards will help, but it will be young Lucian Snuzz that will help the change in Pogglinburg."

Chancellor Silverore looked somewhat confused by this reply to his question. He noticed a look in Murren's eye that told him to ask no more and the old Chancellor held his tongue.

"Should I then ask King Vardiemar to stand down our armies if Pogglinburg is safe?"

"I did not say Pogglinburg is safe, Torryn," smiled the Mage "I merely say that whatever happens will have young Lucian in the thick of it. A wise person does not act on all that he sees and hears. Some actions are written by the hand of Fate and can never be changed. One must use one's own counsel, and judge which are changeable and which are not; then one must decide the best course of action to take from there."

"Yes, I see what you mean," replied Silverore, pulling at his long moustache as he pondered the words of the old Mage. For a while, neither spoke; they sat and listened to the echoes of the water as it dripped in the pool, and the whistle of a light breeze as it passed through the stalactites on the cavern roof.

"Yorgrinn the Sly is digging up the Eastern lands of Dondymaria," said the Chancellor quietly.

"He is seeking the Rune-Stone of Thremgould," replied the old Mage calmly.

"But he seeks in the wrong place, which is to our advantage, Torryn. I have tried to see the Rune-Stone, but it is shrouded from my sight. It must be very deep in the bowels of the Earth, but some nights I can hear it talking to me. Try as I may, I cannot gain a fix on the location."

"I have ordered excavation tunnels to be started at all compass points around the mountain. Soon Elgyn Kloons and his band of adventurers will be leaving to find the Rune-Stone."

"I understand that Elgyn will be taking young Bartielink Quartz with him on the expedition?"

"That is so," replied the Chancellor.

"That's good," smiled the old Mage. "He will be a very useful addition to the party!"

Again, they fell silent, neither really wanting to break the spell that resounded around the cavernous grotto and each enjoying the others company.

"Has our occupant of the cells decided to talk?" asked Murren after many minutes.

"Nay," replied the Chancellor with a frown. "He is stubborn, but it is early days yet. He will talk eventually!"

"But time may not be on your side, Torryn. Have you considered that; I wonder?"

Silverore cocked an eyebrow. "Nay I had not. I considered time would be on our side; you think not?"

"It would help our cause in finding the Rune-Stone if we knew Yorgrinn's plans sooner rather than later. You cannot rely wholly on your network of spies on this occasion, Torryn."

The Chancellor thought on this. "What do you suggest?"

"Have you considered a Dwarvemite?"

"Nay, I have not, my Lord!" he smiled.

The old Mage whistled lightly, and instantly a noise of running paws filled the grotto and a small dog-like creature came running to Murren's side. The animal was a Dwarvemite: he was snow-white with extremely large, pale blue ovoid eyes, and he resembled a cross between a Tapir and a Dog with a stumpy tail. The Dwarvemite sat down, its little tail wagging.

Murren the Mage and Chancellor Silverore with Remy; the Dwarvemite in the holy Grotto of Thremgould.

Murren patted the little creature's head and smiled, "Put Remy here into the cell with the prisoner, Torryn. I can guarantee that he will be only too willing to talk after a few seconds alone with our little friend."

The old Mage got to his feet, helping himself up with his staff. He laid a hand on the old Chancellor's shoulder.

"Now I must leave you, my friend; I must turn my attention to Thremgould and his Rune-Stone. Will he show me the path?" He patted his friend's shoulder gently.

"I will leave you to think about my words. Remy will go with you if you require him. I am lucky as I have only the mysteries of the Universe to ponder, and you, my friend, must ponder what is right for the King and his realm!"

Chancellor Silverore watched the old Mage walk along the edge of the pool, before he turned back for one final observation. "And Torryn, I think you would be wise to have the King station the army at the foot of the Copper Mountain." He then disappeared under the arch of rock and out of sight.

Silverore smiled on these words, and then he leaned forward and patted the little Dwarvemite who wagged his tail enthusiastically.

Chancellor Silverore stood up, leaning on his staff. "Come along, Remy. We have a meeting of great importance to the realm. The King may not agree with the method, but it's for his good and the good of his people."

He walked slowly off toward the grotto's exit, with little Remy padding along by his side.

★ ★ ★ ★ ★

Colour-Sergeant Nagg looked at the clock on the wall: only half an hour remained before he was to go on escort duty. He scratched the end of his jutting chin. "Nah, summink definitely ain't right!" he thought to himself. "Nah sign of the Field Marshal or Colonel Tanttermount, hall day, and now these dodgy horders hof *not* escorting the King!"

He walked around the mess, his boots clumping loudly on the flagstones. He tapped his chin with his fingers, still pondering the matter; "The Palace Guards 're hall jumpy like fleas hon a griddle! Oho woz that bloke in the General's hoffice? Wot woz 'is name hagain?" He stuffed his hands into his pockets, thinking so hard that he gave himself a headache. Meanwhile the door opened, and Corporal Dunsden-Puke entered.

"GIT HOUT!" roared Nagg, and the Corporal quickly exited!

"Is name woz Sir Nausious summink," he thought, "Sir Nausious Nojj, that woz it! Now, where do I know 'im from?" He stomped around the Mess table again, eyeing the clock.

He suddenly slapped his forehead, knocking his hat flying; "HOF COURSE!" he roared out loud, and then hushed himself to a whisper; "E's the Royal *Remover*, the Master hof Hassassins!" Then he stopped and posed himself with another question. "Wot's 'e going wiv the King for?"

Now so far, this was an amazing feat of brainpower on the Colour-Sergeant's behalf: even by most Dondymarian standards, most officers couldn't produce enough brainpower to light five candles!

He sucked on his teeth as he thought, distorting his face into even higher levels of ugliness. He picked up his hat and plonked it on his aching head. Then the *ping* moment; he hit the jackpot, lighting nearly ten candles!

"THEY HARE GOING TO HASSASSINATE THE KING!"

★ ★ ★ ★ ★

Meanwhile, Lucian and his party were racing along the Plain of Uoplaax, the great Fungoid Forest on their right flank and the rocks at the foot of the Zelgemar Stairs insight. "Let's have a breather, Snuzz. It's been hours since we left the Lake of Wonders." puffed Sir Septimus.

"No, Sir Septimus, I would rather we rest at the foot of the stairs. It's not far now. We would be safer when we are under cover of the rocks." puffed Lucian in reply.

So, on they all ran.

Artimus took out his watch as he hurried along. Looking at it, he shook his head. The time was passing quickly; they had been running all night. The Night Husk siren had sounded off twice, so it was now the morning of the 15th July, and doubts really started to rise in his mind that they would miss the deadline. He replaced the watch in his pocket, and ran with even more urgency.

★ ★ ★ ★ ★

In the courtyard of the Royal Palace stood the steam-powered Royal coach. It looked like any other coronation-type coach, except this one was made entirely from iron and steel, and mounted on its two doors were the sub-machine guns!

The coach driver sat high up at the front of the coach with the long shaft of the steering column between his legs. He was dressed in Palace livery, and had large gauntleted hands that were waiting impatiently on the steering wheel.

At the back of the coach, the steam engine puffed away, billowing black smoke into the air. A red carpet was rolled out from the Palace entrance to the coach. Either side of the carpet stood a row of six soldiers standing not so smartly to attention. By the door of the coach stood Colour-Sergeant Frampton Nagg: he frowned menacingly, with his jaw thrust forward.

Six royal trumpeters came out and stood either side of the carpet and got ready to play the royal fanfare.

Nagg readied himself.

The King appeared in the doorway frowning, dazzled by the afternoon sunlight.

"PREEEESENT, WAIT FOR IT, WAIT FOR IT, HARMS!" bellowed the Colour-Sergeant to the soldiers, who gave a rather slovenly display of arms.

The King stepped down onto the carpet, followed by Sir Nausious Nojj as the royal trumpeters struck up with the fanfare.

"Buurrrgerrrphhhhhhhh!" burbled a trumpeter as King Mumbeldok slapped the trumpet away with a mutter of "Get that bloomin' thing out me ear!" His Royal Highness marched up the carpet towards Nagg, who saluted him. His Most Serene Majesty meanwhile, was still shouting obscenities to the trumpeters. "Shut that claptrap up!" is the only printable phrase he uttered.

The Colour-Sergeant opened the door of the coach for the King, and the King put his foot upon the step and jumped into the coach. Suddenly the Colour-Sergeant slammed the door shut behind the King, locking it tight, and at the same moment gave Sir Nausious a shove in the stomach, bowling him over and sending him flying into the soldiers and knocking them down like ninepins!

Quick as a flash, the Colour-Sergeant swung up to the Coach Driver's seat and pushed the driver off it. The driver fell and hit the courtyard flagstones like a sack of potatoes. Meanwhile, from within his locked carriage the King could be heard protesting furiously. "Nagg? NAGG! What the blooming 'ell's going on!?!"

Rather than waste valuable seconds in an explanation, the Colour-Sergeant started the steam engine and the pistons that drove the wheels of the coach slowly started to move. Ashe took off the handbrake, the coach lurched forward, gaining speed as it puffed down the hill from the courtyard.

Lord Creep leapt up from his seat when he heard the commotion in the courtyard below. He threw open the casement and saw all the soldiers and Sir Nausious Nojj trying to get to their feet. He saw the coach puffing down the hill towards the Palace gates.

"**Stop that coach**!" he raged at the top of his reedy voice.

No one attempted to stop the coach.

"OPEN FIRE!" he bellowed, in the hope the gatehouse watch would open fire on the Royal Coach with their cannons, but nothing happened.

Too late for anything, he watched in frozen horror as the coach steamed out under the gate.

He slammed the window shut with such force that it caused one of the panes to shatter. His swift movement caused his wig to spin slightly on his head and slip over his eyes. He turned purple with rage and ripped the wig off his head and threw it on the floor. Like a small child throwing a tantrum, he jumped up and down on it!

★★★★★

Lucian dropped down by the rock, the foot of the Zelgemar Steps just behind him. The run had been too much for them physically. Lucian had never felt so tired: of all the adventures he had been through, this one was the most strenuous, dangerous and exhausting!

Zontahl, unaffected by the journey across the Plain, sat next to him.

"Five minutes' rest and we'll have to move on!" said Lucian, puffing loudly.

"By Obadiah Thrasskin's beard, I never want to have to run like that ever again!" moaned Sir Septimus as he sat down and leaned against a rock for support. Sweat was streaming down his face and he whipped out his handkerchief and wiped his forehead. Artimus lay beside him, gasping for breath: he was followed by Fengook and his scouts, and lastly the three cats.

Artimus lightly patted Sir Septimus' belly. "The good thing is you've lost weight!" he joked.

"A Pogglin, sir, should never be thin!" retorted Sir Septimus, rising to Artimus' joke.

"This is where we met your brother, Zontahl," said Lucian.

"That's right," agreed Artimus. "Just before we were attacked by that vile Acid Slug!"

For a moment they said nothing while they caught their breath.

"Well, we managed it, my friends," said Artimus cheerfully. "We have been to the Moogem Tree and back – we survived!"

"Yes, thanks to our Mushroom brother," added Fengook with a smile.

"So, Lucian, are you going to tell us just how you managed to save us from the Seeker?" enquired Artimus.

Lucian shook his head. "No, Artimus. I want to be well away from this land before I think it safe to tell. One never knows who might be listening!"

Sir Septimus nodded in agreement with his friend, remembering a time on a previous adventure when that very mistake had been made.

"What are we going to do now, what's your pla...?" Artimus was interrupted by one of the cat scouts, who was holding up its paw.

"Acid Slugs! Move!"

A shot of acid suddenly hit a rock close by and dissolved it! The group bolted, not sure of the direction of the attack?

"There!" cried Zontahl and as the great bulk of the Slug heaved into view.

"And there!" squealed Fengook as another great Acid Slug slithered out of the Fungoid forest.

Lucian quickly jumped over a rock, and landed squarely on his feet, tapping his staff on the ground. "***Mortalitas Cos Cotis***!" he shouted, and the gemstone on his staff turned white.

Instantly the writhing Slug turned to flint and moved no more!

"Look out, Snuzz!" Sir Septimus cried as another Slug appeared. Acid flew through the air, Lucian being its target. He flipped backwards and tumbled to the ground, avoiding the acid, and he somersaulted back onto his feet. The gemstone on his staff was already shining brightly as he brought it to bear on the attacking Acid Slug.

"*Mortalitas Cos Cotis*!" he cried again, turning the second Acid Slug to flint.

There was a scream of pain from Dargook as a jet of acid from the third Slug hit him, causing his right arm to dissolve instantly and scarring his face and belly! Lucian spun around, wielding his staff just as the Slug was bearing down on him.

"*Mortalitas Cos Cotis!*" He roared at the Acid Slug. The Slug was caught as it was jetting out the acid from the puckered sack above its head, which, like the other slugs, was turned instantly to flint!

Lucian rushed over to little Dargook, who was writhing in agony in the dirt, and he dropped to his knees beside the little creature. Quickly he doused the acid wounds with the water from The Lake of Wonders.

"By the stars above and the Sun internal, let the waters of the Lake release their secrets," he said quietly. The blue aura appeared around the stump of his arm and wounds, which instantly healed. The agonised expression slowly passed away from Dargook's face.

He smiled up at Lucian, who looked down at the little creature with tears pricking his eyes. Lucian was so sorry; he had hoped that there would be no more pain caused to his party after the encounter at the shore of Lake Naara. He then quickly took out the Moogem fruit cut a wedge from it and got Dargook to eat it.

"Mmm, it's juicy!" said the little Fungiglook with delight.

"This will cure your internal injuries and finish the healing process," he said quietly and cradled head in his arm. He turned to Fengook. "I think the time has come, my dear little friend, to call a Snail; it's time I got you safely home."

Fengook smiled and nodded. He then cupped his hands to his mouth and called, "*Bar-yorooo! Bar-yoroo! Bar-yoroo!*" Some way off a reply came: "*Bar-yoroo! Roo! Roo!*"

"The snail is on the way, my Mushroom brother; it will be here within minutes."

Lucian smiled, "That's good," he replied, "Because if any more slugs appear, we are in deep trouble. My power to repeat that spell on them has been depleted. Three times was my absolute limit!"

Lucian called the other Fungiglook scout to come and comfort his friend. As he went to stand up, the injured Fungiglook took hold of Lucian's arm.

"My deepest thanks; for you have saved me from death once again."

Lucian patted his hand and nodded his head in thanks, to overcome to speak. He took Fengook to one side, and told him quietly, "I want to thank you and your friends for helping us on our quest. I also want to apologise for not being able to protect those who have died and been injured. You have shown us nothing but kindness, and I have not been able to repay you for your loss." Tears welled in his eyes.

Fengook smiled and reached up to wipe a tear from Lucian's cheek. "You have nothing to apologise for: we wanted to help you save the Queen's life, and you protected us as much as you possibly could. You saved us; none would have survived the journey if it were not for your protection. You are wise, you brought forth light where there was no light and you even made the white face with no mouth flee in fear."

He turned and gestured to the three slugs. "You even turned the Acid Slugs into stone, statues that will remain forever after as monuments to your bravery." The little Fungiglook turned to face his friend again. "You have performed deeds that will enter into Fungiglook tales, and the stories will be told for centuries to come so long as my kind remains in the world." Fengook hugged the Pogglin. "True, I am upset at our parting... but I am filled with joy that we met!"

Lucian hugged his little friend back. "Your words have helped heal my pain, my little friend." He said quietly to the little Fungiglook, "Your sacrifice in our quest will be told to our King, country and its inhabitants, and we will be forever grateful to the kind and brave Fungiglooks of Mushentar."

A Giant Snail arrived at the scene, his eyes peering curiously at the stone Slugs. "Goodness me, what's been happening here?!" he said, looking at the group for an answer. "Oh, it's you three!" he said, blinking in surprise.

"You must be Sidney," said Artimus walking towards the snail. "I want a few words with you about making us roll in that slime!"

The snail brought his huge eyes down to inspect the little Pogglin, and the eyes bounced a little as the snail gave a little chuckle. "Well, you look to be a fellow who can take a joke!" Despite his annoyance, Artimus couldn't help but laugh at the snail's cheeky reply.

Lucian came over to the Snail and spoke, "As you can see Sidney, our friends the Fungiglooks have been on a quite a perilous journey. Some of them have been killed and this little chap here has taken a grievous wound." He gestured to Dargook. "He has lost an arm due to those vile Acid Slugs."

"Did you do that?" asked Sidney, gesturing with an eyestalk towards the stone Slugs. Lucian nodded his reply. Sidney smiled broadly at the little Pogglin.

"Then you can ask anything of me!"

"I would like you to take Fengook, Dargook and Songook back to Mushentar. I want you to get them there safely – no stopping off for mushrooms on the way!"

Sidney nodded his head and agreed that he would take his little passengers safely home.

Once again Fengook hugged his friend, then it was Sir Septimus' turn to say farewell. "Goodbye, Fengook, and many thanks for your help. We wouldn't have made it through the Fungoid Forest, were it not for you and your friends."

"You are welcome, my mushroom brother!" replied Fengook and smiled.

Artimus shook Fengook's hand and thanked him. The Pogglins then helped the injured Dargook aboard the snail's back. They thanked him and Songook for all their help and wished them well for the future. Fengook then jumped aboard and helped his friends into the shell with their injured party. Slowly Sidney turned and started to head off into the Fungoid Forest. Fengook crawled out from under the shell and ran up the Snail's back and waved a last farewell to his friends.

"I shall come back Fengook, I promise you! I have unfinished business in Empraktos-Larris!" called Lucian, waving back to his friend.

"Bar-yorooo! Bar-yorooo!" He called back with joy.

The Pogglins waved to their friend until they lost sight of him and could only see the large shell moving slowly, deeper into the great Fungoid Forest until it was lost amongst the giant Mushrooms. "Wonderful chap!" said Artimus to Lucian, who nodded. "Yes, I shall miss him." Sir Septimus blew his nose, never one for showing his feelings. But the other two knew he was just as upset at parting company with their Fungiglook friends.

"I am sorry to say that the time for farewells is not quite yet over," said Zontahl. "It is time for my scouts to return and report back to my brother Fontahl."

The three scouts walked over to the Pogglins and bowed their heads in farewell; each of the Pogglins patted the cats in turn and thanked them for all their help. Like the Fungiglooks, they too set off into Fungoid Forest, when Parrdoo stopped and returned to the group, walking up to Lucian.

"I will never forget your gift of giving me a second chance at life, my friend," she purred. "When you return to this land of Empraktos-Larris I shall be at your side. Until then, good speed, and fare you well my friend Snuzz." She bowed low and then bounded off into the forest after her companions.

"Which just leaves us!" purred Zontahl. "You three certainly have left your mark on the face of Empraktos-Larris. One wonders if it will ever be the same again!"

The three Pogglins smiled at the cat's remark; Empraktos-Larris definitely had left its mark on them!

"Rest, or crack on to Sol-Larris?" asked Sir Septimus.

"Sol-Larris I think, Sir Septimus – time is running extremely short! We'll rest after climbing those stairs!" replied Lucian.

They hurriedly made their way up the steps, with Zontahl taking the lead.

★ ★ ★ ★ ★

The Sun was setting in the west behind Dunbruan's Wall and the Royal steam coach sped on into the dusk. Colour-Sergeant Nagg had the engine running at full steam; they had journeyed through the streets of Dondymar City and were challenged at the entrance to "Border Bridge". They were even fired at by the cannons in the Rotunda that guards the entrance to the bridge!

"That woz a close call!" thought Nagg to himself; he even had to tell the King to "KEEP YA BLOOMIN' 'EAD DOWN!" for sticking the aforementioned appendage out of the coach window when the Rotunda opened fire.

The coach got through Border Town without any problems, making Nagg think that maybe the conspiracy on the King's life hadn't carried through to the rest of the Kingdom. But if Lord Creep was behind the conspiracy, then nowhere in Dondymaria would be safe for King Mumbeldok.

Taking this into account, Nagg had decided against going to Grodium City, as word of the King's escape would have reached the Governor by now. So, the Colour-Sergeant was now steaming along the Grodium Road, heading towards the Grodium Mountain in the hope that his King would still find Yorgrinn the Sly his ally.

Their only obstacle was Fort Tanttermount that lay on the road ahead, which was so heavily fortified with cannon against Atenartian attack that, if they chose, they could have blasted the Royal coach off the planet! Nagg could see the lights of the Fort up ahead and he gritted his teeth as he steamed along the road towards it, and hoped against all hope that they had not received word of the King.

To his amazement, the Royal coach went unchallenged and he sighed with relief then smiled to himself. They were almost at the Grodium Mountain, where he was banking on the protection of Yorgrinn the Sly.

Minutes later he brought the coach to a halt at the gates of the mountain, where two Grodium Dwarf Guards watched him suspiciously. He jumped down from the driving seat and walked over to the Guards.

"COLOUR-SERGEANT FRAMPTON NAGG, HOF THE ROYAL DONDYMARIAN ARMY, CRAVES A HAUDIENCE WIV 'IS LORDLINESS YORGRINN ON BE'ALF OF ME ROYAL SIRENESS, MUMBELDOK THE SECOND HOF DONDYMARIA."

One of the guards' slipped off to report to Gorgrinn, while his fellow guard watched Nagg closely. A few minutes later the guard returned with Gorgrinn, who gazed at the Colour-Sergeant with great suspicion. He looked around to see if there were any other Dondymarians in sight before speaking to Nagg.

"My brother will see your king, and he gives you leave to park your conveyance in the Hallgate," he said in the thick accent of the Grodium Mountain.

The guards opened the gates and allowed the coach into the Hallgate, and closed the doors upon it. Nagg jumped down from the driving seat and opened the door for the King to disembark. The King stepped down, and he eyed the Colour-Sergeant with new respect. Before the rain of bullets and the breath-taking escape from the trap set for him, he had always thought of Nagg as a boring brainless dullard!

"We would like to convey our thanks to you, Colour-Sergeant," said the King, and smiled as Nagg came to attention and saluted. "MY PLEASURE, YA ROYAL SIRENESS!" he bellowed with pride, not able to keep a smile off his face.

The King turned to follow Gorgerin's stout and broad figure, and Nagg followed behind his King.

Shortly they were led into the throne room, where sat Yorgrinn the Sly, stroking his moustache. Next to him stood the little figure of Ikbold the Bitter, his hand firmly clasped to his axe-half. Although they had been allies for many years, this was the first time either of them had ever met; King Mumbeldok had been in the habit of leaving such boring affairs to his Lord Chamberlain, Fangdom Creep.

Yorgrinn the Sly did not attempt to stand in the presence of the King, although Yorgrinn was not a King himself (a Dictator, in fact). He thought himself higher than the King. Yorgrinn's eyes twinkled like pieces of jet, as he looked King Mumbeldok over, whilst continuing to gently stroke his moustache.

"What brings the little King of Dondymaria into my presence?" he finally said.

The King couldn't believe his ears. He was not used to being addressed in such a manner! "That's no blooming' way to talk to a king!" he thundered in reply.

Yorgrinn's wide-set eyes narrowed, and pure rage sparkled within them. His hand shot from his moustache to his axe blade, and he gently rubbed the crescent of steel with his thumb.

"You forget where you are, my little King. You now stand in my domain. I would have had a Dwarf's head for showing me less insolence than you!" he said coldly.

For the very first time in his life, King Mumbeldok began to think that he really should have taken more of an interest in ruling his realm, and his allies! Yorgrinn saw the change in the King's expression and smiled, although his huge, black moustache hid this.

He slicked back his hair. "Yes, I see that you have realised the extent of Creep's treachery to his King. I like gold, my little King, and Creep has given me plenty to turn my coat against you!" His hand returned to his moustache and he continued to gently stroke it. The many bejewelled rings on his hand, glinting in the light of the torches around the chamber.

"Now what is to stop me from turning you over to Creep?" He pondered aloud, causing Ikbold the Bitter to chuckle with delight.

"Our many years standing as an ally!" retorted the King, "After all, Creep seems to have paid with my gold for your treachery!"

Yorgrinn smiled again. Mumbeldok was not such a fool as Creep had painted him, nor was he lacking in courage to stand up to him in this way. He sat forward in his throne; "I like you!" he said "But I don't like Creep. So, I'll tell you what I am going to do; I will not hand you over!"

The King smiled, but prematurely, as Yorgrinn continued. "But I am not going to give you protection from him either!" The smile dropped from the King's face.

"Flee while you can, my little King, as it will be interesting to see how far you get before one of your subjects betrays you to Creep!"

Colour-Sergeant Nagg stepped forward. "WE WILL NOT GET VERY FAR WIVOUT COAL, ME LORD. WILL YA NOT EVEN 'ELP 'IS ROYAL SIRENESS HON THIS POINT?"

Yorgrinn winced at the loudness of Nagg's voice and was amused by his loyalty to his King

"You can have your coal if you can pay for it!" replied Yorgrinn.

"WE LEFT IN HAN 'URRY, ME LORD! WE DO NOT CARRY HANY GOLD COIN TO PAY FOR THE COAL. WILL YA NOT 'ELP THE KING IN 'IS HOWER HOF NEED?"

"Only if you can pay!" came Yorgrinn's cold reply.

The King removed two rings from his hand and threw them at Yorgrinn's feet. Ikbold the Bitter scurried after them like a rat after scraps, retrieved the rings and presented them to Yorgrinn for inspection. He took the rings, still keeping a hand to his axe-half. He nodded, pleased with the quality of the gold and the stones; he was well-placed to appreciate the quality, as they were after all manufactured in his own smithies and exported to Dondymaria.

"They can have their coal," he said to Ikbold and turned his attention to King Mumbeldok. "Now go, before I have a change of mind! The coal will be brought to the coach."

Ikbold the Bitter indicated to the Colour-Sergeant and the King to follow him, while Yorgrinn and Gorgrinn watched them leave the chamber.

★ ★ ★ ★ ★

Chancellor Silverore opened the viewing grille in the cell door and looked in at the occupant. It was a small cell, hewn from the rock of the mountain and opposite the door was a stone slab that had also been carved out the rock. On it was lying a very bad-tempered looking Grodium Dwarf.

"Go away! I have nothing to say to you!" said the Grodium Dwarf venomously.

"So, thou art still refusing to talk to me?" The old Chancellor replied gently.

"I will not speak to scum such as you, Old Dwarf!" came the reply.

"Then thou leav'st me no choice. I am sorry to say I will have to gain the information from thee by force."

The Grodium Dwarf laughed mockingly at the Chancellor. "No amount of torture will loosen my tongue, Old Dwarf! The pain you could inflict on me would be nought compared to the agonies that Yorgrinn would put me through if he knew I had talked. No, Old Dwarf, your threats won't frighten me so, stop wasting my time and leave me in peace!"

"Oh, it certainly won't come to that!" smiled the Chancellor. "We do not stoop to Yorgrinn's level of treatment towards his prisoners. Thou wilt see that here at the Brown Mountain we do things differently."

The Grodium Dwarf heard the key turn in the lock, and slowly the door opened, and into the cell trotted the little Dwarvemite, Remy. The door closed. The Grodium prisoner looked at the little creature with some amazement and then burst out laughing. The Chancellor stood at the other side of the door, listening to the Grodium Dwarf's laughter.

The amusement of the Dwarf made the old Chancellor's raise his eyebrows and smile. Suddenly the prisoner's laughter stopped abruptly and was replaced by terrified screams! They pierced the old Chancellor's ears they were so loud and they echoed around the hall of the cellblock. The Chancellor unlocked the door and opened it, and little Remy came padding out, his tail wagging. The door was shut and locked behind the Dwarvemite.

The Dwarvemite is a creature of metamorphosis and telepathy. It read the Grodium Dwarf's innermost fear and changes itself into the thing that terrorised him the most!

Silverore opened the viewing grille. "Now art thou ready to talk to me?"

The Grodium Dwarf looked at the Chancellor with wide panic-stricken eyes and he shivered with pure terror!

"YES!" he screeched in fear, "I'll tell you whatever you wish to know! Just keep that creature away from me!"

"Then we have a bargain! Thou canst begin by telling me Yorgrinn's plans for the invasion of Pogglinburg. Then, my little bird, thou canst sing to me about Yorgrinn's plans on finding the Rune-Stone of Thremgould!"

The Grodium Dwarf eagerly nodded his head.

★ ★ ★ ★ ★

Colour-Sergeant Frampton Nagg had stoked the boiler with coal bought from Yorgrinn and made sure it was coming up to pressure. The gates of the Hallgate were opened for them. Ikbold the Bitter stood by the doorway and watched as the Royal coach puffed its way into the still air of the night. The guards barred the gates to the mountain. One of the Guards came over at Ikbold's beckoning.

"Have you sent word as Yorgrinn ordered?" he asked.

"Indeed," replied the Guard.

Ikbold the Bitter smiled evilly at the good news, "Then Fort Tanttermount is at the ready!" The Hallgate echoed with his laughter as he returned to report to his cousins.

★ ★ ★ ★ ★

When he had put some distance between the coach and the Grodium Mountain, Nagg pulled up and jumped down from the driving seat and climbed into the coach to face his monarch.

"What is it, Nagg?"

"YA ROYAL SIRENESS, I DON'T..."

"For blooming' sake keep your voice *down,* Colour-Sergeant!" winced the King. "You are not addressing the parade ground now!"

"Sorry ya Sireness, I forget!" saluted Nagg, and he continued, "I don't trust Yorgrinn. I think 'e may 'ave betrayed us to the garrison at Fort Tanttermount?"

The King looked at Nagg with some admiration; he really *wasn't* a boring dullard at all. "Good thinking, Nagg; it was something I didn't consider." He found himself becoming quite trustful of his Colour-Sergeant. "Then what do you propose, Colour-Sergeant?"

Nagg scratched his long chin. He was getting used to all this thinking, and he rather liked it. "Hassumin' Yorgrinn 'as tipped hof the Fort, we hargoin' to come under some 'eavy fire, ya Sireness. So, I think ya goin' to 'ave to give us some covering fire hon the sub-machine gun."

The King smiled. It was his opportunity of shooting at his subjects. King Mumbeldok thought back to those halcyon days when his Daddy used to shoot at his subjects when bored by a long coach journey!

"Yes, that's no problem! And if we should get through?"

"That's the 'ardest bit, Ya Royal Sireness. Hafter the Fort there really is nowhere we can go. Creep 'as a price on ya 'ead it seems, throughout Dondymaria."

The King slumped back into his seat, his crown slipping to one side upon his head. "Then we are finished, Nagg; there is no place we can find sanctuary! Why was I so foolish enough to leave the running of the realm to Creep? Daddy—the Old King told me I'd mess the Kingdom up if I didn't take an interest in it. I may still have the crown, Nagg, but it is Lord Fangdom Creep who wields the power!"

"Not all har hon the side of Creep, Ya Sireness – *Hi* for one ham not!" replied the Colour-Sergeant, jabbing his thumb into his barrel-chest.

The King smiled, nodding his head in agreement. "You are a surprise to me, Nagg; I would have had you down for Creep's man!"

"Wot Me!" retorted Nagg with affronted surprise. "Nah, not me, Ya Sireness; I never could stand the bloke. I swore hallegiance to King and Country, not to the likes of Fangdom Creep. I am a King's Dondymarian, halways 'ave, halways will!" He gave an ugly grin. "Now the only way we har going to get back ya throne is to look for 'elp, and there is only one road open to us."

The King went white, "No! I will not put myself in the hands of the Atenartians at any cost. I would rather be taken by Creep than travel to Megnos City for help!"

"Nah, never the Hatenartians!" shuddered Nagg, "I would rather come to han 'orrible end at Creep's 'ands than go to Hatenartians for 'elp!"

"Then who do you have in mind; not the Pogglins?"

"Nah, we could never get there in this thing," replied Nagg. "Halthough eventually that may 'ave to be hour destination at journey's end. Hour honly 'ope is that we can make it to Dwarveshire. The Brown Mountain Dwarves may be a bit more merciful when they know that ya now count Yorgrinn the Sly as ya enemy!"

"I don't really like having to face Vardiemar III and ask for sanctuary, but I have to agree with you, Nagg. That is now the only road open to us."

With the plan agreed Nagg left the coach, returned to the driving seat and set the coach in motion. King Mumbeldok readied himself on the Sub-machine gun. If they managed to run the gauntlet past Fort Tanttermount then they had a clear road ahead to the kingdom of Dwarveshire. The Royal coach sped along the Grodium Road at full steam, the engine made a lot of noise so there was no way they could get past the Fort by stealth.

As the coach drew near to the Fort, Nagg could hear a lot of activity coming from its direction.

"So, they do know we har coming!" said Nagg to himself.

Suddenly on the wind, he heard a single word: "Fire!"

He saw a flash of red in the darkness and then the roar of the shot. The ball exploded at the side of the road several yards away. The King opened up with covering fire from the Sub-machine gun mounted on the door.

"THEY 'AVEN'T FOUND HOUR RANGE!" bellowed Nagg over the noise of the Sub-Machine gun. As the coach steamed closer to the Fort, they came into range and a shot thumped into the ground very close to the coach, which was closely followed by another!

"We'll never make it!" shouted the King, nonetheless giving the Fort another burst from the gun. Suddenly Nagg careered off the road and onto the rough ground, so the Fort was now on their left flank.

"I'M GOIN' TO 'EAD FOR TANNTERMOUNT 'ILL, IT BACKS HONTO THE FORT. IT WILL GIVE US COVER AND THERE IS FEWER CANNONS HON THE FORT'S SIDE!" roared Nagg as he zigzagged the coach to avoid the cannon shot.

King Mumbeldok had moved over and was now covering fire with the left-hand side machine gun. A few minutes later the cannonballs were coming less frequently as they neared Tanttermount Hill, and soon they were out of range and undercover from the hill.

"Yahoo! we did it, Nagg!" cried the King in excitement; he hadn't had so much fun in years!

Nagg smiled broadly, "WE DID YA ROYAL SIRENESS, HAND YA MAKE A GOOD GUNNER, SIR!"

The coach rattled over the rough ground as it steamed along. In the distance, to their left, they could see the lights of Grodium City as it sprawled across the horizon. It was the second-largest city in the kingdom, and home to Dondymarian's industrial facilities. Even from this distance away, they could hear the countless clangs and bangs that came from the numerous factories that the city housed. They never closed and worked around the clock, twenty-four hours a day, seven days a week. An hour on and they were still passing the city, but at last, they were coming to the end of it.

After Grodium City it would be nothing but open country, and then they would follow the Mumbeldok River westward, keeping it on their right flank, onto the Falls of Gromm. Here they would have to veer north past the Copper Mountain and into the Dwarveshire forest and the eastern gate of the Brown Mountain. But all this was many miles ahead of them.

★ ★ ★ ★ ★

Lucian and his party had reached the halfway point up the Zelgemar Staircase. Zontahl wanted to head the way, and he effortlessly jumped from stair to stair. His energy and dexterity on the whole journey never ceased to amaze the Pogglins. Lucian followed, puffing heavily. The battle with the Slugs had drained him of energy and magic.

The calves at the back of his legs and his thighs ached with burning fatigue. He was finding the journey of climbing the stairs much harder than descending them.

Behind him was Artimus. He was very hot and sweating profusely. Because of the sweat, his pince-nez kept slipping off his nose, so he put them into his waist-jacket pocket. He had his handkerchief in his hand, which was now very damp, and he wiped his face intermittently. So much so, that the damp cloth was beginning to make his face a little sore. It was too much, he had to rest, and he sat down on the step. He mopped his face again with the handkerchief and then checked his watch.

9.12 PM.

He gasped. Even if they were to make it up the stairs by morning, they would be too late to save the Queen!

His heart sank. He looked up and saw that Zontahl and Lucian were quite a few flights up, and it galvanised him into making an effort! He got up and started climbing the steps as quickly as he could; even if time was slipping past, he was going try his best to get back to Pogglinburg.

Catching up with Lucian, he said, "I've been thinking about the properties of the Moogem fruit. Do you agree that it holds a major property for revitalisation and healing?" His eyes were full of hope in his friend's reply.

"Most definitely, Artimus," nodded Lucian in agreement.

"Then do you think that if we eat some of the fruit ourselves, it would energise us and relieve us of our exhaustion?" suggested Artimus.

"What a good idea, Artimus!" beamed Lucian, "I never thought of that!"

He stopped and quickly took the fruit from his pouch and started to cut a wedge from it. "Sir Septimus, come here, quickly!" he called to his friend.

The Pogglin climbed as quickly up to his friends as he could.

"Artimus has had a terrific idea! Have a piece of Moogem Fruit!" And he gave the slice of fruit to Sir Septimus, who took it. Lucian began to quickly cut a wedge for Artimus. Sir Septimus bit into the piece of the fruit and instantly his mouth tingled from the juice of the fruit.

"It's delicious! It tastes like Elderflower cordial!" And he eagerly ate the rest of his portion of fruit. He felt it tingle inside him as he swallowed it, and the effect it had on his body was immediate. He felt refreshed as though he has slept for a week! He smiled broadly at his two friends. "Goodness me, that's good stuff. It really works!"

Artimus took his piece from Lucian. "It's excellent!"

Lucian called to Zontahl, who came and took a piece from his friend. Zontahl nodded his head, "Better than mushroom, but it is still not as good as fresh meat!" he smiled, yet for all his doubts he started to spring up the stairs four at a time. Lucian laughed and turned to his two companions, "He's going to take some catching!" and he ate his own piece of the fruit, smiling broadly at the flavour.

"Tis very good indeed and I feel the goodness of it already! I feel that I too can take four steps at a time! Come, my friends, let us catch up with Zontahl and double our efforts to be away from this accursed stairway!"

With renewed hope, the three Pogglins bounded up the steps after Zontahl.

★ ★ ★ ★ ★

Lord Fangdom Creep could not sleep, and so sat wigless at his desk in his dressing gown. He impatiently rapped the surface of the desk with his fingers. That confounded Colour-Sergeant Nagg had spoilt his plans. "Why is it that all the dullards around here turn out to be the brains of Dondymaria!" he fumed to himself.

He had put every military installation around the country on alert: they were to kill the King and Nagg on sight! Their last sighting was at Border Town, so Lord Creep assumed that they were making for the Grodium Mountain. He had sent a Gweeley Bird off to Fort Tanttermount ordering them to blockade the road and stop the coach. He didn't trust Yorgrinn to return the King to him if he fell into the hands of the Grodium Dwarves. He had been waiting for news for the past four hours, and still nothing!

There was a tap at the casement, and Creep whirled around to see the Gweeley Bird sat hunched on the windowsill. He stomped over to the window to let the bird in and it flew into the Chamber and landed on his desk. Creep hurriedly walked back to his desk and plonked himself down in the chair. "Well?"

"The news is not good, my Lord," squawked the Gweeley Bird. "I did not arrive in time; the Royal coach had been and gone by the time I arrived at Fort Tanttermount."

Lord Creep thumped the desk with his fist, and looked at the Gweeley Bird in anger. "I knew I should have sent Shrigg instead of you! You slow-flying oaf!"

"Not my fault, my Lord! The wind was against me!" protested the Gweeley Bird.

Creep grabbed hold of the Bird's beak to shut him up. "No matter!" he said coldly. "The King has escaped me! Mumbeldok must have met with Yorgrinn, and yet Yorgrinn did not retain the King or return him to me!" He let go of the bird's beak.

"Mumbeldok must have had carried a secret supply of gold about his person and bought his freedom from Yorgrinn? Even so, there is still nowhere else he can run Mumbeldok must have gone to ground!"

He turned to the Gweeley Bird. "You are to fly directly to Shrigg. Tell him that he is to send all of your scouts around the land. Find me Mumbeldok! You will soon receive your reward: when I have finished with the Pogglins, you will have as many carcasses on which to feed as you like!"

The bird nodded. "I shall give your message to Shrigg, my Lord."

Creep returned to the window and opened the casement for the bird to leave. "And *hurry*!" he called after the bird, before closing the window. The sun was rising in the east above the Blendaraak Mountains.

★ ★ ★ ★ ★

Wing Commander "Ginger" Wingnut was just pulling on his flying gauntlets as he strode along the path leading to the take-off strip of the Royal Pogglin Flying core. Red the Hobbdrak was waiting for him, ready for the Dawn Patrol.

"Morning Red, old chap; sleep well? It's a beautiful morning!" he said cheerfully as he hopped up into the saddle mounted on the creature's back.

"Mornin' Guv, and yus, I slept very well thanks!" The Hobbdrak replied with a smile. The Wing Commander pulled a leather strap across his lap and buckled it up.

"All buckled up?" asked Red, pulling down his flying goggles over his eyes.

"Roger that, Red!" replied Wingnut, doing the same.

Two great wings started to unfurl from the Hobbdrak's back (the same way as a snail unrolls its eyestalks). Soon Red's wings were fully extended.

"Front arms in, Red," called Wingnut.

Red began to retract his arms into his body (again, just like a snail's eyestalks). "Front arms in!"

"Chocks away!"

"Chocks away Red!"

"Roger!" replied Red and started to run along the airstrip, while beating his great red and orange wings. He beat his wings faster and his running speed increased, and in seconds they took off and soared upward up into the crisp clean air.

"Tally Ho!" cried Wingnut, as they rode the wind and glided over the town.

They gained height rapidly, and Red beat his great wings as he banked in the clear, blue morning sky. Ginger Wingnut did not need to direct Red; they had been on this patrol many times in so many years together, and the Hobbdrak circled and headed off towards the Copper Mountain. Far below was Pogglin Town, and Red followed the line of the high street. Very soon they were over the Royal Palace and the Copper Lake beyond. It truly was a beautiful morning, and what little cloud hung in the sky was highlighted in yellow by the rays of the sun.

★ ★ ★ ★ ★

Zontahl and the Pogglins came to the narrow bridge: Zontahl slowed his pace as he lightly trod on the bridge and a few rocks cracked from underneath and fell into the empty void below. "Better cross one at a time." He shouted to the Pogglins, "The bridge is very weak, so step lightly!"

Lucian lightly ran across the bridge and some more rocks crumbled from the underside of the bridge. Then Sir Septimus was next to cross, walking very slowly whilst holding his breath, and thinking at every step that the bridge would collapse underneath him! He got to the other side before he opened his lungs again, taking deep breaths of the roasting air in sheer relief.

Artimus was the last to cross: he ran as fast as he could over the stone bridge while holding his overcloak that was still on the stairs where he left it. More rocks crumbled from the underside of the bridge as he crossed. Artimus looked over his shoulder, half-expecting the stone to give way and fall into the abyss below. But the bridge remained intact, and soon they were racing along the tunnel that leads from the Zelgemar Stairs through Mount Zelmekh.

They rounded the corner and for the first time since the 8th July, they saw daylight at the end of the tunnel. Zontahl stopped as if in shock.

"What's wrong, Zontahl?" asked Lucian, surprised by the cat's sudden halt.

"That light, Lucian I have never seen the like of it before!"

The Pogglin patted his friend. "That is the light coming from the rays from the sun Zontahl, a great ball of fire that hangs way up in the sky. There will be many things that will be strange to you in Sol-Larris."

They raced along to the end of the tunnel and stood in the warmth of the Sun. It took quite a while for their eyes to become accustomed to the bright light, and Zontahl breathed in the cool air. "I never knew that air could smell so sweet!" he said.

Soon they were marching down the grey sands towards the pile of rocks. Next to it stood Artimus' flying machine. He beamed with delight at Sir Septimus. "I told you it would be safe to leave it here!"

"A good job for us too, if we are to get back on time!"

The friends hurried down towards the Flying Machine, Artimus getting the key ready that was on his watch chain. On reaching the machine Artimus ran up the steps to the cockpit and unlocked the door, while Lucian and Sir Septimus pulled out the winding key stowed away under the machine. They put the key into the mechanism of the machine and began to wind it up. Meanwhile, Zontahl sat by the rocks, squinting, his orange eyes still not accustomed to the sunshine. His attention was torn between looking at the landscape about him and watching his friends with interest.

The three Pogglins hurried up the steps of the Flying Machine and into the cockpit, closely followed by Zontahl. After they had all squeezed in, Artimus started up the machine. There was a whirring sound of the clockwork mechanism, and then it stalled and stopped.

"What's wrong?" asked Lucian.

"I don't know!" replied Artimus at a loss.

"Try it again, old boy." cut in Sir Septimus not believing the hand that Fate was dealing them. Artimus tried again, and the same thing happened!

Artimus looked dejectedly at his companions. "We're going to have to get out while I look at the mechanism underneath."

With a sense of dread, they all filed out of the cockpit.

★ ★ ★ ★ ★

Colour-Sergeant Frampton Nagg sat at the steering wheel of the Royal Coach, his prominent chin jutting out with a fixed determination of saving his King. He blinked, his eyes red-rimmed with tiredness, but he kept a focus on the rough ground that they were travelling. They were now well out of Dondymarian territory and beyond the reach of Lord Creep. It was the first time Nagg had ever left the confines of Dondymar City and Dondymaria, and he was surprised how pleasing the landscape was to the eye. His face cracked into a smile, enjoying the experience. On his left was the Copper Mountain, and to his right, Lake Gromm and the opening to the Grey Waste. Before him, he could see the trees of the Copper Wood and, rising from its centre, the imposing bulk of the Brown Mountain.

Making their escape in the steam powered Royal Coach.

He fixed his sights on The Copper Wood. "Halmost there, me 'ol son," he whispered to himself, and he caught the sound of King Mumbeldok snoring in the back of the coach. Nagg grinned at the sound. "That's it ya Sireness, 'ave a good sleep, it's been a long day and night for ya!" he thought. Suddenly he heard a noise that rang a bell in his soldier's brain and he looked up towards the direction of the noise.

"CRIPES!" he said, as he saw a Hobbdrak flying along the line of the Copper Mountain. "IT'S A BLOOMIN' POGGLIN PATROL!" Then he stopped.

"Wot are ya hon about Nagg!" he said to himself, "I need to get to Pogglinburg eventually!" And he waved up to the Pogglin pilot and his Hobbdrak mount as he steamed along towards the Copper Wood.

★ ★ ★ ★ ★

"Did you see that Guv?" said Red to Ginger Wingnut.

"Roger that, Red! Looked like the Royal Coach of Dondymaria to me, but what the blazes is it doing this far out of Dondymaria? What do you make of that eh, Red old boy?"

"I dunno Guv, but did you see the driver was a-waving at us?"

"I did Red, very fishy that! Better get back to Pogglinburg methinks, this needs reporting. Abort the patrol, Red; we're going home!"

"Roger that, Guv!" Red banked steeply, flapped his impressive wings, and headed back to Pogglinburg.

★ ★ ★ ★ ★

But Wing Commander Wingnut and Red were not the only ones to have seen the Royal coach. It was also seen by Dwarvish scouts from within the Copper Wood, but also by the beady little eyes of a Gweeley Bird! It squawked and flapped into the air from the bough of a tree and headed towards Dondymaria.

Nagg caught sight of the bird, "CRIPES!" and he turned around, "YA ROYAL SIRENESS! WAKE UP!"

The King started to wake, his crown and wig falling to the floor. "What is it, Nagg?" he said anxiously, sticking his head out of the window.

"GWEELEY BIRD AT THREE HO'CLOCK, TRYIN' TO GET AWAY! SHOOT IT DOWN, YA SIRENESS!"

The King slid up the seat to the butt of the sub-machine gun that was mounted on the right-hand side door. He opened up on the Gweeley Bird with a burst of machine-gun fire and totally missed it! The Gweeley bird squawked in panic, and a flurry of feathers billowed behind it as the bird sped along. The King opened fire again, but his target was now well out of range.

"Curses!" cried the King angrily.

"THAT WAS A STROKE OF BLOOMIN' BAD LUCK! THAT FLIPPIN' BIRD WILL REPORT HOUR WHERE-HABOUTS TO CREEP! I WOZ 'OPIN' TO KEEP HOUR DESTINATION TO HOURSELVES: KEEP THE UPPER 'AND LIKE. KNOW WOT I MEAN, YA ROYAL SIRENESS?"

"I do indeed, Nagg a damn pity that blooming' bird got away! Still, even if Creep does know we are heading for Dwarveshire, there's nothing he can bally well do about it!"

"TRUE YA SIRENESS, BUT I WOULD 'AVE SOONER CREEP DIDN'T KNOW HABOUT IT!" Nagg thrust his chin forward and steamed on towards the woods.

★ ★ ★ ★ ★

Shrigg, the chief of the Gweeley Birds, skipped along the desktop which was littered with maps and old manuscripts.

"He's taking a time!" he thought to himself, and squawked with impatience.

The door opened and Yorgrinn the Sly entered the room holding a plate of the reddest, rawest chunks of meat Shrigg had ever seen! He clacked his beak in anticipation. Yorgrinn put the plate on the desk, followed by his Axe. Shrigg instantly hopped over to the plate and started to guzzle down the chunks of meat – but, with a sudden move, Yorgrinn grabbed the bird by the throat!

"You are sure Creep has no idea that you and your birds are *my* spies?" he said gruffly.

Shrigg shook his head. Yorgrinn released him and pushed the plate towards the bird. "Eat then!" he commanded.

Shrigg quickly gulped down the chunks of meat while he warily eyed Yorgrinn.

"As I have always said, every creature has a price and they quickly turn their coats to receive it!" he said mirthlessly to the bird. Shrigg had polished off the plate in double-quick time. Yorgrinn waited for the bird to talk.

"Creep has lost sight of Mumbeldok after he escaped the attack from Fort Tanttermount."

Yorgrinn stroked his moustache as he silently listened to the bird.

"Creep has now put all my birds on alert, and we are to watch for any sightings of the Royal Coach."

The Dwarf brooded on the Gweeley Bird's words. "And there is still no word of Mumbeldok?"

"No, I am still waiting for a report of a sighting."

"Then you will tell *me* before it is reported to Creep!" growled the Dwarf and the bird bowed. "I will!" he replied.

"What of news on the missing Dwarf? Have there been any sightings or whisperings of him?"

Shrigg's eyes narrowed. "I have had whisperings from the earth crawler of The Copper Wood. They talk of a Grodium occupant residing within the cells of The Brown Mountain!"

"WHAT!" he roared. "I will have the Cur's guts if he talks!" The bird jumped as Yorgrinn's fist hit the desk.

"This he may have already done! The earth crawlers tell of many war drums being beaten in the halls of the Brown Mountain!"

Yorgrinn's face turned purple with rage and indicated the bird to continue.

"The footfall of many boots has also been heard moving towards the eastern gate of the mountain. One must assume Vardiemar is expecting an attack to come from Gromm Bridge!"

"I will have the rogue's bladder for a swimming hat!" exploded the Dwarf, and stomped off to the door and opened it. "Gorgrinn! Ikbold! Get in here quick!" he bellowed, his voice echoing around the corridors and chambers of the mountain.

Yorgrinn returned to his chair in front of the Gweeley bird, and he looked at the bird menacingly while he waited for the arrival of the two Dwarves. Presently they hurried into the room, expressions of uncertainty fixed on their faces.

"You took your time!" growled Yorgrinn as they entered. "Ikbold, get a guard to take our *friend* here back to the surface. We wouldn't want him to *hear* anything that could be of use to Creep's ears!"

Ikbold left to find a guard and moments later returned with one in tow.

"You will report to me *first* on any news of the subjects on which we spoke!" Yorgrinn warned the bird.

Shrigg nodded in answer and then squawked as he was grasped by the guard and taken out of the room.

Yorgrinn waited until the guard and Shrigg were well away from his room before talking.

"The Brown Mountain has our Dwarf!"

Gorgrinn and Ikbold looked at each other on hearing the news and then back at Yorgrinn, who was back to stroking his moustache.

"Can we get to him?" asked Ikbold the Bitter.

"Not for the moment, Ikbold. As a prisoner, he is held too deep within the mountain: we cannot afford the loss of Dwarves it would take to get him out. Maybe an opportunity will arise? Then I can wreak revenge on the loose-tongued cur!"

"Then what do you want us to do?" Gorgrinn said, exasperated by his brother's obtuseness.

Yorgrinn gave his brother a silent warning to curb his tongue, with a look that could freeze the fires of Mount Blendaraak. "What is important about this news is that Shrigg spoke of an impending invasion of Pogglinburg via the Gromm Bridge!"

"Now that is bad news indeed!" said Gorgrinn angrily.

"Exactly Gorgrinn, and if my information is right, Vardiemar is massing his army on the Eastern Gate, very close to The Copper Mountain. Our surprise attack is lost, and we don't have enough forces to get through now that our surprise attack has been blown!"

"You could pull some Dwarves off the Rune-Stone excavations tunnels?" offered Ikbold the Bitter.

"I could, but I won't!" roared back Yorgrinn, "The snivelling cur could've also told the Brown Mountain of our plans for the Rune-Stone. If he has, then I want that to take priority! You are to take some dwarves from the invasion tunnel and put them into the Rune-Stone excavation gangs."

"So, what of your pledge to Creep? Will you fulfil your side of the bargain and invade Pogglinburg at the appointed time?" asked Gorgrinn of his brother.

"I may or I may not, Gorgrinn," Yorgrinn replied. "I will have to weigh the situation carefully, then decide my action!"

★★★★★

Artimus had unscrewed the brass bottom plate of the flying machine and was under it, tinkering with the mechanism.

"Well, what is wrong?" asked Sir Septimus, while polishing his monocle.

"I think sand has got into the crank box! I am going to have to dismantle it and clean it!" Artimus called exasperatedly from underneath the machine.

"And how long will that take, Artimus?" enquired Lucian, pulling at his beard.

"How long is a piece of string? I have no idea, Lucian. You are all just going to have to wait!" The obvious tetchiness in his voice betrayed the despair he was feeling at yet another disastrous set back and the thought that because it was his machine it was somehow his fault.

"This is bad, Lucian. The Queen is lost if Artimus can't get his contraption to work!" whispered Sir Septimus to his friend.

"It is a very worrying possibility!" nodded Lucian in agreement, still pulling at his beard.

"Is there nothing in the secret book that will help us?"

"Even if I could summon a Hobbdrak to our aid by using the book, Sir Septimus, we still wouldn't make it back in time to save the Queen. The Hobbdrak wouldn't be able to fly us there in time. No, I think we will have to be patient and hope upon hope that Artimus can fix the problem – and fast!"

Chapter Six

The Great Hall of Thremgould was filled with the Captains of the Dwarvish Army. King Vardiemar stood before the throne, clenched fists on his hips, looking resplendent in his battle armour made of black steel, gold and copper. To the front, on the left of the steps leading to the throne, stood Queen Ellgah and Crown Prince Vardiemar; to the right stood Chancellor Silverore and Borryn Cobalt.

Standing on the eighth step down, facing the assembled Captains, was Marshal-General Eygon Cavernhollow. He was an imposing sight in his black steel coat of chain mail trimmed with dark green leather. Beneath it, he wore a padded tunic of grass-green, trimmed with white piping. His helmet was tucked under his left arm and he wore brown leather boots with black steel plating up to the ankles. Cavernhollow had long yellow hair, which was flecked with white, and was swept back over his head. He had a beard of orange-yellow, a long moustache under a large, aquiline nose and deep-set blue eyes hiding beneath yellow eyebrows. On his left cheek was a mottled grey-blue birthmark which turned a deep red whenever his temper was roused.

"So, stand at the ready and be prepared. Thou canst expect to be called into action at any given time. Good luck, and may Thremgould look kindly upon us!" he said in a deep, husky voice.

Suddenly, there was a disturbance towards the back of the hall as a guard moved his way through the Army Captains to the stairs. He whispered something thing in the Marshal-General's ear, making his eyebrows rocket. He turned to the stairs and called."If you please, my Lord Silverore, I think you should come here a moment?"

The old chancellor walked down the steps to the Marshal-General and the guard, while the gathering talked amongst themselves. The guard gave his story again to the Chancellor.

"Then bring them in," said Silverore on hearing the news, and then added, "Make sure they are well-guarded, mind I want no accidents!"

He waved the guard on his way and then made his way back up the stairs to the Throne. King Vardiemar sat down when he saw the Chancellor returning.

"I have some very interesting news, your Majesty!" said Silverore, his eyes twinkling.

"What is it?" replied the King.

"The Copper Wood scouting party have just had Mumbeldok II of Dondymaria surrender to them. He is claiming sanctuary and wishes an audience with your Majesty. The Guards have him and his companion outside."

The King raised his eyebrows in surprise, "Well this is a turn up for the books to say the least, Chancellor. This audience should prove interesting. It will be the first time I have ever seen a Dondymarian of the Royal line!"

Chancellor Silverore thumped his staff on the ground several times as a signal to the guards to escort King Mumbeldok and the Colour Sergeant into the Great Hall. The Hall was instantly hushed of noise as the guards entered with their charges. Then some of the captains began to hiss and utter curses at the two Dondymarians: the two sides had been bitter enemies for centuries.

Chancellor Silverore thumped his staff and addressed the Hall. "Silence! I will not have such a disorder; remember where you are. These two are here under truce. Do not dishonour your King by transgressing such a truce with bitter words!"

The Hall became silent again as the Guards and their escort came to a halt at the foot of the stairs leading to the throne. King Vardiemar III stood up from his throne and walked to the top of the stairs.

He looked at the Dondymarians, the Colour-Sergeant being the taller of the two, and he curtly acknowledged Nagg's salute.

"So, what brings thee to our realm?" said King Vardiemar. "It is a strange request, for an enemy to ask sanctuary from the people with whom his kind has been warring against for centuries?"

Mumbeldok looked uncomfortably ill at ease in the midst of so many Dwarves. Although the king was the shorter of the two Dondymarians, he stood a foot and a half taller than the tallest Dwarf in the room. He massaged his throat; it was dry, and he found it difficult to answer Vardiemar's question.

"Your Majesty, I come to you for sanctuary from my own people. My own Lord Chamberlain, Fangdom Creep, has plotted against me. Gor lummy, he's turned out to be a right one! Creep has robbed me of my realm and my dignity! He has destroyed the trust I placed in him and misused his power to displace me from my own throne, in fact, 'e's attempted to do away with me altogether!"

"That's no excuse, Sir King! Do not unload thy own desertion of Kingly duties onto your Chamberlain. A feckless King who does not wield his power is always overthrown by another who *will* use that power!"

"I didn't come 'ere to be lectured on kingly duties, Dwarf!" exploded Mumbeldok. Borryn Cobalt, not being able to take this insolence from the Dondymarian King, started toward the steps, with a determined expression on his face, but the Chancellor stopped him with a hand on his arm and a shake of his head.

"Watch your tongue, Sir King; remember you are a rabbit amongst wolves!" King Vardiemar continued. "Why did you come to me and not to your allies in the North?"

King Mumbeldok stuck out his bottom lip petulantly, quietly sulking. He wasn't used to being questioned so, and especially not by Dwarves. In the space left by his silence, Colour-Sergeant Nagg stepped forward and saluted King Vardiemar.

"MAY I BE ALLOWED TO SPEAK HON BE'HALF HOF 'IS ROYAL SIRENESS?" Nagg bellowed, taking off his hat, his voice echoing harshly around the stonewalls of the Hall.

King Vardiemar nodded his approval.

"PLEASE EXCUSE ME ROYAL SIRENESS FOR 'IS ILL MOOD. WE 'AVE 'AD A LONG HAND TIRING JOURNEY FROM DONDYMARIA, YA ROYAL KINGSHIP. WE CAME 'ERE HAS WE 'AD NAHWHERE ELSE TO GO."

Nagg shifted uncomfortably throughout all of this; he wasn't used to addressing his ancestral enemies in such polite terms. He fumbled with his hat as he addressed the court.

"WE DID INDEED TRAVEL TO THE NORF, BUT YORGRINN IS NAHLONGER ME ROYAL SIRENESSIES ALLY. 'E HAS TURNED 'IS COAT IN FAVOUR HOF CREEP. YORGRINN IS NOW HALSO HAN HENMEY OF ME ROYAL SIRENESS!"

King Vardiemar listened to the Colour-Sergeant with interest; he had great difficulty at first in trying to understand the Dondymarian's coarse accent, but the Colour-Sergeant was so loud of voice that he got his point across to all assembled.

"Yorgrinn the Sly is not called *the sly* for nothing," said Chancellor Silverore."Your King has discovered that he is not to be trusted! But your King can take solace in the fact that, like him, Yorgrinn will also betray Creep in the end!"

King Vardiemar nodded in agreement with his old Chancellor's wise words. Even King Mumbeldok also found himself nodding in agreement.

"THAT WOZ A SHROOD HOBSERVATION HON YA 'CCOUNT ME LORD!"

He gave them a smile, which was not returned by the Dwarves.

"Due to thy foolishness in handling thy realm," said King Vardiemar sternly, pointing at King Mumbeldok, "thou hast caused it to fall into the hands of a ruthless personage that shows all the signs of a tyrant! Creep is preparing to invade Pogglinburg with the help of the Grodium Dwarves. Thus again, as through all Sol-Larris history, the Dondymarians have broken the *age of peace* treaty."

"I never wanted a blooming' war; it was Creep!" Mumbeldok went on the defence, rather petulantly. "Creep was always pushing me to invade *here*, try startin' a war *there*. He bored me to death with his warmongering!" Mumbeldok threw his hand out, in the hope of gaining some pity for his hopeless situation, but he received none.

"It's no excuse; again, thou couldst have stopped it if thou hadst put thy mind to it!"

"IF I 'AD NOT SAVED ME ROYAL SIRENESS FROM THE ROYAL REMOVER, CREEP WOULD 'AVE AD 'IS SIRENESS DONE IN! MAYBE ME ROYAL SIRENESS DID 'ANDLE THE REALM A BIT LACKADAISICLE LIKE, BUT IF YA 'ELP 'IM GET BACK 'IS THRONE, 'E CAN MAKE A CHANGE FOR THE BETTER IN DONDYMARIA," said Nagg in defence of his King.

"He has a point there," said Chancellor Silverore to King Vardiemar.

King Vardiemar stroked his beard while he considered the matter. "Did you know that Creep ordered the Grodium Dwarves to poison Queen Grizzelda?"

"Blow me down and hit me over the head with a fish fork!" exclaimed King Mumbeldok, shaking his head. "No, I did not!"

"What do you know of the tunnel that Creep has ordered excavated from Grodium City?"

"What tunnel's that then?" replied King Mumbeldok with bewilderment and shrugging his shoulders.

"Thou hast indeed lost control of thy Kingdom!" said King Vardiemar coldly. He turned to Queen Ellgah and Chancellor Silverore and asked them to the throne, and the three of them went over to the throne for a discussion about the Dondymarians.

After a few minutes they returned and King Vardiemar spoke his decision. "I have decided to grant both thee and thy Colour-Sergeant sanctuary in my realm. Thou wilt not be harmed and wilt be kept safe whilst under my patronage. Thou, Highness, shalt be kept as befits thy royal station, but for thine own safety thou and thy Colour-Sergeant will both be locked into the chamber made available to thee."

King Mumbeldok was smiling up until the part where King Vardiemar spoke of being locked up, and then his face fell. He was about to say something, but a hand from Nagg restrained him from doing so.

"They hare fair terms, considering hour past footing wiv the Dwarves, ya Royal Sireness," whispered Nagg out the corner of his mouth. "Creep wouldn't hof given the Dwarves such good terms if the boot woz hon the hother foot!"

"I suppose you're right, Colour-Sergeant," replied King Mumbeldok in a deep sulk.

"Guards, take the King and the Colour-Sergeant to their quarters in the south-west corridor," ordered Chancellor Silverore. The guards nodded and escorted their charges from the Great Hall, with many murmurings from the Dwarvish Captains.

The Chancellor thumped his staff to the ground for silence.

"This matter should not be spoken of outside of this Hall. You will all take an oath to Thremgould that you will not speak of it to the massed ranks of the army," said the Chancellor, holding up a hand. "Swear the oath of Thremgould!"

"WE SWEAR BY THREMGOULD, FATHER OF THE DWARVES, THAT WE, THE KING'S LOYAL CAPTAINS, WILL SAY NOTHING OF THE EVENTS THAT UNFOLD IN THIS HALL!" came the massed reply of the Army Captains.

"Excellent!" smiled the Chancellor.

"The King was to address you, but now this matter needs the King's undivided attention. So, you will assemble here later today for the King's address. You are dismissed!" said Marshal-General Cavernhollow, and the captains began to withdraw from the Great Hall, leaving the King and Queen with their councillors.

★ ★ ★ ★ ★

Balferzaar the Black hurried along the corridor of the Royal Pogglin Palace; very soon he arrived at the audience chamber and entered. Inside, Grand King Pooley sat on the throne. Either side of him stood Chancellor Dore and Royal Secretary Sir Grunther-Pulpit. Before the throne stood Field Marshal Mandergast and Wing Commander Wingnut. The King returned his attention to Ginger Wingnut.

"Now tell Balferzaar what you saw this morning, Wing Commander."

"Thank you, Your Majesty," he said in his clipped tones and bowed. He continued, "While out on patrol I did spy the Dondymarian royal coach traversing the land beyond The Copper Mountain. It was steaming along, at full speed, I might add, and towards The Copper Wood and the realm of Dwarveshire. Something damn fishy going on me thought, so I aborted the patrol and came back to report. So, what do you make of that, eh, what?"

Balferzaar considered for a moment, "It is the first time I have known Mumbeldok to have crossed the borders of Dondymaria, so it is surprising that he has chosen to have done so now! Perhaps it would be wise to send for Sir Gilliethrum, Your Majesty. He may have received a report from Dwarveshire and can let us know what this all means?"

Grand King Pooley nodded in agreement with the aged Wizard and sent the Royal Secretary to fetch Sir Gilliethrum Anvilhammer.

★ ★ ★ ★ ★

Artimus was covered in grease and grime; he had finished cleaning the crank box and reinstalled it back into place. He crawled out from under the flying machine and wiped down his face on his handkerchief.

"That's all I can do, my friends. I've completely stripped down the crank box and cleaned out all the sand, the blasted stuff!"

His two friends patted him on the back and Zontahl smiled with relief, as he had thought his dream of getting to Pogglinburg had been dashed!

"Now if you can give me a hand with getting the brass plate back into place, we can be off!" he smiled over his pince-nez, with his fingers firmly crossed behind his back.

★ ★ ★ ★ ★

Sir Gilliethrum Anvilhammer now stood before the throne of Grand King Pooley. "Aye, it is true that King Mumbeldok II and his Colour-Sergeant arrived in Dwarveshire early this morning. They have asked protection and sanctuary from His Highness, King Vardiemar. King Mumbeldok was going to be assassinated on the order of his Lord Chamberlain, Fangdom Creep. The plans would have been carried out if it were not for the vigilance of one Colour-Sergeant Nagg, who had the wits to save his King from the treachery of Creep. Nagg belies the eye, as he looks as though he has not the brains to open a door, let alone foil an attempt on his King's life!"

"Has he given you any information as to how and when the plans for the invasion will happen?" asked Balferzaar the Black.

"I am sorry to say that King Mumbeldok is completely ignorant on matters when it comes to the affairs of state and what is going on in his realm!" replied the Dwarf. "All I can tell you is that he tried to seek help from Yorgrinn the Sly, but he turned Mumbeldok away. Yorgrinn is now in the pay of Creep, and there is strong evidence that Yorgrinn is planning to attack Pogglinburg via the Gromm Bridge."

"Yes, we know all this, Sir Gilliethrum. We discussed it at the council meeting when Mr Kloons first discovered the news. Can you not add anything to that?" enquired Grand King Pooley.

"Sadly no, Your Majesty. I can only advise that you be prepared, as the invasion could start at any time. King Vardiemar has Dwarveshire on a war footing, and he has most of the army stationed at the eastern gate of the realm."

"Please send my thanks to His Highness, King Vardiemar, for standing fast on our treaty of old. But we have the defences left to us by Dunbruan the Great, which Balferzaar the Black has assured me is infallible. I hope that your armies will not have to move out to our defence," King Pooley replied to the Ambassador.

★ ★ ★ ★ ★

"That's that! Now let's see if the little beauty starts for us!" Artimus said, more to himself than anybody else. Lucian and Sir Septimus wound the mechanism once more with the brass key while Artimus climbed up into the cockpit followed by Zontahl. After they had finished winding and stowing away the key, Lucian and Sir Septimus joined the others in the cockpit.

"Here goes, fingers crossed!" said Artimus as he started up the machine. With a whirr, the great rotary blades began to turn and soon became a blur. With a cheer from his companions, Artimus let go of the brake and the flying machine shot into the air and started flying east.

Whistlecraft's flying machine sped towards Pogglinburg; Artimus was at the controls of the machine, and Sir Septimus sat next to him. Lucian stood next to Zontahl, who was looking out of the back windows in amazement as the land rolled by beneath them. It was a little cramped with the addition of the cat, but the atmosphere inside it was not one of happiness or success. In fact, all were full of melancholy as the crew slowly began to come to terms with the unbearable fact that they had failed in their quest to get back in time. They knew that with the constant attacks and interruptions on their journey, and now this last unexpected turn of events with the clockwork mechanism, their expedition had taken them beyond the Queen's lifeline.

"I have set course for Pogglinburg via the direct route through the Copper Wood; we should be arriving in Pogglin Town in four hours. We'll only need to stop once to rewind the mechanism," said Artimus gloomily.

★ ★ ★ ★ ★

King Pooley sat by his Queen's bed, holding her hand as he mopped her face with a damp cloth. He was alone in the room as his advisers were holding another council meeting. As he mopped the Queen's brow, his thoughts turned westward and to Lucian and his party.

"Come soon," he prayed. "Come soon, or it will be too late for my beloved Grizzelda!" Quietly, he began to sob.

★ ★ ★ ★ ★

"Time to land and rewind!" Artimus announced, and started to take the flying machine down to land on the edge of the Grey Waste. They landed near the banks of The Green River, which was the western most border of Dwarveshire.

Lucian, Zontahl and Sir Septimus disembarked down the steps and pulled out the brass key and placed it into the winder and started to wind up the mechanism. Zontahl stretched his legs and looked across the babbling river to the trees of the Green Woods beyond. He sniffed the sweet air and was thrilled by all the wonderful new scents that he could smell, very much different to the realm of Empraktos-Larris which mainly smelt of sulphur and the stench of Lake Naar. Yes, he knew he was going to enjoy this land of Sol-Larris very much.

Artimus came to the door of the Flying Machine and checked his pocket watch. "We shall be home in another fifty to seventy minutes!"

"I can hardly bear the thought of returning home after failing in our duty," Sir Septimus said sadly.

"Come now, Sir Septimus, we have done everything we possibly could and, to a point, have been successful. We have the fruit we went for, we met and fought dangers we never expected to, and we are lucky to be alive. It was always going to be an extremely tight timeline to meet," said Lucian to his friend. He tried to uplift his companions, but he was hiding his own feelings of desolation.

They called Zontahl, who was drinking the clear water of the river, and he bounded back and up into the machine. The two Pogglins followed him, and Lucian closed the door behind him. Artimus checked that everything was locked down and then pulled on the control stick. The rotary blades began to turn, and shortly they again took to the air, speeding towards their homeland.

★ ★ ★ ★ ★

"When are you going to let me out of here?" called the Shadow to his guard.

"Keep the noise down in there!" came the reply.

The Shadow kicked the door and then went huffily over to the bed and sat down.

"How long have I been in this cell?" he thought to himself. The last thing he could remember was reporting to Lord Creep about the goings-on in Pogglinburg on the 5th July. "Next thing I remembers is I'm in this cell!" He rubbed his nose through his black mask. "I'm going to have to use all my cunning if I am to get out of here. Now what clever scheme can I come up with?"

With that, he started to scribble some notes down in his diary.

★ ★ ★ ★ ★

Whistlecraft's Flying Machine flew over the Copper Wood on course for Pogglin Town. Below, the trees surrounded a massive pyramid-like object of white, iridescent marble capped in gold at its zenith. Zontahl looked at the building in wonder. "What is that? I have never seen the like of it before!"

"That is the tomb of Dunbruan," replied Lucian.

"He must have been a great Pogglin indeed, to warrant such a tomb!"

"Dunbruan the Great was the saviour of Pogglinburg, Zontahl; he defeated the whole of the Dondymarian Army in the invasion of 51 AD by throwing up a great mountain range before them!" Artimus nodded towards the purple mountains in front of them. "Those there are the mountains that Dunbruan the Great conjured up before the Dondymarians; Dunbruan's Wall!"

Zontahl marvelled at the mountain range, and at the building that was coming into view.

They were soon flying over the Aerodrome of the Pogglin Flying Corps, and Pogglin Town was beyond in all its splendour. Zontahl was wide-eyed with the beauty of the Pogglin architecture, the Royal Palace, the Black Tower and the Reeveburg's House. Pogglin Town was nothing like the dark, cramped, ugly buildings of Naarunkesh.

"What makes me wonder is why the Hobbdraks haven't been sent out to look for us?" said Sir Septimus, looking back at the Pogglin aerodrome.

"A good question, Sir Septimus. I would have thought they would be actively looking for us, seeing as we have failed in our mission and thinking us lost or worse," said Artimus, speaking aloud.

Then they saw that Pogglin Town was deserted of all people. The streets were quite empty. "They must have gone into two weeks of mourning," groaned Sir Septimus unhappily.

"There would have been people to meet us if we'd been successful," said Lucian glumly, feeling sick to the stomach.

Artimus brought the machine into land next to the Royal Palace. He landed the craft on the grass-covered ground between the old city wall and the Frog and Bottle Inn, since it was nearer the Palace than Bandstand Green. They disembarked from the Flying Machine, and Artimus locked the cockpit door behind him.

"What by Obahdire Thrasskin's beard is going on? Where on Sol-Larris is everybody? Exclaimed Sir Septimus.

"I don't know?" replied Artimus.

"There isn't even a Guard posted outside of the Royal Palace!" Lucian observed, as they made their way to the Palace gate. They felt sick with desolation at their failure to save the Queen's life, as they entered the court yard of the Palace. They could hardly bear to face the King, but face him they knew they must. They looked up when they heard the sound of Sergeant-Major Trumpp drilling his soldiers.

Trumpp stopped with surprise when he saw Lucian and his Party. "They are back!" bellowed the Sergeant-Major, and quickly ordered Private Schnozzle to go fetch Sir Grunther-Pulpit at once.

Balferzaar came out into the courtyard, as he had seen the Flying Machine land, and quickly made his way over to Lucian. "Lucian my boy, where have you been?"

Lucian could hardly look the old Wizard in the eye. "I am sorry my Lord, we have failed you!" was all he could say, as he and his friends bowed their heads in sorrow.

"What?" exclaimed the old Wizard, "Then there was no Moogem Tree, no fruit?"

Lucian looked puzzled. "Er, yes my Lord, but we failed in our duty to get back in time to save the Queen's life."

Now Balferzaar looked puzzled. "I don't understand; you have the fruit?"

"Yes, my Lord. We have it here."

"Well don't dawdle, boy! Quick! Follow me!" the old Wizard called, as he turned and hurried back into the Palace.

"But we are too late! According to my calculations, this is the afternoon of the 17th July!" Artimus said, as they chased after Balferzaar.

"But your calculations are wrong, my dear Artimus! Today is the afternoon of the 15th July!"

Lucian and his friends couldn't believe their ears as they hurriedly went after Balferzaar who was moving very quickly for a Pogglin of his age.

"How can this be?" asked Lucian, and Artimus added, "But my calculations couldn't have been that much out!"

"Never mind about all that my friends, just follow me as quickly as you can!" called the old Wizard.

★ ★ ★ ★ ★

King Pooley was sat by his Queen's bed, holding her hand as Sir Cecil Grunther-Pulpit hurried into the chamber. He was smiling from ear to ear!

"Excellent news, Your Majesty, Lucian and party have just arrived! They are coming with Balferzaar to administer the antidote to her Majesty the Queen!"

"That is wonderful, wonderful news, Sir Cecil," said the King, a sparkle of life returning to his eyes. He leaned over to the Queen. "Do you hear, my dearest? You will soon be back with us again!"

The Chamber door opened and Chancellor Dore entered. "Your Majesty: Balferzaar the Black, Sir Septimus Pulpit, Mr Lucian Snuzz, Mr Artimus Whistlecraft and a cat are without the door, and all crave audience with your Royal Majesty."

"There is no time for standing on ceremony now, Chancellor Dore! Let them in, quick!" replied the King with exasperation.

The old Wizard, the three Pogglins and Zontahl entered the chamber before Chancellor Dore could ask them to enter, and Lucian, Sir Septimus and Artimus bowed deeply to their King. Grand King Pooley was a little taken aback by the appearance of a cat in the Queen's bedchamber, but then smiled a warm greeting.

"You have done us a great service, my friends. Please, there is no need to stand on ceremony," replied the King, and the Pogglins raised themselves at his bidding. Lucian took from his pouch the glass jar containing the Moogem Fruit, which glowed intensely (even in daylight) with its amber light.

"Why, it shines just like the Amber Stone!" exclaimed the old Wizard.

A vial of the water from the Lake of Wonders followed this, and he offered them to Balferzaar to administer to Queen Grizzelda. The old Wizard smiled and shook his head.

"No, Lucian. You journeyed to the land of the Moogem Tree to get the antidote; you may have the honour of administering it to the Queen."

Lucian looked a little shocked, and then smiled at his mentor and nodded. "Thank you."

The King moved aside and let Lucian sit by the Queen. He took his quill-knife from his waist-jacket and then opened the jar and removed the Moogem Fruit, which was fresh as the day it was picked. He then cut a wedge from the fruit; it dripped with juice as the knife pierced the skin.

"That's good it is still very fresh!" he thought to himself as he cut a small piece from the wedge. With help from the King, he sat the Queen up in bed and dropped the little piece of fruit into the Queen's mouth.

He massaged her throat, to help her swallow. Her eyes flickered, and she coughed a little as the piece of fruit slid down. "By the stars above and the Sun internal, let the fruit release it secrets," he said quietly. Quickly Lucian cut another piece and carried out the same procedure, and then again. With each piece of fruit, the Queen ate, the colour began to return to her cheeks and Lucian could feel the warmth returning to her body. He continued to feed the rest of the wedge of fruit to Queen Grizzelda and then he cradled her head in his arm while he got her to drink the vial of water from the lake. While he did so he murmured words of magic to help the properties of the water work faster. The Queen's breathing had returned to normal by the time he had got her to drink the contents of the vial. He laid her gently back on the pillows and waited.

The Queen's body seemed to emit an amber glow as the colour gradually returned to her face and hair. The fruit and the water were revitalising and healing those areas of her body that had been damaged by the poison.

Presently Queen Grizzelda's eyes flickered open for the first time in eleven days, and they were as bright and as blue as they were before the poisoning. She smiled as everyone gave an exclamation of joy, and she sat up in bed as the King rushed to her side and they embraced. Tears of joy welled in the King's eyes, and he kissed her tenderly on the cheek.

"I have been so worried! I thought I had lost you forever my love."

The King then turned to Lucian, Sir Septimus and Artimus. "You three have given back to me my Queen, a service for which I can never repay you; but I can show my gratitude!"

Everyone in the room applauded the three Pogglins as they smiled and bowed back their thanks. "As from today, Lucian, you will no longer be Mr Lucian Marius Snuzz, but *Sir* Lucian!" continued Grand King Pooley as the applause stopped.

Lucian gasped in shock and went very red with embarrassment at the King's announcement. The King then bestowed a Lordship on Sir Septimus, a knighthood on Artimus and the Medal of Honour for the cat!

"His name is Zontahl, Your Majesty, and if it were not for his help we would not be standing here today," said Lucian.

"Yes, for Zontahl, who has of been of great service and courage to us all!" The King said happily. "There will be a banquet this evening in your honour, my friends, and as of today the 15th of July will be forever known as The Return of the Questing Three! Tonight, my friends the whole of Pogglinburg will honour you, and then I shall bestow on you your rewards. The celebrations will take place after the six o'clock skiffle; Chancellor Dore, will you see to the arrangements?"

As the Chancellor left the chamber, Lucian suggested that they should withdraw and let the Queen rest. He left the Moogem Fruit in the jar and told Queen Grizzelda to eat the rest of it as soon as possible, more for his own peace of mind than anything else!

★ ★ ★ ★ ★

"I still cannot believe it's the 15th July," Artimus mused. "How did I make such an error in my calculations?"

"Yes, you are usually spot on with things like that," nodded Sir Septimus in agreement.

"Maybe time runs slower in Empraktos-Larris than it does in Sol-Larris?

And you were not quite feeling your best, either."

Artimus thought on this for a moment.

"Yes, I think you could be onto something there, Sir Septimus. Perhaps, because Empraktos-Larris is at the centre of the Earth, the days are shorter; say, only ten to fifteen hours long?"

"Possible, indeed very possible," agreed Sir Septimus and turned to Zontahl. "Are your days shorter in hours, old chap?"

Zontahl didn't answer; he was too engrossed by the beauty of the Royal Palace. "Hmm?" he said, turning to face the Pogglin.

"Are your days shorter in hours, old chap?" repeated Sir Septimus.

"We cats are only aware of the time when we are hungry; we have little need for timekeeping. Only the Subterranians keep time in Empraktos-Larris, as do the Fungiglooks. I believe they base their time scale on the Subterranian scale of time measurement," replied the Cat.

"Which is?" asked Sir Septimus eagerly, a little exasperated by Zontahl's long-winded reply.

"I understand that they have a time scale of twelve hours to the day." smiled the Cat.

"That's it!" replied Artimus excitedly, "That how I made the error! When Fengook said we had slept the day away, I just assumed he meant a twenty-four-hour day like ours!"

"Well, that's solved that little mystery," laughed Lucian, "Thank goodness we didn't slow down! We could have easily done so, after thinking we were out of time, and therefore there was no point in rushing back!"

★ ★ ★ ★ ★

Now fully clothed, and red-eyed with lack of sleep, Lord Creep sat at his desk waiting for news. There was a knock at his chamber door.

"Enter!" he roared huskily.

General Sidok entered his face in a fixed frown – an expression that Creep read as the portent of bad news! "What is it now?" he asked the temper showing in his voice.

"The Shadow has escaped!"

"WHAT!"

"I sent Major Jumpp to execute him as you ordered. He had vanished without a trace and we can only assume he's headed back to Pogglinburg?" replied the General, sitting down.

This was too much for Creep. "How dare you sit down without me ordering you to be seated? Get up! You will not be stopping *that* long!" he roared, thumping the table.

The General grumpily got to his feet.

"How did an imbecile like the Shadow escape your clutches? Why do idiots surround me! Why does nothing go right this day?" Creep raged, shaking his fists in the air.

"How ridiculous you look!" smirked the General to himself. Aloud, he remarked, "Remember, Lord Chamberlain, that the King is not dead, and you are not yet the leader of this country! I should try to nurture your friendships, if I were you. You understand my meaning? One leader can be as easily disposed of as another!"

The General's implications hit their target, and he attempted a smile. "Yes, quite General, forgive me," he said. "Please, do sit down," and he gestured to the chair. The General shook his head.

"Not on this occasion, Lord Chamberlain. I am not in the mood for talking about the future of Dondymaria!"

Creep flushed purple at the General's snub, and then gave him a hideous yellow smile. "I quite understand, General. You must be very busy. So, don't let me detain you on that account!"

The General gave Creep a curt nod and stomped out of the room, slamming the door behind him. Creep thumped the desk with suppressed rage! He drummed his fingers on the desk, and his long pointed black nails clacked noisily on the wooden surface.

The Shadow had escaped and was probably halfway back to Pogglinburg, if not there already. "Now what would I do if the chap returned who I suspected of poisoning my wife? I would have him killed!" he answered himself. "Therefore, the stupid Pogglins would do the opposite to any Dondymarian logical reasoning, so King Pooley will not kill the Shadow when he returns to Pogglinburg. Curse those Pogglins for their high-standing morals!" And he thumped the desk again!

He growled to himself in annoyance, then marched over to the patched-up window and looked for any signs of a Gweeley Bird, but saw none on the horizon. He did, however, observe that the Pogglins Air Corp had all three of their Hobbdraks out on Patrol.

"That's strange; they never put up a patrol at this time of day." He checked his watch.

"Three o'clock – now that is strange! What's going on over there beyond Dunbruan's Wall?" He rubbed his chin, deep in thought thinking of all the devious things that could be going on. He gave up pondering the matter, knowing that nothing devious would actually be going on in Pogglinburg! Was seeing the three Hobbdraks on an unscheduled flight an ill omen? What more could go wrong so early on in his plans for the conquest of the world?

He went over to the refreshment table and poured himself a drink and then for something to occupy himself he went into his bedchamber to feed the gold fish.

★ ★ ★ ★ ★

Shrigg was sitting on his nest of twigs, waiting for one of his birds to report. Since his meeting with Yorgrinn the Sly, he was beginning to wonder if being a double-dealer was such a good thing after all, but then he thought of all the meat Yorgrinn had fed him and of all the corpses he would be feeding on after the battle, and he made up his mind that it was a very good thing indeed! He cackled to himself as one of his birds finally flew into the roost.

"What is it?" asked Shrigg.

"The three Pogglins have returned in that strange contraption, my Lord. Word is they have brought an antidote to save Queen Grizzelda's life!" replied his subordinate.

"Hmm, neither Yorgrinn nor Creep is going to be pleased with this news!" said Shrigg, shifting uneasily on his nest. "I've also got to tell Yorgrinn that Mumbeldok has made it to Dwarveshire! Are you sure the Pogglin Queen is saved?"

"It must be true, my Lord, because the school bell is ringing on a day when there is no school. And they are also playing the Der-Werga-Werga machine on Bandstand Green!"

Shrigg winced at the mention of the Der-Werga-Werga machine and then grimaced.

"That thing puts my beak on edge! It sounds like a banshee being throttled!"

He got out of his nest and stretched his wings and legs. "Right, I'm off to tell that pig Yorgrinn the news! Give me ten minutes, and then you leave and give that fat Oaf the news in Dondymaria!"

The Gweeley Bird nodded and watched Shrigg take to the air in the direction of the Grodium Mountain.

★ ★ ★ ★ ★

Outside the Palace gates stood Lucian and his friends. The crowds were just dispersing, and after the drama of the past few hours the four of them were now feeling very tired.

"Well, I'm off home for a good scrub and some sleep! I will see you, my good Sirs, later!" Sir Septimus winked, and headed off for Pulpit Manor on the hill.

"See you later, *me Lord*!" shouted Artimus, laughing. He stretched and scratched his head. "I'll see you later Lucian sorry, *Sir* Lucian. I too need a nice bath and some sleep!"

Lucian winced at the *Sir* and blushed. "It's so good to see you smiling again, Artimus," he said to himself. He returned Artimus' wave and then turned his attention to Zontahl.

"Well, Zontahl, we have a long walk ahead of us to Hill Square or we could wait for the Gronk coach. What would you like to do?"

"I should like to walk my friend, to take in the beauty of your homeland, but as I know we are pressed for time, then we'll go by *Gronk coach*?" His pronunciation implied that he didn't fully understand. Lucian smiled and explained exactly what a Gronk and a coach were to the cat.

Suddenly a pair of hands appeared from behind Lucian and covered his eyes!

The intruder alarmed Zontahl, who was about to pounce when he saw Lucian smile broadly and then laugh.

"Miss Dore, you really shouldn't creep up on somebody after they have just returned from an exhausting and perilous adventure, in a land where one must forever watch one's back!"

Sara Dore looked more beautiful than ever.

He turned and smiled; she looked more beautiful than ever! Her pretty face was framed by her raven-coloured hair, and her large eyes sparkled with the joy of his return. They embraced and she kissed him on the cheek.

"I like your beard; you should keep it. And how did you know it was me?" she asked with a mischievous smile.

"Well, I didn't think it was your father!" he replied, laughing, and she giggled with delight. Remembering his manners, Lucian introduced Zontahl to Miss Sara Dore; she curtsied and shook the cat's paw in greeting

"I have seen many wondrous and beautiful things since my arrival here in Sol-Larris, Miss Dore, but you are by far the prettiest jewel I have yet seen!" purred the cat.

"Oh, thank you," she replied, blushing.

"When I saw the love-light in your eyes, I knew the world had nought but joy for me!" said Lucian quietly.

"I too felt the same, Lucian," she smiled.

"Father has told me the wonderful news of your knighthood, Lucian. He is very pleased and proud of you!"

"Proud of me?" he chuckled, "Who would have thought it, Chancellor Sir Amius Dore proud of me; a common Pogglin!"

She playfully slapped his chest, "You know very well my father likes and respects you, Lucian!"

"Especially now he thinks I'm getting a knighthood, eh?" raising an eyebrow.

"Tut, why Lucian Snuzz! There's no *thinks* about it, you're getting knighted this evening!"

"Sir Lucian Snuzz doesn't sit on my shoulder's too well Sara. After all, it wasn't just my doing that saved Queen Grizzelda; I wouldn't have got to Empraktos-Larris at all if it were not for Artimus."

"And he is being rewarded too," she said in reply, arching an eyebrow.

"That is true, but my contribution to the quest was only a part. Once we got to Empraktos-Larris we would have not survived had it not been for the selfless sacrifice of the Fungiglooks and Zontahl's scouts. Now do you see, Sara, why I feel uncomfortable with this honour? I, Sir Septimus and Artimus are the lucky ones who came back. There are Fungiglooks and a cat who will not be returning home: the only reward to their relatives will be the grief of their loss. We must remember that they died for us to succeed in saving Queen Grizzelda, this was a person they didn't even know, yet they still helped us and suffered dreadful consequences. I cannot and will not forget them; I will not be accepting the knighthood."

Sara Dore looked at him, shaking her head, and then smiled broadly! "Lucian Snuzz you really are a unique and upstanding Pogglin!" She hugged him warmly, "And that's why I love you so! I loved you before and I love you even more for refusing it. My Mr Snuzz does not need such trinkets such as a knighthood to make him a better Pogglin!"

They embraced again and Lucian kissed her, and Sara returned his kiss.

"But I don't know what my father's going to say!" and they both burst out laughing. "I think you two had better be making a move back to Hill Square; time is running short, and you have to be back for the six o'clock skittle." She waved them goodbye and she turned and went back into the Palace.

"It's strange, isn't Lucian," said Zontahl as they crossed Pooley 1ˢᵗ Square."How, since we met, time has always been a factor!"

"Indeed!" nodded Lucian in agreement with his friend. They made their way to the Gronk stop and waited.

★ ★ ★ ★ ★

Gorgrinn entered the throne room of the Grodium Mountain, with Shrigg perched on his arm. Yorgrinn was sitting on his throne talking to Ikbold the Bitter when they entered.

"What news, Shrigg? Tell me!" He demanded as he started to stroke his massive black moustache.

"The news is not good," replied Shrigg. "Mumbeldok made is safely through to Dwarveshire. I am told Vardiemar has granted him sanctuary!"

Yorgrinn's jet eyes narrowed at the news, and he slowly stroked his moustache, while inwardly his anger mounted. The only outward sign he gave was gripping the handle of his Axe more tightly."Pray continue!" he murmured in his thick Grodium accent.

"Creep's plan to poison the Pogglin Queen has failed, and the Pogglins are celebrating the Queen's recovery!"

"WHAT!" Yorgrinn roared, no longer able to contain his rage, and threw his axe at the Gweeley bird! It whizzed past Shrigg's head, just missing it by a couple of inches and smashed into the door of the chamber. Splinters flew into the air in a cloud of shattered wood. "GUARD!" shrieked Yorgrinn, turning a vivid shade of red.

The door hurriedly opened and the guard entered; "My Lord?"

"GET THAT STINKING BIRD OUT OF HERE!"

Gorgrinn handed a terrified Shrigg (thinking his end was nigh) over to the Guard, and hurriedly left the room with the Gweeley Bird.

"Ikbold, fetch my axe!" he commanded the diminutive little Dwarf.

"Yes Yorgrinn!" replied Ikbold.

"How far now has the tunnel to go under Dunbruan's Wall?" Yorgrinn asked them.

"They have about six feet to go," replied Gorgrinn.

"Then get them out and onto Ikbold's excavation gangs!"

Gorgrinn nodded, "And what of the invasion of Pogglinburg, Brother?"

"Creep can fight his own wars! It is his fault Mumbeldok escaped; it is his fault my Dwarf got captured! The Brown Mountain knows we are going to attack via Gromm Bridge. Well, there IS GOING TO BE NO ATTACK! LET'S SEE HOW CREEP FARES WITHOUT MY HELP!" He thumped his fist down on the arm of his throne.

★ ★ ★ ★ ★

Lucian and Zontahl descended from the Gronk Coach and walked across Hill Square to number 2. Number 2 was a tall, three-story town house with sash windows either side of the front door.

Zontahl was impressed. "Very beautiful," he commented as they passed through the gate and up to the path to the front door. Lucian took out his key and unlocked the door. He pushed it open for Zontahl.

"Please treat my home as your home," he said to Zontahl with a smile as the cat passed him and entered the house. Within was a large, oblong hallway and there were two double doors, one either side of the hall. Lucian hung up his hat and placed his staff in the stand by the front door. He opened the left-hand side door; "This is the sitting room," he said to Zontahl, and moving over to the other side of the hall, Lucian opened the second set of doors. "And this is my study; probably the most used room in the house!"

Zontahl padded into the study, his eyes wide with the glory of the decor. To Zontahl's right was a magnificent fireplace in the shape of a Pogglin House, the doorway being the fire grate with windows to either side. Above the fire grate was carved two Pogglin figures. They were brightly painted like the rest of the fireplace. Under the mantelpiece were exquisite ceramic tiles that mimicked those going around the Black Tower. On top of the mantelpiece was a superb clock, crafted by Artimus Whistlecraft, and on the wall above there was a portrait of Sara Dore. It was an excellent likeness, and Zontahl did not need to ask whom it depicted. The rest of the room was painted bright yellow, with wooden panelling that stretched halfway up the wall, and this was inlaid with ceramic tiles of orange, blue and green. The floor was carpeted in a bluebird colour.

In front of the fire was a large circular rug. "A gift woven by the Brown Mountain Dwarves," said Lucian when asked. Hanging to the left of the fireplace was a great double-headed battle-axe. It was wrought in the purest gold and silver; on top of its hilt was an Anvil. The handle was made of ebony and inlaid with gold and silver thread. The hilt was solid gold and encrusted with the whitest diamonds to be found in the Brown Mountain.

"That too was a gift from the Brown Mountain, from a dear friend of mine, Chancellor Silverore."

To the left of the door was another portrait of an old Pogglin with spectacles, Lucian saw the cat looking at the portrait quizzically.

"My Uncle, Dr Erazmus Snuzz," he said. There was a desk with a high-backed, ornately carved wooden chair opposite.

At the other end of the room was a great L-shaped bookcase, filled with many books, and it ran along the whole wall opposite the study entrance, up to the large window. They then moved out into the hall again and to the door by the stairs, it was the Kitchen. Lucian then showed his guest around upstairs: master bedroom, guest bedroom and bathroom. The third floor was one large room which contain a telescope and a chair. "I like to look at the stars when I have the spare time to do so," he said to the cat with a smile.

"So that's my home, Zontahl. Do make yourself at home, I want you to enjoy your stay here," smiled the Pogglin.

"Now, I am going to have a nice bath. So, if you want to get some sleep whilst I bathe, I won't disturb you and I'll call you when it's time to leave for town."

He left Zontahl on the third floor and went down stairs and into the bathroom and started running a bath. Zontahl padded downstairs to the ground floor and entered the study: he liked the welcoming feel of the room, and its welcoming air reminded him greatly of his host. He walked over to the circular rug, and curled up and went instantly to sleep.

★ ★ ★ ★ ★

Lord Creep watched the Gweeley Bird flying away, returning to the Gweeley Birds roost in the Blendaraak Mountains. His face burned red, and he shut the window casement with a crash as yet another pane of glass splintered to the courtyard below. He stomped across the room and opened the door. "PEATREA! COME HERE AT ONCE!"

That done, he crossed to the refreshments table, poured a large drink and swallowed it down in one. He was pouring another drink when Peatrea the Jester hurried into the room, the bells on his hat jingling.

"Yes, Lord Creep?" asked the royal jester.

"Is Gittoid back from Grodium City?"

"Sir Kyaphaas Gittoid and Captain Gunkfopp are still inspecting the tunnel that is being excavated by the Grodium Dwarves," came the reply.

"They are taking their time in reporting back!" snapped Creep, and he moved over to his desk and flopped in the chair. "Bad news Peatrea. Mumbeldok has escaped and has handed himself over to the Brown Mountain Dwarves!"

The jester's bells jingled as he moved his head with dismay.

"Yes, it's sickening, isn't it?" grumbled Creep into his glass.

"Who would ever have thought Vardiemar III would have granted the fool sanctuary!"

Suddenly Creep leapt to his feet and rushed to his bedchamber and flung open the door. "KEEP IT DOWN IN THERE!" he bawled, scarlet-faced, then slammed the door shut. He stomped back to his desk, his hairpiece all askew. "Damn Goldfish!"

Peatrea was rather alarmed by Creep's surreal behaviour, and he leaned forward and looked at him closely with his crossed eyes. "Are you alright, Lord Creep?" he asked in his servile manner.

"Of course, I am not alright! Not only has Mumbeldok escaped me, Peatrea, but I have just also learned from the Gweeley birds that the Pogglins have succeeded in saving the life of their wretched Queen!"

He wheezed at the jester, panting for breath, and then continued with his monologue, "All my best-laid plans have gone awry, everyone and everything has fallen flat at every turn! Yorgrinn the Sly will most probably betray me, having robbed me of my gold I do not know if he will stick to the agreed plan of attacking Pogglinburg via the Gromm Bridge! Without Yorgrinn's attack to draw off the Brown Mountain Dwarves, I cannot launch our surprise attack on the Pogglins from the – AND YOU ASK ME IF I AM ALL RIGHT?"

The jester was trying hard not to laugh in Creep's face because the more he raged, the more that stupid wig moved around his head and finally came to rest in its usual place in such circumstances - over his eyes! Peatrea was saved from the disgrace of laughing in his boss's face by the entrance of the Royal Secretary, Sir Kyaphaas Gittoid.

"Peatrea, get out of here!" said Gittoid. The jester hurried past him, legs akimbo and bells jingling, doing his best to stifle his laughter.

Sir Kyaphaas slammed the door behind him just as the jester broke up into peals of laughter outside in the corridor. Lord Creep was fixed to the desk in the same position as when Gittoid entered, the wig still over his eyes. Slowly, Creep sat down and pushed back the hairpiece, and put his fingers to the bridge of his nose and squeezed hard. Then he coughed and opened his eyes, and smiled at Sir Kyaphaas as if nothing had happened.

"So how goes the tunnel under the Dunbruan's Wall, Sir Kyaphaas? Are the Grodium Dwarves almost through?"

Sir Kyaphaas removed his spectacles to polish them; he was trying not to meet Creep's eyes as he made his report. "I'm afraid not, Lord Creep. The Grodium Dwarves have returned to the Grodium Mountain, on the orders of Ikbold the Bitter. Apparently, there is urgent work to be carried out at shoring up the mines, or some such thing." He continued to polish his spectacles.

Creep leaned forward on the desk and linked his fingers together, "They have definitely gone back to their Mountain?" he said, sounding slightly puzzled.

"Yes," replied Sir Kyaphaas, putting on his spectacles.

"Oh! Right!" Creep replied calmly. "I had better bring you up on the latest reports too," he continued as he moved over to the little table of refreshments. He poured two drinks and returned to the desk, placing a glass in front of the Royal Secretary. "Vardiemar III has Mumbeldok: he has granted him sanctuary! There is not much that we can do about that for the moment." He continued.

"I have just received news from the Gweeley Birds that the Pogglin Queen isn't dead!"

Sir Kyaphaas did an excellent impression of a fish as his mouth flapped open in dismay. Finally, he stuttered, "N-n-not dead? That's impossible! The old bag swallowed enough poison to wipe out half of Sol-Larris!"

"Exactly!" said Creep, throwing his hand out. "Nonetheless, those blasted Pogglin Wizards have managed to save the miserable bint from the grave!" Creep played with his lip as he thought on his next move. Then he banged the desk as he came to a decision. "How far has the tunnel to run before we breakthrough into Pogglinburg?"

"The surveyors say about six or seven feet," replied the Royal Secretary.

"Then we will have the War Robots drill out the rest! I am sure Professor Frumpton-Stone or Doctor Meltabossokk can fit them with some drill type thingy. I am certain Yorgrinn will not attack as agreed. No matter I will deal with him later but the important thing is that we still have the element of surprise on our side. Sir Kyaphaas, go and get the Field Marshal and General Sidok. WE ATTACK AT DAWN!"

★ ★ ★ ★ ★

An ornate clock crafted in the shape of a tower clicked, a door flicked open, and a tiny Pogglin figure in painted pewter came out and struck a bell repeatedly with a little hammer!

Lucian sat up quickly in bed and turned off the alarm clock. He peered at the time: 5.10 PM. He rubbed his eyes; he was having a very strange dream indeed. He shook his head awake and then got up and changed into his clothes of dark and pale blue.

He looked into the guest room to wake Zontahl, and was surprised not to find him there, the bed not having been slept on. So, he closed the door and went downstairs to look for him. Lucian found Zontahl asleep on the rug in the study. He smiled, and then went over to the cat and gently woke him.

Zontahl opened his eyes and smiled, "I was having a wonderful sleep!" He stretched out his legs and arched his back as he yawned, and then got up and stretched again.

"Right," said Lucian to the Cat. "Are you ready?"

Zontahl nodded and they went into the hall, where the Pogglin collected his staff and put on his best black 'mushroom' hat. Leaving the house, they walked down Hill Square to the Golden Hill Road and waited for a Gronk coach.

★ ★ ★ ★ ★

In Pogglin Town no one noticed a bulky figure duck into the shadows. He pressed himself flat against the dark wall, his eyes looking through the holes in his cloth mask. No Pogglins about, he surmised, so he darted over to the next shadow and mingled with it.

The only thought that filled his mind was that he had to get to Grand King Pooley tonight!

★ ★ ★ ★ ★

"Excellent news, Your Majesties! Lucian returned from the land of Empraktos-Larris with the antidote. I am pleased to report that Queen Grizzelda is safe and well," Chancellor Silverore said happily to King Vardiemar. "Tonight, there is to be a banquet of celebration to which Your Majesties are invited."

Queen Ellgah stood next to the King's throne, characteristically straight-backed and with her hands on her hips. Her bright red hair was plaited, and her green eyes sparkled like emeralds. She looked resplendent in her battle dress and black steel chain mail trimmed with copper, silver and gold.

"That's superlative news, Lord Torryn!" she declared, clapping the old chancellor across the back with such force that his hat was knocked to one side. If the Chancellor had any complaints about his duties, his only niggle would be that he wished Queen Ellgah wasn't so heavy-handed whenever she clapped him across the back when complimenting him; he always had to straighten his hat! In fact, Queen Ellgah clapped everyone across the back in agreement; she was a bit of a Valkyrie, and had a voice like thunder. But unlike any other Queen in Sol-Larris, she fought by her husband's side in battle, and for that the old Chancellor loved and respected her deeply. He smiled to himself, and quietly straightened his hat.

"Sadly, we cannot attend this happy celebration, and I would like thee to send our good wishes," said King Vardiemar. "Go and choose something nice from the treasury and have it sent to Queen Grizzelda with our compliments and best wishes."

"This will be done, your Majesty," nodded Chancellor Silverore. "Would you like me to travel to Pogglinburg myself, or have it sent via courier?"

The King thought on this for a moment. "Best have it sent by courier, my Lord Chancellor. During this crisis, I would prefer you to remain here in Dwarveshire."

"I shall see to it right away, Your Majesties." He bowed and descended the steps, walked across the great hall and exited via the main portal.

"Why will you not attend the celebrations, Vardie?" asked the Queen.

"Because of Yorgrinn the Sly! I wouldn't put it past the old fox to attack Dwarveshire while we were away in Pogglinburg. Remember there are three items of interest for Yorgrinn here that he would like to take from me: the

Hammer and Anvil of Thremgould, and the Dwarvish guest that occupies our best cell! Nay lass, we are on a war footing, and will remain so until all is resolved!"

"Yes, you're right as usual my love," she replied and bent down and kissed him.

★ ★ ★ ★ ★

Lucian and Zontahl arrived in Pogglin Town at 5.45 PM, where they were welcomed off the coach by the town folk and where everyone present made a great fuss of Zontahl. Thanking them, they quickly moved on and called at Dr Snuzz's house and Lucian introduced his friend to his aunt and Uncle.

"Could you take Zontahl to see the six o'clock skiffle?" Lucian asked his aunt and Uncle.

"Why are you not going to it yourself?" They enquired of their nephew, who told them there was something that needed his immediate attention in the records Library. He asked Zontahl's forgiveness, that it really was most urgent, and he excused himself leaving his friend in the company of his aunt and Uncle.

Lucian made for the Reeveburg's House, which was difficult as every few steps passers-by chose to stop him and enquire about his travels. Eventually, with many interruptions of "Do excuse me" and "Pardon me, but I must hurry," Lucian closed the door of the records Library behind him.

He breathed deeply and moved over to his usual table, the paper and manuscripts were still where he had left them before his journey. The Pogglin smiled to himself. Thankfully Mr Monkclencher hadn't tidied away after Lucian was called away. He sat down at the desk and started rummaging through the papers. A few minutes later, he found what he was looking for.

"Now where did I see that little inscription in code?" he said aloud to himself. "Ah-ha! There it is!"

On an ancient piece of parchment, scribbled down the length of the page was a coded message. It had taken Lucian two years to crack that code, and it told him of a secret that not even Balferzaar the Black knew. The coded message was directions leading to a secret room which Dunbruan had built centuries before.

It was in this room that Lucian had discovered the Secret Book. He refreshed his memory of the directions, and then tucked the parchment back in the file. Lucian then made his way to the door and out into the corridor. There was nobody around as they were all at the skiffle, so he made his way quietly down the corridor and out into the Square.

He made his way towards the Palace, where much to his surprise, he found Sir Septimus. He had also changed his clothes, and was now wearing a suit of black with a fine gold check pattern on the jacket and breeches.

"I knew you would turn up if I waited at the back here!"

"Pardon?" replied Lucian vaguely to his friend.

"Don't give me all that innocent stuff, Snuzz, I've known you too long; you're up to something, my lad!"

"Oh well, I just had to look up something in the Records Office for my own peace of mind," he replied to Sir Septimus, who still wasn't satisfied with his friend's answer.

"Look Snuzz old boy, you've been acting a bit strange. How can I help you if I don't know what is causing the problem?"

Lucian smiled, "Thank you, Sir Septimus. I know you want to help, but there is nothing you can do. I need to discover the missing pieces. Once I have discovered what they are, I can promise you that you will be the first to know."

"Very well, my friend. Have it your way, but you know where I am when you need to talk to me."

Lucian nodded his head in thanks and went to move off, but Sir Septimus stopped him by placing a hand on his arm; "I know you are going to refuse the knighthood, and I fully understand why," he smiled, "It will be for the same reason that I will not be accepting the Lordship!"

Lucian patted his friend's hand and headed off for the Palace door.

★ ★ ★ ★ ★

Doctor Munggo Meltabossokk was screwing in the last bolt on the War Robot when his new assistant Taddmoor De'ath entered the lab.

"De'ath! Can't you see I am working?"

"I am sorry to disturb you Doctor, but Professor Frumpton-Stone is here to see you on urgent business."

"Oh good! Show him in, De'ath!" The small Doctor ran over to the workbench, and returned the spanner he was using; he then hurried back to the three War Robots.

Professor Frampton-Stone entered and examined the three War Robots; the Rotary blades had been replaced with rock-boring drills. Frumpton-Stone nodded, impressed by the new additions. "That will cut through Dunbruan'phs Wall like a kniphfe through butter!" he proclaimed, thrusting his finger into the air in his melodramatic way.

Meltabossokk nodded eagerly, and rubbed his hands together with vigour. "They are diamond-tipped and made of titanium infused with pig iron they will bore through anything!"

The little Doctor scurried over to a large machine in the corner of the room. On its side was a large metal lever, and the mad old Doctor hopped up and down pointing at it.

"Would you like the honour of switching on the drills for the test run, Professor Frumpton-Stone?"

Frumpton-Stone stabbed the air with a finger. "It will be an honour indeed, Doctor Meltabosphspkokk!" he lisped, and moved over to the side of the machine and struck a dramatic pose.

"Fphor the greater good of Dondymaria!" he announced, and pulled the lever.

Immediately the drill heads mounted on the War Robots slowly began to turn!

★ ★ ★ ★ ★

Lucian entered the circular chamber that had served as the book room in the Black Tower. It was Balferzaar the Black's study now, and had been Dunbruan's before him. By the window was a small reading desk, Balferzaar's favourite place to sit when he was working. In the centre of the chamber was the conference table where eleven days ago it had been decided that Lucian should take on the journey to Empraktos-Larris. Beyond this was a stone, spiral staircase leading to the upper chamber of the Tower, and a place where only the Six Wizards of Pogglinburg might enter.

Lucian quickly moved to the north side of the chamber, and looked for a certain piece of carving that was on the sides and fronts of the bookcases. These carvings depicted Fiddoks (a type of shellfish that was a favourite on the Pogglin food menu), and Lucian pressed the left eye on the tenth Fiddok down on the left. Instantly a small panel in the bookcase creaked open.

Lucian chuckled. "You were a clever rascal, Dunbruan!" He tapped his staff on the marble flooring; "***Minimus Lumen***!" and the gemstone on his staff began to glow with a pale light. He entered the portal and closed the panel from the other side.

A narrow passageway ran between the inner wall of the Chamber and the outer wall of the Tower. The stepped path went down at an angled gradient into the darkness. Mr Snuzz held his staff aloft, put his hand against the wall and walked down the path. It was only his second venture into the passage, the first being many years ago when he had first cracked Dunbruan's coded message on the parchment. Of course, he had told Balferzaar of the discovery of the Secret Book, but he refrained from telling him of the passage or the secret room. The light from his staff illuminated the passage enough to see where he was going, and his mind went back to the Pogglin histories.

"Now, let me see? Mr Dewbin Throbb built the lower part of the tower in 4524 BD. It was a watchtower back then, I believe. Dunbruan had this portion of the tower built in 62 AD; he must have been working on this passage when he went missing for all those months," he mused to himself as he made his way along the path which spiralled evermore downwards. A few minutes later, Mr Snuzz noticed that there was a change in the masonry of the outer walls, from circular in shape to square-shaped walls.

"This must be the original watch tower built by Mr Throbb. Now this does confirm what little remains of this period of our history at the Records Office," he smiled, as he did like to confirm the truth of the written word in the old documents.

Down he went, the path now going at right angles to the walls until he finally came to an arched doorway. This was facing northwards, and was the original entrance to the old watchtower. Lucian scratched his head, trying to remember the secret words that opened the portal.

"Ah, yes of course; ***Expositus Ostium***!" he said, and the portal slid open and another dark passageway lay before him. The air smelt even damper than his last excursion into the tunnel all those years ago. He put his glowing staff before him, and entered into the cramped passageway. He hurried along, and was soon swallowed up in the darkness.

This tunnel was cut out of the solid earth: though the walls and ceiling were reinforced with hewn sandstone blocks, the path remained just beaten earth. When Lucian first discovered the passage and the room that it led on to, he took some bearings, applied them to his trigonometry skills and discovered that the secret room lay beneath the Copper Lake which was located behind the Royal Palace! He chuckled: only he in all Pogglinburg knew of its existence! After several more minutes he arrived in a dead-end – a clever trick on Dunbruan's part, just in case the passage was ever discovered.

Lucian turned to his right and moved four paces away from the end of the passage; "***Patefacio Foris***!" he muttered, and a portal in the side of the passage slid open before him. He hurriedly moved into the next stage of the passage and continued his journey that was leading him ever deeper: he was now well under the lake.

The walls were very damp and he knew he was now very close to the Secret Room's position. Finally, the passage opened up and at the far end was a flat circular stonewall. Incised into the stone was the seal of Dunbruan; it was off-centre to the wall, so that the bottom of the seal was a few inches off the earthen ground. At the centre of the Pyramid on the seal, a small hole had been drilled. Mr Snuzz reversed his Staff and inserted the silver base of his Staff into the hole and said the magic words known only to Dunbruan and himself: "**Phasmatis Humus Advoco Ego**!"

The whole of the circular seal of Dunbruan receded from the surface of the wall, and rolled aside to reveal another dark portal. He thrust his illuminated Staff into the darkness and entered.

The seal closed behind him.

Inside, Lucian found himself standing at the edge of an immensely large square room. The walls were lined with sandstone masonry, which had green mildew covering the surface, due to the penetration of the water from the lake above after many centuries. The underground chamber was so wide that the light from the staff wasn't enough to see into the corners, so he held it aloft: "**Susicivius Lumen**!"

A blazing light emitted from the staff and illuminated the entire room.

"Now that's thrown more light on the matter, I can see what I am doing," said Lucian to himself. The room was almost totally bare apart from a table and chair in the centre of the room, a bookcase running along the back wall and a writing desk in the left-hand corner. Lucian shook his head, "Why would Dunbruan want to excavate a room like this? What did he do in here?" he asked himself aloud. He wandered over to the writing desk.

It was in a secret compartment in the desk that he discovered the Secret Book.

He looked through the desk again to see if anything had escaped his eye from his first visit. But there was nothing of any interest: just blank parchment, dried up bottles of ink and an old quill. He moved over to the bookcase and looked at the titles of the books that were deposited on the shelves. Most were ancient volumes written in old Pogglish and Dwarvish. There was a volume on Forician medicine and chemistry. Lucian pulled at his little beard as he read off the titles, but no tome jumped out at him with any clues to the mystery he was trying to solve.

Then he saw a book that had no right to be there. "Hmm, Book of the Thirty Words. That *is* interesting!" He picked it up, and his fingers squidged into the damp sodden leather binding of the book. He tried to look through the book, but it was so damp that the pages were stuck together and tore as he turned them.

"This is an alchemical and occultist book on the worship of Sonoth, God of the Karaarsin. Why would Dunbruan have a book like this amongst his collection?"

He was about to replace the book on the shelf when something else caught his eye; a brown-edged corner of a piece of vellum was sticking out of the pages towards the back of the book.

Lucian's heart skipped a beat.

He placed the book on the table and carefully teased out the piece of vellum from the book. On it was a few lines of ancient Pogglish, and in some places, the ink had almost vanished. It was written in Dunbruan's own hand, Lucian noticed. It was very difficult for him to read what it said and he could only translate a little, and what he couldn't read was badly faded anyway. He looked into the air as he thought, murmuring what he could read of the message. "So, it's something, something and the then *Power*, something, something...*to go to the dark city of the Elders and face the Old One.* Then something, something, and then, *for more on this see The Book of the Golden Toad.* I wonder what that could mean?" He turned around and looked again at the bookcase, but he could find no volume entitled "The Book of the Golden Toad".

Time was running short, as he had to get back for the banquet. He replaced the book on the shelf and put the slip of vellum into his over-cloak pocket. He stood by the table, tapping his fingers on the wooden surface while he thought. "This room possesses more secrets than it can reveal to me," he said and then a thought struck him.

"If the passage to this chamber can have a false ending... Why not this room!"

He started gently tapping the end of his staff around the south wall by the chamber entrance; it was solid. He moved onto the east wall and did the same; again, the wall was solid. He didn't bother with the north wall because of the bookcase, so he tried the west wall and, in its centre, he received a hollow ring to his tap!

"An entrance to another chamber! Problem is, how does one open it?"

He stood back from the wall and pondered the problem. He could think of no other opening spell that would be of use in this situation. So, he decided to make a guess.

"If I am wrong, I can always come back later when I have more time," he said as he placed the staff on the wall. "If these words opened the portal in the passage, then just maybe they will be the same for in here?"

He took a deep breath. "***Patefacio Foris!***"

There was a low rumble and a portal opened in the wall before him. He beamed with satisfaction, "Well I'm jiggered, and I wasn't expecting that to work!" He looked through the portal. "Not a chamber, but another passage. I wonder where this leads too." Lucian entered, and the portal slammed down behind him.

★ ★ ★ ★ ★

Around the table were sat Lucian's Aunt and Uncle, Sir Septimus, Artimus and Zontahl. It was the table of honour in the Hall of Celebrations. Before them, on the High Table sat Grand King Pooley and Queen Grizzelda, along with the table of the Six Grand Wizards.

Artimus glanced at his watch and replaced it in his pocket. "Lucian is late. Unlike him to miss the first course!" he said to those sat around the table.

Sir Septimus frowned; he was worried about Lucian, and their previous adventures around Sol-Larris had never affected him so. He could see Sara Dore, sat on the next table opposite, and she also looked concerned at Lucian's absence. In fact, everyone in the Hall had noticed the absence of Lucian.

Admiral Loomboggle snorted with contempt. "Dashed un-gentlemanly of the chap to be late to a banquet held in his honour!" Lady Loomboggle nodded in agreement with her Husband. Chancellor Dore, who was also sat at the table, remained silent. "What do you expect from a damned scribbler?" added Field-Marshal Mandergast.

Sara Dore, unlike her father, couldn't remain silent any longer! "I didn't see you rush off to Empraktos-Larris, Field-Marshal, to help save Queen Grizzelda's life! It's not that you would have been missed, after all – you only have the command of thirteen soldiers!"

The Field-Marshal's face reddened with anger and embarrassment.

"Sara, you will desist at once!" commanded her father. "And you will apologise to the Field-Marshal this instant!"

"I will not apologise, father! Not until the Field-Marshal apologises for the remarks he made about Lucian!"

Sir Grunther-Pulpit, the Royal Secretary, had been listening to the conversation from the next table, leaned over and said, "I think Miss Dore has a point, Field-Marshal; you were undermining the accomplishments achieved by Lucian on this venture. I think you should withdraw your comments and apologise."

The Field-Marshal turned purple with rage; his dignity as an officer and a gentleman had been called out by the Royal Secretary. Sir Grunther-Pulpit had the confidence of the Grand King Pooley, and so he felt it was an order. His mouth stiffened as he quietly murmured, "I did not mean any disgrace upon the character of Lucian Snuzz, Miss Dore. And I withdraw my comments." He nodded his head stiffly as he apologised and turned an even deeper shade of purple.

Sara graciously nodded her thanks to the Field-Marshal, and the meal continued in silence. Sir Septimus looked to the entrance of the Hall, but there was still no sign of his friend.

★ ★ ★ ★ ★

The portal opened in the west wall of the secret room. Lucian staggered through into the room, and the portal slammed closed behind him. His hat was askew on his head and his face was ashen, his eyes wide with fear and shock. He moved over to the table; his body was trembling all over as he sat down. It took him several minutes to recover and to gain his composure and bearings. He got up and made for the entrance to the passageway. He had to get away from this place as quickly as possible!

★ ★ ★ ★ ★

Creep looked out from his window. The city below was a hive of activity: lights blazed brightly in the darkness of the night, and he could see the steam transports shuttling back and forth on the monorail to Grodium City. A smile crossed his ugly face and he chortled, rubbing his hands together. At last, something was going according to plan. He moved over to the refreshments table with a bounce in his step, and poured himself a large drink.

He thought back to the last meeting of the conspirators. Yes, it had gone very well indeed! Even old Field-Marshal Gunkfopp had fallen into line and was an asset to the meeting, now that he had an invasion to organise and a need to prove that his military mind was still as sharp as ever. General Sidok had forgotten about their earlier disagreement and backed Creep's plans to the hilt. Thankfully Colonel Tanttermount was busy in Grodium City, so the meeting wasn't spoiled by his presence!

He went back to the window to watch the military might of the Dondymarian forces being deployed. The eight hundred and fifty steam-powered War Robots were already trundling down the tunnel excavated by the Grodium Dwarves: three had been fitted with drills to bore their way through the last six or seven feet of rock.

Now the whole of the Dondymarian Army was being shuttled by the steam transporters to Grodium City. They were to follow after the spearhead force of War Robots, and their aim was the utter destruction of Pogglinburg. Creep smiled, nodding his head: nothing could stop the might of his armed forces, not even the Six Grand Wizards. Very soon he would be Emperor of the whole of Sol-Larris!

The chamber door opened and Queen Baalshibah entered Creep turned around and smiled, but his face fell when he saw the Snoog had accompanied her. "She's brought that blasted creature with her!"

His smile flicked back onto his face as the Queen moved over to him.

"I've missed you, Fangy! You haven't been hiding from your Queenie, have you?" she pouted at the Lord Chamberlain.

"No, my dearest," Creep replied and gestured towards the window. "See, I have been planning our future. Tomorrow, my beloved, will be the dawn of a new Dondymaria, and I shall, er, *we* shall reign supreme!"

He leaned forward and kissed her, much to the annoyance of Lug-Lug, and he protested loudly. "Pppphrrrrrrrrrrrrrrrrrrph!"

His lips still pressed against the Queen's, Creep tried desperately to kick the horrid creature, but was missing by miles.

The Queen pulled away. "What're you doing, Fangy? You're not having a fit, are you?"

"No, my dear, just foot-loose to be in your divine company once again!" lied Creep.

"Ooh, Fangy, I do love you!" She giggled, threw her

arms around his fat neck and kissed him.

"Pppphrrrrrrrrrrrrrrrrrrrph!" said the Snoog in disgust.

Chapter Seven

Lucian hurriedly made his way towards the Hall of Celebrations. His mind was on fire with the revelation beyond the passageway of the West Wall portal!

Outside the massive double doors leading into the Hall, Lucian brushed himself down and did his best to compose himself. He opened the doors and entered, closing them behind him. Walking down the Hall, he acknowledged the greetings from all around him, then waved and smiled back. He smiled at Sara when he passed her, but he noted the look of distress on her face. Then he walked up to the Wizards' table, behind which was the High Table. He bowed deeply to the King and Queen and each of the Wizards, and gave his apologies for being late. They all nodded their heads in response, and he couldn't but notice that they too were looking at him with some concern.

He sat down in his place at the table next to Zontahl. He gave them his excuses, and begged forgiveness for being so late. Again, he noticed how they looked at him.

Sir Septimus couldn't contain himself any longer. "What on earth have you been up to, Lucian?"

Lucian smiled: it was a weak smile, but it was the best he could muster under his present duress. "Oh, nothing of any importance, Sir Septimus," and he tucked into his cold main course. "Mmm, I'm hungry!" he tried to say as cheerfully as possible.

"Don't give me that Fiddockswollop! You look like you've seen a ghost and it's worried you sick!" said Sir Septimus, his monocle popping out from his eye socket.

"Really there is nothing wrong, Sir Septimus!"

"Have you seen yourself, Snuzz? You're as white a sheet! So don't tell one of your oldest friends that there is nothing wrong!"

"Sir Septimus, there is no..." But Lucian didn't have a chance to finish his sentence, because the Hall doors burst open and a figure clad from head to foot in black came running in!

"It's the Shadow!" roared Field-Marshal Mandergast, jumping to his feet. "Guards, seize that Dondymarian!"

Four Palace Guards rushed forward and restrained the Shadow. Dondymarians are a little taller than Brown Mountain Dwarves, so he was a lot taller than the Guards restraining him.

"I have come to protest my innocence!" bellowed the intruder. "Fangdom Creep has tried to fit me up and discredit me with the poisoning of Queen Grizzelda!"

"Silence!" shouted Field-Marshal Mandergast, and gave orders for a fifth guard to go fetch Captain Rumsbiggot and the Town Guards.

"Allow him to speak," said Grand King Pooley. "We will hear what the Dondymarian spy has to say." The Guards escorted the Shadow before the High Table and the Wizards.

"I have come, as I said, to clear my name of the poisoning of the Queen. Creep hates me, as I do not bring him enough information on Pogglins and their secrets!"

"Pogglinburg has no secrets!" retorted Balferzaar the Black.

Lucian looked over at the old Wizard. "But there is a *secret*, a secret festering at the very heart of Pogglinburg, Balferzaar!" he thought to himself.

"Nevertheless," the Shadow continued, "Creep wanted rid of me, and the best way he could think of was to implicate me in the murder of Queen Grizzelda! If I was guilty of the act, why would I come here like this?"

"There is a truth to that statement," agreed Baaras the Brown.

"Although we are enemies, you have shown a certain amount of kindness and hospitality. I always thought that was because you never suspected that I really was a Dondymarian spy."

This statement was met with silence, as no Pogglin could believe that the Shadow was anything but a Dondymarian spy!

"And over the many years that I frequented the Frog and Bottle Inn, I came to realise that I felt more at home amongst Pogglins than I did among my own kind back in Dondymaria."

Mr Obadiah Antwhistle, the landlord of the Frog and Bottle, stood up. "I have known the Shadow for many a year, and have got to know his habits pretty well and I would say that it was not he in the Inn on the day our dear Queen was poisoned. I should say it was an impostor!"

The Hall erupted into a buzz of conversation. Pogglins debated amongst themselves as to whether the Shadow was guilty or not. Balferzaar held up his hands for silence, as Captain Rumsbiggot and the Town Guard arrived to escort the Shadow to the Town Barracks.

The King rose to his feet. "The Shadow will be held until we get to the truth of the matter. If he is proved innocent as he claims, then he may walk freely in our Kingdom. We Pogglins have never quarrelled with Dondymaria; it is they who have consistently been the ones to attack throughout our history. If you be found guilty, however, you will be marched to the border and will never again set foot in Pogglinburg. Captain, take him away!" Captain Rumsbiggot saluted his King, and he and the Town Guard marched the Shadow away as the Pogglins' murmur echoed around the great Hall once again.

Sir Septimus got to his feet and addressed Grand King Pooley. "By your leave, Your Majesty?"

"Granted, Sir Septimus," replied the King graciously.

"I have always found the Shadow a strange, but a likeable cove. The blighter may be working for the other side and all that, but I would hate to see a miscarriage of justice done. I can add evidence to Mr Antwhistle's statement, for on the afternoon of the poisoning, The Shadow spoke not a word to anyone in the Inn! This was very strange, because the real Shadow would never stop talking!"

Sir Gilliethrum Anvilhammer agreed. "I can vouch for Sir Septimus, for I was there when he mentioned it. He speaks the truth, Your Majesty."

Lucian stood up. "I too believe that the Shadow seen in the Inn on the afternoon of 5th July was an impostor. I was also with Sir Septimus and heard him say that to which he has just testified. Not only that, the impostor was seen drinking his ale through a straw, something I have never seen the real Shadow do. It was out of character."

The King thanked them, and said he would bear this in mind when he and Balferzaar the Black questioned the Shadow. The King then began to speak about the journey to the lands of Empraktos-Larris for the antidote to save the Queen. A round of applause and cheering followed, as Sir Gilliethrum presented the get-well gift from King Vardiemar and Queen Ellgah of Dwarveshire.

Queen Grizzelda then spoke of her thanks for the bravery of Lucian, Sir Septimus and Artimus; she also gave a special thanks to Zontahl for his help in the venture. The Queen then gave each of the three Pogglins a small gift of gold, and when she came to Zontahl she put a collar of gold and diamonds around his neck. Chancellor Dore then came forward with a ceremonial sword, while Grand King Pooley moved to the front of the Wizards' table.

"We now give thanks to our three friends by bestowing on them honours of the realm. Lucian, please would you come forward and receive your gift?" the King smiled.

Lucian came forward and asked the King if he might have a few words before they continued with the ceremony. The King nodded in agreement, and stepped aside to allow Lucian to speak.

"My Lords, Sirs, ladies and Gentlepoggs; my friends. I took on the honour of this venture for the love of my Queen and my country; I did not expect such a ceremony and honours on my return. The thanks of my King and Queen are reward enough for me. But there is one thing that you must never forget, and that is the quest was never a 'one Pogglin act'. I had the help and support of my friends, Sir Septimus and Artimus. I might add that I am honoured to count them amongst my friends, for a Pogglin could not ask for better friends!"

There were loud cheers and applause, and Lucian held up his hands and called for quiet.

"Please do let me finish. The venture started with just us three; we little suspected that we would meet such brave and courageous new friends and comrades along the way. And it is to these selfless folk, the Fungiglooks of the Great Fungoid Forest and the Cats of Empraktos-Larris that I dedicate this evening. I should like you to honour them. The trip across the desert of Empraktos-Larris was a tiring and perilous journey, and we had help from the Cats and the Fungiglook to make it to our quest's end: the Moogem Tree. If it were not for the unselfish sacrifice of these remarkable friends, neither of my two companions nor I would be here this evening. They died so that our Queen could live. Please remember that I didn't make this quest a success by my own doing."

There was dead silence while he spoke: no cheers, no applause, just a silence born of deep respect.

"I have been on many an adventure, with fellow Pogglins, Dwarves and Foricians, but not one of them has affected me as has this quest to Empraktos-Larris. There are evil deeds that go on beneath our feet, and suffering that you could never begin to imagine. I discovered something that has totally changed my outlook on life and the land we live in. I have made an oath that I shall return to Empraktos-Larris, to put right the terrible wrongs and to release those who suffer in great torment. Remember, my friends that we may live in such a happy, peaceful land, but others are not so lucky. And remember those who died in the cause of saving our Queen. I started by saying that thanks were enough and reward for me; so, I feel, with the greatest respect and gratitude, that I must decline the King's kind gift of Knighthood. If anyone in this room deserves your praise, look no further than Zontahl, chief of the Cats of Empraktos-Larris!"

He bowed and returned to his seat. There was a silence of amazement from the onlookers until Queen Grizzelda started to clap and Sara Dore shouted, "May Dunbruan the Great praise and look down on Lucian with good favour!" The Hall erupted with cheers and applause, and calls of thanks to Zontahl and the fallen cats and Fungiglooks.

Sara rushed over to Lucian and hugged him, while Chancellor Dore flashed an angry gaze at his daughter. Sir Septimus smiled and turned to the King. "I am sorry, Your Majesty, but I am with Snuzz on this one. Totally agreed with what the old boy had to say. So, I would like to thank Your Majesty for your kindness, but I too will respectfully be declining my Lordship." He bowed, then went and clapped Lucian across the back. "Excellent speech and well delivered, my friend!"

The King looked at Artimus. "I suppose that you will not be requiring your Knighthood either, Artimus?"

The watchmaker bowed and replied, "Not for me, Your Majesty. Sir Artimus Whistlecraft, watchmaker to his Majesty Grand King Pooley VI, doesn't quite roll off the tongue." He bowed again and returned to his seat next to Lucian and patted him on the back. "Well done, Lucian!"

★ ★ ★ ★ ★

An hour later the Pogglins had reassembled in the Ballroom for the celebratory dance. Yorik opened the event, with the Jester performing great feats with his Yoyo.

"It is amazing what he can do with that Yoyo!" commented Grand King Pooley to Admiral Loomboggle, who nodded in agreement, "Truly amazing indeed, Your Majesty – it quite defies the law of physics!"

Sir Septimus man-powered Lucian into a corner for a private word. "What was wrong with you this evening, Snuzz? You looked more worried tonight than at any time during the journey to the Moogem Tree, and that is saying something!"

Lucian shook his head. "I am sorry, Sir Septimus. I can't tell you for the moment; the implications are distressing in the extreme! I still haven't been able to come to terms with it myself, so I really do need to take stock and think about it before discussing it."

"It can't be that terrible, surely Snuzz?"

"Worse than you could imagine, Sir Septimus– but when I can talk about it, I will tell you: I can promise you that, my friend!"

Lucian took a sip from his glass, rather more for something to do than for thirst. Sir Septimus twirled at his moustache, deep in thought; then he raised his eyebrows, at a loss at what could be "worse than he could imagine!"

"Very well Snuzz, I won't press you until you are ready, but I think you are taking on more than you can handle at the moment."

Lucian looked at his friend. "Have you ever wondered how the defences laid down by Dunbruan work?"

"They're supposed to be automatic, or so I understand it – keeping the nasty blighter out if they're an enemy of the realm and all that sort of guff."

"Quite," Lucian agreed, "So how comes it that the Shadow can just walk in and out of Pogglinburg at will?"

Sir Septimus thought for a moment before answering. "Because the system knows he's not a threat. He's been coming here for years and has done no harm to us!"

"You don't see it, do you? He was sent here originally to do us harm. He was a known enemy."

"I don't see what you're driving at, Snuzz? I'm a bit of a thicko when it comes to things like this."

"Very well, I'll put it another way. How could a Dondymarian impostor and a Grodium Dwarf get by the defences and still manage to poison the Queen?"

The monocle flew out of Sir Septimus' eye-socket; the penny had dropped! "By Obadiah Thrasskin's beard! You mean the defences put in by Dunbruan the Great are useless?"

Lucian nodded slowly, "Yes, Sir Septimus. They may have worked at some point, but I doubt it, and they do not work now. Dunbruan has duped us!"

His friend winced at his usage of words, "Careful, Snuzz old boy, you don't want Balferzaar to catch you saying things like that!" Then he suddenly stopped. "There's all this talk of invasion in the air. Sir Gilliethrum told me earlier that even the Dwarves are on a war footing; they are convinced Creep is going to make a move against us, now Mumbeldok is out of the way. We're in danger, ain't we Snuzz?"

"I am afraid we are, Sir Septimus. For the very first time in centuries, Pogglinburg will be invaded!"

"Then we have to call a council of the Wizards, tell everything to Balferzaar!"

"Balferzaar was – is – my mentor, Sir Septimus. I've been his student for many years and I know he will not listen to a word said against Dunbruan. Especially as Dunbruan was *Balferzaar's* tutor!"

"Why do you never call him 'The Great' anymore? He was your hero, everything you aspired to!"

"Because I have since discovered that he wasn't 'The Great', far from it! I have always had an inquiring mind, Sir Septimus, but sometimes one delves too deep and finds a devastating truth. Unfortunately, I have discovered too many truths about Dunbruan in an afternoon to last me an eternity. I have been thrice paid for my curiosity!"

★ ★ ★ ★ ★

In the sub-basement of the R.U.F.A.T.A.S. building, Doctor Munggo Meltabossokk was examining a dial on a massive steam-powered generator. He nodded with approval all was going to plan.

He turned to his assistant. "Is the boiler well stoked De'ath?"

"Yes, Doctor. All is in readiness for the switch-over."

"Excellent, De'ath. Very soon I will be proven to be the greatest scientific mind in the history of Dondymaria..." He cackled gleefully and went over to the clock on the wall and rubbed his rubber-gloved hands vigorously. "Not long to go. Soon I will activate the transmitting aerial!" He scurried over to the door. "Come, De'ath, let us partake of some refreshment and return at the appointed time."

De'ath followed the Doctor out of the room.

★ ★ ★ ★ ★

King Vardiemar III was looking at a great map, which was laid out on a large intricately carved stone slab, in the battle chamber of the Brown Mountain. He stroked his beard as he studied the map; on it stood little brown figures. They were beautifully carved and each depicted a Dwarf, all of whom were stationed around the Mountain. Each figure represented a unit of fifty Dwarves.

"You are pleased with the defences, Your Majesty?" asked Marshal-General Cavernhollow.

The King nodded in agreement. "Aye that I am, Marshal-General, but one can never be too careful where Yorgrinn the Sly is concerned," and he picked up one of the figures and placed it at the north gate to the mountain. "You never know if the old fox will come at you from the rear!"

"I do think that a wise move, your Majesty," said Chancellor Silverore.

"So, we have most of the heavy fighting forces at the east gate, dug in on the edge of the Copper Wood and more stationed along the ridge of the Copper Mountain." He liked what he had seen, and congratulated his Marshal General and advisor on their strategy.

"If Yorgrinn is fool enough to try and attack by the Gromm Bridge, then he will get a bloody nose!" said the King, and laughed heartily.

"Mr Elgyn Kloons –to me, if you please!" called the King, and Mr Kloons zoomed into the room and stopped dead in front of King Vardiemar.

The King pointed to the map. "See this unit of Dwarves? Get through to Blue Captain, and have him send a detachment to the North Gate. When it's done, get yeeself back here lad and let me know! This battle room will have to run like clockwork, we'll need constant updates of intelligence." The King gave him a look. "Well, off you go lad!" and Elgyn zoomed out of the room to carry out his orders.

"Right then, Lord Chancellor! Once I have this place up to speed, I am off to join the Queen on the front line." He slapped the old Chancellor across the back. "Just think, Lord Torryn, today may be the day that Thremgould grants me the head of Yorgrinn! It would get rid of many nagging problems, in one fell swoop of my axe-head through the old fox's neck. Eeh, that would be poetic justice indeed, my old friend!"

At that moment Elgyn Kloons returned, confirming that the unit was now at the North Gate. The King was in an excellent mood. "Right, I'm off to the East Gate, Lord Torryn. Keep that map updated with the latest incoming intelligence!" With that, he left the battle room in the capable hands of Marshall-General Cavernhollow and Chancellor Silverore.

★ ★ ★ ★ ★

Sir Septimus and Lucian were still talking in a corner of the Hall; this had not gone unnoticed by Sara or Balferzaar the Black. Sara knew it must be important and so she didn't disturb them. She stayed in the company of Artimus and his son, Zontahl, and Lucian's Aunt and Uncle. Balferzaar, however, was more quizzical and interested to discover what was so important that they should choose to closet themselves away in a private corner during the celebrations in their honour.

Roondar the Red and Bableglum the Blue distracted him in conversation, but his mind was on Lucian. Eventually Balferzaar excused himself from the two Wizards and walked over to Lucian and Sir Septimus.

"You are both being very unsociable this evening. Come, tell me, what is wrong?"

For a moment neither replied, and then Sir Septimus spoke up. "Snuzz and I have been going over a few things, and something has arisen. Dunbruan's defences are at fault and not working, Balferzaar."

The old Wizard was somewhat taken aback by Sir Septimus' failure to use the correct title for the old saviour of Pogglinburg. "Dunbruan *the Great* laboured for many years to make Pogglinburg safe from Dondymarian attack.

It will not fail, Sir Septimus! You forget that Dunbruan the Great himself trained me in the arts of magic. He instructed my fellow Wizards and me in the workings of his great defence, his legacy to the realm and the people of Pogglinburg."

"Look at the evidence, Balferzaar! The magical defences are supposed to be automatic and stop any evil blighters from entering Pogglinburg, yes?"

"Correct," nodded the old Wizard in agreement.

"Then how is it that the automatic barrier did not keep out the Shadow, the impostor Shadow or the Grodium Dwarf? The Shadow has been coming and going for years, the magic never stopped him —and Creep still managed to get his agents into Pogglinburg and poison Queen Grizzelda!"

Balferzaar's back stiffened at these comments.

"Please listen, Balferzaar," Lucian said gently. "You have been my mentor and friend since I was a Pogglet, and you are also wise. Think on Sir Septimus' words and weigh the evidence put before you, and do not let your faith in Dunbruan blind your judgement. Remember you and the Wizards are here to protect the realm."

"You have indeed changed your opinions since your return, Lucian: before the journey you would never have suggested such a thing! But I will consider that which you and Sir Septimus have put before me." And the old Wizard left them and re-joined Roondar the Red and Grand King Pooley.

Sir Septimus looked disappointed. "Do you think he will listen, Snuzz?" he said flatly.

Then to their surprise, they saw Balferzaar the Black leaving with the other Wizards!

"Do you think he has heeded our warning, Lucian old boy?"

"It's possible, Sir Septimus, it's possible! As I said, one can never tell how Balferzaar will react. Maybe I was being a little hard on the old chap after all," said Lucian with a smile.

★ ★ ★ ★ ★

In the tunnel under Dunbruan's Wall, the last of the War Robots were moving into position. They were three abreast, and at the front of the column were the three robots fitted with the drilling devices. Behind them were the three Spearhead Leaders. They were identical to the other War Robots, apart from their heads were painted black as opposed to red.

The eyes of the War Robots glowed dimly in the darkness of the tunnel as they waited for the order to begin the invasion.

★ ★ ★ ★ ★

Meanwhile, the celebrations of thanks had ended and all the Pogglins filed home in a merry mood. Lucian and his three friends were talking outside the Palace gates, and the Pogglins bid them "Goodnight!" as they passed. The three Pogglins and the cat smiled and nodded their thanks. Soon the revellers had gone and Lucian and his friends were alone.

"Well, are you going back to Hill Square tonight, Lucian, or will you and Zontahl be staying with Dr Snuzz?" asked Artimus.

"If Zontahl doesn't mind, I think we will be stopping at my uncle's tonight?"

"Whatever you feel is best, Lucian," replied Zontahl.

"Thank you Zontahl," said Lucian, and he continued, "I think we would be wise if we didn't sleep too soundly, my friends! I sense something on the Ley lines; there is something afoot!"

"You think the Dondymarian attack is imminent then?"

"I do, Sir Septimus—and we should not be caught napping, otherwise Pogglinburg will fall!"

"Then maybe we shouldn't go to our beds but keep watch?" suggested Artimus."The loft above my workshop has a clear view of Dunbruan's Wall."

"Sounds a good idea to me," agreed Sir Septimus.

"Very well. Do we need to bring any blankets, Artimus?"

"No, Lucian, I have plenty to go around, but first, I will have to contact my brother Orlando and ask if he could hold onto little Marius for a while longer for me. Back there at the Lake of Wonders, it bought home just how much my son means to me, I missed him more than I have ever done before...and also the realisation that Marius is part my darling wife as well. It has taken me to be near death to show me what is really important."He smiled at Lucien.

As the group started across the Square, Sara came running out of the Palace."You four are up to something and I want to be part of it!" she said.

"I think not, Sara; I think you will be much safer for the time being at the Palace. Also, we do not want to give your father an excuse to refuse our engagement."

"Fiddlesticks! My father doesn't have to give his permission: I'll marry who I want, and that is you, Mr Lucian Snuzz! If there is danger ahead, then I want to face it by your side." And she kissed him on the nose.

"I want your father's leave to marry you, Sara; he could make things quite difficult for you if you do not comply with his wishes. And as much as I would like you by my side, it is really no place for a Lady Pogglin to be. Now please return to the Palace, which will be the safest place if the Dondymarians attack."

"I want to be with you!"

"Please Sara, for me, return to the Palace." He said smiling deeply into her eyes.

"Lucian, I didn't know whether I would ever see you again during your dangerous quest for the Queen, you could have died, so I am not letting you out of my sight. So no, I am coming with you and that's flat!"

Lucian laughed and kissed her on the cheek. "Then so be it; you are your father's daughter!" he said and turned to follow his friends.

As he turned, the lights in the upper chamber of the Black Tower caught his eye."Look my friends!" he called and pointed at the Tower.

"By Obadiah Thrasskin's beard, would you just look at that! So Balferzaar did take some notice of us this evening!"

"Well, my friends we can only hope that he has realised that there is truth in my words that Dunbruan's magic is tainted or he could just as easily be telling the other wizards I have committed treason!"

Sara was going to enquire what Lucian meant by "Dunbruan's tainted magic" when Sir Septimus shook his head and waved a finger not to ask. Zontahl wondered what was so important about the lights, and he asked Sir Septimus their meaning.

"Oh, it's the meeting chamber of the Six Grand Wizards. Only they are allowed to enter the chamber. If they are meeting at this hour of the night, then something of great importance has arisen!"

Thank you, I understand now," replied the cat with a smile.

"Right! I'm off to Orlando to see if he will look after young Marius for the evening. I'll meet you outside the workshop."

★ ★ ★ ★ ★

In the Chamber of Wizards, the six Wizards of Pogglinburg were seated around a massive stone table in the centre of the circular room. It was round in shape: the carvings on the tabletop divided the surface into seven segments and around the border were incised words of ancient Pogglish. At the bottom portion of each segment was a counter-sunk gemstone, each colour-coordinated to the colour of the Wizard positioned at each of the segments. They sat in high-backed thrones of wood which were also topped with a matching-coloured gemstone.

Towards the centre of the table, the seven segments met. At this point there were seven holes, one per triangular segment, and each about six inches away from the centre point. In these holes were placed the staffs of the Wizards. The holes were carved into the stone at an angle so that the staffs pointed inwards. Above this was a clear globe of crystal that was suspended from the ceiling by a shaft of blue crystal.

"I have called this meeting, my brothers, because yet again the legacy left to us by Dunbruan the Great has been called into question," said the aged Wizard as he looked about the table.

"What, again?" said Roondar the Red. "This is quite outrageous! Never in all my centuries have I ever heard so much doubt raised over the Great Dunbruan!"

"Brother Roondar speaks the truth," agreed Glondin the Green. "This is what happens when we allow too many to freely travel the land of Sol-Larris! The outside world has given them too many ideas; next they will be wanting a steam-powered generator!"

Balferzaar raised an eyebrow at this comment. "So, you think it was wrong of me to allow Lucian Snuzz to wander the land? Do not forget, Brother Glondin that Dunbruan the Great himself travelled around Sol-Larris for his early training. Also remember that we ourselves have also ventured here from the confines of Quistorrisia to our home of Pogglinburg, travelling all those centuries ago."

"I do not question your authority, my Lord Balferzaar—just your judgement, since you are a little too lenient toward Lucian Snuzz and his friends."

Roondar nodded in agreement. "Allowing Artimus Whistlecraft to build that flying contraption was totally against the teaching of the Great Dunbruan!"

"That flying contraption, Brother Roondar, was precisely the thing that saved the life of Queen Grizzelda!" cut in Baaras the Brown.

Balferzaar the Black raised his eyebrows, "Thank you, Brother Baaras. I need no other to defend my decisions, but it is nice that others of our Brotherhood recognised the usefulness for such a machine!" and he turned to Roondar. "Brother Roondar, if we had the magical power to fly, I am sure one of us would have flown to Empraktos-Larris! As we do not possess such power, then we must rely on the engineering genius of young Artimus. Granted, some of his ideas are totally against the laws laid down to us by the Great Dunbruan himself, but others I allow if I deem them useful to our interests."

Roondar the Red jutted his jaw, not liking this experience of being put in his place, especially by the leader of his order. Westerin the White folded his arms.

"As interesting as the subject is, this is not why the meeting was called. What were the doubts tabled, my Lord Balferzaar?"

"The doubts raised, my brothers, is the fear that Great Dunbruan's magical barrier is not going to work. Tonight, I was told that it has failed to protect us."

"That is complete nonsense!" Roondar the Red rebuffed the notion.

"Such a thing could never happen!" agreed Glondin the Green.

"That does sound quite unlikely," added Westerin the White.

"I have total faith in Dunbruan's wizardry!" said Bableglum the Blue.

"Are these young Lucian's feelings on the matter?" asked Baaras the Brown.

"But what are your feelings on the matter of the defences, Brother Baaras?" asked the old Wizard, ignoring the question.

"My Lord Balferzaar, I know Lucian Snuzz very well," replied Baaras the Brown. "He has been a guest at the Brown Tower on many occasions. I know how deep his feelings are on Dunbruan the Great; they are unquestioned! If he now questions what has been laid down by the Great Dunbruan, then something serious is amiss."

"But you still have not answered my question, Brother Baaras. Your fellows of the order have given their feelings – now I want to hear yours."

"My Lord Balferzaar, I cannot answer– as I cannot now truly answer one way or the other."

Balferzaar leaned back in his throne and linked his fingers across his belly. "So, we have four ayes in favour of the Great Dunbruan legacy and one abstainer. Is that not interesting?"

"You have not given your feelings on the matter, my Lord Balferzaar. What are they?" enquired Roondar the Red.

"Until this evening I thought as you, but now I am like Brother Baaras: I cannot answer."

There was an outburst of surprise and dismay from the four Wizards, but Baaras the Brown was silent and unsurprised by the old wizard's reply.

"What evidence has Lucian Snuzz, my Lord, to doubt the very word of Dunbruan the Great?" Again, it was Roondar the Red that put the question.

"We believe that the magical defences installed within these great towers were automatic against enemies entering the realm. In such times of an all-out attack, we would boost our power by assembling at this table, correct?"

"That is what we believe, as told to us all by Dunbruan the Great himself," replied four of the Wizards.

Balferzaar nodded in agreement. "This is true. It is also written in our Legends that the finding of the Amber Stone would bring an end to the mortal life of the Great Dunbruan. As we all know, Ignatius Hossenfefarr found it in the mines of the Copper Mountains in 80 AD."

He leaned forward onto the table, "And on the 23rd December 87AD, I found the Great Dunbruan dead in the chamber below; the cause of death a mystery!"

"Every Pogglin knows this, my lord Balferzaar—they teach every Pogglet the histories in school!" replied Roondar the Red.

"But what every Pogglin doesn't know, Brother Roondar, is that The Great Dunbruan left me a note that the Amber Stone was to be buried with him in the event of his death. That in death it would bestow great power on Pogglinburg, and whilst it rested with him, we shall never more be attacked or invaded!" His voice rose a little, and it was very unlike the old Wizard to lose hold of his temper. "The Amber Stone now lies with Dunbruan the Great, sealed in his tomb of marble that stands within the Copper Woods. What if the Great Dunbruan was wrong? That the Amber Stone has had a *reverse effect* on the Magic held within the Gemstones on the Roofs of our Tower?"

The four Wizards sat back and remained silent as they pondered on the questions put to them, but Balferzaar did not give them time to ponder!

"Tonight, my brothers, the facts were given simply and plainly to me by Lucian and Sir Septimus Pulpit. Those simple facts are; how did the Shadow manage to enter and walk abroad in our realm? How did the Shadow's impostor and the Grodium Dwarf enter our lands, without the magic of Dunbruan the Great preventing them from doing so? They were all enemies of the realm —and yet none were stopped, no warning alerted us of their presence. We had become so complacent with the Shadow sitting in the Frog and Bottle Inn that none of us, my brothers, never thought to question how he got in there!"

★ ★ ★ ★ ★

Artimus and his friends had made themselves quite comfortable in his workshop loft. Each was wrapped in a warm blanket and from the window they had a good view of Dunbruan's Wall (which was lit from the back by the lights burning in Grodium City). Zontahl had a blanket over his back and a bowl of hot syrup. Artimus poured four steaming mugs of syrup and passed them around to Lucian, Sara and Sir Septimus.

"You are certain that the Dondymarians will invade, Lucian?"

"I do believe so, Sara. Fangdom Creep has been trying to force King Mumbeldok into war for years. Now that Mumbeldok has fled to Dwarveshire, Creep has a clear hand to do as he will! I think he tried to murder the Queen in the hope of demoralising us and would have attacked during our traditional two weeks of mourning."

Sir Septimus nodded, "Yes that would be as low as Creep is willing to stoop. The chap is an out-and-out cad and bounder! I will give him a good thrashing should we ever meet!"

"What's the time, Artimus?" asked Lucian.

Artimus looked at his watch. "It's 3.45 AM Lucian," and he put it away in his pocket.

"Right, I think some of us should get some sleep, whilst one stays up to keep watch. We'll change shift every hour and a half."

"Fine by us," the friends agreed.

"I will take the first watch," offered Zontahl.

★ ★ ★ ★ ★

Red the Hobbdrak had a good stretch while he was waiting for the kettle to boil on the stove. On the side three tin mugs were prepared, and each mug was the size of a dustbin. By the side of the enormous mugs was an even bigger enamelled Green Teapot, with chipped paint around the lid and the spout.

The kettle came to the boil, and Red proceeded to pour the water into the immense teapot. He stirred the pot with a long wooden spoon and replaced the lid. He poured out the tea into his white tin mug, which had *RED* painted on it in black paint. Picking up his mug of tea, he walked over to the lounge area of the Aerodrome and plonked it on the table. He then walked down towards the sleeping quarters of the dome.

He kicked the bed. "Get up, Bluey! Ya knows the Wing Commander has ordered us to get out on patrol early. So, get up, ya old snake!" he said with a grin.

Bluey was out of the bed, laughing and making his way towards his early morning starter; a nice hot cup of tea! Red made for Greenie's bed, but Greenie was up and sitting on the side of the bed already. "Ooo, I 'ate these early mornin' starts!"

Red smiled: he was always an early riser and that was why Ginger Wingnut picked him for the dawn patrol duties. "There is a nice hot steaming brew awaiting you, Greenie me old mucker, and you will be raring to get into the air after 'aving such a revitalising drink to start ya day!"

Red returned to his mug of steaming tea, sat down in his chair and started reading the early edition of *The Pogglin Times* newspaper. "We've got ten minutes, boys, to wake up and start our duties for the day."

★ ★ ★ ★ ★

In the sub-basement of the R.U.F.A.T.A.S. building, Doctor Munggo Meltabossokk was once again standing in front of the massive steam-powered generator, his eyes on the wall clock.

"It is three minutes to four AM. De'ath, time to activate the transmitting aerial!"

De'ath nodded and moved over to a large lever, then pulled it down with both hands towards the stone floor. A mechanism was set in motion: up on the roof, a massive steel pole started to rise above the building. As it rose, little steel bars began to spring out at its sides and then the top unfolded and a mesh-like dish expanded and unfolded to its fully extended state. The transmitting aerial was now fully operational!

Meltabossokk cackled with glee as he read the meters and dials. "I am going to switch the War Robots over to self-control: they will become self-thinking, self-supporting entities!" He threw a switch on the machine and it hummed as it sent the signal up through the aerial, and a light began to blink on the control panel.

"It is done, De'ath; my positronic steam-powered brains are now under self-control! It will be interesting to see the results of the War Robot's capabilities, now that it is a self-thinking machine!" Once more he rubbed his rubber-gloved hands hard together with glee.

★ ★ ★ ★ ★

In the tunnel, the War Robots' eyes flashed twice and began to glow with a fierce intensity.

"Orders-Have-Been-Received!" chanted one of the Spearhead leaders.

"Start-Up-Drilling-Devices!" chanted another.

"Operate!" replied the three drilling War Robots as their drills started to whirl around, and they moved towards the rock face, where they bored into the surface. Chunks of rock began to fly about like a snow storm as they started to excavate the tunnel's end.

As the column of War Robots began to move forward, the Spearhead Leaders began to chant their orders to the rest of the Robots: "The-Pogglins-Will-Be-Destroyed!" "Nothing-Will-Be-Permitted-To-Stand-In-Our-Way!"

"The-Pogglins-Will-Be-Annihilated!" War Robots chanted their reply, "Attack! Attack! Attack! Attack!"

Soon the Drilling Robots burst through the final layer of rock and the War Robots swarmed into Pogglinburg, bent on the total annihilation of their enemies. The Spearhead Leaders and the War Robots trundled towards The Green Tower and Didock Farm.

★ ★ ★ ★ ★

Red, Bluey and Greenie Hobbdraks were waiting on the runway for the Pogglins. Shortly, the Wing Commander and his two cadets joined the Hobbdraks with a cheery greeting – "Morning boys, sleep well? Good!" and they mounted their saddles and were soon ready for the off.

"Chocks away!" called the Wing-Commander.

"Roger that, Guv!" replied Red and he started to race along the runway. Soon they were circling in the air. Shortly Bluey and Greenie joined them and the three started their patrol of the Pogglin borders.

★ ★ ★ ★ ★

Artimus was slowly nodding off while on watch. Suddenly, his head jerked up as he heard a strange sound of chanting on the breeze blowing over from Dunbruan's Wall. He looked out of the windows and could see hundreds of pairs of red lights swarming towards the Green Tower! He jumped to his feet and shook his friends awake.

"Wake up! Quickly! The Invasion has started!"

Lucian, Sara and Sir Septimus jumped to their feet and looked out the window. They could see the circular red lights flashing about and great sparks flying from the base of the Green Tower.

"What are they, Snuzz? That is no Dondymarian out there!"

"I have no idea what it could be, Sir Septimus! But I suggest we get ourselves over to the Black Tower and let the Wizards know that something has bored its way through Dunbruan's Wall!"

"So, you were right, Lucian – Dunbruan's defences do not work!" exclaimed Sara.

"I am just so sorry I had to be proved right in this way!" replied Lucian to the others. "Look you had better both stay here with Zontahl and keep watch. Come on, Sir Septimus– we have things to do!"

The two Pogglins climbed down the hatch while Sara, Artimus and Zontahl remained on watch in the workshop loft.

"Do you think they will reach the bridge, Artimus?"

"I don't know Sara. If they do, then we are going to have our backs to the wall trying to defend the town from whatever THEY are!"

★ ★ ★ ★ ★

King Vardiemar III was standing on the ridge of the Copper Mountain, his eyes cutting through the darkness. Dwarves' eyes are better for seeing in the dark, more than any other race in Sol-Larris. He could see nothing in the direction of Gromm Bridge. So Yorgrinn was not fulfilling his oaths to Creep – not from this direction, in any case. Then he turned his head towards Pogglinburg, as he had caught strange noises on the breeze.

"Do you hear that, my Queen?"

"I do, Vardie. What could it be!?!"

"Devilry is afoot in Pogglinburg!" he turned quickly to Elgyn Kloons. "Report to Cavernhollow and Silverore! I am taking half the reserves into Pogglinburg; the Dondymarians have started their attack!"

Elgyn Kloons shot off towards the Brown Mountain at breakneck speed, while King Vardiemar and Queen Ellgah took the Dwarvish reserves over the ridge of the Copper Mountain and across Gromm Bridge into Pogglinburg.

★ ★ ★ ★ ★

The Six Wizards were still in a deep debate when Lucian Snuzz and Sir Septimus entered the chamber via the spiral stairs leading up from the chamber below. Balferzaar's back was to them, and he looked in surprise as Roondar the Red roared with anger, "You defile this chamber! You are not of the order of the Brotherhood; get out this instant!"

Balferzaar the Black turned around and saw Lucian and Sir Septimus. "You must leave, Lucian– you know only the Order of the Six may enter here!"

"I cannot, Balferzaar! Dunbruan's defences have failed us!"

"GET OUT BEFORE I THROW YOU OUT! I WILL NOT HAVE SUCH BLASPHEMY SPOKEN IN THIS SACRED CHAMBER!" bellowed Glondin the Green.

Suddenly the Tower was rocked by a mighty crash, and the six Wizards looked at each other in startled amazement!

"Hearken to my words!" warned Lucian. "That was the Green Tower falling to its destruction! The Dondymarians have come under Dunbruan's Wall. If you do not act now, Pogglinburg will fall!"

Baaras the Brown rushed to the eastward-facing windows and looked out.

"Lucian speaks the truth; The Green Tower has fallen. What are those red lights?" he asked.

"They must be some new invention of the Dondymarians. They move fast and, if you do not act now, they will reach the bridge!"

"This cannot be happening said Glondin the green. "Why has Dunbruan the Great forsaken us to our enemies?"

"Those lights are heading towards the Didock farm!" shouted Baaras the Brown from the window, and then added, "They have paired off, and a group is heading for The Red Tower!" He hurried back to his throne and sat down. "Lucian is right, my brothers –if we do not act now, then all will be lost!"

"The Great Dunbruan has punished us for weakening his laws! Those such as him," said Roondar the Red, pointing at Lucian, "Have brought this destruction upon us!"

"NO!" said Lucian in anger. "We all brought destruction upon ourselves for relying on a Pogglin who was corrupted and bent his will to other means! And if you shall not act, then I will! Come on Sir Septimus, we will leave these old Pogglins to their fate!"

With that, he dashed down the stairs.

"You should have listened to us, Balferzaar!" Sir Septimus, his pointed finger raised in accusation. "You have all failed in your duty as Wizards. Lucian is right: you are nothing but old Pogglins, wrapped up in your legends of a worthless Pogglin. There is no greatness in Dunbruan!" With that, he turned and followed Lucian down the stairs.

★ ★ ★ ★ ★

Farmer Didock sat up in his bed, wide awake, and leapt over to the window. His eyes widened in terror as he saw twenty of the War Robots steaming through the yard towards the house.

"Henrietta! Henrietta, wake up!"

His wife sat up with a start. "What is it, Elisha?"

"There's something horrible out in the yard! Go and get Suzie and Jessie, take them to the back room and lock the door!"

The sound of splintering wood resounded through the house as a War Robot smashed through the front door! Henrietta rushed into her children's room and they were huddled together in one of the beds, white with fear. Their mother took them and they ran to the back room of the house and locked the door. The room was specially prepared for such an event; the thick wooden door was reinforced with strips of Black Steel.

Two more War Robots entered the house and started smashing their way through the various rooms of the house, which made the children scream with fear. The Farmer ran out into the hall in his striped pyjamas and waved a large wooden club above his head as a War Robot turned its head to face him, its eyes glowing in the darkness. It loomed menacingly above the farmer.

In the back room of the house, Mrs Didock and her children listened in wide-eyed horror as the Farmer confronted the menace.

"Get out of my house and off my farm!" he shouted. For a moment there was silence, and then they heard a whirl of metal blades. The farmer screamed in agonised terror. Mrs Didock huddled herself in the corner of the room, her daughters clinging tightly to her as she silently sobbed.

182

Suddenly the door started to splinter as the War Robot tried to smash its way through. The three terrified Pogglins screamed in terror.

It battered at the door, but was stopped by the reinforcements of Black Steel. The War Robot backed away, and Mrs Didock could hear nothing other than the terrifying howls from her young daughters. She tried desperately to comfort them as she fought back her own tears.

Suddenly three War Robots smashed through the wall, causing the ceiling to fall in on them. Despite the collapsing masonry, they kept making for the three terrified Pogglins in the corner of the room. Mrs Didock screamed in fear of her children's lives as she saw the red eyes of the War Robots bearing down on them.

"Please, do not harm my girls! Take me, and leave my girls be! For mercy's sake, have pity!" she pleaded with the metal creatures. The War Robots' rotary blades began to turn and rapidly pick up speed. Screams filled the air, and suddenly everything fell silent.

The War Robots trundled back out into the yard, leaving death and destruction behind in the now silent farmhouse.

★ ★ ★ ★ ★

King Vardiemar and Queen Ellgah rushed down into the plain of Pogglinburg with their troops and stopped dead. What met their eyes were hordes of War Robots steaming towards Pogglin Town.

"By Thremgould, these are not Dondymarians! What devilry has Creep set forth from Dondymar City?" said the King in amazement. They looked to the Green Tower; all that was left of it was rubble, beside the half-gutted house of Glondin the Green. There was a tremendous crash as the Red Tower was brought down by the War Robots!

"Will we have enough troops to hold them?" Queen Ellgah said.

"More are on the way, but we will be well occupied until their arrival," replied Vardiemar, raising his Battle Axe. "For Thremgould and the Brown Mountain!" he cried.

His troops replied with a thunderous cheer. With his Queen by his side Vardiemar charged off towards the War Robots, his Dwarves following behind.

King Vardiemar smashed into the side of the nearest War Robot with his mighty battle-axe. The blade ripped through the iron monster like paper, and a great burst of steam spewed from the mangled metal. The King jumped back and managed to dodge the jet of boiling steam as he brought down his battle-axe again. This time it smashed through the robot's head, the glass eyes shattering with the blow. The hulking robot slowed to a halt and became dormant. The King laughed with glee: the Dwarvish heart for battle had been rekindled within him, and his eyes shone with the wonder lust for war.

"These iron monsters will be easily dealt with by my Dwarves; victory will be ours!"

By this time the War Robots had diverted from their orders to take Pogglin Town, and started to turn towards the Dwarvish King and Queen and their troops.

The sun began to rise in the east, and the first rays of daylight hit the tops of the War Robots' heads as they steamed towards the Dwarves. There were more of them than the King had anticipated, and there was still more coming down from Dunbruan's Wall and so he quickly came to a decision.

"We must outflank them, my brave Dwarves, or the battle is lost!"

Queen Ellgah shouted the ancient battle cry of the Brown Mountain rallying call and, with her battle-hammer tightly in her grasp, charged off after the King. The Dwarves raced around in a crescent and hit the War Robots side on. Queen Ellgah smashed through the shafts of a War Robot's rotary blades, which went spinning into the air and one stuck into the side of another War Robot. She spun around with her Battle-hammer, crying the Battle rally as she did so, and sliced off one of the upper exhaust pipes on the back of the Robot. She ducked just in time as another War Robot shot out its propeller-like blades towards her. In mid-duck, the Queen smashed her battle-hammer into the tracks of the robot and it buckled under the blow. The battle was fierce: the Dwarves fought desperately against the War Robots as more of them swarmed onto the plain.

Queen Ellgah stoves in a War Robot's head with her Battle-hammer.

Lucian and Sir Septimus arrived at Battlehorne Bridge and ran across the ancient covered causeway and came to a halt on the eastern bank of the Copper River. To their astonishment, there was no sign of the War Robots.

"I would have thought they would have been here by now?"

"They would have been, Sir Septimus. Look over there," said Lucian pointing to the north, "The Dwarves have come to our aid and drawn them off!"

"By Thrasskin's beard, you are right, Snuzz! If we don't do something quickly, then our friends will be massacred!"

"Then we shall help them!" said Lucian with steadfastness, and the two Pogglins hurried off towards the Didock Farm where the battle raged.

★ ★ ★ ★ ★

Balferzaar the Black was stood at the tower window and was observing what little could be seen of the battle. He put his hand to his chin and rubbed it as he thought on Lucian's words. He turned to his fellow Wizards.

"The Dwarves have honoured the ancient treaty; they have engaged the Dondymarian War machines to the North. Lucian and Sir Septimus have gone to join them. It is time, my brothers, to act. We must fulfil our pledge of protecting Pogglinburg!"

He crossed the chamber and sat down in his throne at the table. "Whatever has gone wrong with Great Dunbruan's plan, we must now amend. The time has come, my brothers, to fulfil the oaths of our office."

Thus saying, he placed his hands on the black gemstone in front of him, and the other Wizards did the same on theirs. And as they did so, they all began to hum quietly, as Balferzaar spoke the words of incantation along with the other Wizards that was given to them by Dunbruan the Great all those centuries ago. The Wizards' incantations rose in pitch and came to a crescendo!

Suddenly the gemstones on their staffs lit up. Shafts of light sparked from them to illuminate the crystal globe above the stone table with a kaleidoscope of rainbow colours. The crystal globe glowed with energy as it travelled up the crystal shaft to the great gemstone on the tower roof. Suddenly a radiant burst of blue light shot out of the great black gemstone on the roof of the tower. The beam of light shone across to the west of Pogglinburg and struck the gemstone of the Brown Tower. Immediately the great brown gemstone on the roof emitted a golden light that ballooned out across the hill and down over Hill Square until the whole area was under a canopy of golden light and encapsulated the land in a bubble of gold!

While this was happening, the very same thing went on at the White and Blue Towers, until the land that surrounded them was enclosed in bubbles of White and Blue light. Around the Black Tower a pale blue light covered the whole of the town: it stretched westward to cover the Royal Flying Corps Aerodrome, and it also stretched eastward to Battlehorne Bridge. Apart from the land where the Red and Green Towers had been destroyed, the rest of Pogglinburg was encapsulated in four protective bubbles of magic light. Balferzaar opened his eyes and smiled, thankful that at least that part of Dunbruan's plan had worked.

★ ★ ★ ★ ★

Sir Septimus stopped and looked on in awe as the dawn sky lit up the power of the magic bubbles. His mouth dropped open and his monocle popped out of his eye as he looked on in wonder at the wonderful display of colours.

"Snuzz, look at Pogglin Town! I have never witnessed such a thing in my entire life!"

Lucian pulled his friend to follow him. "We'll have plenty of time to wonder at the power of the Grand Wizards later, Sir Septimus. Our friends are in serious need of our help. Now come!"

The two little Pogglins raced along the eastern bank of the Copper River towards the battle between the Dwarves and the Dondymarian War Robots.

The Dwarves were now fighting for their lives. The War Robots outnumbered them five to one and the reinforcements from the Brown Mountain still had not arrived. Many Dwarves had fallen valiantly, and their bodies littered the plain along with the burnt-out carcasses of the iron War Robots. The War Robots had virtually surrounded the Dwarves and were hacking into their number. King Vardiemar and Queen Ellgah were in the thick of battle, fighting back to back and holding off the deadly propeller blades of the War Robots.

"I am sorry we shall depart this world together like this, my love, but we shall enter the Hall of Thremgould in glory!" said the Queen to the King as he fought off another of the War Robots. The Queen stoved a War Robot's head in with her Battle-hammer and it exploded in a cloud of steam.

Lucian was running as fast as his little legs could carry him. As the two Pogglins drew nearer to the scene of battle they could see what a desperate fight the Dwarves had been putting up. It was a scene of carnage, and it hardened Lucian to the task in hand and overcoming the enemy. Suddenly he dropped to the ground with his staff and thumped the gemstone into the dew-covered grass as he roared the magic words: "*TERRA PROSTERNO*!"

The ground trembled, and a torpedo-like bolt of energy ripped through the grass-covered plain towards the oncoming War Robots. The soil smashed into them, sending them hither and thither in all directions. Some smashed into each other and exploded on impact, while others sank into the soil like it was quicksand!

The explosion of the earth caused the Dwarves to pause in wonderment, his attention distracted; King Vardiemar did not notice the War Robot that was bearing down on him! Instantly the rotary shafts of one of the blades shot forward, but Queen Elgar's lightning-quick reflexes saved him as she shattered the shaft with her Battle-Hammer and then staved in the robot's head with a single blow. A great jet of steam shot out of the top of its metal head and it ground to a halt. The King escaped with a minor flesh wound to the top of his arm. In exhaustion, he looked deeply into the Queen's eyes and smiled his thanks.

Seeing more of the War Robots bearing down on the Dwarvish King and Queen, Sir Septimus picked up a Battle-Axe from one of the fallen Dwarves and charged in, waving the axe about his head. The stout little Pogglin smashed down the axe into the tracks of a War Robot that was almost upon the King and Queen of the Brown Mountain. He roared in fury as he swung the axe down again, cutting through two of the exhaust pipes. Steam jetted out the back of the robot as it tried to turn to lay a death blow on the little Pogglin's head, but its damaged track caused it to grind itself into the soft earth.

"Allow me, Sir Septimus!" said Queen Ellgah as she leapt forward and dealt a heavy blow to the robot's head, watching as it fell, dormant.

To the right flank of the Dwarves, Lucian thumped his staff on the ground, "*Mortalitas Cos Cotis*!" There was a flash of blue light and a War Robot was halted in its tracks, turned instantly to stone. Suddenly a boulder fell from the sky and smashed down onto a War Robot to the right of Lucian. Quickly, he looked up to see Wing Commander Wingnut and Red swooping up in an arc.

"THANK YOU!" he called as Flying Cadet Thaddeus Morton-Chump, mounted on Bluey, swooped down and knocked out another War Robot with a boulder. Even with the intervention of the Pogglins, the battle was still in the War Robots' favour as still more of their number swelled the plain. Suddenly there was a huge explosion as one of the Robots was hit by a cannon ball. Lucian turned to see Admiral Loomboggle in his two-seater man of war, The Diamond! He had sailed from the Copper Lake and down into the Copper River to give battle. The Admiral let off another broadside into the approaching War Robots, and another exploded on impact.

"How many more of these steam-driven metal devils are there?!" shouted King Vardiemar, as he fought off another Robot. As soon as a War Robot was destroyed two more seemed to take its place. The War Robots had lost their pincer attack on the Dwarves, but still had them pinned down. Sir Septimus stood beside the King and Queen and fought as bravely as any Dwarf warrior. Never before in his lifetime had the Dondymarians invaded his homeland: he was angry, angry enough to pay with his life to his defend his King, his country and his friends. The little Pogglin hacked, chopped and pummelled with his battle-axe in a frenzied attack on the relentless War Robots.

Lucian saw another wave of War Robots coming over the ridge toward King Vardiemar's group, which was hacking into the robots with equalled vigour. Lucian quickly dropped to his knee and thumped the gemstone atop his staff into the ground; "***TERRA PROSTERNO***!" he shouted, sending another earth torpedo off into the group of War Robots. The soil smashed into them, causing two them to explode in a mass of flames and steam.

Just then the Royal Pogglin Flying Corps swooped down again and dropped three boulders down on the War Robots. Two hit their target with direct hits, while the third boulder hit the ground, bounced into the air and took out three more of the Robots like skittles in a bowling alley. "YOHAY!" shouted the Wing Commander with joy, and Red swooped up into the early morning sky.

"TO ME!" called Lucian over the din of battle to Sir Septimus and the Dwarves. "TO BATTLEHORNE BRIDGE WHILE WE HAVE THE CHANCE!"

The Dwarves and their little Pogglin Companion fought hard against the few robots that remained around them, then broke out and ran westward towards the river. They were covered by Admiral Loomboggle in the Diamond, who let off shots to cover the Dwarves' backs. The Dwarves quickly caught up with Lucian and they hurried down along the eastern bank of the Copper River, hotly pursued by yet more War Robots. They were supported by air attack from Wing Commander Wingnut and his cadets: the Hobbdraks picked up the boulders from the nearby mountains with ease and, guided by their pilots, released them onto the pursuing robots, then broke off and sped back to collect more of their heavy ammunition.

Admiral Loomboggle followed the Robots along the banks of the Copper River, firing on them at will. It was enough to slow the robots up, and the Pogglins with their Dwarvish allies made it back to the safety of Battlehorne Bridge. The magic bubbles encapsulated the bridge and the land about. Only those of pure heart and no malice had the power to pass through the magic bubble.

"What wonder is this, Lucian?" enquired Queen Ellgah, rather breathlessly.

"Dunbruan's magic, my Queen," he replied, also out of breath, "And if it had been working as we were led to believe, none of this would ever have happened. The Dondymarians would not have entered Pogglinburg. But we are safe within the confines of the barrier, and they cannot get in!"

He turned to King Vardiemar, who was trying to strap up his injured shoulder with little success. "My Lord King and my Lady, you have fought bravely for my homeland, and your Dwarves died valiantly to save our land. Many songs will be sung in Thremgould's Hall of valour. I thank you!" He bowed deeply.

The King patted the Pogglin's back. "Aye, Lucian, my Dwarves fought bravely and died with honour, and there will be many songs sung in Thremgould's Hall with whom they now sit at his high table." He smiled and then thumped down his hand on Sir Septimus' shoulder, noting that he still carried the battle-axe. . "But this one here, my friend Lucian, has shown his mettle on the field of battle, and fought as bravely as any Dwarf!" He laughed a hearty laugh, "And he shall be thrice honoured when he comes next to my Great Hall of the Brown Mountain!"

Sir Septimus beamed as he bowed to King Vardiemar, and, nodding with thanks to having such honour placed on his shoulders, he popped his monocle back in his socket.

"LOOK!" shouted one of the Dwarves in amazement, and all turned to see the War Robots bouncing off the magic bubble. "They cannot penetrate the sorcery of the Black Tower!" A cheer of joy went up from the exhausted remnants of the Dwarvish advance guard.

"Just what are these steam-powered war machines?" enquired King Vardiemar, while Queen Ellgah attended to the King's wound.

"The new storm-troops of Dondymar City, I would suggest, my Lord King. And I would say it is just the spearhead of the main attack: somewhere beyond Dunbruan's Wall, the entire Dondymarian army stand poised to attack!"

The King looked grimly at the little Pogglin. "Well, the magic of the Pogglins has given us a respite from these steam-powered devils at least, and once we have recovered, my friend, I and my Dwarves will take to the field again!"

Suddenly, from behind them, Lucian and his party heard the pounding of running feet over the wooden bridge; they turned to see Sara, Artimus and Zontahl.

"Thank Dunbruan you are safe!" cried Sara with relief.

"There were still more of those War Robots pouring out of Dunbruan's Wall when we left the workshop loft. We and Zontahl have come on ahead to let you know that King Pooley is just behind with the Town Guard and the Royal Palace Guards."

The King and Queen of the Dwarves nodded their thanks and they went amongst their Dwarves to attend to their needs and sort out the walking wounded.

"Sir Septimus fought like a berserker!" said Lucian to Artimus.

"Good old Sir Septimus!" replied Artimus, and patted his friend on the back whilst Sara kissed him on the cheek.

"Only doing my duty, old fruit," said Sir Septimus modestly.

"I was sorry to have missed out on the battle, but I have come prepared for the next," said Artimus, and with that he brandished a strange, stick-like object made of wood and brass. "It will give me a chance to try out one of my little inventions!" and he smiled broadly at his three friends.

"What's that going to do against those War Robots?" exclaimed Sir Septimus with surprise.

"Wait and see, Sir Septimus, wait and see!" came the reply.

"I think I'll trust in my Battle-Axe, thank you!" said Sir Septimus as he patted the Axe-half. "We've become close acquaintances in the last forty minutes," he explained to the watchmaker and, beaming, patted the Axe again.

"Well, I am feeling rather redundant! What can I do to help?" enquired Zontahl.

"I'm afraid there's not much you can do to help against these iron machines, Zontahl, so I suggest you stay within the protection of the magic barrier until all is done. You have played a valiant part in our adventures; it's time for you to rest," said Lucian kindly to the cat as he stroked Zontahl's head.

"As do you, Snuzz! You are looking drawn and tired," said Sir Septimus with concern. "You have overused your magic back there, and it shows, my friend. You should rest before our counter-attack."

"I will do – as we all shall do, my friend, after the job is done this day."

The four Pogglins and the cat looked out over the river towards the Eastern bank; the morning sun was now quite high and the green fields were clearly lit by its rays. They could see a great line of gleaming red metal as the War Robot spearhead steamed towards them. Now and then, some would explode as boulders that were being dropped by the Royal Flying Corps crushed them and whenever the Diamond fired a broadside into them. Every time this happened a great cheer went up from the Dwarves, who stood waiting for their orders to start the counter-attack to drive the War Robots back to Dunbruan's Wall.

At that moment Grand King Pooley arrived with Field-Marshal Mandergast, the Town Guard and the Royal Palace Guards. He checked to see that Lucian and Sir Septimus were well.

"It is good to see you safe, my friends!" he smiled, "The Grand Wizards are still within the Tower chamber, and all their powers are focused on maintaining the magical barriers that protect us from these iron monstrosities! Now if you will excuse me, I must see if there is anything that can be done to help our Dwarvish friends."

King Pooley made his way over to King Vardiemar and Queen Ellgah, where they were tending to the wounded and rallying the spirits of their warriors.

"Thank you for coming to our aid, Vardiemar. Pogglinburg may well have been lost if it were not for the efforts of you and your warriors," he said as he shook King Vardiemar's hand, and Queen Ellgah shot King Pooley a look. "And, of course, the sterling efforts and bravery of your courageous and lovely Queen Ellgah!" he added quickly, and the Queen graciously nodded her thanks.

"There is an old Dwarvish saying that you will do well to remember Pooley, and that is, *there is nought that one can rely on in this world other than the steel of your axe head*!" King Vardiemar exclaimed. "The treaty between our two Kingdoms stands older than Dunbruan's Wall, and on the Dwarves' help you can always rely."

King Pooley smiled and flushed with embarrassment at the failure of the Great Dunbruan's defences to protect his Kingdom. Quickly he said, "I have brought Field-Marshal Mandergast, the Town Guard and the Royal Palace guards to help swell your ranks, Vardiemar. I know they add only twelve more to your number, but they are well-trained, if a little rusty in the arts of war. I shall of course be at your side when we muster for the counter-attack."

King Vardiemar beamed at the little Pogglin King and laughed heartily. "Then our friendship will be forged even stronger in the heat of glorious battle. I say one thing, Pooley, for little folk you have stout hearts of Oak. Why, Sir Septimus fought more fiercely than a cornered terrier!"

The four Pogglins and the cat returned to observing the War Robots after King Pooley had left them. The robots were testing the perimeter of the magic barrier, but still they bounced off the curved wall of the magic bubble. Their tiny positronic steam-powered brains just couldn't cope with the concept of being unable to enter. So, they filled their time with milling about the eastern side bank, destroying what little there was left to destroy. Zontahl's sharp and keen eyes were the first to spot it: a blur of light moving rapidly along the bank of the Copper River towards the Bridge.

"What is that which this way comes?" he said pointing out the strange manifestation with his paw as it was now rapidly advancing.

"Why, it's Elgyn Kloons!" answered Lucian. "I would know that blur anywhere!"

Elgin Kloons came to an abrupt halt before King Vardiemar and Queen Ellgah. Bowing low in salutation, he gave greetings to Grand King Pooley.

"What news do you carry, Elgyn?" asked King Vardiemar.

"Marshal-General Cavernhollow has just crossed over Gromm Bridge and asks where he is to attack the enemy?"

"If Cavernhollow can draw off some of those metal misfits from the Bridge, we can break out and attack them from the rear, while the Royal Flying Corps and Admiral Loomboggle can pin them down by the Didock Farm. If we can sweep them towards the Gromm Falls we can wheel around and mop up the Dondymarian Army, and push them back down the rabbit hole that they have bored through Dunbruan's Wall!"

Grand King Pooley agreed with Vardiemar's plans, and sent Captain Rumsbiggot out onto the western bank to signal Wing Commander Wingnut and Admiral Loomboggle.

"Hey, Guv, you're being signalled!" called Red, back to his Wing Commander.

Wingnut looked down to the ground and saw Captain Rumsbiggot waving with his large red bicorn hat.

"It looks important, Red. Take us down and see what orders he has for us." Red swooped down towards the west bank in a long arc and penetrated the Magic barrier with ease. "Good morning, Captain Rumsbiggot, and what can me and my boys do for you?"

"New orders from Grand King Pooley, old chap. The Dwarves are coming over Gromm Bridge and are going to draw off the War Robots. You and your cadets are to keep them pinned down up by Didock Farm, and the King and the Dwarves will counter-attack from the rear."

"Wilco, Rumsbiggot old bean. We'll just go and load up and then start our attack run. Come on Red, back to Copper Mountain for some more boulders, and we'll try and get some nice biggan's this time!"

"Roger that, Guv!" said Red and flapped his wings and started to make for the Copper Mountain.

"What are my orders, Captain Rumsbiggot?" asked the Admiral.

"The same, sir – keep the machines pinned down near Didock farm," replied Rumsbiggot.

Elgyn Kloons dashed off, leaving the safety of the protective magic barrier and weaved his way through the War Robots that stood between him and Marshal-General Cavernhollow. He was way too quick for the robots to attack, but they sensed that someone was there and the Robots turned and started to steam back towards the Didock farm. The plan was beginning to work!

Marshal-General Cavernhollow was lying flat on the ground: he watched the War Robots attempting to puncture an entrance into the Magic barrier, and he saw them turn away and start to move towards the Didock farm. He turned to his Captain who was lying next to him. "That will be Elgyn on his way back; prepare to make the signal."

Just then Elgyn skidded to a halt beside Cavernhollow. "They're on the way!" he said calmly.

"Well done, Elgyn! The plan is working." The Captain of the Guard made the signal to the Dwarvish warriors lying down behind him, and they all stood up with their Battle-Axes at the ready. One thousand dwarves stood ten abreast and dominated the horizon.

Marshal-General Cavernhollow got to his feet and stood in front of his Dwarves. "Let them get within thirty feet – and then let them have it!"

The Dwarvish warriors roared back. "For King Vardiemar, and the honour of The Brown Mountain!"

Cavernhollow smiled. "That's the spirit, boys!" and he turned to watch the War Robots that were now streaming by the Didock farm. Wing Commander Wingnut and his mount swooped down and dropped the first of the boulders onto the robots, hitting his target, and then circled tightly towards the Copper Mountain for another boulder.

Cadet Thaddeus Morton-Chump came next in on Bluey, though his boulder missed its target. "Botheration!" he said in disgust at himself.

"Never mind mate, we'll get them on our next run," said Bluey cheerfully, in an attempt to rally his young pilot.

Cadet Ignatius Ffaph swooped in low on Greenie, above the heads of the War Robots and let loose two boulders, which hit a robot that exploded on impact and disabled another. While the Hobbdraks were gathering more boulders, the Admiral opened fire in the Diamond and took out two more Robots.

The Pogglins and their Hobbdrak mounts kept up a heavy bombardment on the advancing Robots, but it did little to slow them up. Cavernhollow gave the signal to Wing Commander Wingnut to withdraw, and then he and his Dwarves charged into the War Robots. The counter-attack had begun! King Vardiemar, Queen Ellgah and Grand King Pooley had already moved off from Battlehorne Bridge with their small army of troops behind. They marched at an easy pace until they were halfway to Didock Farm, then they picked up to a trot. Not too far off ahead of them, they could see the line of War Robots advancing towards Cavernhollow and his Dwarves.

Grand King Pooley's mouth and throat were dry as dust; it was the first time he had seen war and had taken up arms. He tried to swallow, but nothing happened: he was too tense with anticipation and fear. Before he knew what was happening, he and the Dwarves were in the midst of the battle and fighting with all their might.

★ ★ ★ ★ ★

Meanwhile, Lucian and his three friends had other plans. After saying farewell to the two kings, the Queen and the troops, they hurriedly set off towards Dunbruan's Wall.

"I don't think Zontahl was too pleased at being left behind," said Artimus.

"He will be better off back there. Teeth and claws are no good against an iron enemy, no matter how brave he is."

"Yes, you're right there," said Sara, "but I think you still should have let him come with us."

Lucian stopped and turned, "Sara, this isn't a walking party! There are many of our friends out there who could be killed or dying for us. We have an important job to carry out, and I did not want the extra weight on my shoulders worrying about Zontahl's safety. Now let's get on!" He turned and started to move off quickly towards the White Tower.

"Don't mind him, Sara; he's got a lot on his plate at the moment. You know what Snuzz is like, he'll get over it," said Sir Septimus, resting the battle-axe across his shoulder.

"What have you brought that Axe along for?" enquired Artimus.

"In case those iron blighters show up! I think it better protection than your stick!"

"It's not a stick, it's a..."

"No time for explanations, Artimus. We've got to move!" said Sir Septimus as he hurried off after Lucian.

Soon the four Pogglins were standing on the hill by the White Tower, where they could see the ferocious battle in the distance. Even from up there, they could see many dead lying in the fields about the farm.

"It's going to be a massacre if I can't find the correct Ley lines from here!" said Lucian in distress.

"Sorry, I don't understand. What've Ley lines got to do with it up here?"

"Everything, Artimus! Why do you think Dunbruan was able to raise up that Mountain range? Because he made his stand on the convergence of Ley lines: he drew his power from them, and focused it into his sorcery. The Ley lines converge on Dunbruan's Stand, the hill where he cast the spell. I need them to do something similar and stop this bloodshed!"

Sir Septimus, Sara and Artimus raced down the hill after Lucian, who was zigzagging down the hill and running in different directions holding his staff before him.

"There must be a convergence about here somewhere. But it needs to be as close to the tunnel as possible, otherwise I could lose control of the magic forces and end up destroying our friends and ourselves in the process!"

All his three companions could do was watch as Lucian ran frantically about, trying to find the Ley line convergence. Suddenly his staff began to grow warm in his hand, and he shouted with joy and he started racing off nearer to the edge of the magic bubble generated by the White Tower's gemstone on its roof.

Chapter Eight

It was a long, hard and bloody fight; Grand King Pooley saw many brave warriors fall and die beside him, as the rotary blades of the War Robots caused horrific wounds, amputations and death. He had many near-misses from the fatal blades himself, but, as he later recalled, it was amazing how quickly one remembered the art of combat when one's life is at stake! He had discarded his sword, which was hardly causing a scratch on the surface of the robot's bodies, in favour of a Dwarvish battle-axe which he had claimed from a poor soul who no longer had need of it. The black steel of the Dwarvish smithies was the hardest known metal of Sol-Larris, and it sliced through the War Robots as if they were made from paper. That said, they were still a formidable foe and could strike out their rotary blades at lightning speed. Also, the escaping steam was a hindrance, he had seen many a Dwarf caught up in its blast, and seen how it caused their skin to boil and blister.

The sun had slowly risen in the sky. It must have been almost noon, and still, the battle raged on. The machines were relentless and numerous. Grand King Pooley continued to hack away at the War Robots with his Dwarvish allies at his side.

★ ★ ★ ★ ★

Lucian had finally found the convergence of Ley lines. "At last!" he exclaimed, as he stood squarely on the spot. In the distance, he could see yet more War Robots steaming out of the tunnel at the foot of Dunbruan's Wall. A column split off from the main body and headed towards him and his friends. Lucian threw out his arms and was about to cast his spell when he stopped abruptly.

"I can't cast the spell! The Magic barrier of the Grand Wizards will bounce my spell back at us. The barrier has to be brought down before my magic will work!"

As in answer to his words, the voice of Balferzaar the Black echoed all around the hill.

"You have been heard, Lucian, and your request shall be granted."

The magic bubble seemed to fizz and then it disappeared, leaving the four Pogglins in the path of the approaching War Robots!

"What a time to drop the barrier!" grumbled Artimus as he moved forward with his strange contraption at the ready.

"I'm afraid I can't help you, my friends—all my powers will be needed for my spell, you have to hold them off for as long as possible!"

"You can rely on us, Snuzz old boy," said Sir Septimus as he rushed forward, waving the battle-axe above his head.

The War Robots accelerated and steamed towards them, their rotary blades at full speed. Sir Septimus was about to wade into armed combat with the first War Robot when Artimus stepped forward and released a small catch on the side of his invention, causing it to extend a few inches and a trigger to drop down towards the handle. He aimed the 'stick' at the incoming robot and gently pressed the trigger. A small black magnet shot out of the end and stuck to the robot's head, just above the left eye. It had an instant effect on the Robot; it went crazy and spun out of control, smashing into its fellow robots!

Sir Septimus stopped dead in his tracks and looked around at Artimus in amazement. "I want one of those!" he beamed.

"Well, I have one too!" exclaimed Sara, and activated the trigger mechanism, took aim, and fired at the incoming War Robot. Like Artimus, her aim was exact: hitting one directly between the eyes, she sent it spinning off like an oversized toy.

Meanwhile, Lucian had been muttering magical words. He then threw out his arms and as the gemstone glowed pale in the sunlight the threw back his head. He shouted "*MAGNETICUS PILA PRO EXITIUM!*" then thrust his staff into the ground.

On the impact of his staff hitting the ground, there seemed to be a miniature earthquake. It caused the four Pogglins and the War Robots to be jostled about, but Lucian still stood firmly on the spot, his chin jutting out in determination and defiance. The War Robots regained control as the quake subsided, and bore down on the Pogglins once again.

"For Pogglinburg's sake, keep them off me!" called Lucian through gritted teeth, his cheeks trembling under the great strain of the spell he had cast.

Once more Sara and Artimus bravely started to attack and pick off the Robots: they fired their magnet guns at the robots and any direct hit sent the robots veering off instantly into the other War Robots around them. The magnets seemed to confuse and muddle their mechanical brains, and they started to attack each other.

Sir Septimus, breathing hard, rested his battle-axe on the ground and leaned on it. "I definitely want one of those, Artimus!" he said, feeling a little redundant.

While the crazed War Robots tore into its companions, a small white orb had appeared at the mouth of the tunnel. It crackled with energy and slowly began to grow, expanding to the size of a football in seconds. Lightning forks began to flash from it; the wind began to sweep around it, circling like a tornado, and all the time it was expanding. The colour had drained from Lucian's cheeks and he was sweating profusely, his eyes were clamped shut and his teeth were clenched in the monumental effort to infuse the orb with his power. The orb began to spin, gently at first, then with gaining speed, and all the time it was continuing to expand in size. It was now the size of a small house, and a storm of lightning flashes raged all about the orb.

It was then that Sir Septimus saw that the War Robots were losing control, and great ruts in the grass began to appear as they were being pulled back towards the spinning white orb. Suddenly the magnetic pull of the orb wrenched them from the ground, and they went hurtling towards the mouth of the cave!

★ ★ ★ ★ ★

Meanwhile, the battle of Didock Farm was still as hard and ferociously fought as when it had started. The Dwarves and the small band of Pogglins had managed to destroy half of the War Robots' forces, but they had still lost many warriors to the robots even though the Dwarves outnumbered them this time around.

King Vardiemar was hacking off the shafts of the rotary blades when the robot before him suddenly jerked backwards; Vardiemar looked at it in surprise and wondered what was happening to it. The robot's head turned from side to side, as if in frustration of not being able to move forward. Suddenly, all the robots in the vicinity followed suit and they too all jerked backwards. The grass and mud were being ploughed up under the heavy resistance of the machines as they were being dragged away by some unseen force! Then a robot was suddenly pulled up and seemed to leap into the air, releasing its grip on the ground. Another robot flew into the air followed by another and they smashed into each other, causing them to explode.

"By Thremgould, what is this?!" said the King in astonishment as the all the robots on the field were dragged backwards to Dunbruan's Wall.

A Dwarf warrior was hit, and seriously wounded, by one of the flying War Robots.

"GET DOWN ON THE GROUND AND STAY DOWN!" roared King Vardiemar. Everyone hit the ground as the War Robots were ripped off the ground and hurtled off towards Dunbruan's Wall. Suddenly the king's helmet flew off his head and shot off in the same direction! He felt a force pulling at his battle-axe and it tried to wrench itself from his grasp, but the wily old King kept his head and evoked the power of the rune symbols on his battle-axe, Dwarvish magic that brought the weapon back under his control. All around him the Dwarvish warriors were doing the same thing and keeping a firm grip on their precious battle-axes, although all had now lost their helmets to the unseen force.

The fields about the farm were now totally devoid of the War Robots. Had it not been for the fallen warriors and the ruts in the ground, it would have seemed as though the battle had never taken place there.

★ ★ ★ ★ ★

Sir Septimus' Battle-Axe was pulled from his grip, and flew off towards the white orb at the mouth of the tunnel. It grew no bigger, but it was spinning faster and the magnetic draw was phenomenally powerful. Now, like a sun it had many satellites spinning around it. Every War Robot, together with destroyed shells and parts of robots, a few battle-axes and many Dwarvish helmets, were hurtling around the outer edge of the white orb.

Lucian now looked like one of the living dead: his eyes had sunken in, and he looked like all his life's energy had been completely drawn out of him.

"I can't hold... it much... longer!" he said with extreme effort through clenched teeth. "Sara... Are there any more... war robots...left?"

"No Lucian, you have drawn them all off with that white orb at the tunnel mouth."

"Thank Thremgould!" sighed Lucian. "If I can.... just muster the last remnants ....of strength I have... for one final effort, I must.... close the breach!" With great effort Lucian drew his arms together, grasped his staff in both hands and thumped the staff twice hard on the ground. "*PILA EXITIUM!*"

Instantly the white orb began to decrease in mass, and the colour darkened from white to red. As the orb shrank, there was a horrible sound as the War Robots were being crushed into all manner of deformed shapes as they were sucked into the orb's maelstrom. Then as the orb shrunk down to the size of a tennis ball, it fell heavily to the ground and rolled down into the mouth of the tunnel. Suddenly there was a massive ground-shaking explosion, and a mass of belching flames and steam shot out of the tunnel entrance. Mixed in with the sounds of explosions were screams from the remaining Dondymarians that had been waiting in the tunnel for their orders to attack.

There was one final, mighty explosion that brought down the mouth of the tunnel, and the top part of the mountain seemed to sink under its own weight. The tunnel had been completely sealed and the Dondymarian army units that were on standby in the tunnel had been crushed. It would be a very long time before the Dondymarians could even think of mounting an attack from that direction again!

Lucian's eyes flickered open; he swayed, and then fell, lifeless to the ground.

"Lucian!" cried Sara in shock and ran over to him, quickly followed by Artimus and Sir Septimus.

He was cold and as white as marble. Sara, convinced he had killed himself to save his people, started to sob uncontrollably. "Sara, help us, we must get him to Dr Snuzz without delay!"

"He doesn't seem to be breathing, Sir Septimus!" cried Sara.

"Come on! We MUST TRY!"

Sara cradled Lucian's head in her arms and then his anxious friends took their fallen friend's feet and arms between them, while Sara picked up his staff. They then hurried off down the hill towards Battlehorne Bridge and Pogglin Town as fast as they could possibly run.

★ ★ ★ ★ ★

Creep lowered himself down onto the comfy cushioned seat of the Royal Throne, where he nestled himself into it like a hen on a clutch of eggs. "Yes," he thought to himself, "I could take to this quite easily; this will be my throne when I am the emperor of the world!"

Just then the whole of the palace rocked to its very foundations, causing Creep's wig to slip down over his eyes yet again. The earth tremor subsided after a short while, leaving Creep in the dark. For a terrible moment he thought he had gone blind, but soon realised it was the old problem of his wig falling over his eyes. "I must get a new one when I am Emperor," he thought to himself as he straightened the bothersome hairpiece.

Then his eye caught a glimpse of an explosion! He trotted as fast as his bowed legs would carry him to the window that looked northwest out towards Pogglinburg. Above Dunbruan's Wall, he could see what looked to him to be a tornado, from which thundered great bolts of lightning. Suddenly there was a flash of white light and a massive explosion that again rocked the Royal Palace. He saw a portion of the Dunbruan's Wall sink into the earth. His instincts told him instantly that his plan for the domination of Pogglinburg had failed; the tunnel was destroyed.

"Damn those filthy Pogglins!" he screeched as he tore off his wig and threw it to the marble floor with rage.

The door opened and Sir Kyerthaas Gittoid entered the throne room, his face long and mournful, and Creep knew that he carried news that his plans had failed utterly.

"The tunnel has collapsed, many of our soldiers were killed and we believe the War Robot spearhead has been wiped out. Doctor Meltabossokk has lost all contact with the spearhead, and asks when shall we attack again? He says he will have another fifty War Robots ready by this evening."

Meltabossokk can sti…" Creep was about to say when Queen Baalshibah entered with her pet Snoog.

She gasped with surprised to see the Lord High Chamberlain of Dondymaria with his head laid bare. "Oh Fangy, what's happened to your lovely hairpiece?"

"On the blooming' floor like the rest of my plans!" he barked back sharply and caused Lug-Lug to snarl at him in hatred, "Pppphrrrrrrrrrrrrrrrrph!" which didn't improve Creep's disposition one bit!

★ ★ ★ ★ ★

Dr Snuzz and his wife took Lucian to the school that was being used as a field hospital where the many wounded and dying were being attended to. To everyone's relief, the doctor announced that he could feel a pulse, but it was extremely weak. There was no change in him by the following day and so he was moved into the spare bedroom at the Doctor's house where he remained in a coma for six days.

In that time Sir Septimus, Artimus with Marius, and Zontahl visited him. Sara sat by his bed, holding his hand and talked to him constantly. She stayed with him around the clock, and prayed to the great Dunbruan for his recovery. He also had visits from both Kings and Queens, and even old Chancellor Silverore paid him a visit from Dwarveshire. The visitors talked to Lucian gave him news of the work being carried out on the reconstruction of the destroyed Red and Green Towers, and bathed his brow. They did everything they could to bring him back from the coma and hoped upon hope that, if they managed to, then permanent damage was not the result.

Then, on the afternoon of the sixth day, Lucian's eyes flickered; seconds later he blinked and then opened his eyes for the first time. He found himself looking up into the big orange eyes of Zontahl, who had been keeping vigil while Sara, Sir Septimus, Artimus and Marius were downstairs with the Doctor and Aunt Samantha.

Lucian smiled, and the cat smiled back. "Hello, Zontahl old chap," he said with a smile and then rubbed the sleep from his eyes.

"It's so good to see you back in the land of the living," replied Zontahl with a grin.

Zontahl jumped off the bed onto the chair alongside it, as Lucian started to sit up. "How long have I been asleep, Zontahl?"

"This is the sixth day, my friend," replied the cat.

"Did we manage to overcome the invasion?"

"We did indeed, and it was a glorious victory. The War machines of Dondymaria were totally destroyed by your magic, and you have sealed the breach in Dunbruan's Wall. You have even had visits from all six of the Grand Wizards. Sara has been constantly by your side, and has naturally been desperately worried, as indeed we all have."

Lucian smiled. "That's very kind of you. It was strange, but while I was asleep, I had a strange feeling of being in another place, another time. I was dreaming that I was a sculptor of clay figures it was all very strange indeed!"

With that Lucian made to get up out of bed, but Zontahl jumped on the bed to stop him.

"No! You are to remain in bed on your uncle's orders."

"But I have urgent work to do! I must speak with Balferzaar."

"That can wait; you must have complete rest, my friend." The cat jumped off the bed and made for the door. "The others are downstairs, and I shall go and tell them the excellent news of your awakening. They will be overjoyed".

A few moments later they were all standing around the bed in the small bedroom. Apart from Sara, who stood beside Lucian and held his hand. "I thought you were never going to wake up, Lucian. I am so pleased to see you awake! How do you feel, my love?"

Lucian looked into Sara's bright, sapphire-blue eyes, smiled and squeezed her hand with thanks.

"I feel rejuvenated," he said and continued, "When I first saw the love light in your eyes, I knew that the world had nought but joy for me." He said quietly with a smile, and she smiled and nodded her head.

"Tis true for me too, my dearest Lucian Snuzz!" she said with joy and kissed him.

"Now then you two love birds, there's plenty of time to plight your troth later," said Dr Snuzz moving forward, putting the stethoscope in his ears in readiness to listen to Lucian's chest. After a few moments later he rose. "Nothing wrong there, Lucian, you seem as fit as a fiddle!"

Then he added, "But I recommend you rest and remain in bed the rest of the day." Dr Snuzz turned to his wife; "We had better go down and make a drink for our guests, Samantha." Both left the room.

"Look whose here to see his Uncle Lucian!" said Artimus joyfully.

Lucian held his arms wide, and Marius jumped into his arms. "Hello, you little rascal, and how is my favourite nephew?"

"I am fine, I love you Uncle, and I don't want Daddy or you to go away ever again!" The young Pogglet smiled, and Lucian found it hard to give a reassuring reply to Marius' statement, but just said, "No, we won't be going away for a long while yet." He smiled and Artimus picked up his son from the bed, and gave Lucian that look. "We have all missed you greatly," he said.

"Now you are awake, Snuzz old boy, how about a few answers. What was that thing you summoned, was it a giant magnet?"

"Oh, gosh, no," replied Lucian to his friend. "Although it was magnetic, it was not a magnet as such. All I did was focus all the Earth's magnetic forces into that iridescent orb. That's why I had to find the conjuncture of the Ley lines. It was also by the same means that Dunbruan was able to throw up the mountain range that we now call *Dunbruan's Wall*. Not the same magic, mind you, but the same forces of the Earth. Although I am not as powerful in magic as Dunbruan, and that's why it very nearly killed me!"

"All the magnetic forces of Earth, eh? No wonder the War Robots flew through the air like so many pins to a Magnet!" said Artimus with a smile.

"And talking of magnets, those sticks of yours, Artimus - now weren't they firing magnets?"

"Indeed, they were, Sir Septimus! The War Robots, being entirely made of metal, gave me the idea that a magnet would affect them, but I didn't know just how much damage to them it would do. I assumed that they had some sort of brain: probably a positronic one most likely. So, if you stuck a magnet on one, it would seize up. Well, that was my reasoning anyhow."

Artimus found Sir Septimus looking at him with a glazed expression: he obviously hadn't grasped onto the explanation.

"The positronic brain would become magnetised and would stop working. That's why they lost control and started attacking themselves when a magnet was attached to their heads."

198

"I see, I see," replied Sir Septimus nodding his head, not entirely sure that he did see.

"In short, Sir Septimus, the magnets confused their metal brain. You could say that they had a complete *metal breakdown*," he said with a smile.

Sir Septimus winced at the joke. "I've heard that one before somewhere!"

"Lucian, you must be so proud of your Sara! The way she handled that magnet gun was incredible, and she was fearless and strong until she thought she had lost you for good," Artimus said.

"Oh shush!" said Sara, "I was no better or braver than anyone else, and probably had more luck than anyone else."

Lucian smiled and said, "I can't say that I was too happy to see her risking her life like that, but yes, I am so very proud of her: she was amazing."

★ ★ ★ ★ ★

In his rocky lair within the Blendaraak Mountains, Shrigg was once again sitting on his nest waiting for news from his scouts. He was very hungry and pined for food, his stomach rumbled in protest.

Shortly a scout came to report, and it wasn't the news that he wanted to hear.

"I come with tidings of bad news, my Lord Shrigg. The fallen dead have been removed from the field of battle. If it were not for the ploughed-up grass and a destroyed farm, no being would have assumed a great battle to have taken place!"

Shrigg squawked with hunger. "What I am to eat if there are no dead on whom to feast?!" Then his black beady eyes fell upon the scout, and if a bird's beak could produce an evil smile, then his did!

★ ★ ★ ★ ★

Colour Sergeant Frampton Nagg and King Mumbeldok II sat at the beautifully carved Dwarvish wooden table. They were playing a game of chess, and Nagg was letting the King win for the sixth game when a knock at the door interrupted them and Elgyn Kloons entered.

"I bring you news from King Vardiemar III! The Dondymarian force of War Machines has been crushed, and the Dwarves and the Pogglins are victorious."

Mumbeldok looked unmoved by the news "So?"

"'Ow many Dondymarians were killed?" asked Nagg.

"None on the battlefield," replied the Dwarf. "Only the War Machines took part on the field of battle. Although how many Dondymarians died when the tunnel under Dunbruan's Wall collapsed, I cannot tell. You have been ordered to present yourselves at the court of Grand King Pooley VI of Pogglinburg. I shall return tomorrow at nine – be ready!" With that, Elgyn left the room.

"So, they used the secret weapon!" said Nagg, getting up from the table. "I said to General Sidok a 'ousand times that those blooming' robots har no replacement for ya Dondymarian soldier wiv a sword pike hand some guts be'ind it!"

"It was Creep that wanted them. Now I can see why!" retorted the King, knocking the chess pieces flying.

★ ★ ★ ★ ★

The following morning was one of deep sorrow and mourning in Pogglin Town. The whole of Pogglinburg had come out to mourn the fallen Dwarves and Pogglins. They were to be laid to rest within the grounds of the Didock farm rather than the Pogglin Fort Cemetery. All the arrangement was left in the capable hands of the Pogglin Undertaker, Mr Sampson Fillmore-Graves.

The coffined bodies were brought from the schoolhouse to the farm. A great pyre had been made for the fallen Dwarves, as it was Dwarvish tradition to cremate their glorious dead. The coffins of the Didock family were buried where the Farmhouse once stood. After the burial ceremony conducted by the Six Grand Wizards, King Vardiemar lit the funeral pyre of the Dwarves while the surviving Dwarves sang the funeral dirge for the dead. It was a very mournful but beautiful melody, and it brought a lump to Lucian's throat as he remembered those who had sacrificed their lives for the freedom of Pogglinburg.

Behind the graves of the Didock Family, a great stone plinth which had been carved by the Dwarves was erected in honour and remembrance of the dead. Upon it was carved many runes of the Dwarvish language and many words of Pogglish which marked the date and the event of the battle. The six Wizards moved the War Robot, which had been turned to stone by Lucian at the height of the battle, onto the plinth to complete the monument and the ceremony. It was a standing memorial to all of those who had died from both races. Then the congregation sang the hymn of rejoicing and thanks for their victory.

Grand King Pooley stepped in front of the stone monument to address the assembled congregation. "My dear Pogglins and Dwarves, I should like to say a few words of thanks to my dear friend, King Vardiemar Ironhammer III of Dwarveshire. He and his glorious warriors came to our aid in our hour of need, and kept the oaths of his grandfathers before him. He showed great courage on the field of battle, and he stared into the jaws of death to keep this land of ours free from Dondymarian domination. Also, I would like to add a word of thanks to her gracious Majesty Queen Ellgah of Dwarveshire, who can hold her own on the battlefield as strongly as any Dwarvish Warrior. May Vardiemar's beard grow longer and may Elgar's beauty never fade."

A momentous cheer went up from the crowd and when it subsided, he added, "Twice – nay, thrice – Queen Ellgah saved me from a grisly end. It was the first time I have taken up arms in the defence of my realm. I hope I will never have to do so again, but I will gladly do it again if the freedom of this wonderful land of ours is again in danger from outside forces! I would also like to say to our glorious allies the Dwarves that you can count on us in your hour of need as you have with us, should you ever need it."

The crowd erupted with applause and cheers. "Long Live Grand King Pooley!", "Long live King Vardiemar Ironhammer III!", and "Long Live Queen Ellgah!"

After King Pooley came Balferzaar the Black. For his speech, he went to the foot of the monument and the crowd hushed with reverence for the old Pogglin Wizard.

"Your Majesties, Arch-Dukes, Lords, Sirs, Ladies and Gentlepoggs, my friends. Sixteen days ago, our lives and our country were turned upside down by the attempted murder of our gracious Queen Grizzelda by the Dondymarians. The Dondymarian master spy had been impersonated to gain access to the realm. King Pooley and I have questioned the Shadow, and we agree that he had nothing to do with this devilry of Dondymaria. He has been freed and welcomed to stay. Three Pogglins volunteered to take on the quest of finding the cure for the poison and they – my friends, as you know – succeeded admirably in this task. And it is to Mr Lucian Marius Snuzz that I wish to add my thanks, for he had the courage to question the "secret" laid down to us by the Great Dunbruan and to question the six Grand Wizards' beliefs. If it were not for Lucian Snuzz, Pogglinburg could already have been totally razed to the ground. His diligence of thinking called something into question that we all took for granted. He and his friends made a stand against all the odds and won!"

The crowd then erupted with cheers and calls of "Hurrah for Lucian Snuzz!", "Up with Sir Septimus!", "Hurrah for Sara Dore! Hurrah for Artimus!" and "Hurrah for Zontahl!"

"Come here, Lucian, my boy."The old Wizard beckoned the Pogglin forward and Lucian joined the Wizard at the monument.

"You declined the honour of a Knighthood, my dear Lucian; I now bestow on you an honour that you cannot decline. My friends here bear witness that I decree that Mr Lucian Marius Snuzz be made the seventh Grand Wizard of Pogglinburg!"

Lucian was quite taken aback by this unexpected announcement. The crowd again applauded and cheered with joy as Balferzaar presented him with a small ring. It was a little ring (it looked a bit like a signet ring) of silver mounted with a small gem of Amber stone.

"Why, why, thank you," he said. "I am deeply honoured."

As the old Wizard placed the ring on Mr Snuzz's finger, he whispered, "Use it wisely Lucian." He smiled, his eyes twinkling.

The crowd grew silent as Balferzaar placed a sash of bright orange and red around his waist. "You shall be known as the seventh wizard, named Osrick the Orange." He then pushed Mr Snuzz forward, and the crowd listened to what the newly-appointed wizard had to say.

"My dear friends, I will not keep you long – but when you go home tonight, think of those who are absent from their own firesides. Think of the grief of their families. War is an ugly thing and above all remember the fear. I would like to show my thanks to the Fungiglooks of the Fungoid Forest, the Cats of Empraktos-Larris and the Dwarves of the Brown Mountain. If it were not for their selfless sacrifices, none of us would be here this morning. So, praise their deeds, and never, never forget what they stood for and did for us. Thank you."

There was silence and then the congregation erupted in loud applause and cheered, "Long live Lucian Snuzz! Long may he live, the seventh Grand Wizard!"

Then, as was the Pogglin tradition, Lucian laid a single white lily at the foot of the newly consecrated monument, and everyone in the crowd filed past and laid a lily in thanks. The Pogglins and the Dwarves then retired back to the Frog and Bottle Inn where a wake had been prepared. Whilst there was sorrow for the many deaths, there was also much rejoicing and happiness in the knowledge that their land was safe once more.

Lucian and his friends were at a table near the entrance to the bar, opposite from where he had sat with Sir Gilliethrum on the outset of this chain of events. And for all the horrible things that had happened since then, he still managed to smile and laugh: there was a feeling of contentment about him, stronger than before, in fact. As the afternoon drew on, and there were no signs of the merrymaking drawing to a close, the six Wizards took their leave of the proceedings. Each gave their thanks and goodbyes to Lucian and his friends as they went out – all except Balferzaar.

"I haven't forgotten what you said in the chamber of the Black Tower, young Lucian. Your words have caused me to think over ancient history, and the wisdom of the Great Dunbruan. I know you have discovered something of which we know nothing. It has changed you my young Pogglin—and I think for the better."

Lucian smiled and shook the old Wizard's hand.

"Thank you, Balferzaar. I was afraid I had broken our friendship with the harsh words I uttered within the chamber of the Black Tower. But, as you know, I can sometimes be a little brash under extreme conditions."

"You have nothing to worry about, Lucian," the old Wizard smiled back. "It was those words that have caused me to rethink old times and what they mean now."

"Are you busy tomorrow afternoon, about 2.00 pm?" enquired Lucian.

"No, but I think I will be if you are thinking of paying me a visit!" laughed the old Wizard.

"Very well, smiled Lucian. "Expect Zontahl and me for two o'clock!"

"Gladly," replied Balferzaar and left the Inn.

"Well," said Lucian. "I'm feeling rather tired. We've all got a long day ahead of us tomorrow, so I suggest you two had better get an early night too."

"Why is that?"

"Because, Sir Septimus, we have a meeting with Balferzaar at two, and there is something I want to show you all. I've discovered something under the Copper Lake!"

"Right!" said Sir Septimus, and drank down his ale and banged his pot down on the table. "I'm ready to go!"

Artimus was just finishing up his ale too. Lucian and Sara got up from the table to let out Sir Septimus, Zontahl and Artimus.

Lucian waited until his friends were out of earshot and then said, "Sara, I can't tell you at the moment what is troubling me —but once I have seen it through, I will go and see your father and ask for your hand in marriage. Even in my darkest moments, a vision of you brings me light and hope." He smiled at her rather shyly. "Do you still want me as a husband?"

"Hmmm, I don't know, are Grand Wizards allowed to marry?" said Sara playfully, and then added "Of course, I still want to marry you, you silly! I've never wanted anyone else from the first time I saw you in the school playground, I knew that I wanted to be your wife." And she chuckled and kissed him on the cheek.

"I see the lovebirds are at it again!" mumbled old Grandpa Snodpack to no one in particular from the opposite table.

Lucian and Sara said their goodnights and then Lucian left the Inn, stepping out into a cool summer's evening where his friends were waiting for him.

"Well, I'll see you three tomorrow at the palace," said Sir Septimus and he made his way across the Square towards Pulpit Manor on the hill.

Artimus walked with Lucian and Zontahl to his shop, and there he said, "Goodnight Lucian, and to you Zontahl, I'll see you on the morrow." The key turned, and he let himself inside.

As the Pogglin and cat walked off down the road together, the setting sun hung low and red in the sky.

Lucian turned to Zontahl. "You know something, my friend?"

"What is that, Lucian?" replied Zontahl.

"It's going to be a beautiful morning tomorrow!" he smiled.

And with that, they turned the corner and made their way back to 2 Hill Square.

Lucian Snuzz in his ceremonial robes of Osrick the Orange.

Acknowledgements

My warmest thanks go to Carol Barnes for all her help and support, and her kind encouragement to finally get the book into print. I would also like to thank Karen May for her valuable and generous assistance. Last but not least my thanks to Monica for her help.

About the Author

Robert Kew was born in Hammersmith, London in 1964 and started drawing at 2 years old.

He was sculpting in plasticine from the age of 5 and started having dreams of Sol-Larris from the age of 7 years old, that's when Lucian Snuzz came into his life and was his guide around the ancient world of Sol-Larris. At 8 he was sculpting in clay and in 1982 he became a professional sculptor.

In 2006, Robert had two successful exhibitions revealing the world and creatures that populate Sol-Larris. The first exhibition was held in Kettering and the second in Boston UK. Robert now lives in Northamptonshire.